Darker than Dark

A Story Of The Vietnam War

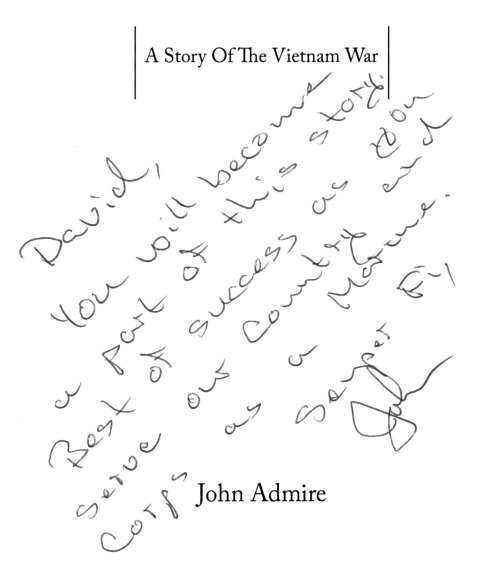

John Admire

ISBN 978-1-942451-04-4

Published by
Yorkshire Publishing
6271 E. 120th Court
Suite 200
Tulsa, Ok 74137
www.yorkshirepublishing.com

Text Design: Lisa Simpson

DEDICATION

This story is dedicated to my daughter, Katelyn Eileen Admire,
who is the blessing and inspiration in my life
&
to the Marines and Navy Corpsmen of Company M,
3rd Battation/3rd Marines. It was my honor and privilege to serve
with them in Vietnam in 1966-67.

John Admire has written a brilliant story about young Marines in Vietnam. As a highly respected veteran of that war and a top leader for decades in the Corps, he knows battle, how men deal with the challenges of combat, and the raw emotions that rip through the souls of warriors. John has captured all that and more in this book. He has also given us a remarkably insightful account of Vietnam from the grunt's perspective. This is a must read for vets who will immediately relate to what he has written and for those who want to understand this conflict from an honest, straight forward front line view.

General Tony Zinni
USMC (Retired)/Combatant Commander/
Author/Middle East Peace Envoy

This story of infantry combat in the Vietnam War rings true. Its brutal honesty will both anger and inspire readers. Reading it I felt it was part of my story, part of my struggle to survive, part of my combat horrors and miseries. It reminded me I was one of the lucky 19 year-old Marines to survive…thanks to the brotherhood of those with whom I served.

Ray Calhoun
Vietnam Marine Lance Corporal/CEO Silver Bridge Tech

It's a bold story accurately depicting war and Marines in combat, especially their selfless devotion and dedication to their mission and survival. Their brotherly love beyond personal safety evokes memories of those with whom I was blessed to serve and remember with respect decades later.

Richard Ashton
Sergeant Major, USMC (Retired)/
Manager Premier Logistics Solutions

John Admire's book validates the everlasting truths about the nature of war and its profound impact on both the warriors who wage it and the society that sends them to fight it. He takes the reader directly into the heart of war: the realm of human emotions, motivations and behaviors. His depiction is raw, authentic, unflinching and mesmerizing. As Americans, we have the inalienable right to abhor violence and hate war. But, as citizens of a democracy, we also have the duty to understand the burden society imposes on the warriors it sends to fight in its name. Reading this book is an important step toward fulfilling this moral obligation.

Ms. Lani Kass
Senior Vice President, Corporate Strategic Advisor,
CACI Int'l/Former Senior Policy Advisor to the Chairman,
Joint Chiefs of Staff/ Author/War College Strategy Professor

ACKNOWLEDGEMENTS

John G. Admire, my father and blue collar oil field worker, and Earline M. Admire, my loving mother and housewife, taught me to work hard and dream hard. This story is one of my dreams for them. They had a hard life during the Great Depression, Oklahoma Dust Bowl, and World War II, but shared much love with my sisters, Carol and Susan, and me.

Coaches Bill Allen and Gene Shell, my Tulsa Webster High School basketball coaches, introduced me to the challenges of leadership. Coach Allen is a defining part of my life and his influence has been an everlasting one. I am proud to be considered one of Coach Allen's "Boys."

Tulsa Webster High School, Oklahoma Christian College, and the University of Oklahoma provided me the teachers so critical to my education. I will forever respect their patience and understanding.

Bonnie Allen Williams and Gary Dale Rosson, University of Oklahoma classmates, encouraged me for years to write a novel. Without their perseverance it's doubtful this story would have ever been written.

Ed Goodin and Ann Habeeb have been more than friends to Katelyn and me. They and their families became part of our family and our family a part of theirs. They were the brother and sister who would critique me and console me, especially during a challenging time in my life.

The Soldiers, Marines, Sailors, Airmen, and Coast Guardsmen who served in Vietnam have my eternal respect. While it was a challenging time for our nation, you represented it with dedication. You never quite received the support and appreciation you deserved, but maybe this story will help our nation better understand your sacrifices and the war.

The Marines and Navy Corpsmen in our Vietnam War infantry platoon represented our Country and Corps with honor. Marines Ray Calhoun, Jr, David Cooper, II, Joe Cordileone, Bill Early, Don Hossack, Bill Lindholm, Bob Moffatt, Ricky Smith, Ken Snider, and Tom Wheeler, as well as Navy Corpsmen Sam Leathes and Lynn Thomas, are but a few of those with whom I was honored to serve. This story is about them and for them and for those with whom we served who gave their lives for us and our country. May God and peace be with them and their families.

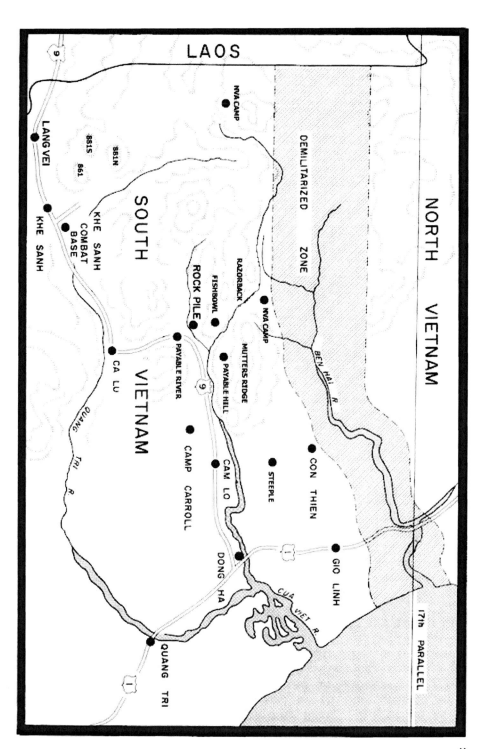

Contents

Author's Note

This is a story of the Vietnam War and four young Marines. It's about fighting and killing. Compassion and love, however, are defining parts of the story. The story personalizes what war does to those who fight it and what they do to survive it. Enduring and caring relationships forged in combat are as much a part of their survival, maybe more, as their combat skills. While the book is fiction, the majority is based on actual battles and personal experiences.

Vietnam was a challenging war for those on the battlefield to fight as well as for those on the home front to support. The conflict was a limited war and the complex nature of such war was confusing and contentious to many. The combatants' frustrations with the war's limitations and the miseries they endured are captured in the actions and thoughts of the Marines. Their story is about living and dying in combat. But it's also about the love and loyalty they share in a truly unique relationship. It's a story that testifies to the human spirit and will as well as the belief that love and friendship conquer all…even the hatreds and animosities of war.

The Marines share with you their hopes and dreams as they struggle with the despairs and nightmares of Vietnam. They take you into their battles and bunkers. They acquaint you with combat's horror and humor. The story is the universal infantryman's story for most all who have fought in war—the challenge of defying death daily while fighting to survive till tomorrow.

This is also, however, America's story. In the aftermath of Vietnam the consensus was that the war's true legacy would be the lessons learned from it. Vietnam was insidious as well as instructive. Today, the war on terror and the dysfunction of various states and the ideological rivalries in the international community pose serious threats to the stability and security of our world. Then, as well as now, the conflicts of our time and the future present us with challenges similar to Vietnam. We must understand them to protect our freedoms and nation and peace.

PROLOGUE

The limitations are just one big kabuki dance. We just tip toe and lightly kabuki dance around targets we should be stomping to holy hell. We're dancin' this little ballet with soft slippers and the North Vietnamese is Texas two-stepping the hell out of us with clod hoppers.

— Marine Private First Class Dominic Hawkins

In war, young infantry combatants quickly mature beyond their years. Their lives depend on it. Corporal Dark Pale Thunder, Lance Corporal Aaron Wiley, and Privates First Class Dominic Hawkins and Brad Clary were no exception. They were four young Marines, 17 to 19 years of age, assigned in 1966 to a fire team in the Vietnam War. While they learned that to live, others may have to die, they came to accept it. War did that to them. Accepting the eventual unpopularity of the war, however, was harder to accept. Initially confident, America's later doubts about the war confused them.

In March 1965 the United States deployed ground forces to South Vietnam to counter communist aggression by North Vietnam. The noble goals of protecting the independence and freedoms of South Vietnam were initially supported by the majority of Americans. In time, however, discontent with the war eventually contributed to the distortion and disintegration of such support. In a prolonged war, characterized by questionable policies and strategies as well as the lack of public support and resolve, the Vietnam War later became symbolic of the futilities and frustrations of war.

In the half-a-world away airline flight to Da Nang, Vietnam, Lance Corporal Aaron Wiley had time to think of a world and situation far different from any he had ever known. *War's not necessarily what I want to be doing right now, right any time,* he thought, *but I want to do what I believe is right and helping people be free is right.* Wiley is black. He, his family, and his race understood freedom's struggle. He was fighting for freedom. In time, however, propaganda and innuendo became the trademarks of the war instead of freedom and liberty.

"Hell No, We Won't Go," protestors shouted and signs proclaimed after years of frustration. Similarly, the chorus of a popular song admonished, "War, what is it good for? Absolutely nothin'!" Streets and campuses became awash with protests to the war. It was a time in which many championed civil rights as well as promoted civil disobedience. It was the 1960s in America.

The Vietnam War became the epicenter of a raging firestorm that edged America closer to the swirling abyss of chaos. The political and social and cultural fabric of America became frayed. The past and present values and beliefs of America were repeatedly attacked and challenged. America became polarized by protests, fragmented by factions, and divided by dissent. The protests were Anti-War, Anti-Establishment, Anti-Government, Anti-Cultural, Anti-Authority, Anti-Draft, and Anti-Most Anything and Most Everything. It was the Vietnam War, however, that became the lightning rod for the disenchanted and for Anti-American sentiments.

"What makes Vietnam so hard to understand," Corporal Dark Pale Thunder exclaimed in early 1967 after months of frustrations that endangered his team on patrols, "is because of the complexities and contradictions of what the politicians and generals call 'limited war'. It's a type of war we're not used to fighting. Most think war is war, but there're different types of war with different types of rules and challenges." The team's leader, he sighed remembering the young South Vietnamese girl afraid to walk to school on trails booby trapped by Viet Cong guerrillas.

The constraints of limited war challenged and confused the team, "Jesus, the North Vietnam sanctuaries, no-fire zones, ceasefires, and other dumb-ass constraints just handicap the hell out of us and make fightin' unfair for us," Private First Class (PFC) Dominic Hawkins exhorted in a tirade after mourning the loss of a friend killed in an ambush, "When I get home from this war I'm gonna protest, too. I'm gonna protest all these damn limitations that are killing us. Yeah, I'll protest to beat all hell." He was a rebellious Boston Italian under no illusions that war was fair, but he believed in similar rules for all combatants. Hawkins witnessed Marines die from the restrictions and thought it wrong. It was that basic and that personal to him...*to all of them.*

After one too many battles in which one too many limitations jeopardized their combat effectiveness and survival, battle weary Private First Class (PFC) Brad Clary groaned, "It's just that everything's pretty easy or simple in theory or in books. But it's damn hard and just plain complicated on the battlefield. It's just hard as hell to take good theories and good words and fight a bad war with them." He had recently returned from a patrol in which restrictions from firing or engaging the enemy because of the possibility of collateral damage or civilian casualties resulted in severe injuries to a Marine friend instead.

In battle after battle they were bloodied and bruised, but their hearts and souls willed them to overcome searing and scaring tragedies. "We want to fight," Corporal Thunder once explained to his platoon leader during a patrol debrief, "but often the rules just won't let us fight the way we want to fight. We just want to fight to survive." He was an Osage Indian from the Oklahoma prairies and familiar with the history of unfairness in war and his tribe's fight for survival.

Surviving the war was their constant struggle. Understanding it was their ultimate darkness. They endured incredible sacrifices and miseries. Adrenalin charged battle exhilarations shattered absolute boredom, while brutal and ruthless combat assaulted their youth and innocence. Torrid tropical temperatures and the cool monsoon rain wetness plagued them. The deprivations of decent meals and sleep bore hard on them. Living in filth, they stank from the poverty of their dank musty bunkers and relentless exposure to the elements. Fifty plus pound packs rubbed shoulders raw until they became calloused. Ceaseless patrols in triple canopy mountainous jungles exhausted them.

It was, however, the frequent deaths and heartbreaks that overwhelmed them. Death and danger stalked them constantly. The killings dehumanized them. The fear terrorized them. They learned war is painfully cruel. But what hurt most was the loneliness and subsequent sense of lack of support from their country...they were the cruelest pains of all. In time, they came to feel alone and misunderstood. The loneliness was the worst. It was an indignity they never deserved.

The four Marines devised a plan to conduct frequent bunker talks to help them understand the war and to survive it. Speaking plainly and listening intently, they honed their fighting skills while striving to understand the confusions and contradictions of the divisive war. They talked during card games and night watches, while on patrol and cleaning weapons. The talks bonded them into a team and more...*they became family.*

Together, they became a potent and charismatic force. They survived one battle only to have to survive others. They patrolled and fought one day, only to have to patrol and fight the next day...and then into their tomorrows. It was war. It was what they did. They patrolled and fought relentlessly...till they were either killed or they completed their tours and rotated home.

"We're killing to survive and live. You learn to kill real fast or you die real fast. It's just the way the war is," Wiley once proclaimed. The son of a sharecropper farmer-preacher, he struggled with theoretical oppositions to killing, but balanced it with the practical desire to live. The killings became old and weary burdens they bore despite their young and exuberant ages.

"Ain't no good days in war or Vietnam, except for the days you survive," Hawkins frowned.

"Yeah, everyday in Vietnam is a lifetime. I just hope we got more lifetimes than we got days in Vietnam," Corporal Thunder concluded with a paternal look as he led the team on yet another potentially deadly patrol. "Saddle up. Let's move out." They fought and moved on; they moved on and fought. Patrols were their life...*and death.*

CHAPTER 1

The Inescapable Darkness

While we learned that to live others may die, we came to accept that. War did that to us.

—Marine Private First Class Brad Clary

Marine Corporal Dark Pale Thunder squinted his eyes almost shut and then quickly opened them wide and blinked twice. Nothing. Shaking his head to clear his vision he blinked again. Still he saw nothing. His world at that moment was one of total darkness. He tried again to discern something, anything, in the murky night. Squinting and blinking one last time he again saw nothing. Now he was satisfied with the darkness. It was darker than dark.

Darkness was sometimes his friend; sometimes his enemy. Now it was his ally. On Vietnam night ambushes there was a degree of relief in the black darkness of the mountainous triple canopy jungles in the far northern area of South Vietnam near the Demilitarized Zone (DMZ).

Sometimes the darkness was unnerving, but Corporal Thunder knew survival depended on controlling emotions. He was an Oklahoma Osage Indian and the dark nights on the plains and prairies accustomed him more than most to the darkness. He was comfortable with nature and the outdoors. They were kindred spirits to him, but in war the darkness caused certain discomforting emotions despite familiarity. He was only 19 years old, yet the oldest and most experienced Marine in his four-man team. The team trusted and depended on him. He was the team's leader.

Darkness was one chilling description of the lonely mountainous jungles. *Deadly* was another. Both descriptions applied to Corporal Thunder's fire team of Marines who lay prone, silent, and fearful in ambush positions along the treacherous and taunting jungle trail. Dense bamboo thickets, shoulder high elephant grass, forests of giant broad leafy trees, and tangled vines obscured light even in daylight. The indigenous and fiercely independent Montagnards, known as "Mountain People," referred to the mountainous jungles as "Crouching Beasts." The mountains and jungles were poised to pounce. *Chilling* and *deadly* aptly described this nighttime drama Corporal Thunder's team experienced during ambushes in this remote area of Vietnam.

Individually, they grappled to overcome the darkness, silence, and fear. The struggle was like the steady drumbeat of a funeral procession. The deathly drone wore on them. The Corporal's nerves throbbed, but he fought the urge to twitch as he remained motionless. Private First Class (PFC) Brad Clary's haunting stare into nowhere revealed the depth of his exhaustion. Fatigue swept over the tired aging lines of PFC Dominic Hawkins' teenage face. Lance Corporal (LCpl) Aaron Wiley sweated profusely as salty flavors dripped onto his quivering lips.

Clary burrowed into the wet foliage and soft mud to wrestle into a comfortable position, but there was no comfort on jungle ambushes. He was a 19-year-old Southern Californian much more at home on beaches and athletic fields with adoring young ladies and cheering crowds than muted mountainous trails. Attending one year of college on a football scholarship caused the team to nickname him "Socrates." He was the team's *intellect* and *idealist*.

The jungle was as eerily silent as it was dark. Clary endeavored to open his ears with a wide yawn and repeated clicks and stretches of his jaws. His sense of hearing in the darkness was critical to survival. He cupped his palm over his ears one at a time and pressed gently to create a vacuum to clear his hearing. At home he would have welcomed noise, especially the pounding waves of the surf or the blasting music of a Beach Boys tune. In Vietnam, however, he was comforted more by silence than by noise. Now he heard nothing, which was exactly what he preferred the enemy hear—nothing. Silence and surprise were critical to successful ambushes.

Wiley's uniform was virtually pasted to him with sweat from the arduous patrol and the later unrelenting cool monsoon rains. Shuddering as the cold wet night pressed on him, he accepted them as minor nuisances. He was from a Mississippi sharecropper family with roots deep into slavery and the land. Wiley was far too familiar with the physical discomforts of hard work and poor conditions to be too affected by the cold and wet. He was reared on hardships. His familiarity with austerity was an advantage in the wretched poverty of war.

Wiley was the Assistant Fire Team Leader and patrol by patrol his leadership was becoming as formidable as his brute strength. The team affectionately referred to him as "Baby Brute" because he resorted to power wisely and only as a last resort. He was 18 years old, but he had a child's innocent kindness and an adult's super human strength. He was the team's *conscience.*

Hunkered down low near Wiley and Clary, Hawkins quickly hugged his stomach with his forearms as it began to rumble. Perpetual hunger and thirst manifested themselves with strange sounds emanating from his shrinking gut, often at the most inopportune times. Only 17 years old, he was the youngest and the mutt and the runt of the team. A North End Boston Italian, he constantly dreamed of pasta and pizza…when he was not dreaming of fighting or girls. Thoughts of Italian cuisine were so vivid that he sensed the increase of moist saliva in his mouth in remembrance of his mama's cooking.

In deference to Hawkins' small size and ethnicity, the team nicknamed him "Little Italy." It had been months since any of them had enjoyed a home cooked meal, but Hawkins discovered solace in battles. Battles whet his appetite almost as much as his mama's pasta…maybe more. He was the team's *fighter* and *rebel.* He was a street fighter at heart—*with heart.*

Corporal Thunder, Wiley, Clary and Hawkins were one of three four-man Marine fire teams, part of an eighteen-man squad ambush. The wet cold monsoon rains plagued them. Exhausted from the strenuous patrol to the ambush, hunger and thirst shadowed them constantly. Yet, their miseries became secondary thoughts. Now they prepared to kill and killing was their primary thought. It was why they were here where they were. It was why they were doing what they did.

The dense jungle foliage camouflaged the Marines as much as the silence and darkness. The dark silence surrounded them as a heavy acoustic veil. It protected and soundproofed them. It was their private shroud for masking their presence and thoughts. In preparing for the physical battle, they also had to prepare for the psychological one. The twin battles contained, consumed, and cloaked them in their own private universe, in their own personal hell of their emotions.

It's darker than dark. The darkness is blinding, Wiley thought as he took minutes to slowly slide by fractions of an inch to settle into a better firing position. He squinted and glanced repeatedly to and fro to prevent fixating on false movements. Raking his eyes back and forth across the darkness, he knew steadily staring eyes could play tricks on him in the night jungle.

It's quieter than quiet. The silence is deafening, Clary pondered as he slowly cocked his ears to aid his hearing. The steady rain splashed on the crisp leaves, but the drumming staccato thumps blended with the silence. Soft splatters of rain pooled in muddy depressions and echoed in melodic rhythm to complicate his hearing for enemy movements. He had learned from his patrolling experiences that some sound was better than no sound. Clary alleged in their bunker talks, "Too quiet is too quiet." Some noise contributed to alertness. No noise contributed to fear. It was always a delicate balance between silence and noise; between alertness and fear.

The fear's too real, Hawkins mulled, *Ain't no escapin' the damn fear. It's here with us. It hangs on us. It's here on us and in us. It's unnervin', but it jacks me the hell up. I ain't scared to fear, but not fearing really scares me.* The darkness, the silence, and the stark realities of war were fear inducers, but that was good. No fear was bad. Hawkins was aware that the absence of fear bred complacency and complacency beckoned carelessness. He was never complacent.

The fear was bittersweet, too. It was both intoxicating and sobering. In the aftermath of battle, Hawkins once claimed, "Fear creates this little buzz of recklessness while also givin' me a hint of caution for the danger." Nonetheless, he was more into fear's intoxication than its sobriety. It was the fight, though, that was more intoxicating to him than the fear. The fight was his elixir.

The four Marines lay silently and close in teams of two in 50-50 buddy system arrangements. It was their ambush routine. In the dark silence of the ambush, as in many past ones, their teamwork became their reliance and trust. As the steady rain pelted them, their bodies molded into the supple mud. While one was on alert, one dozed or relaxed at arm's length. They lay immobile and absolutely no one or nothing moved, except for a tap on the body or silent signal from a teammate to alert them to danger. Their eyes and ears constantly scanned the ambush killing zone.

They lay in the dark, quiet, fear, and waited. They waited to kill. They prayed silently to live, too. They learned to allow their minds to wander to avoid the drudgery of war while also remaining vigilant to its exhilarating dangers. As they waited their minds drifted to various thoughts. Wiley uttered a silent *Amen* to his prayer for the team. A spiritual man, he often debated or philosophized the biblical conflicts of "Thou Shall Not Kill" and "An Eye for an Eye." The practical reality for him, however, was simply to kill to live; to fight to survive.

Hawkins frequently recalled, either during patrols or in their bunker talks, "We're always either killin' or prayin'. Ain't war just something?" Killing and praying simply seemed contradictions to them at times. *Sorta like startin' a war to win a peace*, Hawkins thought.

Corporal Thunder focused exclusively on the mission and his team. He simply wanted them to stay alive through the darkness, silence, and fear. *Let's stay alive until sunrise*, he thought.

Clary maybe summarized their quest for survival best after a particularly brutal battle with multiple killings when, he confessed to the team, "While we learned that to live others may die, we came to accept that. War did that to us." These were the constant emotions and actions that plagued and motivated them throughout countless and ceaseless ambushes and patrols.

In pre-ambush briefings, Corporal Thunder always cautioned, "If you absolutely must move you better move slowly and deliberately and imperceptibly. Very imperceptibly. Otherwise, I might shoot you myself." Then he would smile, "I heard the Lieutenant say 'imperceptibly.' You probably understand it better than me." Corporal Thunder was anything but pretentious.

But no one ever smiled in return. They were confident that anyone who jeopardized the mission or the lives of his Marines would answer to him. Once a Marine from another squad claimed, "I doubt the Corporal would shoot anyone who makes noise or screws up a mission."

Hawkins simply asked, "Well, shithead, why don't you test him on it?" No one ever did.

Clary rustled as silently as possible, but held his breath after every broken twig. He was situating his tall frame into his fighting position to avoid further moves for the remaining long arduous hours of darkness. Frustrated because it took profound patience and discipline, he nonetheless knew both were preferable to other alternatives. It was hard, but surviving was hard.

Time drifted slowly and somewhat "imperceptibly." Clary smiled remembering Corporal Thunder's reference and honest unfamiliarity toward the word.

Corporal Thunder periodically glanced at his watch's luminous face as the dark hours passed. Then the ambush was almost over without enemy contact. Wiley smiled as the sun began to rise and slivers of sunlight broke the darkness. The jungle came alive with sounds of leaves gyrating in gentle breezes and insects and wildlife awakening to a new day. The Corporal, however, motioned with silent hand signals for his Marines to hold their positions and remain quiet.

Corporal Thunder's regular patrol brief and warning included, "In the triple canopy jungle with few trails the enemy mostly moves at twilight or at sunrise." Trails were the expressways of the jungles. Although paths were dangerous, they were, at times, less dangerous than hacking noisily through the dense and tangled vegetation. The decision to use trails or unbroken terrain was always a carefully considered one. On paths, patrols could often move quicker and quieter than over unbroken ground, but both had their inherent dangers. Sometimes there were no options. It was now a critical time on the trails. They were the hunters—but they were the hunted, too.

The Marines waited patiently for about an hour before deliberately abandoning their ambush positions to assemble on the trail for their return to their base camp. Wiley bent and twisted his body slowly from the sluggish and stiff night. Clary yawned and stretched to relieve tightness. Hawkins stifled groans and moans caused by sore and tingling muscles. Suddenly, the silence gave way to noise and commotion. They instantly froze. Their eyes and ears sprang to high alert.

Corporal Thunder and his Marines quickly kneeled with their weapons at the ready. They waited. Seconds later PFC Williams from Fire Team One walked up the trail with a Vietnamese in tow. Corporal Thunder motioned his Marines to hold their positions as he stood and cautiously moved forward onto the trail. He always moved and spoke with poise, power, and purpose.

"My Corporal told me to bring this Vietnamese to you," PFC Williams said innocently.

"Why me?" Corporal Thunder asked with a steely gaze on him and the Vietnamese.

"He said you'd know what to do with him," Williams replied naively.

"Who or what do you think he is? Is he a Viet Cong or VC? Is he a North Vietnamese Army soldier or NVA? Is he a prisoner or local civilian?" he asked with a glaring stare. Corporal Thunder's rapid fire questions flustered Williams, who stood confused with his eyes blinking in rhythm with his hesitant stammering.

"You don't know do you?" The Corporal grilled.

Williams meekly whispered, "No, Sir."

"Well, Williams, first, you don't 'Sir' me. I'm a Marine Corporal; a Non-Commissioned Officer. I'm proud to be an NCO. I'm no officer," he punctuated his words with special care and effect. His voice rose with certain words. He was baiting the Vietnamese.

Without verbal orders or direction, Corporal Thunder's fire team slowly formed a wide circle around the Corporal, Williams, and the Vietnamese. Their weapons were trained on the prisoner. Meanwhile, Marines on the ambush gathered, but kept their distance. The Corporal motioned them to maintain an alert and steady watch up and down both ends of the trail.

"Damn," Hawkins whispered to Clary, "we're on this godforsaken trail in the middle of this godforsaken enemy-infested country and Corporal Thunder's dressin' down Williams like a godforsaken stepchild with a lecture on godforsaken Marine Corps protocol and discipline."

"Wait a second," Clary rebutted in a barely audible voice while keeping his eyes and weapon trained on the NVA, "Corporal Thunder knows what he's doing. I think he's acting a bit or something. He's messing with the prisoner more than Williams."

"Acting? Messing?" Hawkins asked, "What da you mean by that?"

"Hell, I don't know!" Clary smiled, "I'm not the Corporal. Be quiet. Let's listen and learn."

"Second," Corporal Thunder emphasized, "you don't bring any Vietnamese to me if you don't know who or what he is without taking a few precautions," as he shrugged in total disgust.

Williams was about to ask, "Why?" or "What precautions?" but realized he was probably about to be told why and what in no uncertain terms.

He frowned with embarrassment knowing he had faced enough indignity for now without inviting or heaping more upon himself.

In seconds, Williams and the others learned exactly why. It was swift and silent. It was fast and furious. It was as delicate as it was deadly, too.

While the Marines were focusing on Corporal Thunder's tirade, he was obliquely watching the NVA. The Vietnamese had Corporal Thunder's undivided attention. It was mostly by peripheral vision, but his eyes never left him. The enemy probably guessed he was temporarily unnoticed with everyone distracted by the Corporal's words and actions as he cautiously inched his hand into his right front black pajama pocket. The NVA guessed wrong; Corporal Thunder guessed right. Unnoticed, the Corporal slowly repositioned his right hand across his body to lightly grasp the hilt of his machete on his left hip to inch it upward. The NVA began to slowly withdraw his hand, but Corporal Thunder glimpsed the glint of metal from the grenade in the morning sunlight as the NVA quickly raised both his hands up toward his chest.

As the Vietnamese's movements accelerated and became more pronounced, so did Corporal Thunder's. The NVA's movements were now fast. The Corporal's were faster. With lightning speed and precision, the Corporal drew his machete from its sheath amid a screeching sound.

In one powerfully swift circular motion, Corporal Thunder raised his machete up, around, and down. It was so fast it almost ended before it began. The razor-sharp machete sliced the left arm of the Vietnamese above the wrist with such speed and force his hand was severed from his arm. His hand and wrist fell to the ground with a bloody and damp *thump*. Blood splashed wildly and spurted onto the wet leaves with a disturbingly melancholy echo.

But amazingly, the Vietnamese was not done. Neither, however, was Corporal Thunder. Although dazed from excruciating pain, the NVA lowered his head slightly while rapidly raising his right hand upward. Corporal Thunder anticipated this move, too, and with a full and complete 360-degree rotation of his bloody and keenly sharpened machete he delivered the fatal blow.

The impact of Corporal Thunder's second machete blow was faster and harder and more violent than the first. The bloody machete sliced through the early morning mist with a whistling sound. This time the machete caught the Vietnamese at the back of the base of his bent neck and decapitated him. The whining sound was replaced by sounds of blunt force severing crisp bone and pliable tendons and sinew. It was surgical…precise…crude. It was ugly and devastating.

Decapitations were ugly and unexpected. They created involuntary revulsions and voluntary reactions. Despite their becoming familiar with the horrors of war, Wiley gasped and Clary turned away. It was unnatural to feign indifference. Death was always hard. Decapitations were among the hardest. But Hawkins simply shrugged in defiance. He was street hard. Death had touched him powerfully hard before—he was hardened to it.

The Vietnamese's head slammed onto the jungle trail with a louder thud and with more blood than his hand. It was gruesome. Wiley stepped back as blood sprayed and splattered on his muddy boots in a cascade of crimson. Clary did his best to look away, but involuntarily glanced at the NVA's head only to be repulsed by the ghastly look of terror in his frantic eyes. The partially upright NVA body convulsed once, twice, and then heaved forward in a lump. *Splat.*

The Vietnamese fell into the fresh patch of his blood, twitched once, and then laid still. But the hand grenade he had held in his right hand rolled for a few feet before coming to a halt. The sight of the grenade caused the Marines to instantly take two rapid steps away and quickly dive head first away from the grenade and onto the ground.

Staring at the mutilated NVA body, Clary later observed the Vietnamese had attempted to first pull the grenade's pin with his left hand and later his teeth. He knew pulling a pin with your teeth was hard—it was almost impossible unless the prisoner had straightened the pin earlier. Noting the NVA failed in his efforts to pull the pin, Clary witnessed Corporal Thunder succeed in his. The Corporal anticipated the prisoner's actions. The Marines survived. The NVA died.

"That's why you never bring a Vietnamese to me without knowing who or what he is," Corporal Thunder said somberly, as he pointed toward the grenade. He suspected Williams had wanted to ask him why, but he was confident Williams and the others now knew why.

"There's a lot more we need to talk about and learn from this," he noted, "because we're just beginning to learn the thinking and tactics of the NVA. We have lots to learn." At that moment he nonchalantly grabbed a swath of wet jungle leaves, wiped the blood from his machete, and carefully replaced its shining blade in its sheath. The killing was done. It was over—*for now.*

Then, in an almost professorial tone, Corporal Thunder softly whispered, "I don't pretend to know a lot about war or killing, but I know that if we don't do our best to learn about them we'll die. We won't survive. And we ain't dying. We just ain't. We're surviving and living."

Training his gaze squarely on Williams, Corporal Thunder again paused, "We'll learn from one another, too. Thanks to Williams, we just learned a good lesson." This brief thanks restored Williams' dignity and he smiled gratefully.

Corporal Thunder was aware Williams bore the brunt of his earlier criticism. He concluded he now must correct it to make Williams feel a valued member of the unit. Williams had been an unwitting, maybe unfortunate, pawn in the incident, but a critical lesson had been learned thanks to his innocent help. Corporal Thunder wanted the Marines to respect Williams.

Clary intently watched and listened to their team leader with admiration while thinking, *It's vintage Corporal Thunder. It's leadership; it's what Marines do.* He quickly recalled, *you rarely, if ever, punish in public. You praise in public and punish in private.* You avoided public criticism, but sometimes it had to be done. Sometimes there was a reason. This was one of those times there was a reason, but then it was time to praise. It was Corporal Thunder.

"One more thought before we police up and pack up for our patrol back to our base camp," Corporal Thunder added, struggling to forget and move on from the killing, "Killing another person is never easy. It's hard. I killed the NVA only to protect us. I shouldn't have had to kill him because we should've searched him before we brought him into our ambush. But then I found out he had a grenade. Then he tried to use it to kill us. Then I didn't have much choice."

"That grenade would've wounded or maybe killed a few of us, too," Hawkins interrupted, "but I had my rifle aimed at him and I'da killed him if you hadn'ta."

"That's why I acted fast," Corporal Thunder politely but forcefully corrected, "I didn't want any of you shooting him because the rifle fire would have alerted any following NVA force that something was wrong. We'd either be fighting a bigger force or racing out of here right now instead of policing up like we should. We got time to do this right, but we also have to hurry."

The philosophy Corporal Thunder had come to accept since his arrival in the war-torn land—"Nothing is ever truly over in Vietnam. Nothing. Zero. Zilch."—he had introduced to them early in their tour. They believed it now more than ever. But they knew, too, Hawkins thought, *It's really over only when we stop learnin' and we stop learnin' only when we're dead. So, let's keep on learnin' and makin' sure nothin's ever over. It just means we're livin'.*

Corporal Thunder then patted Williams on the back with thanks and turned away and ordered, "Okay, now let's police up this killing zone and get ready to get out of here."

These words were a dismissal and release for the Marines to return to their respective teams. They began preparing for the patrol back to their base camp by shouldering their packs and gathering on the trail. The ambush was over, but the learning was continuous and never over. Now, returning safely to their base camp was their new and next mission.

Quietly, in whispers, came the call down the trail for, "Team leaders up." Sergeant Hedquist, Second Squad Leader, was calling his three Fire Team Leaders to his position to issue the order for the squad's and patrol's return to their base camp. He was about ten meters or less up the trail in a bomb crater. Corporal Thunder expected the call, but it came quicker than he estimated, which was good. He was ready. He knew they must depart quickly.

"We need to get out of here as fast as possible," he told his team. "I took a few minutes to explain the incident with the Vietnamese while it was fresh to us," he said, "but we'll need to talk more later. Right now, let's prepare to move on." They paused briefly with cocked ears and searching eyes to listen for and detect any sounds of approaching enemy forces. Assured they were alone, they moved on one by one.

Corporal Thunder wheeled to proceed toward Sergeant Hedquist's location, but quickly turned back and ordered his team, "Wiley, coordinate with the other teams to post Hawkins and Clary back down the trail in the direction the Vietnamese came from to set up a quick and tempo-rary listening post. Hawkins and Clary, you watch and listen for anyone coming up the trail. The dead NVA may have been an advance scout or recon for a bigger force. Be alert."

"Wiley, then police this area fast. Cover all signs of us ever having been here. Take the dead Vietnamese's body down the mountain. Take it about fifty meters or more and hide it in a natural ravine or gorge or crevice. Cover and conceal it with whatever foliage and rocks you can find. Make him disappear for now. Animals will take care of forever." Corporal Thunder quietly whispered in short bursts, "Leave nothing behind. Be quiet and be ready and be alert."

The Corporal then rushed to his meeting, but his footsteps were quieted by the soft mud, wet foliage, and Indian skills he valued. Wiley was proud to coordinate with the other teams. He thought to himself that Corporal Thunder trusted him more and more. After the coordination he went about fifty meters down the trail with Hawkins and Clary to their listening post. He wanted to have a general idea where they would set up their position. While unnecessary, Hawkins and Clary appreciated it nonetheless. It gave them a sense of connection with the squad.

Wiley then disposed the NVA body and policed the area. He located the spot on the trail where Corporal Thunder had last met with them. When the Corporal returned he wanted to be there because he was confident he would have orders for them. He settled into a good position, but it was bad and lonely without the team. Shuddering involuntarily in the solitary silence, he sighed. Alone now, he sat and waited.

"I bet you ten bucks we're the point team on the patrol back to our base camp," Hawkins whispered as he and Clary sat quietly in their listening post.

"I bet you twenty bucks you're right," Clary replied. Clary knew this would temporarily confuse Hawkins. Clary was always testing and teasing Hawkins.

Hawkins thought about this before he smiled, "Yeah, I bet your thirty bucks back." *Maybe Hawkins was catching on*, Clary smiled.

Humor helped relieve the tension, but point was no laughing matter. It was the most critical element of any patrol. It was the first to make enemy contact and Corporal Thunder's team almost always had point, especially in critical times. It was a reputation the team had earned, but it was also the most dangerous place in the patrol. It was contradictory until you analyzed it. You then concluded you wanted the best to take on the worst or the hardest challenges.

Clary and Hawkins alternated listening and whispering softly as they sat in the listening post, but they were acutely aware of the jungle sounds and their eyes were riveted on the trail. "I'll bet you volunteer as point man, too," Clary declared. He knew this was a sure bet because he knew Hawkins always volunteered for point. It was a matter of honor for Hawkins, but it was more than that. It positioned him for the initial contact and fight with the enemy. Clary remembered a Marine recruiting slogan, "First to Fight," and concluded Hawkins was the model for the slogan.

Point was physically and psychologically demanding because the intensity and stress were incredible. Hawkins and Clary rotated at point to alleviate and share the stress and to remain vigilant. The team's anxiety level skyrocketed when on point, but it's where they preferred to be.

Corporal Thunder shuttled back to Wiley's position after the briefing. Wiley was tired and nodding from the long sleepless night. He never heard the Corporal's approach until he ordered, "Wiley, go recover Hawkins and Clary."

Wiley was somewhat embarrassed to be dozing and startled by Corporal Thunder's silent approach. But he had learned that his movements were swift and silent and meant to surprise. It was the Indian in him. It was the hunter in him, too.

Wiley practiced the swift and silent approach on Hawkins and Clary, but apparently he needed more practice. Hawkins spied the lumbering Wiley and took dead aim at him with his rifle by the time Wiley saw Hawkins. "Come on, let's go," Wiley mouthed and motioned to Hawkins and Clary. The three quietly policed and camouflaged the listening post before they tactically withdrew to meet with Corporal Thunder.

As they approached Corporal Thunder's position he was shouldering the second radio for the team to use on the return patrol. Immediately, they smiled at one another. The radio confirmed what they had anticipated. They were point.

"Did you hear or see or notice anything to make you think the dead NVA was a scout for a larger element?" Corporal Thunder asked them. They replied, "No," in unison and proceeded directly to the front of the patrol and moved out. Hawkins was point, then Clary, Corporal Thunder, and Wiley. The squad followed in trace. Within minutes they were on the move.

After the patrol developed a rather steady and comfortable pace, Corporal Thunder plotted six separate artillery fire missions along the patrol's route of advance. They were "On Call" missions to be fired only as required to protect their patrol route. He coordinated the fire missions with Wiley, who had the radio and would call for them if they became necessary.

Hawkins established a demanding pace as the patrol battled the slippery slopes and coarse vegetation, but despite slips and falls no one complained. They were too exhausted and numb to complain. They simply trusted Hawkins at point. It was raining and the splashing sounds, gathering clouds, and early morning fog combined to help mask their movement.

Hawkins periodically adjusted the pace to conform to the terrain, threat, and weather, but they moved decisively. A wet jungle leaf or low hanging branch would occasionally slap their faces or sting their arms to startle them, but they plodded on. They were no longer grinding along the trails; they were gliding along them. Months of patrolling had refined their skills.

As the patrol entered the base camp they could afford to relax. Hawkins thought of food; Wiley dreamed of a nap; Clary considered a quick combat field bath; and Corporal Thunder hummed a country tune. But first one duty remained. Sergeant Hedquist ordered, as he halted and dismissed the patrol, "Report to my bunker in five for our debrief."

Patrol debriefs were standard procedure. They were a time to talk and share lessons learned while the patrol was fresh in their memories. Corporal Thunder warned his fire team, "We have four minutes to stow our gear and report to Sergeant Hedquist's area. Let's go. Let's do it. Let's be more than on time; let's be early. We have a lot of lessons to learn from this ambush." Learning was surviving and Corporal Thunder always made sure they were learning and surviving...as well as punctual.

CHAPTER 2

The Mission Is Paramount

Dead ain't accomplishing the mission and dead ain't surviving.

—Marine Corporal Dark Pale Thunder

The ambush patrol members reported to Sergeant Hedquist's bunker within minutes. His bunker, similar to all the bunkers on the perimeter, was about eight-by-eight feet with three-to-four-foot-high sandbag sides covered with a canvas tarp. It was a fighting position dug into the hillside's defensive perimeter. Only the company and higher headquarters had true and totally sandbagged walled and roofed bunkers.

It was early October, but the area was already haunted by the ghosts of those killed in previous battles. In war, Halloween came early and often. It lingered late and long, too. The base camp had the eerie feel of a cemetery…and more. It was a base camp as well as a battlefield. While it was where they lived, it was also where far too many died.

The surrounding base camp landscape was the site of a former battle and old and new fighting holes were scattered throughout the barren area. It was devoid of dense jungle growth due to frequent NVA mortar attack craters, scorched scrub grass, cleared fields of fire, and the constant digging of trenches and fighting holes. When Clary saw it he sarcastically spouted, "It looks like the bald knob of my high school principal." Somehow, someway, something in Vietnam always reminded them of something back home. It kept them connected with home.

The Marines ambled into the area conscious of maintaining dispersion against enemy snipers or mortars. The first arrivals pulled up large wooden ammo boxes to sit on. Later arrivals located smaller metal ammo cans as seats. The last to arrive either sat on their upside down helmets, packs, flak jackets, or folded ponchos. They rested as comfortably as possible in the light drizzle and austere conditions. *It looks like pictures of the Western Front's No Man's Land I saw in my history book,* Wiley thought as he attempted to relax on his hard wooden box. The Payable Hill base camp was bleak, but it was home for now and they were home from the patrol safely.

After the Marines assembled, Sergeant Hedquist presented an overview of the patrol before he sternly explained, "We had a bad incident on the ambush. We didn't handle it good and we could've lost Marines because we didn't do what we should've done. We made mistakes."

Sergeant Hedquist's frown was hard, but his words were harder. Marine Sergeants were respected for their leadership and none more so than him. His physical presence exuded power and virtually demanded respect. It was his leadership style, though, that truly distinguished him. Tactically proficient and totally dedicated to his Marines, he was a respected small unit leader.

"I've asked Corporal Thunder to talk about the incident to make sure it never happens again," he began, pausing for emphasis, "because if it happens again we'll probably be medevacing some of us in body bags because some of us will be dead as dead." Medevac was the common and salty term for medical evacuation. Its use signified tenure and experience in Vietnam. Once in Vietnam, or in-country, another veteran term, Marines spoke words to identify themselves as combat veterans. Sergeant Hedquist then turned to Corporal Thunder and motioned him to begin.

"Dead ain't accomplishing the mission," the Corporal opened, "and dead ain't surviving." He paused a moment for the Marines to consider the seriousness of missions and surviving. "We have a responsibility to our mission and to one another, but this morning we jeopardized both. This is not what Marines do. We need to learn from it so we never do it ever again."

His grim gaze locked on the Marines as he withdrew a small green government-issued flip notebook from his crusty utility blouse's front pocket. "I keep this over my heart because it's the heart of all we do as Marines," he proclaimed proudly as he slowly opened it while patting his chest pocket. "We've all heard it a hundred times. But it's always worth repeating. Always."

Reading from his notebook while shielding it from the incessant rain, though he knew it by heart, Corporal Thunder declared, *The Marine's Guide to Leadership* says, "The primary responsibility of the leader is to accomplish the assigned mission. Everything else, even the welfare of the men, is subordinate." He slowly glanced at every Marine to emphasize the quote.

"Yeah, the quote's maybe hard and heartless," he agreed, "but so is war. The mission is always first. God has a heart and forgives mistakes. The enemy don't and won't."

Corporal Thunder smiled respectfully before he admitted, "Smarter Marines than me wrote this quote, but I think there's a correction. It should say the mission is the responsibility of every Marine—all Marines, every one of us—regardless of rank or position. It's not just leaders or officers; it's all of us. We're all responsible for mission success. All Marines do missions."

He slowly placed the notebook back in his pocket as he noted a core element of the quote that was personally important to him. "We have another responsibility and that's to our Marines. We all have to care about one another. Caring is critical," he admonished. "The mission and caring are dependent on one another. Take care of your Marines and they'll take care of the mission."

Corporal Thunder always emphasized this as he reflected on the thought: *Your Marines never care how much you know until they know how much you care.* The Marines knew he cared.

Selecting his words carefully, he offered, "This morning we didn't do good at either." The Marines nodded in agreement. "We almost failed the mission and almost lost Marines. We were careless. We weren't smart. Let's talk about what we did wrong and what we need to do right."

He spoke with "we" and never once did he mention names or point the blame at anyone. It was always the collective "we" because they were all to blame and all responsible. It was his leadership style. It was his approach. It worked. It was one of an expanding list of admirable character traits that made Wiley, Clary, and Hawkins proud to be members of the Corporal's fire team. The three of them then rustled in their pockets and took out their notebooks and pens to take notes, which were signals for the other members of the patrol to take notes, too. Corporal Thunder glanced at them and nodded in approval. They were a team in more ways than one.

Then, the Corporal mentioned the morning's bad incident with the fatal outcome. "We brought an NVA into our patrol and it endangered our mission and us," he began. "Three months ago, operating down south, southwest of Da Nang, we encountered Vietnamese on almost every patrol. Some were friendly; some were Viet Cong or VC. It was different then than it is now. It was different then near the villages than it is now in the mountains and jungles.

"Now, here west of Dong Ha, here up north by the DMZ, we rarely ever encounter a Vietnamese. When we do, it's almost always an enemy. It's almost always an NVA." Corporal Thunder had their total attention as he continued, "It's a different enemy and situation. But both the VC and NVA want to kill us. Nothing's different about that. Always remember that. Always!

"We should've known to be a helluva lot more suspicious than we were," Corporal Thunder asserted. "Up north here we should be suspicious and consider every Vietnamese an enemy first. Only later, after we've confirmed he's not an enemy, should we consider him a friendly.

"This morning, however," he said in a more serious tone, "we considered the Vietnamese neither a friend nor an enemy. We didn't know. We brought him right into our patrol before considering who he was. We should've never done that without doing a few things first."

Corporal Thunder then began to list in rapid-fire order the "few things" they should have done. "Be suspicious, keep a weapon pointed on him at all times, always keep two Marines on him, search him for weapons or explosives, watch his every move, notice his eyes and facial expressions, keep him a little confused and off balance, check his clothing and footwear, notice his hands and feet for their toughness, note his physical appearance and possible conditioning, and anything else we can think of or that's important to us. Mostly, just be alert and suspicious.

"We didn't do most of these," Corporal Thunder exclaimed gravely as he raised his hands and arms in exasperation. "Instead, we dropped our guard and our suspicions. We failed to search him for the grenade. We forgot that most Vietnamese men wear black pajama bottoms and sandals, especially the VC, but usually only the NVA wear boots. We failed to notice the boots. We forgot he seemed to be fed and fit, which were other signs he was NVA. We failed and forgot a lot. If we don't start remembering, they'll be nothing for us to forget. We'll be dead."

To encourage the Marines to think and talk among themselves, he said, "You can figure out most of what we should have done and some others, but if you have questions see me later. Think about them. Talk about them. Learn to think. Think hard. Thinking's important. Talking's important, too." Corporal Thunder tapped his temple lightly and repeated, "Think and talk."

Quickening his pace, he proclaimed, "Only after we've done all this do we consider bringing the Vietnamese into our patrol. But even then we should consider dealing with him outside the patrol. It's often not necessary to bring him into our patrol area. But if we decide to bring him in we need to blindfold him, handcuff him with his hands behind his back, and make sure he has a weapon pointed at him at all times. *At all times keep a weapon aimed at him.* It's better to be too suspicious than not suspicious enough. Our lives may depend upon our suspicions. Be suspicious and we'll live longer. Be careless and we'll die sooner."

As an afterthought he added, smiling, "You might even hobble him like we do horses on the plains. Tie his ankles with maybe a couple of belts or ropes. Leave it loose enough he can hobble or shuffle along, but tight and close enough he can't run." Since coming to Vietnam, he always searched his Indian and Oklahoma ranching and hunting experiences for tactics for the war.

Summarizing his debrief, he reduced it to a simple, "Smart Marines have a better chance at living. Dumb ones a better chance at dying. Let's help one another be smarter and survive."

Then, unexpectedly to most, his ambush patrol debrief was over—brief and to the point. He simply stopped talking and walked to his fire team in the splashing mud. As he walked toward them, Clary whispered to Hawkins and Wiley, "Okay, I told you he'd talk only a few minutes."

The assembled Marines involuntarily adjusted their positions and hunched their shoulders as a sudden gust of wind and bristling rain laced into them. Darker clouds rolled in with a vengeance and the rain swatted them unmercifully. The Corporal realized the squad was tired, dirty, hungry, and thirsty. He knew how difficult it was to focus on debriefs in such conditions and situations. So he talked briefly and then it was over.

Thankfully, Sergeant Hedquist quickly released the squad adding, "Well, there's not much else to say, except let's learn from it. Corporal Thunder pretty much said all that needed saying."

As the team strolled to their bunker, their individual thoughts fluctuated between their immediate needs and the Corporal's debriefing. Hawkins' hungry stomach groaned. Wiley's sleepy eyes drooped. Clary felt gritty and stank from the caked filth. Corporal Thunder's emotions ebbed and flowed with thoughts of killing and living.

Wiley, Hawkins, and Clary thought how this latest debriefing was vintage Corporal Thunder. He was always teaching, but he was always more interested in their learning than in his teaching.

They learned from experience that he was a leader of few words. While they had their own explanations for his brevity, they always enjoyed repeating them. "We learned," Clary said after a previous briefing, "Corporal Thunder speaks only when he has something to say. Then he says it and it's over. He moves on."

Hawkins claimed, "Maybe it's the Indian in him. Maybe he's just quiet." He was a prolific talker, but he respected the Corporal's quietness, too. It helped him become a better listener.

Wiley confided after a debrief months earlier, "Sometimes I learn as much from what he doesn't say as from what he says. He's like our ole farm pump. He primes the pump and then wants us to think and talk among ourselves. Then we're all becoming teachers as well as students."

"He never just tells us the way or shows us the way," Clary summarized, "Instead, he walks the way with us. He's right there with us and for us."

"Yeah," Hawkins had interjected, "most times it seems I learn as much from what he does as by what he says. I listen to him, but I watch and observe him even harder."

As the team of four Marines sauntered toward their bunker their miseries were evident. They were always dreaming about rest, cleanliness, food, and drink. These basics, however, were now past realities. They had no such basics in Vietnam—but they had their dreams. The dreams were painfully cruel, yet playfully compassionate. "When all we got's a lot of nothin', dreamin' of a little somethin' is almost everythin' to us," Hawkins often lamented.

The dreams were as diversified as their personalities, yet they all dreamed common dreams, too. Corporal Thunder thought of electricity and gas for heating and air-conditioning and plumbing with faucets for running water. They, of course, had none of these comforts—but they envisioned them daily! Girls, of course, were the dreams of all of them.

Clary probably described it best after months of grueling ambush patrols and the bunker's squalid living conditions. Unstrapping his pack and unbuckling his web gear and repeatedly feeling exhaustion set in after the adrenaline rush of patrol after patrol, he began to complain about the grungy conditions. "I can't recall the last time I had a shower or turned on a faucet or flipped a light switch or opened a door or sat at a table or huddled over a heater or felt the cool breeze of an air conditioner or listened to a radio or watched a television or any such luxury."

Hawkins just stared blankly at him for a moment. When the reality of Clary's tirade sank in, Hawkins cussed and spewed, "I forget the last time I was with a girl or my last pool hustling victim or my last good-night kiss from my mama." It was far too sad for them to recall such absences, yet it made them smile. Thoughts and dreams of home always made them glow.

Shivering with delight at describing and regaling in life's luxuries back home helped them endure their miseries. But as they approached the austerity of their bunker they were jolted back to reality. The bunker was their home now. The muddy close quarters of the sandbag and tarp bunker were ugly and confining. The cruel ritual of their dreams, however, was worth the homesickness it caused because it sustained their hopes and dreams.

The reality of their new "home" hit once again as they stepped into the trench at the front of their bunker and hoisted themselves up and into the bunker's confined sleeping and living area.

Sitting or sprawled out because the overhead was too low for them to stand or sit up straight, Corporal Thunder ordered, "Okay, we know the drill. Let's do it." They began taking care of their household duties and squaring away gear, which consisted mostly of staging equipment in the back of the bunker in ammo boxes and cans and preparing to clean their weapons.

They sighed almost in unison. Miserable in their fatigue and deprivations, they were so physically exhausted none of them seemed of any significance. The miseries were hard on them, however, getting used to them was harder. They were now simply conditions and routines that were a common part of their uncommon lives. It was who they had become—who they would be for many more months.

Corporal Thunder grimaced briefly, primarily to fight the ebbing fatigue, before continuing his orders, "Wiley, you and Clary clean your weapons first. Then let Hawkins and me know when you're finished and we'll clean ours." He then briefly massaged his calf muscles.

Whether the team was on patrol on in the base camp the Corporal made it their practice that while two weapons were being cleaned two weapons would be at the ready. They had learned they were safe nowhere in Vietnam and that a ready weapon was part of their survival.

The Corporal and Hawkins assumed positions with their M14s facing the perimeter. They were on watch lost in far away thoughts while their eyes scanned the jungles. The distant western mountains loomed large though partially obscured by the steady and relentless misty rain. The Corporal wondered, *How can such beautiful vistas be so dangerous.* He pulled to tighten his collar to enclose escaping body warmth, but he only shivered from the harassing cold. Hawkins noticed him shiver, which caused an involuntary shudder of his own. They stood together looking and listening and thinking of home. Thoughts of home always warmed them.

Wiley and Clary began cleaning their rifles. The four Marines became lost in their rambling thoughts and relentless fatigue. Wiley recalled an incident from months before and asked, "Remember when that squad was cleaning their rifles at the same time one afternoon. Wouldn't you know the NVA launched a mortar and rocket attack. Then all hell broke loose."

"It's hard to be alert and defend the perimeter," Hawkins smiled, "when you're holding eight or ten parts of your disassembled weapon in your hands. It don't function too good that way."

Clary joked with dead seriousness, "They might as well of dropped the parts and grabbed their peckers because in a fire fight a broken down rifle is about as useless as holding peckers," he paused. "But for some, while holding their peckers at least they knew what they were doing."

"Unless, of course," Hawkins howled, "you'd rather fornicate with the NVA than fight'em."

Wiley always laughed hilariously when Hawkins said "fornicate." It's not the first word Hawkins used to describe the situation, but once he learned Wiley's dad was a preacher he was more careful and respectful with his language.

Wiley noticed Hawkins' attempt to avoid as much profanity as possible. One night, late on watch, the two of them were alone and Wiley had said, "Thanks, Hawkins. I'm not offended by cussing. I've heard it all. I've heard worse, but thanks."

Hawkins, embarrassed by the thanks, simply countered, "Yeah, I know, but my uncle's a Catholic priest. I really try to watch my language around our family." After a brief pause, he admitted, "I owe you and your dad the same respect because now you and me are part of one another's family." Hawkins reached over and gave Wiley a playful shoulder punch.

His tough and rough exterior and persona were believable because it was who Hawkins was and because it was who he wanted the team to believe he was. But there was more to him. There was much more to all of them. They came to know how much more in time.

Wiley was nonetheless touched and surprised. After the incident, he had later divulged the conversation to Corporal Thunder. "It's the first time any white guy ever talked to me about me being part of his family and him being part of mine."

With heartfelt conviction, Corporal Thunder continued sharpening his K-Bar knife and declared, "We're family. We're Marines. It makes us family. There's lots of reasons we're a good team, but a sense of family is probably the best of all of them." Then he pointed the K-Bar squarely at Wiley and repeated for emphasis, "We're family now and always will be."

Twice now, Wiley had been considered family by white Marines. It was incredibly inspiring for him; he had never before been accepted as such by adults outside his own race. The Corporal and Hawkins had unhesitatingly extended their Marine and team friendship to a family one. It would forever change his life. As he and Clary shared a game of blackjack in their bunker one evening, Clary was lost in thought while blankly staring at the dark cloudy sky. Wiley was far away, too, as he had Hawkins on his mind. Suddenly, he smiled at Clary and confided, "Hawkins always wants us to think he's nothing but a Boston Italian outlaw or hood or Mafia bad ass, but there's a softer side to him, too."

"True, but don't ever let on because he'll deny it ten ways from Sunday," Clary smiled.

Wiley was startled out of reminiscing and back in the present when, after weapons were cleaned and gear stowed, Corporal Thunder suddenly suggested, "Okay, let's eat."

"Yeah, if you call eatin' these putrid C-Rations eatin'," Hawkins complained while twisting and contorting his face in revulsion as he selected a can of beefsteak and potatoes. "They got nice sounding names, but they're horrible." Wiley always professed they were "like eating boiled chitlins," a favorite southern hog intestine delicacy he nonetheless detested. Clary ate Cs only to keep from starving. Corporal Thunder ate anything.

"But we get to wash them down with iodine-laced water purification pills," Clary added flippantly as he shook his canteens to help dissolve the pills he had earlier dropped into them. The tablets were bitter, but protected them from disease despite their despicable taste.

"Damn, we're always arguing which is worse," Hawkins teased, "but we always conclude it's a worthless debate. The rations and water are just too awful to argue about."

In between jokingly gagging on their dinner, Wiley injected, "Yeah, but worse is we never get good sleeps." They all realized as long as they were in Vietnam they would never have a full night's sleep—a good eight hours or four hours of rack time. Instead, patrols, ambushes, listening posts, night watches, and the virtual nightly enemy rocket and mortar attacks, among other distractions, ensured sleep was intermittent and on a catch-as-catch-can basis.

Corporal Thunder's observations of his team reminded him of a Marine slogan, *A Happy Marine is a Complaining Marine*, by alleging, "You three complain and bitch and moan as much as any Marines I've ever known. So, you got to be the happiest Marines in our Corps."

Then to really harass them, he said derisively, "Let me see those happy faces." On cue they all frowned sadly before laughing boisterously. Friendly complaining was part of coping and they grumbled further as they ate and settled in for the night by jostling for sleeping space.

As the darkness became darker than dark they began one of their frequent talks. "Our talks settle nothing," Hawkins noted, "but talkin' helps keep me thinkin' and thinkin' helps keep me livin' and livin' helps keep me survivin'."

The bunker became unusually quiet as the four of them considered Hawkins' words. "Well," the Corporal stretched to relieve the tension in his back and emphasized, "maybe the talks do help settle something. I'll take surviving as something. I'll take surviving until our tour ends. I'll take that for now and forever." He stretched, again, thankful his pack was stowed and off his back.

Hawkins started to argue the point, but had nothing argumentative to say. This usually resulted in him saying nothing except, "Yeah, for now, I'll take survivin', too. Survivin's good. Let's talk."

Surprisingly, the usually quiet Corporal Thunder initiated their evening talk. Living involved killing—they all knew it by now. The Corporal, however, was the first to verbalize it tonight. "Today, hell, everyday, we're talking about or thinking about or actually killing. It's wearing on us, but I don't want it to get us worn down or out." He made a point of reiterating the guiding principle he had established at the onset by emphasizing, "I want us to understand it, to do it when we have to do it. I don't want us dying, but I don't want us killing unnecessarily either."

He frowned as he recalled the decapitation earlier that morning. "I'm praying killing the NVA today the way I did was right." His face clearly reflected his inner turmoil and remorse over the unavoidably gruesome action he had been forced to take. "It was nasty, but it had to be a quiet killing. It was the only way I knew how to do it. I didn't want to maybe alert a following enemy force and endanger the mission and us. I won't ever forget it. I'll just have to live with it.

"Killing's always been wrong to us, but now it's what we do." He winced at the remembrance of the decapitation. "The killing's hard, but living in war is harder. The killing's hard to do, but harder is understanding them." He sensed the deaths had disturbed the team's sense of morality and had challenged them emotionally. "Killing ain't easy, but dying is hard," he concluded.

The Corporal was careful neither to legitimize nor demonize the war and killings. He was, however, determined that he and his team would survive. The killings and darkness became old and weary burdens they bore despite their young and exuberant ages.

Corporal Thunder paused momentarily for words to both sympathize and prepare them to repeatedly kill to live. "The killing is foreign to all we've ever known in the past, but now it's all we know. We just have to learn to live with it or it will kill us." They had few options. Options in war were few. Sympathy was fleeting. Death was forever.

"Thinkin' about why we're here and why we're doin' what we're doin' is too much damn stress for me…the killin's just too much," Hawkins confessed as he admitted the trauma of killing was a moral dilemma for him, too. He was the team's fighter, but he was cognizant of the difference between fighting and killing.

"Remember, we're humans and we got to live with ourselves and with others, too," Corporal Thunder concluded. "We know right from wrong. We got to always do our best to do right. We got Marine Corps values and beliefs despite the disgusting and horrible situation we're in now."

While thoughts of killing were depressing to them, they were often compelled to share such thoughts. Curiously, talking about them was often the only way to suppress them and move on.

Clary immediately thought, *Corporal Thunder's focus is always on character and ethics, but his focus is always on us, too. He wants us to do right, but he wants us to survive, too. We're his team.* This was of special importance in Vietnam because the war was essentially a small unit one. The vast majority of the fighting was done by fire teams, squads, and platoons. They did the fighting and the dying. The greatest number of deaths and casualties were from small units.

Fire teams had been the basic foundation of Marine infantry units for years. When the four of them had these talks, Corporal Thunder often asserted, "There are three infantry fire teams per squad, three squads per platoon, and three platoons per company. The larger companies and battalions and regiments are above my influence. But this team is ours. It's ours to make the best." Infantry squads normally averaged about 14, platoons 40-plus, companies 200-plus, battalions 1,000-plus, and regiments 4,000-plus Marines and Sailors.

Corporal Thunder's primary devotion was to his team and his Marines. All beyond that was secondary. But all beyond that was infinitely more critical to him and his team than he would ever possibly know. At his level in the chain of command, however, he only knew what he knew. It was part of the darkness. It was the darkest part of the darkness.

Hawkins interrupted his thoughts as he suddenly blurted, "Corporal Thunder, I have a question if you don't mind." The team paused in surprise while preparing for their "sleeps," which was how Wiley always referred to "sleep." This was serious. Hawkins rarely, if ever, asked if he could ask a question. Usually, he simply and bluntly shouted it out.

"Sure, I'll do my best to answer," Corporal Thunder replied. "What you got?"

"What made you the most suspicious about the Vietnamese this morning?" Hawkins asked.

"Well, most all those reasons I mentioned in the debrief," Corporal Thunder explained, "but there were some other signs I noticed, too.

"At first the Vietnamese was more scared or afraid than he was angry or hostile. He just looked more meek than defiant," he continued, "but then I noticed his attitude change. He seemed to become less afraid and more angry. My dad taught me to be more wary of an angry animal or critter than a scared one. My dad says a scared animal or opponent wants to get out of the situation if he can because he wants to live. But once his fear changes to anger it kind of means he's resigned himself to losing or, in this case, dying. Then he's just angry and hostile and that's when he no longer cares too much about living but only killing. Once I noticed he was angry, I knew he'd be hostile and that he'd given up on living. I saw it in his clinched fists and grinding teeth. In his glaring eyes and sullen expression. Then I knew he was a danger to us. Does that make sense?" he asked.

Hawkins thought for a few seconds and then exclaimed, "Jesus, that's right. That's the way it is in boxin' and fightin', too. I'd rather fight a scared guy than an angry one. Yeah, that makes sense to me. I'll remember that."

The Corporal's care for his Marines surfaced again as he requested, "Well, talk about it with other Marines, too," he requested. "Maybe it'll help them understand and learn, too." It was momentarily quiet as the team reflected on another lesson from Corporal Thunder.

"It's darker than dark," Lance Corporal Wiley said as the team began to randomly talk about and reflect on last night's ambush. He changed the subject to help relieve Corporal Thunder's guilt over the killing. He expected his dark observation to be good naturedly challenged. Pausing for the usual challenge, he was surprised when none came. He was cautiously relieved and shrugged his relief with a sigh as he pounded his pack into a pillow for his sleeps.

About the time he thought his darkness view had been accepted, Hawkins countered by asking jokingly, "But is it as dark as your black Mississippi ass?" Wiley was a Black Marine, but he was relieved. When Hawkins, an Italian, joked with him it was his way of extending friendship as well as respect. Wiley had worked hard to be accepted in their brief time together. He was beginning to feel a part of the team. They were all beginning to feel a sense of team.

Wiley thought briefly about countering, but he knew it was useless. Hawkins would continue the banter, the give and take, until they were all either laughing or brawling playfully. Wiley had no desire to brawl in the cool late night mid-October tropical monsoons and temperatures, even if playfully. He could have wrestled Hawkins into defeat, but he knew Hawkins would never quit.

As Clary had once whispered, "Wiley, never brawl with a wild savage and never debate with an insane moron. It's an awful combination." Clary then looked quickly at Hawkins in exasperation.

While Wiley was at times unsure about his leadership and the predictability of Hawkins, he was always confident and certain and protective of his race. He sensed an obligation to respond to Hawkins' black ass comment and counterattacked as he swept the rain from his ebony face with his huge calloused palm while flexing his powerful black forearm.

"Well, it's black and black's an advantage in the jungle darkness, but I'm not too sure about your lily pink butt," Wiley finally countered. He deliberately said "pink" instead of "white." He knew "pink" would irritate Hawkins, irritate him to no end, as he pictured a pink lily.

Hawkins became defensive. "Pink, hell, it's white, pure white. You're color blind." It was a weak comeback and Hawkins knew it, but he was pleased Wiley was becoming more assertive.

As a PFC, Hawkins' "black Mississippi ass" remark could have been considered a breach of Marine protocol or racially intolerant, especially to Wiley as a Lance Corporal and black. But Hawkins was always saying, "There ain't no black or white or brown or red Marines. There's only Marine green Marines." Hawkins was passive toward race, but passionate toward Marines.

Wiley started to counter again. Instead, he thought Hawkins would now have to consider there were pink Marines, too. He decided to let Hawkins dwell on that for a while. Wiley reserved any other comments for later, while noticing the consternation on Hawkins' face.

Hawkins was part Boston Italian and familiar with racial slurs. His devil-may-care attitude was refreshing and comforting, especially in their current combat situation. Forgiving him was better than arguing or fighting with him because arguing and fighting were what he loved.

"You're right about the darker than dark," Hawkins suddenly agreed, but he ignored the pink comment. The agreement surprised Wiley. Hawkins rarely agreed with anyone on anything. At least he usually always pretended to disagree. He loved to fight with words as well as fists.

Momentarily, the Marines in the fighting bunker were overcome by thought. They had been in Vietnam for about three months, since mid-summer 1966. Initially, they had operated in the Da Nang area of southern I Corps, the northern most Corps in Vietnam. They had recently, however, relocated with their battalion north to the De-Militarized Zone, or DMZ, west of Dong Ha. In the new operating area they talked to acquaint themselves with the new area and enemy.

The team initially talked about numerous topics. Hawkins talked of pretty girls and fast cars. Clary spoke about sports and surfing. Wiley remembered cotton season and homeschooling. Corporal Thunder recalled hunting and fishing on the plains. Plus, they all talked of home and family. It was later, after months in Vietnam, that they began to talk of the war and killing and fear.

The war and the mountainous jungles were rarely what they expected; more often what they dreaded and feared. Nothing was as it appeared. Nothing seemed real except the fears and the killings and the contradictions of the war, which were all too real.

Then the reflections were over. Then it was back to reality. The ambush patrol had almost concluded without incident until the hapless NVA stumbled into it. The gruesome killing of the NVA by Corporal Thunder had briefly unnerved those unfortunate few who had witnessed it. Death was, however, what they came to know. Once again, they were simply relieved to be alive.

After the decapitation, Clary had shrugged and sadly proclaimed, "We regret the killing, but rejoice in living." Death was always lurking. It was always present. It was always close. Always.

"It's late. It's time for watches and sleeps," Corporal Thunder announced. "Check your weapons one more time." He was always emphasizing, "Take care of our weapons and they'll take care of us." It was a duty they remembered, one they never forgot. Unfortunately, their nation forgot, but that was in their future and they would come to decry the forgetfulness in time. The forgetfulness was tragic. It was the M16 rifle, but it was a bad memory for another day.

The team jockeyed for sleep positions in the small confined bunker. They wrestled with ponchos liners as blankets, squashed packs as pillows, and cardboard C-Ration case boxes as foundation bedding to keep them out of the oozing shifting mud. It was uncomfortable to sleep with their boots on, but more uncomfortable to be without them should the NVA launch a night attack or mortars.

Corporal Thunder smiled as he thought of them as wild geese twisting and turning to smooth out their nests. Recalling his Pawhuska home and hunting with his dad, he became pensive. Thoughts of family and home on the Oklahoma prairies were always comforting. But the team was now his focus and his family. Proud of his team, he was deeply and fully committed to them. He was an Oklahoman and Osage Indian proud of his state and heritage. But he put aside such remembrances for now. Now he was a Marine fire team leader. He never put that aside.

CHAPTER 3

Friends Despite Diversities

Ask not what your country can do for you, ask what you can do for your country.

—President John F. Kennedy

The team's nightly talks became standard for them, but they remembered one of their first talks as one of their best. The past summer, about two months ago, the first part of August, while down south near Da Nang, Corporal Thunder held a special evening talk. In the shade of a poncho lean-to as a shield from the glaring setting sun, they gazed over the lush rice paddies and spoke simply and plainly about themselves. Clary later remarked to them, "The talks bonded us as much, maybe more, than the war. We're becoming a team and becoming a team is helping us survive."

Total strangers in peace often become forever friends in war. Corporal Thunder had been in the Marine Corps for about two years, Wiley over one, and Hawkins and Clary less than a year. They all came to Vietnam in mid-summer 1966. Arriving as individual replacements instead of with units was the standard process for Marines manning their forces in Vietnam. Marines bonded into teams once in-country with units.

Later, after a lengthy patrol along the gleaming rice paddy dikes and numerous thatched village huts, the team sat on sandbags in the warm twilight and talked about becoming a team.

"We musta arrived in-county within a week of one another," Hawkins estimated.

"Yeah, but I felt bad without a unit," Wiley frowned. "It was good to get assigned to one."

"One day we were strangers; however, the next day brothers in arms," Clary conceded.

After Corporal Thunder, Wiley, Hawkins, and Clary had been together in the fire team for about two weeks, Corporal Thunder announced, "We probably could have talked earlier, but sometimes it takes a few weeks for teams to become permanent. Often Marines temporarily transfer in and out of teams before becoming stable. They change units because of casualties, promotions, tour completions, and other causes," Corporal Thunder summarized, "but I hope we'll be together for months.

"Lieutenant Abrahams asked me yesterday how we were doing as a team," Corporal Thunder continued. "I told him we're good and we'll get better. I told him I wanted each of you, all of you, together on our team." Second Lieutenant Abrahams was the Second Platoon Leader. They had known him for only a few weeks, but they were learning that he was a professional. Most importantly, they sensed he truly cared.

"I told him Hawkins probably needs more help and work than any of us," Corporal Thunder teased, "but that Wiley and Clary could handle him." Hawkins falsely bristled, but then smiled.

Hawkins attempted to interrupt, but Clary was faster, "Damn, you mean we have to carry Hawkins for the next year?" They all laughed because they all knew no one carried Hawkins.

"Seriously," Corporal Thunder injected, "you're who I want with me, who I want as our team."

Hawkins mentally drifted as he calculated: "Now we're officially in the Second Fire Team, Second Squad, Second Platoon, Company M, 3/3." The 3/3 was the abbreviation for 3rd Battalion/Third Marines. The complete abbreviation was 2/2/2/M/3/3, but it was seldom used. Usually, they simply said they were in Mike Second Platoon or Mike Company or 3/3.

It was what they all wanted, but they were so elated with the news they were somewhat stunned into silence. It was their actions and smiles that said more than words could ever say. Shaking hands and hugging one another, these simple gestures bonded them for life.

"Okay, I know it's kind of hard to express our thoughts about this, but let's simply talk about ourselves so we can know one another better. It's part of Marine Corps leadership. It's part of us being Marines," Corporal Thunder affirmed, "for us to know one another, and to look out for one another. Now we're a team we need to know one another good to look out for one another better."

As darkness descended on the poncho lean-to and bunker, the Corporal suggested, "I don't quite know how to do this. I've never had a team in combat, but I want us to share thoughts about our past and who we are and what we think is important for us to know about one another.

"Okay? Simple enough?" asked Corporal Thunder, but before anyone answered he said, "I'll go first, as an example, but you can say as much or as little or whatever you want. It's up to you.

"I'm an Indian," Corporal Thunder began proudly but nervously, "which is pretty obvious, but I'm also part Irish. My dad's a full-blood Osage Indian and my mom's a full-blood Irish woman. But one thing I'm not is what the white man says is a half-breed. I don't like that term. I'm a full-blood American. That's who I am and what I am. That's what counts. I'm a hundred percent Marine, too. Now, that's what counts the most to us, too." He lightly touched his dark and pronounced Indian cheeks and Marine Corps insignia stenciled on his utility blouse.

"My Indian-American name is Dark Pale Thunder. Dark is respect for my dad's plains and sun-darkened Indian skin and lifestyle. Pale is respect for my mom's Irish heritage and soft and smooth coloration. Indians appreciate and respect colors," he emphasized. Clary noted Corporal Thunder's pride when he mentioned his dad and his eyes twinkled when he talked of his mom.

"I have two sisters, Moon Beam and Bright Star, and two brothers, White Horse and Blue Bull. I warned you we Indians love colors. They're all younger than me," he disclosed affectionately.

Wiley, Hawkins, and Clary sat quietly. Corporal Thunder was rarely talkative, but now he believed it was his duty to talk. It was the team's responsibility to listen and they listened.

"My Indian heritage is the Osage tribe, which has a relationship or connection with the Sioux Indians. The Osage Indians are taller than most tribes, which maybe explains why I'm about 6'2," he sat tall and stretched, "but I'm proudest of the Osage Indian's reputation as uncommonly fierce fighters and renowned hunters. My dad taught me to hunt and fight, but now the Marines are teaching me a different type of hunting and fighting.

"Two of my favorite Osage Indian Chiefs are Chief Black Dog and Chief Bigheart. Chief Black Dog was seven feet tall and weighed over 300 pounds. He loaned Indian scouts to the Army troops in the western plains. Chief Bigheart negotiated land treaties with the white man and was among the first to retain mineral rights to the land. It seems the white man always broke his treaties with us and kept relocating us time after time, but Chief Bigheart and oil kind of helped Indians even the score," the Corporal proclaimed with a hint of anger as he recalled the white man's past disrespect for his people. The team unequivocally sensed his pride in his Indian heritage.

"But the two people I'm most proud of are my dad and my mom. My dad has a work ethic like no one and my mom has a compassion and tenderness toward others second to none. They've truly blessed me and I hope to make them proud of me." Corporal Thunder continued, "At times, I probably didn't appreciate my dad's work ethic as much as he wanted, but his beaded leather belt helped change that," he frowned. "My mom's the kindest woman I've ever known, but when I did wrong she was never hesitant to break a birch switch across my butt," he winced and patted his butt, "because right and wrong are important to her.

"I was reared on a Pawhuska, Oklahoma, ranch. I love the outdoors and respect nature. I played football, ran track, and wrestled in school, but my favorite sports are hunting and fishing," he smiled.

"My dad and brothers and me are good hunters. We mostly hunt ducks, doves, quail, rabbits, squirrels, deer, and other small game. All we kill we eat. We never kill just to kill," he confessed.

"I feel most at home on the open plains and prairies, but it's a tough life, a hard life. My dad ranched and farmed and we raised and grew most of our beef, chickens, eggs, vegetables, and fruit, but my mom drew the line at hogs and pigs. No hogs or pigs," Corporal Thunder grinned.

"My dad and two of his brothers were Marines during World War II. They wanted to be in the infantry, but the Marines assigned them as communicators. They were never part of the famous Navajo Code Talkers, but they performed almost the same duties for their units," he proudly related. "My dad never talks much about the war, but maybe when I go home we can talk. I'd like that." Clary made a mental note to remember this.

"College is a dream, but when I graduated from high school our family couldn't afford it" he sighed. "Maybe with the GI Bill I can go to the University of Oklahoma. I'd like that. They play good football at Oklahoma. Plus, I'm Indian and they don't much like cowboys from another state school, Oklahoma State University, but it has a famous wresting history, which we respect, too.

"So, when I got out of high school I knew the draft would be after me, especially with the Vietnam War beginning," he shrugged, "and when my dad asked me what I was going to do I told him I was going to be a draft dodger. My dad frowned until I quickly said I was dodging the draft by joining the Marine Corps." Hawkins smiled recalling what prompted him to join the Marines.

"My dad just grinned and said, 'Son, that's an insane way to dodge the draft, but be my guest'. He later told me he was really proud of me and gave me one of the few hugs he's ever given me," the Corporal conceded. "But mom just cried. Moms cry a lot when sons go to war. They hug you a lot, too. I got lots of tears and hugs from my mom." He glowed affectionately talking of his mom.

"It was hard to leave home because I love ranching and farming and the life of a cattleman on the prairies. I know how hard and tough a life it is, however, after seeing my parents struggle and sacrifice for our family," Corporal Thunder smiled. "So, I told my dad I didn't think I was tough enough to be a rancher and farmer and that I'd just join the Marines and go to war to toughen me up for the hard life as a cattleman. My dad knows what true toughness is from his time as a Marine and farmer. He smiled and told me to come back home when the Marines and this war are done with me and that we'd show the land how tough and hard we Thunders are." It was obvious to the team that the Corporal and his dad had a special relationship.

Corporal Thunder paused while searching for anything he should add before he simply said, "So, that's my story, that's who I am, that's why I'm here in Vietnam. It could be worse and maybe it'll get worse, but together we'll get through this.

"Now, before another talk, you each have to ask me one question," Corporal Thunder blurted.

Hawkins mumbled, "You didn't say nothin' about havin' to ask questions."

"I must have forgotten," the Corporal admitted, "it's an ole trick I learned from Ms. Wilcox, my speech teacher. To ask good questions, you have to listen good. She always made us ask a question after one of us gave a talk. She graded the talker, but she also graded the listener and our questions. She wanted us to be good speakers, but even better listeners. It works. Trust me."

"Okay, trust me." Hawkins smiled, "Do I have your blessing to ask your sister on a date?"

"Yeah, you can ask her, but I doubt she'll say yes," Corporal Thunder asserted, "but if by chance she says yes, which is doubtful, you have my approval on one condition."

"Okay, what's it?" Hawkins quickly asked.

"We all have to help one another survive this war," Corporal Thunder answered.

"I can live with that. I can live with survivin'," Hawkins joked and they all laughed until he pleaded, "Seriously, I got a real or better question. We're now in your team and you're now our team leader. So what's your leadership philosophy or style?"

Corporal Thunder thought briefly before he answered, "My favorite leadership thought is that *Good Followers Make Leaders Good*." Pausing, he looked each of them directly in their eyes and spoke no other words because he wanted them to thoughtfully consider what he had said.

The team was somewhat perplexed and Clary asked, "Don't you mean *Good Followers Make Good Leaders?*"

"Well, that's true, too, but I believe the greater truth is that *Good Followers Make Leaders Good*," the Corporal confidently replied before further clarifying his thoughts. "There's no leaders without followers. Followers make leaders who they are, just as leaders make followers who they are. It's teamwork pure and simple. But my view and my emphasis is that it's teamwork from the bottom up: just as it's teamwork from the top down."

Corporal Thunder detected their puzzled expressions and explained the essence of his beliefs on leadership. "I simply believe that the more time and energy I invest in you, the more I teach and train you, the better you'll become. Then the better you become, the better the team becomes. The better the team becomes, the better I become. You, as followers, will make the team better and you'll make me better, too. That's how I prefer to look at and practice leadership."

The Corporal momentarily paused and concluded, "Leadership's always a good subject for us to talk about. Later, once we've been together for awhile, let's have one of our bunker talks be on your individual thoughts on leadership."

Only beginning to understand Corporal Thunder's leadership philosophy, Wiley, Clary, and Hawkins nodded in agreement. They sensed leaders and followers have an incredible responsibility toward one another. Fulfilling that responsibility, however, would challenge them in terms unimaginable to them at that time. Corporal Thunder then pointed to Wiley to continue with the questions.

Wiley then asked, "You never mentioned your religion. What's your religion?"

"I should've known you'd ask about religion," Corporal Thunder replied. "Well, white missionaries' established churches and religious schools to make Indians Christians, but most Indians have never really belonged to organized religions. We believe strongly in spirits and nature. Our religion is mostly about our Great Spirit and our Great Earth. We believe in our Indian heritage and in the earth, sun, moon, and stars. We believe in avoiding violence and living in harmony with our land," he concluded.

Clary rescued Corporal Thunder by asking, "Your Indian dad married an Irish woman?"

What may have been considered a personal question was accepted in the team. The four had few secrets and their openness helped bond them into the close family they eventually became.

"We don't know much about my mom's family because she never knew that much about them to tell us," Corporal Thunder replied, "but we know they were Irish farmers who had the bad luck to come to Ochelata, Oklahoma, in the mid-thirties during the Dust Bowl era. It was a bad time. It was a hard time. The land turned brown and as much dirt was constantly swirling in winds as was on the shifting ground. Dirt and dust and grit were everywhere. It was in people's ears and noses and mouths. It was terrible. Many people became discouraged and moved on, especially if they had no ties to the land and no families to help them. One day, when my mom was eight, her family was gone and my mom was abandoned at the Matoaka Baptist Church in Ochelata."

Corporal Thunder reflected momentarily on his mom's memories and stories of those devastating times. It was a time when her family was torn apart and the precious land was ravaged. He then continued, "It really hurt my mom and she rarely talks about it, except to tell us how thankful she was when an Indian family accepted her into their family." He paused to quietly reflect on the tragic incident that helped to later define his mom's loving tenderness.

"My dad's family was friends with her adopted family. In time, they became friends. After World War II, they were reacquainted at a Victory Dance in Pawhuska," Corporal Thunder smiled.

"My dad once told us kids that it takes a good woman to help a good man during the hard times of working the land hard," he solemnly stated, "and that my mom was as good and soft as they come…and as bad and hard as she had to be, too. I think my mom had a softness that balanced my dad's hardness. But by damn she could be harder than hard when it came to protecting and caring for our family, especially us kids. My mom's special and she makes me and our family as proud to be Irish as Indian." He then grinned in relief because he was never much into public speaking.

Silence settled upon the four Marines as they reflected on Corporal Thunder's brief but poignant description of himself, his family, and his life. They were touched by his simple and plain words to describe how deeply he believed in his Indian heritage and how he so passionately cherished his family and his life on the Oklahoma plains.

"Okay, who's next?" Corporal Thunder asked as he purposefully broke the silence. Without waiting for a volunteer he asked, "Clary, you want to be next?"

"Sure, I'll go next," Clary rolled his eyes and took a deep breath and replied.

Corporal Thunder sensed Wiley and Hawkins were searching their memories and past for meaningful thoughts to share with the team. He was intuitively aware they would appreciate more time to collect their thoughts. But he knew Clary would be ready. Clary was the most intelligent Marine in the team and the most articulate in expressing his thoughts and ideas. Clary, however, never flaunted his education or intelligence and he never talked condescendingly to them. He had the ability to speak simply about complicated issues, which later became important to them as a team. In talking about himself, however, he was less confident than they had at first suspected.

"I'm a Southern Californian," Clary began hesitatingly, "and that more or less defines both where I'm from and who I am. I don't really know much about my family's past, especially about our heritage. My dad or mom never talked much about our genealogy or lineage or ancestors. I don't know why they never talked much about their past or families, but after learning about

Corporal Thunder's family and past I hope someday I can learn more about my family.

"It seems my family simply began with us. I know my paternal grandparents were from Ohio before they settled in California in the early 1900's. I know my maternal grandparents were from Georgia, but they came to California much earlier. I think they came sometime before the Civil War," he continued, "but before that I don't really know and, worse, I've never really been curious or interested. Maybe it's a uniquely California phenomenon. Maybe it's because most Californians came from somewhere at sometime for some reason and then simply became Californians. We don't seem to think much about being English or French or Italian or Irish or whatever. We seem to think we're simply Californians." Hawkins shrugged wondering how anyone could consider it unimportant to know their ancestry. He was proud to be Italian.

Clary began to believe his talk was more difficult than he initially thought. Then he realized he had to be himself and true to whatever past he knew. Whatever it was, it was his. He had to own it.

"Californians seem to live more in the present and value the future more than the past," Clary announced as he modified his thoughts. "We're diverse in our thoughts and creativity as well as united in our love for the land and environment. We have forests and deserts, we have majestic mountains and lush valleys, but what we have that defines us most are our beaches and sunshine. Plus, we got Hollywood and the Golden Gate Bridge. That's California to me.

"My dad graduated from high school and worked as an auto mechanic before he joined the Marines for World War II," he continued. "My mom was a secretary when they met and they married the month before my dad was transferred overseas for the Pacific Campaigns.

"Tarawa was my dad's most famous battle, but he rarely talks about the war. I'm proud of my dad now more than ever, now that I'm a Marine. I know he received the Silver Star for heroism, but he never talks about it. I hope after this war we can talk together about our combat experiences," Clary declared as he glanced at Corporal Thunder. Wiley grimaced thinking of the boot camp history classes on the bloody battle at the Tarawa beaches. Now he knew from whom Clary received his inner strength.

"After the war my dad came home and attended college on the GI Bill. It was a struggle for our family financially, but dad was determined to become a college professor, which meant many years of study to earn his doctorate to teach at the university level," he proudly but sadly stated.

"Unfortunately, most of my life my dad was preoccupied with his studies and later his students. When he was home he was writing because the 'Publish or Perish' rule for tenured professors seemed to be both a pressure and a passion for him. Our family was close, but we were often apart. We were often in the same house, but in different rooms," Clary sighed, "which was why sports and surfing became such a huge part of my life. My surfing bum friends and sports teammates became my families. I was an only child, but had numerous brothers and sisters at the beach and sporting events.

"The outdoors for me was beaches and mountain ski slopes instead of plains and prairies or these tropical mountains and jungles. I never shot a weapon in my life until I joined the Marines," Clary confessed, "but I loved and lived to compete in sports. My coaches promoted me as one of the best all-around all-star athletes in California, which helped me with a number of scholarship offers.

"I know the value of education because I've seen how it's changed my family from a lower middle class to upper middle class one," he admitted, "but once I enrolled in college I realized I lacked the maturity and commitment to study. My dad and I had one of our best heart-to-heart talks. He explained to me how the Marine Corps changed his life and changed it for the better.

"My dad never encouraged me to join the Marines," Clary acknowledged, "and my mom certainly discouraged me joining. But I realized I needed to change my life to change my future. Now the Corps is my life and I'm learning the degree to which the Marines will change my life.

"But for now I'm thankful you're all a part of my life and family. I was never as close to my family as I am with you, but I've learned that's part of my life I want to truly change," he noted.

"Once I joined the Marines we began to become closer. The Corps' helping me better appreciate family. When we're together again, my goal is to help us become a better family." He smiled.

Corporal Thunder, Wiley, and Hawkins had perceived Clary was different than they were from the day they first met. After Clary spoke they were even more perplexed about the differences, but they all recognized Clary was special. He was different, but he was special.

Clary was taller than Corporal Thunder by an inch or two and his broad shoulders and muscular arms and chest were physically imposing, yet they lacked the brute force of Wiley. Clary's blond-haired, blue-eyed bronze body was in stark contrast to the miniature physique and rough features of Hawkins. He was city-wise and metropolitan compared to the plains and prairies that defined Corporal Thunder. Clary was, as Hawkins later whistled, "The real deal."

Yet, to the team, Clary appeared to lack a certain confidence and a certain driving force in his life despite his unique and special attributes. Clary became more of an enigma than they initially believed. They became convinced, however, that once Clary "found himself and his potential," as Wiley once noted, he would achieve more than any of them. They had exceedingly more confidence in Clary than Clary had in himself; however, in time they conspired to change that. They did, too.

"Okay, who's first with a question?" Corporal Thunder asked as he realized Clary needed closure to his talk and to move on.

Although Wiley had been lulled into quiet reflection by Clary's personal presentation, he volunteered with his standby question, "You never once mentioned religion. Do you have one?"

"Jesus, Wiley, be a little more creative," Hawkins quickly and teasingly growled. "What's with all the bullshit religious questions?"

But before Wiley could answer, Clary spoke, "I was hoping you wouldn't ask that question, Wiley, because I have no good or reasonable answer.

"I've attended church, but never regularly. I believe in God, but I suppose I've shied away from organized religions," Clary explained. "I'm somewhat familiar with the better known Bible stories and the more often quoted scriptures, but I'm certainly not Bible literate. I'm thankful for what I have and sorry for those less fortunate. I make mistakes and I ask for forgiveness. Though I've prayed in the past, my prayers have never been daily or nightly. In fact, they've been sporadic."

Clary paused to collect his thoughts before continuing, "Prayers are now a dilemma for me. In this place, in Vietnam, in this war, when I believe I most need and want God in my life, when I most want to pray, I'm almost reluctant to pray. I'm concerned all those times I was safe and life was good,

I seldom prayed and thanked God for the blessings he'd provided me. But now that I'm in danger and life is bad, I'm more than ready to pray and pray often. God probably thinks I'm ungrateful and self-serving. God's probably asking, 'Where were my prayers when all was good?' I have no good answer," Clary conceded. "But my belief in my God and my relationship with God is one I'm committed to working on if I can survive this war and somehow deserve God's grace. I just don't quite know how to do it right now."

None of them expected such an answer. None of them knew quite what to say. Yet, all of them had similar thoughts. Wiley spoke briefly for all of them when he slowly countered, "Clary, I know something God does not know."

Hawkins instantly thought he should seek cover because God's wrath or a bolt of angry lightning or whatever would surely reign down upon them for such a sacrilegious remark.

Wiley, however, made their nervousness worse when he repeated, "I know something God does not know." Wiley paused while they all considered his remark and then continued, "I know God does not know a single person he does not love.

"Clary, God loves you; he loves us all, whether we pray or attend church or not, God loves us," Wiley declared. "We'll talk about this later if you want, if you'll let me?" Clary nodded to agree.

"Now, it's my turn to ask one," Corporal Thunder said. "Clary, what are your future goals?"

Clary thought briefly before answering, "I definitely want to go back and complete college. I'm considering maybe eventually attending law school or maybe business school or both. Maybe I could use my legal training as a corporate lawyer and become an entrepreneur in innovative businesses. I'd like to be creative and help people succeed in novel and exciting enterprises."

Again, to a degree, Clary's answer surprised them, but they were learning they knew Clary less than they first thought. Maybe they had too quickly and carelessly labeled him as a liberal, carefree, self-centered, or elitist Southern Californian. They were learning none of these applied to Clary.

Hawkins quickly asked Clary, "You never really told us why you joined the Corps. Did you join because of your dad or frustration with college or what?" Clary's answer stunned them.

"I've thought about that," Clary candidly admitted. "I've thought about it a lot. The more I think about it, the more convinced I am that for me it was for the best reason. Some probably thought it was an impulsive or idealistic decision or an escape from something or someone. The truth is, however, it was for what I believe and for how I feel."

Clary paused momentarily as he collected his thoughts, "You may remember, we were all probably in school, when President John F. Kennedy was assassinated in November 1963. We remember where we were and what we were doing that fateful day. It was that memorable to us. It was one of the saddest days in our nation's history. It was a day our nation lost its innocence to an evil we never envisioned or expected. We were virtually helpless and lost as how to react."

"Throughout the following days of sorrow," Clary continued, "President Kennedy's words and actions and accomplishments were reviewed and summarized in the media. But one among many was one we all probably knew, one we all probably remembered without any reminders. It was his Inaugural Address in 1961 when he spoke those few words that challenged and moved Americans: 'Ask not what your country can do for you, ask what you can do for your country.'

"Well, I'm no super patriot or gallant hero," Clary declared, "but I'm an American and those words meant something to me then and they mean something to me now. I believe that for centuries those words have meant something to those who have served and sacrificed for our nation, too. Now it's my time to do what I can do for my country. It's my time to honor those who have done what they've done since our nation was founded. It's what I can do for my country." Clary spoke with conviction, almost daring anyone to challenge his commitment to do what he could now do.

The silence was palpable. They were mesmerized by Clary's words and their own thoughts about the words he had spoken. War was neither a place nor a situation in which they were particularly pleased to be, but they were prouder than ever to be exactly where they were and doing exactly what they were doing. It's what they could do for their country, too.

Clary concluded, "My thoughts are probably unabashed idealism, but idealism is part of America; part of the American dream; part of what has made Americans who we are and who we will be. Our ideals are our America and our America is our ideals."

After Clary spoke, the silence and thoughts persisted longer than normal. Eventually, Wiley asked, "Can I be next? I don't want to be last. I don't want to come from the back of the bus."

They all smiled at Wiley's oblique reference to the ole Jim Crow laws of social segregation and separate but equal rights, which were anything but social or equal. Corporal Thunder quipped, "Wiley, you'll be next, but let's do next tomorrow night. It's late now and we're all beat to hell."

"Thanks for making this a good talk," Corporal Thunder had remarked. "I know girls talk like this because I have two sisters who do it with their friends all the time. But I wasn't too sure if guys would do this. This is a lot different situation, however, for all of us. Thanks."

"Jesus," Hawkins joked. "It's kinda girly, but when we ain't got nothin' else to do but talk and patrol and ambush, well, talkin's kinda fun and we'll talk about anything. Besides, when we ain't patrollin' we ain't got much else to do but talk. We got no radio, no TV, no books. We got no girls, no cars, no sports. We got nowhere to go and nothin' to do. We got damn near nothin' to do but Marine and war and combat stuff. So, I'll talk and listen to about anything."

"But I ain't too thrilled with havin' to listen to Clary talk," Hawkins paused and joked. The team laughed as Clary pretended hurt feelings. Clary and Hawkins had a special emerging and evolving friendship.

The evening talks therefore expanded and became part of their daily lives. At times, their talks and thoughts were fast and fleeting. At others, they were slow and substantial. Always brief interludes from the miseries of war, the talks helped hone them for the actions they had to take as well as healed them from the emotions of those actions.

It seemed too quickly it was then time to return to the darkness, the silence, and the fear. Tomorrow they would talk again. Tomorrow the darkness and silence and fear would again talk to them, too. But tonight they would now think of home and family. Home and family, however, were so far away while the darkness and silence and fear were so near and close.

~

CHAPTER 4

Common Friends in Uncommon Times

We were the epitome of diversity, but we became one. In the cauldron of combat, we became more than friends. We became a Marine Fire Team. We became a family of four. We became as one.

—Marine Corporal Dark Pale Thunder

Corporal Thunder's fire team had in a few weeks become accustomed to their daily routine in combat. It had its moments of sheer exhilaration and spiked adrenaline as well as its absorbing and consuming boredom. At the small unit level their daily existence consisted of combat patrols and ambushes. Patrols dominated their lives, but then their talks became a major part of the team, too.

The next evening, after their mid-day patrol, debriefs, household duties, and weapons care, darkness approached. "Okay, we ready to continue our talks about ourselves?" Wiley asked.

Corporal Thunder realized Wiley had been anticipating his talk all day. In the late afternoon tropical heat, with steaming rice paddies in the background, they sought shade under a poncho lean-to as Corporal Thunder announced, "Wiley, you're up. Let's hear what you got."

"Well, I'm black and I'm from the south, which is both obvious and defining for me," Wiley smiled, "but there's much more to black and to the south." He had obviously listened closely to Corporal Thunder introduce himself as an Indian and Clary define himself as a Californian. His strong ebony features were classic and undeniably African. They exuded stately and substantial strength as well as plowing and planting fortitude.

Hawkins, physically smaller than any in the team, listened while imagining fights if he were Wiley's size. Most probably initially assumed, because of their contrasting physical statures, that Wiley was the fighter and Hawkins the peacemaker. But it was a false assumption that Hawkins used to his advantage. Physical diversity uniquely bonded the two.

"Our family history is one of slavery, but we don't know much about our ancestors," Wiley admitted. "What we know about our family is mostly from the few records in our Family Bible, but they're kinda scribbled. My dad and mom say most of our history was simply passed by words and stories from one generation to the next. They say it's sort of suspect, but it's all we have.

"We believe that our people came from a place in Africa now called Liberia in the 1820's or 1830's. But that's more of a guess than a fact. We do know that slaves at that time were sold and traded and separated from families, which made it hard to keep families together and to know our family history before the Civil War," Wiley disclosed with a look of sadness as he fidgeted.

"President Lincoln's Emancipation Proclamation may have freed the slaves, but it was a long time after the war before blacks felt really free," Wiley declared, "but my dad and mom say we're pretty lucky despite all the struggles.

"After the Civil War slaves were released from their masters, and some had a hard time adjusting to freedom and to new jobs and to new responsibilities," Wiley claimed, "but my past grandparents were asked to stay on the huge plantation near Natchez.

"One day they were plantation slaves and the next day they were hired field hands and domestic help in the home. They weren't paid much at first, my dad says, but they received food and clothing and their basic needs as payment for their work," Wiley continued, "and the best part is that they stayed because they wanted to stay. They were free to go, but they stayed. They were free.

"They stayed," Wiley hinted, "simply because they had more opportunities and more freedoms staying. In time, the owners actually deeded a small plot of land to my grandparents to work as their own if they'd continue to work the plantation. They even helped build a small home for them, too."

"The Old South took a long, long time to change to become the New South and it's still changing. We're changing with it. While the South was hard on blacks, our plantation people were good to us because we worked hard for them," Wiley claimed as he flexed his strong arms.

"Segregated and separate but equal rights were mostly false promises back then," Wiley frowned, "but our plantation lady took care of us. She was so unhappy with the local white school for her children that she hired tutors. My mom offered to pay whatever she could if us kids could have classes with the tutors. The plantation lady said okay, but that mom wouldn't have to pay."

"Well, my dad said it became a standoff between my mom and the plantation lady. My mom insisted she pay. The lady refused any pay," Wiley laughed. "Finally, the lady said if my sisters helped with house chores and us boys helped with outdoor chores that'd be pay enough for tutors."

"That resolved the crisis and that's how we received our education. We earned it, but it was also an earned gift from the plantation lady. It was our greatest gift. My mom always insisted what really changed our lives was we all worked hard and we all earned what we got," he declared. "My mom's not into charity or welfare or getting something for nothing. She opposes entitlements with one exception. She says we're all entitled to work. We worked and work changed our lives.

"I have three brothers and three sisters because, as my dad and mom always teased us, they needed lots of help on the plantation," Wiley smiled as he rubbed his calloused hands together.

"The plantation family had five kids and once we started school with them we became friends, good friends. It seems kids have no prejudices or hates. Color don't matter much to kids, but fun and kindness and respect do. It's only adults who learn prejudice and hate," Wiley nodded.

"It was only later I sort of figured out why all of us kids, blacks and whites, became friends. I think the plantation lady had a lot to do with it," he confessed, "because she suggested all us kids were sort of like Tom Sawyer, Huck Finn, and Jim. At the time, I really didn't understand what she was hinting at, but later I suspected it was because we all just simply got along together and could have fun at most anything."

"So, like in the Mark Twain stories, the plantation lady brought us all together. Soon the plantation lady was encouraging her kids to visit our little home, too, maybe to help them appreciate their big huge mansion. Maybe to help them be grateful for what they had," he guessed.

"But it seemed the lady wanted her kids to do more than study or play with us because she started talking about our chores. She was sly," Wiley shrugged, "and later her children would help us with chores just so we could share more time together. That's how she got her kids doing chores. It was just like the fence white-washing in the Mark Twain's story."

"The plantation lady coordinated with the local school for her kids and us to take graduation tests," he declared proudly. "I took the test and I passed it." It was apparent that education was important to Wiley.

"My mom actually cried, cried lots of tears, but my dad simply praised the Lord and thanked the plantation people," Wiley beamed. "I vaguely thought of college, but we couldn't afford it. That's when I heard about the GI Bill and started thinking about the military, especially with all the talk about Vietnam and the draft and how the Marines could later help me attend college."

"My dad once read or heard someone say, 'Education Will Help Make You Free.' He said it to me, to all of us kids, all the time," Wiley emphasized. "Freedom has been a lifelong struggle for my people. I began to understand and believe that college would help me and my people become freer. So, here I am in Vietnam as a temporary stop on my way to college and freedom."

Wiley sighed in relief. He was glad his talk was over and to have said what he had said. He waited for the questions, especially from Hawkins. He knew Hawkins was anxious to fluster him.

Without Corporal Thunder asking for questions, Hawkins injected, "We know your dad's a preacher, you told us so earlier, but you never mentioned what he preaches?"

"My dad's a part-time preacher at the rural Southern Baptist church near our home. He's not ordained or certified or whatever, but he's self-taught and on-the-job trained," Wiley began.

"My dad works the plantation and our land full-time during the days and preaches on Sundays. He started studying the Bible and becoming interested in preaching after we got a television about six years ago," he remembered. "He began to hear the sermons and talks of Martin Luther

King, Junior, and his encouragement to blacks to be non-violent to end segregation and seek equal rights.

"It was hard because the stinging fire hoses, brutal police baton beatings, fierce and mauling attack dogs, choking tear gas, and other brutalities forced upon blacks were violent," Wiley winced. "But the lynchings and church bombings that killed innocent young girls and boys were the worst. Killing kids is cruel and evil, but many blacks nonetheless wanted non-violent change." Wiley paused for a moment as he recalled such atrocities. He remembered the costs of freedom.

"My dad truly believed that such evil was the acts of cowards. He thought cowards represented a minority and the majority of whites were good people like our plantation people. Dad believed bad and evil shouldn't be allowed to provoke blacks into bad confrontations with good whites," he exclaimed. "My dad began preaching to help Mr. King spread his non-violent messages."

Wiley paused and to move on Clary asked, "Who are your heroes?"

"I have lots of heroes," Wiley confessed. "My first hero is President Abraham Lincoln because he believed that slavery was so evil and freedom so precious he was willing to risk the fate of our nation in war to fight for equality and justice for all peoples. It cost our nation a war, but freedom is truly priceless and worth any cost.

"Joe Lewis, Jesse Owens, and Jackie Robinson are my heroes, too. In their own way, in sports, they helped us eventually become free, too," Wiley continued. "But on a personal level my heroes are the plantation man and lady who helped us with opportunities to work, own land, become educated, and earn our freedom. Also, my dad, mom, and brothers and sisters are my heroes. It's been a hard life, a work hard life, but their love and kindness made us a family."

"Why's the man your hero?" Corporal Thunder asked. "You talked mostly of the lady."

"Well, the lady was on the plantation all the time, but the man was a lawyer and most of his time was in Natchez," Wiley alleged. "As time passed, he trusted my dad to mostly run the plantation, sort of as the foreman, because more and more of his time was in his office and the courts in Natchez.

"My dad would see the man probably once a week during trips to Natchez for supplies and to update him on the plantation, and us kids mostly stayed on the plantation and rarely went into town," he said, "but once when we were older all the boys, white and black, accompanied my dad to Natchez for supplies. It seemed unusual because we rarely got to go to the big city, but we were excited. Later, I kind of suspected why we went.

"Black Freedom Marches spread across the south in the late fifties and early sixties. They were peaceful marches, but sometimes outside goons or thugs were recruited by the KKK, the Ku Klux Klan, to disrupt local marches," Wiley suggested, "and the plantation man wanted no violence or disruptions in Natchez. The man was very protective of Natchez, his land, and his family. So, he asked my dad to bring his sons and my brothers and me into town that day to maybe be a deterrent or to hopefully stop any violence. The plan, however, went bad fast. But it turned out good.

"We were at the farm and feed store loading supplies and minding our own business when thugs came by and noticed us blacks and whites working together to load our truck," Wiley smiled, "and the goons began yelling obscenities, mostly to the whites, about mixing with blacks. My dad told us to be calm and we did until one of the thugs threw a rock and one of our white brothers went down hard with a nasty gash and blood spurting everywhere." Wiley's fists clenched subconsciously as he remembered the horrible wound and his blood drenched white friend.

"My non-violent preaching dad saw who threw the rock and immediately charged him and wrestled him into custody. We all followed," he grinned. "Unfortunately, for the thugs, one hit my dad square in the jaw, but dad didn't flinch. That's when the rest of us tore into the thugs.

"I was as angry as I've ever been, especially after seeing my dad and friend attacked. I beat one of the thugs unconscious. I'd probably have damned near killed him but for my older brother pulling me off the coward," Wiley admitted. "My brothers and me had mule plowed and toted cotton bales and labored hard all our lives. The thugs didn't stand a chance. It was almost over before it began. Those we hadn't beaten down hard or captured just ran like hell." Hawkins grinned unabashedly.

Corporal Thunder, Hawkins, and Clary sat silently for a few seconds. It seemed they were picturing their usually quiet and passive Wiley launching an all out frontal attack on hapless thugs.

"It scared me that I could get so angry and fight so hard, so wild," admitted Wiley, "but it scared me more that there's evil guys out there who can cause me to feel that way, too. Yet, I feel bad for those who preach and practice hatred because it must be sad and bad to live hateful and bitter lives."

Then it was silent. Then it was time for Hawkins. Hawkins destroyed the silence with animated gestures and rabid stories of questionable veracity. Hawkins was anxious to share his stories.

"We've saved the best for last," Corporal Thunder announced. "Hawkins, it's now your turn to talk, but remember the war will be over for us in about a year. We got thirteen month tours."

"Okay, I talk a lot, but when I do it's because you guys really need to hear what I've gotta say," Hawkins smiled, "but you ain't heard nothin' yet." Hawkins never lacked for confidence or humor regardless of the topic. Hawkins talking about Hawkins, however, proved as entertaining as it was enlightening; as sad as it was inspiring.

"I'm Italian, but I really don't know Italy and never knew my Italian papa," he shrugged. "My papa and mama married after the big war, but Papa was killed in a back alley bar fight. In the war, some Italians first fought for Mussolini and Germany and later fought for the U. S. and its allies. It sometimes caused Italians to question the loyalty of one another. It caused bitterness and doubts.

"Papa fought for one side then the other, but he always fought for Italy. A gang attacked my papa because of this. It threatened my mama, too. It claimed my papa fought with a unit that killed some of their relatives and friends in another unit. The gang demanded money. Mama's family was afraid that with Papa dead they'd come after her or them for the money," Hawkins remembered. "So, mama's papa arranged with his brother in Boston to take in my mama who was with me.

"It was a hard decision for my mama and her family because she was their only daughter and three of her four brothers were killed in the war," he sighed, "but life in Italy was really bad after the war. All their lives were made worse because of the hostility from the war and the fear of a vendetta against my mama." Hawkins scowled as he thought of the forced exile from his home and Italy.

"You wouldn't know it from my scraggly looks," Hawkins frowned, "but my mama's beautiful. I ain't prejudiced about it either. She's just pretty as hell and the kindest person in my life, too.

"I have only one sister, Maria. She's a sweet kid," he momentarily reminisced, "five years younger than me and a whole lot smarter and more talented, too, especially singin' and dancin'."

Hawkins paused and proudly pulled pictures of his mama and Maria from his wallet and passed them to the team to confirm their beauty. He was obviously proud of them both and kissed both pictures tenderly, which was the only pause in his lengthy monologue.

They all knew Hawkins was expecting one of them to say something. Corporal Thunder finally said, "Your mama's stunningly beautiful. Your sister is, too. But what the hell happened to you?"

"Yeah, yeah," Hawkins gestured, "I guess my papa was lacking in looks, but my mama was pretty enough to marry one of her uncle's Boston business friends. I always appreciated and respected my step-papa for lovin' my mama and takin' me in the bargain because I ain't no prize.

"Our new family settled in North Boston, which is mostly Italian. It's often called Little Italy because of all the Italians and great Italian food," he bragged. "It's a nice part of Boston. I loved the narrow streets and our stickball games, but most of my time was in the gym boxin' and the pool hall shootin' pool. Boxin' and pool are my best sports," Hawkins boasted as he shadowboxed while sitting on a sandbag.

"Boston became all I ever really knew. If you couldn't get there on the local bus or rail, then I didn't get there. I loved goin' to Fenway Park to watch the Red Sox play ball, especially Ted Williams. I wish I'd seen Joe DiMaggio play, but I was too young for Italian Joltin' Joe. Besides, he was a New York Yankee. Yep, Boston's a nice play to grow up."

"The first time I was ever outta the city and in the country was when I joined the Marines. The Marines sorta helped me outta some trouble," Hawkins admitted with relief.

"It seems I got into one too many street fights and hurt a guy a little more than I should've, not that he didn't deserve a good ass whippin'. Then it kinda came down to jail or the military," he said.

"First, I went to the Army recruiter and after the little test he gave me the Army Sergeant said I didn't do too good on the readin' or writin' and did even worse on the math," Hawkins frowned.

"I told the Army recruiter I wasn't plannin' on readin' or writin' to the enemy or teachin'em math," Hawkins smiled. "I told him I was aimin' to kill'em because that's what I thought Army guys did. That's where I figured I could best help the Army.

"The Army Sergeant rolled his eyes and muttered that I might be a little problem, that I might be a little too rebellious for the Army." Hawkins shrugged his shoulders in disbelief.

"I thought he said I might be a little too 'religious' instead of 'rebellious' and I asked him what the hell does religion have to do with killin'," Hawkins professed. "I told him I wasn't gonna baptise'em for heaven but blast'em to hell.

"I musta confused the hell outta the Army Sergeant because he just stood up and walked me to the door and suggested I see the Marine Sergeant next door," Hawkins confessed. "He even pointed to the Marine door, like I couldn't read, to make sure I knew where I should go.

"Well, that's when I met my first Marine. He was both sorta friendly and not too friendly," he estimated, "because his first question to me was to very loudly ask me why the hell I thought I was good enough to be a Marine. Before I could answer, he growled and said he knew damn well I wasn't good enough. He said I looked a little too puny and too ragged to be a Marine. He asked if I was just wantin' a free meal and some nice uniforms from the Marines.

"I was kinda surprised he thought I wasn't good enough to be a Marine," Hawkins said, "and it sorta pissed me off and made me wanna prove I was more than good enough. I thought about whuppin his ass, but there was three of them and one of me. I didn't really mind the fightin' odds, but I had more important business right then. I wanted to prove I was good enough for the Marines.

"I told him I could eat paper and crap dollar bills and drink lead and fart bullets. I said I didn't need any handouts from the Marines," Hawkins boasted, "but that I needed someplace to fight.

"The Marine looked at me kinda startled, but when I mentioned fightin' he simply smiled and placed his hand on my shoulder and asked me to come sit down because he thought we could just maybe do some business together after all," Hawkins explained.

"The Marines gave me a test, too, and afterwards the Sergeant asked me how many years of college I had because I sure aced the test. He said it was one of the best scores ever," Hawkins contended. "Hell, I didn't wanna tell him the high school graduated me just to get rid of me. I only had one obstacle to attendin' college and that was high school. Yeah, if it hadn't been for high school I'd probably be in college now and be an Oxford Scholar, too, because I thought straight "Ds" was good grades, because that meant no "Fs." Besides, I thought straight "Ds," just like a straight in poker, is really good. But I figured the Sergeant didn't need to know about my grades and high school problems or that I flunked the Army test. Once I mentioned fightin', it just didn't seem to matter.

"The Marine Sergeant told me most everyone was wantin' to get in the infantry, but the Marines really needed some truck drivers, admin types, and supply men," Hawkins reported.

"I figured real fast that the infantry was the most popular and thought it must be the best," he smiled, "and I hinted, maybe pleaded, I didn't want to be screwed out of the infantry." Hawkins glanced at his three teammates, but detected no overly suspicious disbeliefs.

"The Marine Sergeant just sighed and said it'd be hard and was I sure about the infantry because he'd have better luck gettin' me in supply or admin, which were nice cushy jobs," Hawkins announced. "He even said I might like being a cook and could maybe fatten myself up some.

"I'd heard that sometimes tricky recruiters made wild-ass promises to naïve recruits just to fool them into joinin', especially the cushy jobs. But I told the Marine Sergeant that if he could help get me in the infantry that we might have a deal," Hawkins acknowledged. Clary looked bewildered because most enlistees he knew did their best to avoid the infantry.

"The Marine Sergeant just smiled and said it might be kinda hard, but he'd personally talk with the Marine Commandant and the Marine General at Parris Island to tell them all about me." Corporal Thunder appeared doubtful, but said nothing. Instead, he thought, *Hawkins is evidently as free with his words as he is costly with his fists, but it's a priceless performance.*

"Later, after more testing and a whole lotta paperwork," Hawkins declared, "I was in the Marines and the infantry, too. The last thing the Marine Sergeant told me before I got on the bus for Parris Island was to be sure and take my swim trunks and suntan lotion because Parris Island was lots of fun on the beaches and in the sun. He made it sound really nice." Wiley smiled at his innocence or was it his exaggerations or was it his spreading fertilizer thicker than on Wiley's farm.

"After I arrived in Parris Island the drill instructors was running around and yelling like insane inmates in an asylum. But it got crazier. It was more insane than I ever imagined. That's when I kinda figured my Sergeant was teasin' me about the fun beaches because all I ever saw was swamps. He was right about the sun though. Anyway, damned if he didn't get the Commandant to let me in the Marines and infantry and here I am in Vietnam. Who said recruiters don't make good on their promises? He gave me a special deal, too." He tapped his temple to hint he tricked his recruiter.

Corporal Thunder, Wiley, and Clary sat in stunned silence. They were truly baffled by what they had heard from Hawkins and about his experiences and relationship with his crusty Marine Sergeant recruiter in Boston. They knew Hawkins was part mystery and part myth, but now they were dumbfounded as to whether he was total bullshit or one hundred percent naive Italian innocence.

Meanwhile, Hawkins gave them no clue. He gazed upward toward the cloudless blue sky and intentionally never once looked into the eyes of any of them. Hawkins had a resolute poker face with neither a grin nor frown nor hint as to his actual thoughts. One could only imagine. Yet, one could never imagine. Corporal Thunder had thought, *If Hawkins looks squarely at any one of us we'll all erupt into spontaneous and uncontrolled laughter at the insanity of Hawkins' monologue; at the insanity of Hawkins. But then again, maybe it's all true.*

Corporal Thunder broke the silence, "Damn, we're really lucky in our team to have someone with so much pull with the Commandant and Generals. We'll have to remember this when we need help, maybe with an early ticket home or some pretty medals." They burst into prolonged and unsuppressed laughter, but Hawkins never broke a smile.

After they had collected themselves, Wiley asked his usual religious question, "Why do Italians talk so much about both the Catholic Church and the Mafia?"

"Well, Italy, the Vatican, is the home of the Catholic Church. It's also the home of the Mafia. One's a religious organization and one's a criminal one," Hawkins explained. "One's supposedly after your soul. One's mostly after your money. Some say sometimes it's hard to tell one from another because both seem to be after both your soul and your money. Some say one is as good as the other. Some say one is as bad as the other. Some say Italy is the greatest exporter of both Catholicism and crime in the world. Only the Italians! That's Italy!" He genuflected recklessly.

Hawkins paused for a moment for them to consider whether he was serious or joking before he continued. "But both are a huge part of Italy and Italians. I'm a Catholic, but not a good one, at least not a good practicing one. But I'm not in the Mafia even though I kinda want folks to think I'm a practicing Mafia bad ass. Maybe it's the Italian in me, but I blame it on the Catholics.

"But for me, I just sorta take the best of both the Catholics and the Mafia and make it what I believe in and practice. The Catholic Church and the Mafia is mostly about family and the part about family is what I believe in the most. I believe in family and family has kinda become my religion."

It was momentarily silent before Clary asked, "You like boxing or pool sharking best?"

"I love boxin' most and only shot pool because the pool hall was next to the boxin' gym," Hawkins began, "My boxin' coach. My Uncle Gino, always teased me I had a heavyweight mouth and a lightweight body. My sister, Maria, joked I had a bantamweight brain, too," Hawkins smiled, "but both agreed I had a super-heavyweight heart. My family said what I lacked in size I made up for with soul and I never ever gave up. I love boxin', but I love fightin' the best."

"I thought boxing and fighting were the same?" Clary asked.

"Hell, no, they ain't the same," Hawkins exclaimed, "'cause boxin' has rules." The clear implication was that fighting had no rules for Hawkins. This subtle difference was one they would discuss time and time again as they talked about the rules of war, especially the rules of limited war.

Corporal Thunder asked the final question, "You really hurt the guy worse than you intended?"

"Well, I didn't really beat him worse than I wanted because I wanted to beat him to an inch of his damn life. I wanted to beat him really bad and then some," Hawkins countered, "because he'd made a threat to my step-papa and uncle and their business about wanting protection money. He seemed to fancy hisself as some sorta debt collector or enforcer and we weren't, at least I weren't, having any part of that bullshit. Not again. Not after what happened to my real papa.

"But after the beat down, the Mafia that protected the North End without costing any of us Italians anything asked to see me. I thought I was in bad trouble, but learned I was okay," he sighed, "because the Boston Mafia said some Miami or Philly or New York City thugs were trying to come into its outer areas and they'd been secretly watching them until I sorta blew it by making it public.

"So they asked me to get outta town and maybe join the military and learn some skills useful to them, some skills more than boxin' and beatin', and later, in a few years or so, come back to Boston. They said they could handle the jail and legal issues and they did. That's when I sorta made the Marine Sergeant glad to see me, but he never knew how glad I was to see him. It worked out for both of us and here I am a Marine. Ain't life something? Ain't the Marines something? Ain't the Corps and killin' a little like the Mafia? Ain't we a little like Catholic monks, too, cause once we kill'em we can give the enemy dead their last rites?" Hawkins made the sign of the cross.

Hawkins' soliloquy concluded too abruptly. No one had quite known what to expect when the talks began. Now no one was quite ready for them to end.

It was probably beyond them to truly appreciate the significance of their various thoughts and their simple descriptions of themselves and their hopes and their dreams. The synergy of the four became incredibly amazing; however, none of them could have confidently defined synergy and exactly what that intimated. Nonetheless, they truly were collectively more than the sum of their individual selves and together they became a potent and charismatic force.

Instinctively and intuitively, however, they sensed their diversity and their homogeneity, though none of them would have ever used the word homogeneity to describe themselves either. They averaged about 18 years of age and represented the major geographic regions of America's east and west coasts and the prairie plains and river deltas.

One was black, one white, one Indian-Irish, and one Italian-Mafia. One was part-time Catholic and part-time Mafia. One was full-time Southern Baptist. One was equal parts The Spirit Father and Mother Nature. One was sometimes Protestant and sometimes Agnostic. But race and religion were far less important to them than their faith in one another and family.

They joined the Marines for a variety of reasons, too. One was an alleged but joking draft dodger. One was an unabashed idealist. One was confronted by the courts with jail or the military. One was interested in college and the GI Bill's education benefits.

Physically, they were exceedingly diverse, yet complementary. Wiley was huge, the tallest and heaviest. It was his brute strength, however, which defined him. His broad muscular shoulders and chest as well as massive arms and legs exuded power. His brawn was formidable. At Parris Island, he set the recruit bench press record at 472 pounds, but he had never lifted weights in his life.

Clary's physique was one of a sculptured Greek god and an athlete. His lithe and lively frame belied his inner competitiveness. His commitment to conquering opponents on the sports fields as well as battlefields was his trademark. Hawkins always simply said Clary was "silky smooth."

Hawkins was the mutt and the runt. He was wiry and testy with an unrivaled bravado toward even the most physically endowed. He had an unequaled love and passion for the fight regardless of the odds or the opponents. Clary declared Hawkins was "a street fighter at heart, with heart."

Corporal Thunder had none of the singular distinctive physical characteristics of the other three. He was, however, a balanced and blended combination of all of them. But it was his extraordinarily unique talent of physically swift and decisive actions that distinguished him. He was the most feared and revered. He was a pacifist with a killer's instinct. While the most feared, he was the most beloved.

Clary was the most intellectually astute and articulate. Wiley was the steadiest and most thoughtful. Hawkins was the craftiest and the most manipulative with the best street smarts in the team. Corporal Thunder was the most experienced with nature and the outdoors and he demonstrated unparalleled common sense combined with a gift of perception and anticipation.

Corporal Thunder, Wiley, Hawkins, and Clary would have undoubtedly never been friends back home in their neighborhoods, schools, clubs, or in any other such capacity, if by some ironic twist of fate they would have ever been in such a situation. Their respective social and cultural and socio-economic status would have made them more likely adversaries than allies. They almost assuredly would have more likely been strangers than best friends. Their dissimilar lives and interests would have virtually confirmed their anonymity or total and distant estrangement from one another.

In a later letter home to his parents, however, Corporal Thunder explained the team to his parents as sincerely as he could. "We're the epitome of diversity, but we're becoming one. In the cauldron of combat, we're becoming more than friends. We're becoming a Marine Fire Team and a family of four. We're becoming as one." His dad and mom, acutely aware of their own respective racial and cultural diversities, simply smiled and prayed for the team. Their common love for the land made them one; their love for one another made them a family. The team's common struggle for survival made them one; their talks made them family. The talks molded them into who they were and who they would become. The talks also bonded them for the patrols and war they confronted.

CHAPTER 5

Relocation to the DMZ

It's just Vietnam. It's just the way it is. It's just war. What the hell did we expect?

—Marine Lance Corporal Aaron Wiley

While the team's relationship evolved, the war it confronted consistently changed. Corporal Thunder and his team came to know one another the summer their battalion, 3/3, operated southwest of Da Nang in the southern area of I Corps. It was the northern most Corps of the four Vietnam Corps. After patrolling and initiating their talks down south for almost three months, however, the battalion relocated that fall to the northern area of I Corps. Clary observed that while down south, "The terrain was mostly coastal plains and rice paddies. The Viet Cong and booby traps were our primary enemies." The landscape was peaceful, except for the war.

But now they had relocated northwest of Dong Ha near the Demilitarized Zone. "Now it's mountainous triple canopy jungle terrain. The NVA and rockets, mortars, and large units are now our main enemies," Wiley noted to the team as he shielded his eyes from the dull sunlight while conducting a panoramic survey across the monstrous mountains, deep valleys, and rugged jungles. "Whew, it's going to be different." The terrain was frightful and the war made it fearful.

Hawkins equated the situation to his Boston turf wars. "Well, we got new streets and new gangs to battle." The current terrain and enemy, however, were decidedly different and more dangerous. They learned quickly how different and dangerous it would become.

"On our second patrol in our new area near the DMZ, two point Marines were separated from our patrol during a deadly and fierce NVA ambush. The dense jungle limited visibility to a meter or two along the twisting trail," Clary recalled as they discussed tactics in one of their bunker talks. "We fought hard and somewhat blindly to shift the momentum of the battle. After what seemed like a lifetime, we forced the NVA to break contact and they faded into the jungle."

"We secured the area and launched a search to locate the missing Marines," Corporal Thunder sighed, "and within minutes discovered their mutilated bodies in a ravine near the killing zone." They had been shot in the head and killed. Gruesomely desecrated with either knives or machetes or bayonets, their disfigured corpses were hardly recognizable. It was a sight the Marines would remember forever. Brutal and senseless deaths are near impossible to forget. Corporal Thunder never forgot. Furthermore, he swore he would remember.

It was about ten days later that the team's ambush concluded with the decapitation of the NVA. While it was neither retribution nor revenge, Corporal Thunder professed, "It was necessary to save lives from the enemy's grenade. It was to maintain silence should a larger enemy force be in the area. War's war and it's hard to believe, but there's no reason to believe in mutilations." It was simply war and war was often simply violent and evil beyond belief.

Terrain and enemy, either down south or up north, often dictated their tactics. It was, however, the concepts of limited war and the restrictions of such warfare that changed and challenged and confused them the most. "I'm believin' the NVA sanctuaries, no-fire zones, ceasefires, and other constraints handicap the hell outta us and make fightin' unfair for us, too," Hawkins groaned. They were willing to fight and they were under no illusions that war was fair, but, as Hawkins repeatedly rallied the team, "Let's go at it, but let's go at it with the same rules for everyone. Even if that means there ain't no rules for nobody. No rules is better than unfair rules."

The team became acutely aware of this and the decapitation incident reinforced it. Now, occupying its new northern base camp in an area about halfway between the South China Sea coast and South Vietnam's western border with Laos, they were the northern most Marine Infantry Battalion in the area. They were only about 10-12 kilometers south of the DMZ, which separated North and South Vietnam. "Damned if we ain't the point Marine unit in Vietnam," Hawkins professed as the team paused to consider its predicament.

"It's hostile mountains and jungles instead of streets. It's the NVA instead of gangs. It's a bad and nasty area. It'll get worse before it gets better because it'll never get better. It'll only get worse from now on," Corporal Thunder declared and nodded as he peered across the mountains.

After the battalion established its new base camp, Corporal Thunder sat on the bunker's sandbags and briefed them on the terrain. "Company M, Battalion Headquarters, and Company K will occupy a north to south ridge line named Payable Hill." He laid out his map and pointed with his machete to the ridgeline that was now their new home.

"Company L will be located to the west in the valley in an area known as the Fishbowl," he continued as he again pointed out the area on his map and the ground, "and Company I will be located to the south along a road called Highway 9 and the Cua Viet River."

Corporal Thunder continued his description by pointing north and east of Payable Hill. "This mountain range is known as Mutter's Ridge and it's a main route for the NVA traveling north to south." The mountains appeared distant, but ominous as they glanced at them.

After he identified the various company positions on the map and in the distance, Corporal Thunder briefly described other terrain features in their area. "This is known as the Rockpile and this is the Razorback," he noted as he pointed to the two geological anomalies. The Rockpile was basically in the middle of the three camps configured in a triangle. The Razorback extended north up the valley and west of all four company camps. The orientation failed to capture the full extent of the ruggedness and isolation of the prominent terrain features, which were thousands of meters apart. The full impact of their locations and loneliness would become apparent later as they occupied and patrolled them.

But more frustrating than the new terrain and enemy was their emerging confusion with new rules of engagement. They had similar restrictions on one of their last patrols down south, but they had adjusted. Now they would again have to adjust to new rules and also adjust a few rules.

In one of their talks while on a patrol break deep in the lush jungle days after the NVA decapitation, Clary asked, "You remember our patrols down south, down in the rice paddies and the coastal plains?" He paused while they remembered. "We patrolled the same area for months and hardly ever saw a VC." It had been frustrating, but the war was frustrating.

"Yeah," Hawkins reminded them, "but almost every week, almost every day, the VC saw us."

Wiley then joined in, "Yeah, the area was nothing but homemade mines and booby traps. There were bamboo punji pits with those razor sharp bamboo slivers that would pierce or slice you with deep and nasty cuts. There were Chinese Communist or ChiCom grenades and other crude and ugly killing gadgets. The VC were everywhere, but nowhere we could see or know them."

"Don't forget that worthless sniper who'd fire a few rounds every day or so to cause us to go on alert," Hawkins joked. "Hell, he never hit nothin', but he sure made us scatter and scramble."

"That's the point," Clary shrugged, "the VC were killing or wounding our company's Marines several times a week. Maybe more. They were always harassing us, but we hardly ever saw them much less captured or killed one. At least not until later."

Clary reflectively paused, "I kinda knew VC was operating in the area. But…."

"Kinda knew?" questioned Hawkins. "Hell, I knowed it from the beginning. We had casualties all the time from their booby traps. I knew they was there. I just didn't know where they was."

"You're right, Hawkins," Clary confessed, "but what I was trying to say is that while we knew they were there, we were limited in what we could do to uncover them.

"We knew, for example," Clary continued, "the VC was placing mines and booby traps all over the area. We conducted day and night patrols and ambushes throughout the area every day to try to catch them, but after awhile we sort of knew that was not the best way to catch them."

"Yeah," nodded Wiley. "We wanted to patrol in certain areas and search certain places, but they were off limits to us."

Silence interrupted the talk for a few moments while they listened to the jungle sounds and contemplated one another's thoughts while on the patrol break. In time, Clary asked, "Remember our patrol where we finally caught and killed two VC and wounded another, the VC nurse?"

Clary then asked another question, but it was a precision guided laser aimed at the heart of the discussion. "Remember how we reacted when we saw the faces of the two VC we killed?"

"Yeah, I remember. I remember the frustration, but I remember the disgust more than the frustration," Wiley announced.

"Yeah, the disgust makes me want to forget it, but I ain't never forgettin' it. I'm gonna remember it so it don't happen again," Hawkins proclaimed.

"We felt a little helpless," answered Corporal Thunder, "but worse, I felt a little guilty, too."

"I'd seen those two damn VC so many times in the area," Hawkins sighed, "but they were always with kids or older Vietnamese women. They sort of hid behind the kids and women. Looking back they didn't seem too friendly with the kids or women, but now I'm supposin' they'd threatened the locals and the villagers were afraid of them."

"Later, it became a lot clearer to me," Corporal Thunder confessed, "but at the time they were a mystery. A mystery we couldn't do much about without evidence or help from the locals."

"Yeah, I remember they were just here and they were there. But they seemed to be nowhere," Hawkins recalled. "They had ID's and papers from the village elders. So, what could we do?"

"We later suspected the local South Vietnamese were hostages or threatened by the VC," Wiley declared, "and they had to go along to get along or get killed. War's just nasty."

"Well, we eventually did what we had to do," Clary answered. "We had rules and limits for what we could do, but that changed when we discovered who they were. Corporal Thunder made sure of that. He made damn sure." Eager to continue, word was passed to mount up to continue their patrol and they had to defer their talk to later.

The team interrupted its talk, saddled up, and moved out. Patrol breaks were always over too soon. Twisting and tangled jungle trails again beckoned them. Wearily plodding in the slush and mush the patrol returned to its base camp without incident before sunset and darkness.

As day drifted to night the darkness and rains intensified. The team huddled in its musty bunker seeking warmth and dryness. Hawkins lit a heat tab for a hot canteen cup of coffee. Clary asked, "Hawkins, can I have a sip?"

Hawkins passed the coffee and said, "It's hot."

The team then returned to its earlier patrol break talk about the VC they had killed down south. They remembered their squad was conducting a late afternoon patrol in the eastern sector of their operating area. It was a routine patrol, if any Vietnam patrol could ever be considered routine. It was almost over, if anything was ever over in war, but then the normal was abruptly transformed into the abnormal. It was the abnormal, however, that exonerated them.

"As point, I must have surprised the lady VC nurse. I must have spooked her," Clary added to continue their earlier discussion, "because when she saw me it startled her. She jumped up and ran toward the hut yelling."

"That's when the two VC in the hut ran out to see what the woman was screaming at," Wiley smiled, "and that was the beginning of their end." Wiley pictured the blatant fear on the VC faces.

"The only escape for the VC was across the rice paddy on the far side of the hut, but that was a bad one for them," Hawkins declared, "because the second they hit the rice paddy they were in the wide open and totally exposed. At that second they were goners, dead and gone goners."

Corporal Thunder then proclaimed, "Discovering and eliminating the threat was good, but what we learned next was best."

"That's my reason for asking us to remember it," Clary insisted, "it's what we learned."

In the immediate area, the site to which the VC ran to escape, was a religious site. While it seemed neither a church nor pagoda, it was recognized as a local village off limits site. It had a cross and three markers that were grave stones or spiritual symbols of some type, but nothing else.

"It never seemed like much to me," Wiley reported, "but it seemed to mean a lot to someone up the chain of command because we were ordered to consider it a religious site. It was off limits."

"Yeah," Hawkins frowned, "we couldn't even walk into the area much less search the damn place. We respected it, but we learned the VC disrespected it."

"After we'd killed the VC," Clary surmised, "we figured the site was where they were running. Corporal Thunder became suspicious and we now had our probable cause to check it out."

"We secured the area," Corporal Thunder noted, "but before we searched it we asked a local Vietnamese woman to gather neighbors and come with us."

"The women were sort of scared," Clary explained. "We wanted to show them we respected the site, but wanted to search it. Somehow, with smiles and pantomimes, we gained their trust."

"At first they seemed reluctant, but once they saw the two dead VC they seemed relieved. I saw little smiles come to their faces," Corporal Thunder remembered.

"Once we kind of had them and their neighbors' approval," Clary continued, "teams began to carefully and respectfully search the site." The South Vietnamese carefully observed.

"One team discovered a weapons cache with grenades and mines under one of the markers or false graves," Hawkins exclaimed, "we found trip wire, ammo, and other devices under another.

"Damnit to hell," Hawkins muttered, "it was there all the time, but off limits to us. Despite our suspicions we couldn't search it. It was rules and limits that let the VC operate there, but not us."

"The best part of the search was the reaction of the Vietnamese women," Wiley smiled. "While our two languages made it hard for us to understand our different words, smiles and pantomimes helped us talk to one another. The women were shy at first, but frowns blossomed into smiles and then giggles once they saw the VC cache."

"Unknown to us at the time, but a cruel fact we soon learned," Clary testified, "the VC and weapons cache had been a danger to them." The local villagers had suffered, too.

Wiley remembered one of the Vietnamese women simply said, "VC number 10." Number 1 and 10 were common phrases between Americans and Vietnamese to signify the best and worst. Number 10 was the worst. It became immediately evident that the local South Vietnamese disliked the VC, especially the two dead ones. It was, however, equally evident they had feared them.

"Jesus, I remember one of the Vietnamese women signaled for a child, probably her daughter, who was about eight years old, to come forward. The little girl was so cute and so very precious," Hawkins remembered, "but she walked with a crude wooden crutch because her lower right leg below the knee was missing. I thought of my sister, Maria, and it made me mad as hell."

"I suspected what had happened," Corporal Thunder sighed, "but the mother wanted to tell us as best she could anyway. She wanted us to know what had actually happened and how the VC terrorized the villagers."

"With motions and tears and muffled noises for explosions," Clary shrugged, "the mother kind of gestured that her daughter had inadvertently tripped a VC booby trap and lost her leg." The mother's arm flapped upward as she uttered, "Boom." She then pointed to her daughter's horrible injury and missing leg as tears welled in her eyes. Remembering the demonstration recalled sad memories of the VC atrocities.

"The mom pointed to her daughter's ugly stump," Hawkins growled, "and then to the dead VC." She smiled and again said, "VC number 10." Wiley walked to the mother and gave her a hug. This simple act of kindness reinforced to the Marines their reason for the war. It was neither about governments nor politics. Instead, it was about people and their right to live free from fear.

"The South Vietnamese were casualties, too, because the VC terrorized the villagers into silence. The villagers hated them, but they were powerless," Hawkins exhorted.

"Then for the next few weeks before we moved up north," Corporal Thunder proudly recalled, "we never again had a casualty from booby traps or landmines."

"But just as good was the locals were up and about more. We saw them in the fields and in their villages and they just seemed happier," Wiley exclaimed. "It's like we got rid of the bad and they could live their lives good. They could live free and free from fear."

"We sure ain't no officers or diplomats," Hawkins smiled, "and we ain't got no interest in makin' policies or rules. But we sure got interests in survivin' and helpin' others survive."

"Yeah, we worked with the village women and kids to figure out a way to bend a few rules to help them and us survive. We worked it out together and it worked out, too," Clary exclaimed.

Simply by their patrols and experiences they learned lessons and eventually recognized the adverse consequences or, as Hawkins railed, "The stupidity of some of the limitations and rules." They initiated practical actions to save themselves and their fellow Marines and the local village people. It was that simple to them. They saw no need to complicate surviving.

The lessons were often frustrating and disappointing, but, as Wiley said, "It's frustrating and disappointing to our politicians and generals, too, but it's hardest for us fighting this war. It's just Vietnam. It's just the way it is. It's just war. What the hell did we expect?"

It was a simple question from a sincere enlisted Marine. In his innocence, he spoke for many who fought in Vietnam. While unable to articulate the grand strategies and policies of the war, those fighting it expected someone to define the war's strategic goals and expectations as well as to protect them. Unfortunately, no one ever seemed to articulate consistent strategies or define achievable expectations or sufficiently protect them.

Corporal Thunder attempted to explain, "War's just pretty devastating, but most countries have rules of engagement, or laws of warfare, or codes of conduct, or basic principles. But the NVA seem to have none of these. They play by their own rules, but we can play that way, too."

Unable to resist, Hawkins plunged in, "Yeah, well, just remember, in war there's only one rule worth rememberin'." He paused to let them think about possible answers before concluding, "You kick ass and win and you get to make the rules. Winners write the rules. Maybe better. Just know there ain't no rules and let it go at that. Keep it simple. No damn rules.

"There's a lot of ugliness and brutality in war," Hawkins exclaimed, "but the really evil ones take killin', nasty killin', and make it really bad. They kill in the worst way. Sometimes they're just devious and devils or tyrants and terrorists. Hell, in this war, the VC are called insurgents, guerrillas, and terrorists because of the cruel killin's and cowardly acts. Call 'em whatever you want, but I'm callin 'em murderers. They even kill or mutilate innocent kids, like they did that pretty little Vietnamese girl. They think their bad killin' is so bad that good people won't do bad things back to them."

"Yeah, as much as I believe in the Bible and goodness," Wiley countered, "I believe good sometimes has to be bad. It has to be worse than bad. It has to be the worst. Sometimes that's all the bad ones understand. They think because the good have a conscience that they won't do the really bad. But we got convictions, too, and we'll do bad if we have to."

"Yeah, but sometimes it's hard for good people to do really bad. Some good people will say that if they do bad, really bad, that they let the bad people bring them down to their level," Clary injected. "They say that allows the bad ones to bring them down into the shit hole with them and then we're all dirty as all hell. Then we're all wallowing in the nasty filth."

"You're all right," Corporal Thunder agreed, "but sometimes we just got to get down in the manure, like we do on the farm, and spread as much filthy shit as fast and as hard as we have to. Later, because we spread the nasty manure, we got good strong land to help us produce good crops and good grazing grasses for our livestock.

"I feel bad that we got to do bad, but sometimes we just got to be nastier and dirtier than the enemy. If we ain't ready to be the meanest and toughest ones on the battlefield, well, we ain't ready and we'll probably lose to those who are. If we do bad for good, I'm good with it," the Corporal concluded. "I'm okay with doing bad for freedom and family. I'll be as bad as I have to be for us to survive. I pray we'll all do whatever we have to do to make the bad ones know they don't really know bad till they know us."

"Jesus, you ain't gotta pray too hard for that," Hawkins announced, "because we're already with you on that. We'll be worse than the bad when we have to be, but we'll be no worse than we have to be. We ain't losing the good in us and in what we're fightin' for, but we gotta let them know they'll never be as bad as us. Otherwise, the bad wins and we ain't lettin'em win."

"Yeah, it's like an old saying," Clary concluded. "I don't exactly remember it, but it sorta says that bad and evil people win when good and honorable people do nothing."

"Well, I ain't doin' nothing'. I'm do somethin'. I'm doin' whatever bad I have to do for good," Hawkins surmised in another attempt to have the last word, "because that's why we're here doin' what we're doin'. War and fightin' ain't pretty. It's ugly as hell. Sometimes we just have to get down and get ugly."

At this point, the team's discussion was probably neither the most competent nor articulate overview of their predicament. But their talk was the beginning of their personal rules to survive the war despite the complex limitations that frustrated them and their survival.

"Up north we seem to have fewer rules about who's the enemy and who ain't. Down south we had to make sure it was a VC before shootin' to avoid shootin' friendlies," Hawkins moaned a few days later in another bunker talk about the war.

"Jesus, that was sometimes hard, sometimes impossible," Hawkins declared. "Sometimes, I never knew till they shot first and I ain't too damn thrilled about gettin' shot at first." It was that simple to Hawkins; that simple to all of them. The war, however, was rarely, if ever, simple.

"Vietnam is a limited war. We have a responsibility to control our actions to those of limited war and to conduct the war accordingly," or similar words with similar effects, were quotes that appeared in the media or political speeches. The team became aware of them from news clippings and letters from home. The seemingly contradictory words were disheartening. "We're not too excited about maybe dying because of these words," Clary once shrugged as he and Corporal Thunder read a news magazine from home.

"Okay, hell, maybe it ain't total war to them," Hawkins admitted, "but it's World War III to us. It's our asses on the line. It's total war to those of us on some damn lonely jungle trail, or high mountain pass, or rice paddy dike, or dangerous valley. When it's you, when it's us, then it's World War III. The names and numbers of the wars don't matter much. Not much at all. It's our last war if we're dead. Call it World War III or Vietnam or whatever you want, but we're gonna fight it like it's our only fight and our only war. Don't they understand that?" He breathlessly concluded as he took a huge breath in the musty bunker. He expressed his frustrations and angers in rapid fire bursts. He was rarely deliberate or on semi-automatic with his words or rifle. Instead, as with his approach to battles, he was always spontaneous and on full automatic.

Corporal Thunder reminded the team that on the rifle range firing line the commands included, "Ready on the Right; Ready on the Left; Lock and Load; Ready, Aim, Fire."

Corporal Thunder then alleged, "Hawkins just starts out with 'Fire' and only later 'Aim.' "

Wiley attempted to tease or caution Hawkins, "Hawkins, the key to Marine marksmanship is, 'One Round; One Kill.' One well-aimed round. One confirmed kill."

"Jesus, it's one round that usually kills. Hell if I care if it's the first round or the hundredth round," Hawkins growled, "but I aim to fire my hundred rounds at the NVA before they fire theirs at me. I ain't counting rounds. This ain't about math or addition or subtraction. It ain't about saving or spending too much ammo. It's about war and killin'. The more rounds the better as far as I care. The Marines have millions of rounds of ammo, but there's only one me. I damn sure don't care 'bout savin' ammo, but I sure care 'bout savin' me."

"At first, it seemed Hawkins' thoughts on killing were contradictory or pure insanity," Clary later declared in a letter to his dad, "but once we thought about them we agreed he was probably right. Hawkins simply believes that the more we kill and the faster we kill, the sooner the killings will stop." They all learned it was a fundamental lesson of war. Eventually, the killings would become so horrible the belligerents would seek peace, but the war's limitations prolonged the killings and delayed the peace. This was one of their darkest lessons or, as Hawkins lamented, "Someone's a fiddlin' while we're a fightin' and I ain't likin' the fiddler's tune one damn bit."

"Well, I hesitate to halt this talk," Corporal Thunder admitted, "but we got an early morning patrol tomorrow. Let me think about this and come up with a plan."

"Tonight, I'll take the first watch," Wiley suggested. The others quickly scurried to carve out a dry place in the bunker to bed down for the night. It was a futile effort, but eventually the rustling ceased and calm came to the bunker. Wiley stared into the dark silence and silently prayed for the team, *Oh, Lord, you are the light and you are the way. Lead us to the light and away from the darkness of this war. Amen.* He then sighed as his eyes scanned the perimeter and his ears listened for dangers in the surrounding mountains and jungles that embraced them with darkness and death.

Corporal Thunder mentioned over their breakfast of Cs the next morning that he had read in a news article, "Initial public opinion polls in 1965 revealed 64 percent of Americans supported the Vietnam War. A year later 61 percent favored escalation of the war." It lifted their spirits to know they had deployed to Vietnam with the support of their country. Year-by-year, however, increasing anti-war sentiment opposed the war and influenced the character of the war. In time, without American resolve and public support, the war drifted aimlessly. This dashed their spirits.

Initially, unknown to most of those fighting in Vietnam, the dissent and protests in late 1966 would become ever more pervasive in the coming years. While somewhat helpless and incapable of appreciating the war's policies and protests from afar, they vowed to work together to understand them.

Wiley pleaded, "Maybe some don't believe in war, but I hope they believe in and support us," as he hurriedly wrote a letter to his brothers and sisters whose support he could rely on.

"Jesus, we're the ones fighting and dying, but no one seems to care," Hawkins extolled as he opened a box of shotgun shells. *But my mama and Maria care,* he thought.

Achieving an understanding of the war was a dilemma for them. Corporal Thunder was the first to ask, "Well, we want to learn about the war, but what's the best way to learn about it? Clary, your dad's a professor and most of the protests are on college campuses. Maybe he has thoughts."

"I'll ask him to send us newspaper stories and summarize his thoughts," Clary volunteered. "Maybe we could all write home and ask for help from parents and friends. Then we could talk."

Thus began Corporal Thunder's and his team's quest for understanding. They agreed to plain talks to comprehend the war and to practical rules to help them through their sunrises and sunsets. Relatively young and totally inexperienced in the complexities of national political and military objectives, they were nonetheless serious and sincere about surviving. Simple words and plain talk were their guidelines in their search. They understood simple. They were good with simple.

They talked plainly and listened intently. They were right at times; wrong at others. At times, they had no idea whether they were progressing or regressing. At other times, they were confused and overwhelmed. It was a dark time in America, but it was dark time in Vietnam, too.

CHAPTER 6

~

Con Thien's Hill of Angels

You mean the NVA can fire at us from across or in the DMZ, but we can't fire back at them? That's part of limited war? Ain't that some kinda deal? A deal good for the NVA. A bad deal for us. Who's makin' such stupid deals?

—Marine Private First Class Dominic Hawkins

"Okay," Corporal Thunder said as he vaulted into the bunker a few days later after a meeting with small unit leaders. "Gather round. Listen up. Standby for a new mission." Flipping open his notebook he reviewed his notes to pass the word. Rain splashed from his helmet onto his notes as he shuddered from the drenching monsoon squalls and rubbed his hands for warmth.

"Gather round! Why you always say gather round? I'm here. We're all here. We're always here," Hawkins groaned playfully as he jumped to attention and almost poked his head through the tarp atop the bunker. "Jesus, we' ain't got nowhere to go. There's nowhere to go. We ain't got no one to see either. There ain't no one to see but us and us is always here together."

"Yeah, yeah," Corporal Thunder frowned jokingly. "Sometimes you're here, but you're not really here. I just have to get your attention. Lieutenant Abrahams is attending a meeting now and we'll get the details later, but we got a warning order for a mission at Con Thien."

Clary winced at the words "Con Thien," believing the misery of their everyday conditions and everyday routine was about to become drastically altered with greater misery and greater danger. He dejectedly peered into the mist of the valley and partially invisible distant mountains.

"While we're waiting I got other news, too. It's not good, but it's part of our talk last night about the support for and misunderstandings of this war," Corporal Thunder remarked.

"You remember Lance Corporal Wilson from third squad? He rotated home in September after completing his tour," he asked and reminded them. They nodded their heads in recognition.

"Yeah, Wilson had done his time in Vietnam," Clary reported, "but when he left he said he'd write us. Most promise, but then never write."

"Well, Wilson wrote Sergeant Hedquist," the Corporal revealed, "and his letter sort of explains why many never write. It's really kind of sad." Writing from Vietnam was hard at times, however, writing to Vietnam as a veteran was often harder. It was another of the war's mysteries.

"Yeah, a lotta guys probably want to write, but just don't know what to say," Hawkins added.

The common bond dependence and combat friendships were no longer present once Marines rotated home. In a peculiar way they preferred it that way. Only those who had experienced it could understand why it almost had to be that way. Wilson's letter indirectly illustrated the oddities.

"Wilson served his time with us. We went on patrols together. We trusted and depended on him. He was somebody to us. He was somebody special," Corporal Thunder summarized.

"Yeah, Wilson helped teach me a lot about patrollin'. He knew a lot about walkin' point, too," Hawkins admitted, "and in his quiet manner he shared his smarts with me. I listened, too."

"Yeah, well, that may be part of the problem. In Wilson's letter, he says back home no one listens," the Corporal continued. "Worse, they don't ask questions. Worst, they care nothing about it. The war and us fighting hardly exist to anyone but our parents and relatives and friends."

"Damn, that's like experiencing the most significant emotional event of his life and having no one at home with whom to share it," Clary observed as he considered his future homecoming.

Wilson's letter was their first personal indication of the coming turmoil and doubt in America. It was Wilson's final indignity…no one remotely cared. Wilson sacrificed, he endured, and he believed, but back home many were causing him to disbelieve, doubt the war, and doubt himself.

"That's devastating to read from someone who was one of us and part of us," Wiley moaned.

"Well, it gets more devastating," Corporal Thunder frowned, "because in his closing comments he wrote he wishes he was back with us for a second tour, back where he belongs, back with people who care."

As unbelievable and as incomprehensible as Wilson's thoughts were, many later learned there was an element of truth to them. While many were relived to return home after completing their tours, many also regretted leaving friends behind who were still in harms way. It was one of the illogical logics of the war. While civilians and military alike might view such a thought process as incredulous, many who served firmly believed that if they were *serving during a war* that they should be *serving in the war*. Quite simply, it was a Marine and warrior ethos to many.

Whether they were patriots or protestors, it was simply a phenomenon of the war and warriors. Many had wanted to make a difference. Instead, many sensed they had made little difference. Then many felt guilt or failure or both. It was an inexplicable and irrepressible thought, but so much of the war was inexplicable and irrepressible. While in Vietnam many fought the inexplicable thoughts of a second tour as hard as they fought the war, but once home such thoughts inevitably surfaced. In the midst of their combat tours, however, few even remotely considered another tour.

"Okay, now that's total bullshit," Hawkins exhorted as he shook his head in defiance, "I ain't acceptin' that because I'm survivin' day-by-day with the hope of someday goin' home. It's hope that helps me make it through every single day. It keeps me going. It keeps me focused. It keeps me dreamin'. I'm leavin' here someday and I ain't never comin' back. I'll just be good and gone."

"Yeah, I have to hold on to that dream, too. I have to hold it hard and tight," Clary explained, "because it's the dream that helps me through all the nightmares of Vietnam."

Wilson's letter contributed to an erosion of their dream. It was symbolic of the nightmare Vietnam would become. At the time, Corporal Thunder and his Marines embraced the dream because the alternative was the nightmare. The Marines lived for the dream of someday going home. It survived as long as they survived. They refused to let it die. The dream died only when those fighting died, which it did all too often.

"The letter's just one more reason we have to understand this war better. It's why we're writing home to ask friends and family to mail us articles and information about the war and what's going on at home," Corporal Thunder suggested. "It'll probably be December or so before we have a good collection, but then we'll start reading, talking, and learning more about this war."

The team nodded to agree. They acknowledged studying and learning about war and better understanding it would be a daunting task, but then Hawkins candidly said, "War's pretty damn dauntin', too. Studyin' and learnin' ain't got nothin' on warin'. Studyin' ain't killed nobody yet."

Corporal Thunder was summoned to another meeting and departed. "Wiley, you're in charge, watch Hawkins," he ordered. He smiled before Hawkins could rebut. Wiley frowned.

"Gather round. Listen up," Corporal Thunder announced as he returned and sat on an ammo can an hour later. He smiled at Hawkins, who grinned but let the "gather round" comment pass.

"Battalion's still coordinating the official order," he opened with a frown, while Clary involuntarily shivered from either the cool wetness or the pending mission.

"You thinking it'll be that bad? You shaking?" Wiley innocently asked Clary.

"It'll probably be bad. They say Con Thien's just terrible," Clary answered, "but I'm shaking from this cold and wet and miserable rain. I haven't been dry in weeks. My bones are dripping wet. I'm shivering from the cold so much my body just freezes up tight and locks itself down till I can't shake no more. It gets to me. It gets to me bad." He crossed his arms and hugged tight.

While the winter temperatures in Vietnam were never freezing, Hawkins asserted, "Yeah, but when I'm always wet, twenty-four hours a day wet, and it rains forever, I just get cold and stay cold." This was especially so in the high mountains in which the team operated. Maybe the temperatures were only 50 or 60 degrees, but the constant cold rains made them seem worse.

"We've never really operated in Con Thien because it's mostly an outpost with a few South Vietnamese and Special Forces," Corporal Thunder said, "but plans are to make it a fire base. We don't know for sure now, but the intelligence officer said there's talk about the Pentagon wanting to build a fence or barrier to stop the NVA from crossing the

DMZ into the South. The NVA'll probably want to make it hard for us to turn it into a fire base and build the fence."

"Where's Con Thien exactly?" Wiley asked.

"It's only about three or four kilometers from the DMZ," he reported. "It's about 20 to 25 kilometers to our northeast and maybe 15 clicks north of Camp Carroll and Cam Lo."

"It's more open and exposed terrain," Hawkins injected. "I remember it from the convoys from Dong Ha to Payable. It'll be different fightin' in the coastal plains than mountain jungles."

Corporal Thunder nodded in agreement and added, "You're right, which means our worst dangers will be artillery and rockets and mortars. They say Con Thien's a rocket and mortar magnet.

"The bad part," he addded, "is there's rules about us not firing into the DMZ. It's something about counter-battery fire restrictions. I don't know the specifics, but just know there's some."

"Holy shit!" Hawkins exclaimed. "You mean the NVA can fire at us, but we can't fire back? That's part of limited war? Ain't that some kinda deal? It's a good deal for the NVA, but a bad deal for us. Who's makin' such stupid deals? Is the fence guy and restrictions guy in cahoots?"

"Like I said," Corporal Thunder explained, "I don't know the particulars, but I know we'll probably not like them. We won't have to worry about them because we can't do anything about them. The battalion will handle all of that, especially the supporting arms fires."

"We won't worry about them my ass," Hawkins replied. "I worry like hell when someone can shoot rockets at me and I can't shoot back." He threw his hands up in disgust and mock anger.

"You're right," Corporal Thunder admitted. "I didn't mean it the way it sounded, but that's all I know for now. We'll just have to wait for the order and more details about when and where we can and can't fire. We'll be briefed on the exact restrictions."

"Well, one thing I know for sure is what maybe some dumb ass in the Pentagon should know," Hawkins angrily theorized, "and that's if we build a fence to stop the damn NVA that they're just gonna go under it or over it or through it or around it. It won't stop jack shit. Jesus, those strategic Pentagon thinkers are idiots." He then scrunched his face into his wild and stupid look.

"You better stop that look before it freezes like that," Wiley cautioned, remembering one of his mom's favorite expressions. Again, remembrances of home came at the strangest times.

"One last thing," the Corporal remembered and smiled to temporarily ignore Hawkins, "you could probably care, but for what it's worth in Vietnamese Con Thien means *Hill of Angels*."

"It ain't worth much," Hawkins replied, "except us Marine Devil Dogs are gonna go to the Hill of Angels to kick those devil NVA straight to hell."

They smiled at Hawkins' reference to Devil Dogs because it was a favorite nickname of Marines. It was awarded to Marines by the Germans for their fighting ferocity at the Battle of Belleau Woods in France in World War I. It was an iconic Marine battle and victory.

Wiley innocently but mischievously asked, "Is Devil Dogs the reason why we Marines call our metal ID tags we wear around our necks 'dog tags'?" He nonchalantly glanced at the horizon while sipping coffee from a canteen cup and suppressing a smile.

"Exactly," Hawkins quickly and teasingly responded, "except in your case we're gonna call'em Gorilla Tags 'cause you're so damn big and ugly and black." Wiley choked on his coffee, but quickly cleared his throat to cough to avoid laughing.

"Yeah, I asked for that one didn't I?" Wiley smiled. "But if that's so, maybe I should call yours Pink Pekinese Pendants because you're so damn puny and fluffy and lily pink."

In absolute unison they erupted in laughter. Hawkins wiped the tears from his eyes and said, "Well, I guess I asked for that one, too." Wiley was becoming much better with his bantering.

As darkness approached they ate their Cs and talked before their watches. Corporal Thunder commented, "Now that we've been up north over a month our area of operations is expanding from Payable to the east and Con Thien. Later, I'm hearing we'll also go west to Khe Sanh."

The team paused to consider the day's dramatic turn of events. Con Thien was definitely in their thoughts. Khe Sanh was definitely in their future. But it was always one good patrol at a time or, as Wiley always prayed, "It's surviving one sunrise and one sunset at a time."

The Con Thien operation began with a 0300 reveille. In the dark cold Corporal Thunder and Wiley shrugged without commenting, which only opened the serious complaining to Hawkins.

Hawkins gingerly pulled on his wet uniform top, but the frosty clammy wetness slapped him momentarily breathless. While it abruptly jolted him, he was unable to ascertain whether it was scalding hot or freezing cold. He silently let loose a string or profanities for warmth, but they never helped. Within minutes the initial wetness was of no consequence because he was soaked to his core from the pouring monsoon rains.

"Damn, it's cold, wet, raining, and miserable," Clary confessed as he laced up his soggy boots, "but it's always miserable in Vietnam. There's just no relief. Just none at all. Zero."

"Jesus," Hawkins moaned, "just every once in a while I'd like to pull on a pair of dry socks. Just once or twice a week I'd like to slip into a dry warm utility blouse without having to shake my ass off from that first cold wham it gives my back. I'm so wrinkled I'm a damn raisin."

The battalion assembled along Highway 9 and the Cua Viet River before loading onto trucks for the convoy east toward Cam Lo. It was a relatively short distance, which caused Hawkins to say, "It hardly seems worth the trouble to truck us when we coulda just as easy and maybe just as fast walked to Cam Lo." He pranced jokingly as he pantomimed a comedy march parody before slipping and falling on the muddy road. Suppressing a laugh, Wiley bent to lift him up.

"You can walk if you want," Clary responded. "I'll ride because there's lots of walking in front of us." Clary quickly grabbed one of the few seats in the back of the truck covered with a canvas tarp to shield him from the drizzling rain and smiled. He saved seats for the team, too.

Hawkins thought about Clary's comment, but said nothing. He was seldom without a rebuttal, but he knew Clary was right. He would rather say nothing than admit Clary was right.

The convoy arrived at Cam Lo on schedule. After the brief cluster from dismounting the trucks with Marines flailing in the dark searching for their units, leaders began forming their units, moving to assembly areas, and advancing north to Con Thien.

Corporal Thunder once again quickly briefed his team on the battalion's formation for the advance north toward Con Thien. "Our company,

Company M, is on the right flank and Company L is on the left flank." He quickly unfolded and laid out his map and pointed, "We'll be on the east side of this dirt road or trail and Company L will be on the west. Company K will straddle the road and follow as the reserve and security for the Battalion Headquarters."

It was still dark. It was still raining. The Marines were still cold and wet. After a few kilometers of hauling fifty plus pound packs their bodies began to warm up. An hour into the advance the skies began to darken despite the fading night and coming day. The rains increased and the winds howled stronger. Wiley exclaimed, "Well, praise the Lord. It's another sunrise. I can't see it for the monsoon and clouds, but I know the sun's up there somewhere."

Clary later noted, "The terrain's opening up the farther north we go. We'll see the DMZ soon."

"Yeah, and that probably means the NVA can see us, too," Hawkins frowned as he squinted to survey the horizon, "but the rain and mist are making it hard to see too far."

Corporal Thunder later pointed toward the northern skyline, maybe six or seven hundred meters to their front, and asked, "Look, to our front, what do you think that is?"

Wiley, Hawkins, and Clary could only see the top of whatever it was because the sheets of rain and fog partially obscured their vision, but Clary finally guessed, "I'm not sure, but it looks like it might be some type of steeple, maybe to a church or maybe an old village tower."

It was the only structure visible for kilometers and it appeared to be located on a small rise. "Whatever it is," Wiley observed, "from that location one can see forever in all directions, especially in good weather." He bent into the gusts of wind and rain and trudged forward.

Maybe two hundred meters later the word was loudly passed. "Incoming. Incoming." But instincts had alerted them seconds earlier. They had already hurled themselves down and flat.

"Down. Get Down," Corporal Thunder yelled to his team. "Get small; get small fast." By then the danger alerts were unnecessary because they were already frantically clutching and hugging the soggy earth.

It was a natural and instinctive reaction, but they quickly adopted the fetal position and attempted to pull themselves into their helmets. It was too late for Entrenching Tools, or E-Tools, to dig holes. They needed to be flat and not crouched digging. Hawkins philosophized, *It's impossible to hide or disappear into helmets, but there's a helluva lotta comfort in trying.* He wiggled into as small and tight a ball as possible. Then he squeezed himself smaller and tighter.

The mortar and rocket explosions reached a horrific crescendo before slowly dissipating into silence. The silence was shattered, however, by the painful and piercing groans of the wounded.

"Where's Clary?" Hawkins blurted. They frantically searched the area, but no one saw Clary.

Wiley yelled as he scurried, "He was back down the line and maybe just over this little rise."

Corporal Thunder and Hawkins immediately charged after Wiley, who disappeared in the tall grass as he fell to his knees to cradle Clary in his arms shouting, "Over here. Clary's over here."

Corporal Thunder quickly assessed Clary's wounds and ordered, "Wiley, take Clary's first aid kit and stop the bleeding." Then he ordered, "Hawkins, find a corpsman. Tell the doc Clary's not an emergency and to treat the seriously wounded first, but tell him to come soon."

Corporal Thunder then kneeled next to Clary to help Wiley administer first aid and treat his wounds. Clary was bleeding profusely from shrapnel to his right shoulder, arm, and forearm. He thought, *The wounds are more than superficial, but less than life-threatening.*

Corporal Thunder admonished Clary for not calling for one of them. Clary grimaced and smiled, "I thought I was okay and didn't want any of you to expose yourselves to more danger."

Meanwhile, Corporal Thunder suspiciously glanced at the distant tower.

Hawkins appeared in time to hear Clary's answer, shrugged his shoulders, and grinned, "Oh, now I understand. You wanted the Purple Heart all for yourself and for us to just get nothin'."

"That's about it," Clary shook his head, "the team only needs one hero."

"Hero my ass," laughed Hawkins, "this Purple Heart only means you were in the wrong place at the wrong time. Jesus, you just laid there fat, dumb, and happy and took a little shrapnel and now you're gonna get a

Purple Heart. I oughta shoot you myself so you'd earn a real Purple Heart. Then I'd be a hero for shootin' you, too. You slacker."

The corpsman was dumbfounded by the conversation. Doc Timothy understood, however, they cared for and talked to one another with confusing as well as unique and special actions and words. Nonetheless, he thought the team was a little insane.

"It doesn't appear the shrapnel hit any nerve or deep muscle tissue," the Doc explained. "The wounds will bleed like hell, but you'll be okay once you're medevaced. I'll give you some quick field expedient fixes, but they'll probably give you more stitches back at Dong Ha."

"You're kidding us, right Doc?" Hawkins asked, "These tiny wounds are gonna get Clary to the rear for clean sheets and decent chow? He gets to go where it's warm and dry?"

"Yes, and a hot bath and cold beer, too," Clary added for spite and to irritate Hawkins.

Clary was tagged and medevaced. Afterwards, the battalion advanced steadily but sluggishly forward. The closer they came to Con Thien, the closer they came to danger. They advanced cautiously but relentlessly. As twilight approached they viewed Con Thien on the horizon. Its stark ugliness and desolate landscape more than confirmed their preconceived notions. Despicable from a distance, Con Thien's devastation awaited their presence and it was only by their actual presence that its vivid ugliness was revealed.

"Damn, it's just out in the open and it's awfully close to the DMZ," Hawkins observed.

"You're right, but maybe that's why they're planning for the barriers and fences for the area," Corporal Thunder reminded them.

"Oh, yeah," Hawkins remembered, "it's part of that Pentagon and wizards plan to stop the NVA from infiltrating or crossing the DMZ with obstacles and barriers. Yeah, that fence plan."

"Well, I have bad news for the Pentagon," Wiley smiled, "it's too late because the NVA's infiltrating now. Bet they keep infiltrating, too. They're here now and they'll just keep coming."

The battalion was confident the NVA had registered the outpost with artillery and rockets and that dispersion was critical. It halted 500 hundred meters from the outpost and advanced one company at a time into the outpost's perimeter until the battalion was securely occupying Con Thien.

"Okay, let's get serious," Corporal Thunder cautioned as they settled into their bunker. "We'll be here for three or four days to provide security for engineers and electricians and whoever's on the team to survey and study. Then it'll take months to decide if the fence idea is good or bad."

"They can study the fence idea from hell to breakfast, but I already know the answer. Months, hell! It's dumber than dirt. I knowed it in seconds," Hawkins spouted convincingly.

Wiley smiled and asked, "What's electricians have to do with the fence? They going to light it up so the NVA will know where it is in the dark?"

Corporal Thunder vaguely recalled the Lieutenant's summary of the fence as a barrier and answered, "The Lieutenant said something about an electronic fence or one with sensors or radars. Some type of systems to detect the ground shaking or moving, too. Seismic, I think he called it, but I don't know what all's involved. It must be kind of sophisticated or fancy."

"Well, hell, that changes everything," Hawkins smiled. "Put electricity in the fence and the NVA will grab it and electrocute themselves. I'm all in. Maybe that's the Pentagon's secret plan."

"Hawkins, you have a good point," Corporal Thunder smiled as he remembered a joke from his youth in Pawhuska. "One of my favorite Oklahomans is the humorist Indian cowboy Will Rogers. He once said there are three types of learners. Those who learn by reading. Those who learn by observing. Those who have to pee on the electric fence for themselves."

"You pee on an electric fence and it's the shock of your life," he laughed, grabbing his crotch.

"Okay, that seals the deal. I'm now supportin' the fence. I'm now all in for the electric fence," Hawkins declared. "Let's build it and teach the NVA to piss on it. It'll fry their little peckers to a crisp and then maybe they'll stop screwin' with us."

"Well, I doubt it. They'll probably screw with us all night," Wiley sighed as he set the night watches and the team attempted to sleep in the cold wet rain and hot dark fear of Con Thien.

"Minutes after midnight the NVA launched its nightly artillery and rocket barrages into Con Thien. "Damn, it's like they waited till we're so tired and so scared from waitin' before they decide to mess with us," Hawkins complained as he set his M14 to automatic.

"It's just like you said, Corporal Thunder, they fired a few rounds and now have us waiting and wondering what's to come," Wiley exclaimed as he pulled his poncho liner tighter for warmth and positioned his rifle toward the perimeter. Wiley was a bear of a man, but when his hibernation was interrupted he was a grizzly. Fond of his sleeps, he was playfully irritable when denied them.

The waiting and wondering was the worst part of the night, but the best part was the pre-dawn opportunity to actively and convincingly act instead of passively wait and wonder.

"Wiley. Hawkins," Corporal Thunder whispered. "Look, directly to our front. I believe I see movement. It's about 50 to 75 meters in front of our positions. Wait for a flash of light and maybe we can see better. Look low. Scan the area and don't lock onto it. They're low crawling. They're probing. They're preparing to attack. Let's aim in and be ready to fire. Let's get grenades ready, too.

"Stay alert while I pass the word down the line so Sergeant Hedquist can notify the Lieutenant and the company and battalion, too," Corporal Thunder mumbled softly.

Moments later, shattering and thunderous explosions erupted and waves of tremors literally shook the earth. The NVA rounds impacted with such force that shrapnel tore into the sandbags and mud and debris splattered the team's bunker.

The attack prep fires were followed by an NVA ground attack. Hawkins fired first and yelled, "Over there, straight out, looks like a platoon or so." He fired and popped an illumination flare directly behind the NVA to further silhouette the enemy with light. Fears flourished as the fight intensified, but their fears were subdued by their furious actions.

The tracer rounds, with their blazing red arcs from the team's M14s, helped the Marines on the perimeter target and fire effectively on the enemy probe. Within seconds the enemy was engulfed in a massive fusillade of small arms and machine gun fire, M79 rifle grenades, and 3.5 rockets. The aggressive actions by the Marines surprised the NVA, who were caught in the open and exposed.

Corporal Thunder observed the NVA hesitate and then begin to pull back. Then an unexpected action occurred. "Ceasefire, ceasefire," he surprisingly yelled, "Ceasefire."

The Corporal, without warning Wiley or Hawkins, surprised them and the perimeter Marines with his next action. Once the Marines ceased firing, he unhesitatingly leaped from the safety of the bunker and attacked toward the wire and the retreating enemy.

Corporal Thunder zigged and zagged as he wildly attacked forward. He yelled a blood curdling, "Aaahhhaaa, Eeeiiioooaaa," repeatedly as he charged with a primitive savageness the NVA had undoubtedly never before seen or heard. He dropped to a prone firing position in the sodden earth every few meters to aim and fire at the retreating enemy, especially those attempting to recover their dead and wounded. Once he even twirled his flashing machete over his head in a circular motion as he chanted, sprinted, and screamed. It was beyond wild. It was beyond savage. It was insane.

Wiley and Hawkins simply looked at one another in absolute amazement. Without hesitation they lurched forward at full speed to join Corporal Thunder while firing continuously.

At first, the Marines on the perimeter remained in their secure bunkers, but gradually crawled out of their positions and cautiously moved forward. They were initially more curious than courageous, but they were ready for a fight. As they rushed forward the fight and enemy retreat was on.

Corporal Thunder breached the concertina wire barrier at the designated entry and exit point and cleared a safe path for the following Marines as he ordered, "Check every NVA. Those dead leave for now. Search and handcuff and blindfold the wounded as prisoners. Strip them down good before taking them inside the perimeter. Stay alert. Keep firing.

"Quickly, quickly," the Corporal ordered, "we need to do this fast and get back inside the perimeter. Take the wounded and prisoners to our officers because they'll know what to do with them. Our intelligence folks will want to talk to them."

Wiley and Hawkins delivered their wounded NVA soldier just inside the concertina wire and passed him to the Lieutenant who had come to investigate. Wiley told the Lieutenant, "Corporal Thunder said to deliver this prisoner to you because you'll know what to do with him. There's more coming, too." Wiley brushed blood from his hands and uniform and inserted a loaded magazine into his M14. Hawkins knelt to reload his shotgun before tugging on Wiley to return to the fight.

Then, before the Lieutenant could speak or ask questions, Wiley and Hawkins wheeled and rushed back to join their Corporal. By then, eleven NVA prisoners were in custody. Corporal Thunder counted nine dead NVA soldiers and he ordered the remaining Marines, "Drag the dead as close to the concertina wire entry and exit point as possible. Then lay them side by side."

After the NVA had retreated into the darkness, he commanded, "Okay, everyone back to our bunkers, but keep the dead NVA under surveillance in case the NVA come back to recover them."

Corporal Thunder, Wiley, and Hawkins wearily quick-timed to their bunker. The surprise and unexpected episode with the enemy attack required about thirty minutes or less. It had been done quickly without advance warning. It was, however, one wild and wicked action. Then it was silent.

Later, the sun began to rise. They had a patrol to prepare for and they had hardly slept. Tired, dirty, hungry, and thirsty defined them once again. They were excited and proud, however, of their success. In a small but significant engagement, they announced to the enemy Con Thien was no longer simply a minimally manned outpost. Instead, it was now occupied by Marines and as Hawkins exclaimed, "It'll be a little different with Marines here. The NVA better get used to it."

"Well, I'll be honest with you," Wiley contended as he heated a cup of coffee. "At first, I thought we were crazy. I thought we'd lost our minds. I mean, who the hell leaps up from the safety of a bunker and trench and charges across an exposed killing zone while the enemy's firing incoming artillery and launching a ground probe or attack? Who really does that? That's crazy. We're crazy."

"Crazy, hell, it's insane," Hawkins mumbled as he savored a C-Ration crackers and cheese breakfast, "but when Corporal Thunder yelled his Indian dancin' chant and slung his machete around wildly, I just figured he was another savage on the warpath. Hell, I thought he was gonna scalp one of'em and I wanted to be close to see it. Ain't never seen a scalpin'. I figured no use him havin' all the fun to hisself. Yep, it's crazy, it's insane, but you gotta be a little insane crazy to be a Marine."

"Well, if I'd known I was going to attack them like I did I'd have warned you," Corporal Thunder admitted as he sharpened his machete to help relieve his post-battle rush withdrawal, "but when they hesitated I figured it was better to just act fast. I figured it wouldn't be too much of a risk. We already had'em pulling back and thinking about retreating. Besides, something like that, maybe I have no right to ask you to do."

"Well, I bet anything you knew we'd follow you," Wiley declared. "You knew you didn't have to ask us or order us. You knew we'd be there for you and with you." They nodded and smiled.

"Yeah, Wiley, you're right," Hawkins concurred, "he knew we'd be just as dumb as him and dumb enough to do the same. I ain't takin' your bet or bettin' against you. I ain't that dumb."

"This is the first night in over three months we're missing one of us." Corporal Thunder quickly changed the subject and declared, "We're missing Clary."

"Yeah, never thought we'd miss that California surfer dude," Hawkins grinned, "But I feel kinda bad about teasin' him yesterday about his Purple Heart. I hope he knows I was only jokin'."

"He knows," Wiley whispered, "because the last thing he told me as I escorted him to his medevac helo was to tell you to get two wounds so you'd have twice the fun and get two Hearts."

"I ain't gettin' any if I can help it," Hawkins replied. "All the body parts and blood I have now is what I want to go home with. Don't need no wounds and don't need no Purple Hearts."

As the team, minus Clary, talked in their bunker, word was passed for the Corporal to report to Sergeant Hedquist. He pulled on his combat gear, grabbed his weapon, and smiled, "Wiley, you're in charge of Hawkins until I return. Don't let him do anything stupid. I'll be back as soon as possible."

"Hell, after your actions last night, ain't nothin' stupid left to do," Hawkins groaned as he smirked back at the Corporal. "Ain't nothin' but insanity goes on in Vietnam." They exchanged smiles as Corporal Thunder departed for Sergeant Hedquist, but the Corporal's smile faded quickly.

The hostility of the pre-dawn NVA ground attack and bombardment paled in comparison to the combative engagement he was about to confront. Corporal Thunder was oblivious to the events about to transpire, which was best. Sometimes innocence and ignorance are true bliss. He later learned, however, the pre-dawn NVA attack was less hostile than the one he was about to engage.

CHAPTER 7

Mortars, Machine Guns, & Machetes

"Whew, three meetin's! That musta been somethin'. What'd ya do, have a war party and scalpin' or powwow and smoke a peace pipe?"

—Marine Private First Class Dominic Hawkins

Corporal Thunder sauntered to Sergeant Hedquist's position and together they strolled to Second Lieutenant Abrahams' bunker. They were content and pleased with their initiatives to repel the NVA attack. It mystified them, however, to learn their actions were about to be vilified. When they arrived at the Lieutenant's position he was pacing nervously and visibly upset. He notified them, "The Company Commander, Captain Garvin, radioed to order all of us to his position. We have to report immediately to the Battalion Commander, Lieutenant Colonel David. We have to go now."

Sergeant Hedquist and Corporal Thunder then became aware of the impending crisis. They had no idea what it was about, but they sensed it was serious. Serious, however, was an understatement.

Sergeant Hedquist and Corporal Thunder quickly glanced at one another but said nothing. They concluded it was not a good time to talk. It was a good time to be quiet. They strongly suspected all this reporting to here and reporting to there was not good. Reporting to the Company Commander, much less the Battalion Commander, was rarely career enhancing. They waited silently.

"The Captain says the Old Man is hot as hell, really pissed, and really curious as to what the hell's happening on our portion of the perimeter, especially after last night, or to be more precise, early this morning," Lieutenant Abrahams frowned. He controlled his anger by pacing back and forth as he clinched his fists because he was unsure to whom and about what he should be furious.

Sergeant Hedquist and Corporal Thunder remained silent and said nothing. There was nothing for them to say or do. They were clueless and concluded they would be informed in time. Until then, they waited while noticing gray smoldering smoke drift from the numerous rocket craters.

"The Captain thinks we're all going to the Battalion Command Post or CP to have our asses chewed on by the Old Man or maybe worse," the Lieutenant said as he rolled his eyes and groaned, "and none of us are necessarily looking forward to an ass chewing right now. Right damn anytime!

"I'm not sure what the Old Man is enraged about," Lieutenant Abrahams admitted, "and maybe it's best I don't know for now. Maybe knowing is worse than not knowing, at least for now."

Second Lieutenant Abrahams dejectedly hung his head as together they walked to the Company Commander's bunker. They were announced and the Captain emerged from his bunker strapping on his cartridge belt and combat gear. The Captain appeared decidedly more distressed than the Lieutenant. Saying nothing at first, he simply glared with disdain at the three Marines he had summoned to his bunker. The Captain's stare spoke volumes. He snapped his helmet straps together with contempt. He, too, was angry, but unsure exactly why and for what.

The Captain was a Mustang Captain, which meant he was previously an enlisted Marine, in the Korean War, who later received a commission as an officer. Although Sergeant Hedquist and Corporal Thunder had had few contacts with the Captain, Lieutenant Abrahams previously told his platoon the Captain was an extremely no-nonsense and by the book leader. This applied to most Marine leaders and was therefore of no particular insight and fairly meaningless to them.

"He's hard, but he's fair," the Lieutenant said in summarizing the Captain as a leader, as if that provided more depth or perspective into the Captain. That, too, was relatively useless.

The Captain took his time before speaking. Eventually, as his cold stare bore into them, he growled, "The Battalion Commander is livid. The Old Man admits he's only heard a partial report of the antics on the line this morning, but what he's heard appears to him to be totally unprofessional and the result of poor leadership." The Captain was distraught and winced when he said "poor leadership" and "unprofessional." The words were an anathema to Marines. They stung; stung hard.

"I've been in the Corps for almost twenty years and this is the first time I've ever been summoned to the Battalion Commander for any lack of professionalism or leadership," Captain Garvin continued. "Somebody better have one helluva good explanation or we may all be relieved or disciplined or whatever. In combat, this is damn serious. This could be very bad and ugly." He attempted to speak again, but said nothing. Momentarily speechless, he became more frustrated and angry. Slowly, he recovered. His tempered wrath was almost beyond his control. His rage exploded.

"I'm curious as hell as to what exactly happened and exactly why we've been ordered to the Old Man's bunker. But I've been told to ask no questions now because the Colonel wants no collusion. He's ordered none of us to talk together for now," Captain Garvin sighed. "Damn, it sounds like the Old Man's considering legal action. It feels like an investigation or worse." He shuddered twice.

Corporal Thunder had seen the Battalion Commander, but had never met or talked with him. He knew from other Marines, however, that Lieutenant Colonel David was one hard-ass Marine. He had participated in multiple legendary battles in the Marine Corps' famous Pacific Island Campaigns of World War II. The Battle of Iwo Jima, however, was the one which most distinguished him.

Marines who knew him alleged Lieutenant Colonel David's temper was as razor sharp as the texture of the volcanic rocks he crushed and ground the Japanese into on Iwo Jima. Furthermore, his absence of compassion in such disciplinary hearings as office hours and non-judicial punishments rivaled that of satanic cults or rituals.

The Sergeant Major alleged, "Satan ain't got nothing on the CO. Hell, Satan fears the Old Man." The Old Man's standing and stature in the Marines was created at the Battle of Iwo Jima and he was dedicated to ensuring no one ever tarnished Iwo Jima. It was a reputation ferociously and famously earned by Marines with whom he had served. Equally adamant in protecting the reputation of today's Corps and Marines, the Old Man was the epitome of a leader and combat veteran.

Lieutenant Colonel David was a Marine enlisted on Iwo Jima, reportedly a Corporal, but later was awarded a battlefield commission and became an officer. He had bled the dark volcanic ashes of Iwo Jima and belched the island's volcanic sulfur fumes. The Old Man was Old Corps to his core.

Captain Garvin, Second Lieutenant Abrahams, Sergeant Hedquist, and Corporal Thunder were too acutely aware of Lieutenant Colonel David's reputation as they trudged toward the Old Man's bunker on Con Thien. They exchanged no words. They trod dejectedly. It seemed as though they were in a wake or funeral procession. Maybe it was an execution walk. Maybe it was worse.

The four Marines from Company M arrived at the Battalion Headquarters. They reported in and waited outside the bunker for permission to enter. Shifting nervously from foot to foot they became anxious. The Old Man purposefully forced them to wait and wait and wait. It appeared the Colonel was intent on having them stew and suffer while considering their fate. They were suspended in time. The waiting, however, eventually became worse than either. Unknown fates are often feared most. It was a cool drizzling morning, but the two officers were sweating. The desolate red clay landscape of Con Thien paled in comparison to the black desperation beginning to consume them.

Later, in due course, the Battalion Operations Assistant appeared and asked Captain Garvin and his Marines to report to the Colonel. The Colonel was on the radio with Regimental Headquarters. They continued to wait and said nothing. They stared into the distance while considering their fate.

"Yes, Sir, I'm investigating the incident now and will report to you as soon as possible," the Colonel reported to Regiment. This was a bad sign to the four Marines. It was a horrible sign. It suddenly seemed to the four Mike Marines their situation was deteriorating, if that were possible, if it could actually become any worse. But if the Regimental Headquarters was now involved they could only assume the worst.

The Colonel glared at the Captain. The Captain piercingly scowled at the Lieutenant, who stared harshly at Sergeant Hedquist and Corporal

Thunder. The two enlisted Marines had no one to glare at. Instead, they looked straight ahead in the coal black candle lit bunker. The scent of burnt black powder fumes hung in the sandbags.

In time, the Colonel informed them, "It's been reported to my Command Operations Center that rather unusual activities occurred along the Company M defensive perimeter early this morning. By unusual, I refer to Marines risking their lives outside the wire. Marines mistreating wounded NVA. Marines screaming and flashing machetes. Marines defiling enemy dead. Marines acting with total disregard for the safety and security of the lines, especially during enemy artillery and rocket attacks. Marines possibly endangering the lives of other Marines and the reputation of our Corps."

The Colonel paused to inhale deeply before continuing, "Now, is this about it or, God forbid, is there more? Who the hell knows the most about this travesty? Who knows the more, if there's any more? Who's to tell me what I should know? What I damn sure better know and be told."

Respectful of seniority, Lieutenant Abrahams, Sergeant Hedquist, and Corporal Thunder said nothing. Captain Garvin reluctantly but finally spoke, "Sir, I was commanding the company from my bunker and have no direct knowledge of the incident to which you refer, but…"

"Damnit," Lieutenant Colonel David growled as his face turned crimson, "I didn't ask who doesn't know what happened. I asked who knows what happened. I asked who knows if there's any more I should know. Damnit, that seems fairly simple to me. Why can't someone answer a simple damn question?" Every question was louder than the previous one. The meeting began wretchedly.

This time the Captain said nothing. The Lieutenant glanced down. The Sergeant shuffled his feet. Corporal Thunder gazed steadily and assuredly straight ahead.

"Sir, I know," Corporal Thunder finally began, "I know what happened and why."

"Well, Corporal, go on. Let's hear it," the Battalion Commander scowled at the officers.

"Yes, Sir," Corporal Thunder continued, "I did what I did because the Captain and Lieutenant are always telling us small unit leaders that one of the most positive leadership traits is for us to exercise our initiative. Take the initiative. They're always teaching us that. That's why we did what we did."

The Captain and Lieutenant visibly frowned. They were both convinced their Corporal was about to throw them under the 6X6 cargo truck and suggest they were the culprits. It definitely appeared to them as though Corporal Thunder and his Marines did what they did because it was what the two officers trained them to do or, worse, ordered them to do. The officers began to sweat even more.

When the two officers thought the discussion with the Colonel could deteriorate no further, Corporal Thunder's next remarks convinced them he was now intent on destroying them.

"Colonel, most of what you heard is not true. It's just wrong," Corporal Thunder announced.

The Captain and Lieutenant shrank visibly. Corporals never told Colonels they were wrong. Never. Confident the Colonel would bolt from the sandbags he was sitting on and rip into them unmercifully, the two officers took a step backward. They thought this was becoming a suicide mission. Corporal Thunder was sacrificing them and taking them with him became their sole conviction. The two officers' careers flashed before their disbelieving eyes.

The Colonel, the Old Man, however, said nothing. Captain Garvin and Lieutenant Abrahams thought maybe he was so outraged he was speechless. They concluded he was too shocked to respond. The Colonel, however, seemed surprisingly calm and attentive to Corporal Thunder and motioned for the Corporal to continue.

"Colonel, Sir," Corporal Thunder confidently continued. "My team observed enemy NVA approaching our lines. We noticed their artillery and rockets attacks were tapering off as the enemy probed our perimeter. To us it was no risk to attack the enemy probe because we'd disrupted their attack with our accurate fires. They appeared temporarily confused and hesitant. To us at that time it seemed no risk, but we thought it simply a bold decision to attack them. We attacked and the NVA retreated. When we counterattacked they seemed even more confused, too, and retreated faster."

The Colonel said nothing, but unknown to the four Mike Company Marines the Old Man was searching his memory for one of his favorite war quotes. It was one from General Erwin Rommel. General Rommel was the legendary German Panzer Commander often referred to as the Desert Fox because of his World War II North Africa Campaigns. General Rommel, the Colonel recalled, was famous for his boldness, his use of surprise, and his willingness and readiness to accept risks.

Corporal Thunder paused before continuing, "We exercised our initiative and our boldness as the Captain and Lieutenant trained us and it worked, too, just like they taught us. I believe they trust us to take the initiative and to act boldly. I believe all Corporals appreciate it when their officers trust them to take the initiative and to act timely and aggressively and boldly."

The Colonel was now remembering his time on Iwo Jima, his time as a Corporal in combat. He remembered precisely his respect for those seniors who trusted him and who willingly encouraged small unit leaders to exercise initiative. It was a trust, a sacred trust, shared between the best leaders and the best followers. It required incredible training and discipline to achieve that trust in units, but once earned and shared those units became the best.

The mood in the bunker seemed to perceptibly change. The Mike Company officers appeared encouraged by a slight softening in the facial expressions of the Old Man. But questions remained.

"But what about attacking beyond the wire?" the Colonel asked. "Is that true and why?"

"Yes, Sir, that's true, we did it," Corporal Thunder pointedly replied. "We attacked."

"Why the hell did you attack the NVA outside the wire?" Colonel David interrupted.

"We attacked outside the wire because that's where they were," Corporal Thunder answered. "We just attacked them where they were. No sense attacking them there if they weren't there."

The Mike Marines, except for Corporal Thunder, frowned and cringed. They were convinced the previous blaze of anger that seemed to have been reduced to a simmer was about to reignite into an inferno. His remark, "that's where the NVA were" seemed too flippant under the circumstances. It was too nonchalant. It was maybe even disrespectful. Nonetheless, his words now raged on.

"Sir, we knew we'd wounded a number of enemy and our officers are always telling us prisoners of war, POWs, are good for intelligence and to capture them when we can," the Corporal exclaimed without pausing. "The NVA were trying to recover them, but we wanted to stop them and recover them first. So we went outside the wire to get them." Corporal Thunder was now beyond calm. The Old Man thought, *He's either totally unconcerned…or totally confident…or totally fearless of the NVA as well as of me. He's got a warrior's ethos.*

The Colonel only nodded and asked, "What about any mistreatment of the prisoners?"

"No, Sir, no mistreatment," Corporal Thunder replied. "We just handcuffed them with their belts and stripped their trousers off and tied the bottoms together and slung them over their heads as a hood to blindfold them before escorting or carrying them into the perimeter. We just made sure they had no grenades, or knives, or weapons, or explosives on them. We probably saved the lives of several of them, too, because they needed emergency medical aid. We got them medical help fast."

The Colonel only nodded, but this time the nod appeared to be a nod of approval.

"What about defiling the dead?" the Colonel asked.

"Sir, what exactly does defiling mean?" Corporal Thunder innocently asked.

"It means to dishonor the dead," the Colonel smiled and answered.

"No, Sir, we never dishonored the dead," Corporal Thunder responded, "we collected them and laid them side by side at the wire so that later they could maybe be turned over to the South Vietnamese. Maybe later returned to the North for burial or whatever they do with them."

"You're an Indian, aren't you son?" the Colonel inquired.

"Yes, Sir, I'm Osage Indian and Irish. I'm a Marine Corporal, too," Corporal Thunder confided.

He thought he probably did not have to tell the Colonel he was a Marine or Corporal. The CO already knew, but then again he wanted the Colonel to know he was proud of being an Indian and Irish as well as a Marine and a Corporal. He asked his question; he received his answer.

"Where're you from?" the Colonel asked.

"Sir, I'm from Pawhuska, Oklahoma," Corporal Thunder replied proudly.

"Indians respect the dead, don't they?" the Colonel inquired.

"Yes, Sir, Indians honor the dead and burial grounds are sacred," Corporal Thunder explained. "The dead can never harm us, but their spirits can haunt us. We respect the spirits of the dead, too."

The Colonel nodded again and groaned, "What about the damn machete?"

"Yes, Sir, I have a machete and I use it when I have to," Corporal Thunder admitted. "I have all my team carry a second weapon in addition to our M14s. Clary has a M79 grenade launcher. Wiley has a .45 pistol. Hawkins has a shotgun. We just believe in having different types of weapons and the more the better. Actually, we all have a third weapon, too, because we all have K-Bar knives."

The Colonel considered asking Corporal Thunder who authorized or approved second weapons, but he remembered from Iwo Jima most Marines carried a second weapon or more. He decided maybe it was best he neither knew about nor questioned how they came to have second weapons.

Corporal Thunder paused while the Colonel appeared deep in thought, but eventually he broke the silence by commenting, "I learned from our Marine history classes how the Japanese officers would carry samurai swords and sometimes lead night banzai charges to try to scare the Marines on Guadalcanal or Iwo Jima. But the Marines would kill them and use the swords in attacks of their own to demoralize the Japanese soldiers. It worked then and it seems to have worked last night, too."

The Colonel nodded once more, but this time with a strong glance of approval. The Colonel again remembered Iwo Jima and his actions, which were very similar to Corporal Thunder's in Vietnam. He particularly remembered a samurai sword incident, one in which he was personally involved, one in which he brazenly yielded a samurai sword, but he made no mention of it.

Corporal Thunder started to speak to continue his explanation, however, the Colonel held up his hand to motion him to remain silent.

The Colonel was again lost in thought; lost in memories. The Old Man considered maybe Corporal Thunder was a master at pulling all the right strings by referring to Iwo Jima and to his time as a Corporal; maybe he was an expert at punching the right buttons related to similar past experiences; maybe the machete and samurai stories and the talk about initiative and boldness and risks were more than coincidences.

The Colonel decided it was virtually impossible, very improbable, for the Corporal to know that much about his time on Iwo Jima. No Corporal could know that much about his experiences on Iwo.

"Son, what did you say your name was?" The Colonel finally asked, surmising maybe a relative or family friend of Corporal Thunder's had been on Iwo Jima.

"Sir, Corporal Thunder, Corporal Dark Pale Thunder," Corporal Thunder straightened.

"And you're from Oklahoma?" The Colonel again asked.

"Yes, Sir. Pawhuska," Corporal Thunder again answered.

The Colonel was searching his memory for a connection between Corporal Thunder and Iwo Jima, but he discovered none. He expected none, but he was astonished and curious about all the coincidences. Suddenly, an expected thump requesting entrance hit the sandbags to Colonel David's bunker. Colonel David ignored the thump. Another louder thump irritated him.

Colonel David bellowed, "We're busy in here. Unless it's important, damn important, come back in about five minutes." Now the Colonel was angry at being disturbed.

"Sir, it's me, Major Lloyd from the Ops Center. It's very important," Major Lloyd exclaimed.

"Enter," Colonel David commanded, but he was obviously displeased by the interruption.

Major Lloyd entered the bunker smiling, which confused everyone. The Colonel signaled for him to report on whatever it was that was more important than his talk with the Mike Company Marines. The clear impression was that it had better be good. It had better be damned good.

"Colonel, we just this minute received a radio call from the regiment. The radio operator wrote down the message from regimental ops as best he could and I called back to confirm its content," Major Lloyd announced. "I talked briefly but directly with Colonel Miller, too."

Colonel David stiffened when Colonel Miller's name, the Regimental Commander, was mentioned. Mayor Lloyd continued, "Colonel Miller said to relay his congratulations to you for successfully repulsing the NVA attack last night and for capturing prisoners."

Major Lloyd paused briefly before concluding, "Colonel Miller says the intelligence folks are interested and excited about interrogating prisoners from this area. He said they're the first prisoners from Con Thien and will be invaluable to them. Finally, and this is verbatim, Colonel Miller said to tell you, and I quote, 'Keep up the good work. We're proud of you and the battalion.'"

Corporal Thunder noticed the previous somber and sullen and serious atmosphere in the bunker immediately transition to relief, maybe cheerfulness, maybe even elation. But he remained erect and expressionless. He stood tall and steady and stoic. He was Osage.

The Colonel surveyed the bunker and Marines slowly while searching for an appropriate response. Remembering Corporal Thunder's lack of concern when he had entered the bunker, he now accepted his lack of enthusiasm over the good news from regiment. The Corporal appeared totally unfazed. He had never once apologized or made excuses. It was ever more obvious to the Colonel that Corporal Thunder came into the bunker confident his alleged bad or questionable actions were good ones.

Corporal Thunder was, therefore, unmoved by the news from regiment. He had done what he had done because he believed it was what he had to do. He did it and believed he had done right. Nothing any of them thought or said, including regiment, seemed to really make much difference to him. He had his beliefs about right and wrong. The Corporal never preached them, but he practiced them.

The Colonel understood instinctively that any praise about the incident, an incident that minutes before conjured thoughts of punishment, would probably be embarrassing to Corporal Thunder. So the Colonel simply stood, held out his hand to shake the hand of Captain Garvin, and quietly stated, "Good job, Captain Garvin. You have a good company and it's doing a good job for the battalion and for the Marine Corps. I like what you're teaching your small unit leaders and how you're training your Marines. Thank your Marines, on my behalf, for their professionalism."

Lieutenant Colonel David turned to Corporal Thunder and smiled, "Corporal, you just keep doing what your company and platoon commanders teach and train you to do. Good job. Damn good job."

The Colonel then faced Major Lloyd and asked, "Can you get me Colonel Miller on the radio?"

'Yes, Sir," Major Lloyd replied, which was the signal for the Mike Company Marines to depart.

Captain Garvin was silent and speechless during their return walk to the company area. The preceding stroll across the muddy red landscape was a depressing and demoralizing one, but now they were walking tall and proud. The two officers initially expected to be pillared, but they were eventually praised. Captain Garvin thought, *This war is harder and harder to understand.*

As they arrived at the Captain's position, the Captain faced them squarely and simply said, "Good job. I'm still trying to figure out how you worked the Colonel the way you did, Corporal Thunder, but it seems you just told the truth as you know it. I'm proud of you. Tell your Marines that, too."

Corporal Thunder returned to the bunker about the time Wiley and Hawkins were waking from a brief morning nap. "Gather round. Listen up," Corporal Thunder announced.

"Gather round?" Hawkins asked. "Hell, we're already gathered. We're always gathered. We're right here. Where'd you think we'd be or go? Where else is there to be? Where else is there to go?"

Hawkins then blurted, "Okay, Corporal Thunder, what the hell was the meetin' all about?"

Corporal Thunder replied coyly, "There was no meeting."

"What the hell you mean no meetin'?" Hawkins moaned.

"No meeting. It was meetings. It was three meetings," Corporal Thunder clarified. "We met with the Lieutenant. Then we went to meet with the Captain. Then we went to meet with the Colonel."

"Whew, three meetin's," Hawkins whistled and asked, "That musta been somethin'. What'd ya do, have a war party and scalpin' or powwow and smoke a peace pipe?"

"Well, yeah. At first, the Colonel thought we'd violated rules last night and he was scalping mad," Corporal Thunder smiled, "but finally I had to tell him what really happened."

"Well, okay, hell, what'd you tell'im?" Hawkins pestered as he became agitated by Corporal Thunder's repeated stalling.

"Well, I finally had to tell the Colonel one of my Marines, named Hawkins, rushed forward like a crazy wild man, screaming and scaring the poor NVA, twirling a machete like a drum major parading in a marching band, and shooting anything that moved. I just admitted temporary insanity for you and told him we'd asked for an appointment with the psychiatrist for a psych evaluation to have you checked out and possibly committed to an institution. I apologized and asked for forgiveness and he gave it to us. That's it. Then it was over."

"Yeah, well, I have you know I know that's bullshit because you know I've already been committed to the world's foremost institution for the insane. It's the Marine Corps. Yeah, look around who's right here with me. It's you and Wiley and Clary after he returns from his vacation in the hospital and rear. Now, tell me who's crazy!"

The team grinned at first and then laughed. Without their laughter they would probably at times be crying. They created opportunities to laugh simply so they could forestall their tears.

"Seriously, what the hell happened," Hawkins pleaded.

"Seriously, that's what I said," Corporal Thunder winked to Wiley. "Ask Sergeant Hedquist."

"You can bet you're ass I'll ask him," Hawkins smirked.

"Let's be ready to saddle up and move out in a few minutes to meet the squad for today's security patrol," Corporal Thunder quickly alerted the team to change the subject. He wanted to move on and move on quickly, but Hawkins had other thoughts.

"Saddle up and move out," Hawkins giggled, "sounds kinda cowboy. I thought you was Indian?"

"You know damn well I'm an Indian," Corporal Thunder replied, "but Marines saddle up, too."

"Okay, but as a Bostonian and Italian type I'm tryin' to figure out why they call cowboys by the name cowboys," Hawkins inquired, "because that seems kinda girly to me. It seems kinda feminine. Cows and boys seem kinda prissy and sissy to me. Why not bulls or cattle or men?"

"Well, they call them cowboys because they herd cattle. They punch cows on the open range," Corporal Thunder explained. "They're cow pokes. You know, they punch or poke or prod cows."

"They punch cows?" Hawkins further baited Corporal Thunder. "That sounds kinda sexual to me. They prod cows? They're cow punchers? They poke and prod cows? Whew, that sounds kinda nasty to me. They must be some damn good lookin' pretty cows? They must be awfully sexy cows, too.

"It must get some kinda lonesome on the prairie. It must get damn lonesome. Do the cowboys call that cowulation instead of copulation?" Hawkins finally laughed.

Corporal Thunder realized Hawkins had backed him into a corner with the cowboy talk. He preferred to ignore Hawkins, but he was challenging to ignore. The Corporal was intent on extricating himself. Hawkins' final question rendered any escape nearly impossible.

Corporal Thunder pondered carefully and proclaimed, "Well, that's the cowboys for you. We Indians call ourselves horsemen. We ride horses. Indians who own cattle call themselves cattlemen, too. We don't use the term cowboy. It's a white man's term. We're horsemen and cattlemen."

The banter continued as the team saddled up and later provided security for the patrol with the surveyors studying and evaluating the barrier proposal. The team patrolled for three days and withstood devastating NVA artillery and rocket barrages for three nights before returning home to their Payable Hill base camp. There were, however, no more ground attacks. The NVA had evidently decided to delay additional ground assaults until they had departed Con Thien. They departed Con Thien, but Con Thien never again departed them.

The barrier fence Hawkins so desperately despised and ridiculed never quite materialized. Con Thien became, however, a critical strategic point. Its significance was validated throughout the war by the tenacity of the fighting. The exceedingly high casualties were testimony to its bitter and protracted struggle. Corporal Thunder and his team were a part of the initial process to enhance the Marines' presence at Con

Thien. But unknown to them, as they returned to Payable Hill and slept another fitful night, they would return to Con Thien in the future.

In the coming months, Con Thien would be transformed from an outpost into a firebase. In time, it would become an ever more dangerous and deadly duty and location. Marines over time would endure incredible sacrifices in what would come to be known respectfully as the Battle of Con Thien and the Siege of Con Thien.

Within the coming year, 1967, Con Thien would inspire legends of lore within the Marine Corps. The Marines and NVA hotly and highly contested the valuable terrain and over 1,400 Marines were killed and 9,300 wounded on its few acres. NVA losses were estimated at 7,600 killed and 169 prisoners. The continuous artillery and rocket attacks and threats of NVA ground assaults were among the most physically and psychologically challenging of the Vietnam War.

On a later foray to Con Thien, Hawkins referred to Con Thien as "Our Turn in the Barrel." The nickname stuck, but it was also infamously called "The Meat Grinder." The artillery and rocket duels became so intense that the Marines alleged DMZ, Demilitarized Zone, actually stood for "Dead Marine Zone."

Con Thien became so treacherous battalions would be rotated into the firebase for thirty days at a time and then be withdrawn because of the intense physical and psychological stress of the constant barrages. The bombardments were emotionally devastating. Wiley later remarked, "Con Thien was ugly the first time we were there, but with each visit it just got uglier."

It became decidedly more deadly, too, as Corporal Thunder and his team learned in the coming months. But tonight they were back home on Payable Hill. Now they could sleep as best they could. Con Thien would wait and it did. Con Thien waited for them time and time again.

CHAPTER 8

Payable Hill Rocket Attack

Yeah, everyday in Vietnam is a lifetime. But some days in Con Thien can seem like days or weeks of lifetimes. I just hope and pray we got more lifetimes than we got days in Vietnam.

—Marine Corporal Dark Pale Thunder

It was raining and cold as Corporal Thunder, Wiley, and Hawkins settled back into their bunker on Payable Hill. Wiley tossed his drenched poncho into the back of the bunker and uttered, "This poncho's more like a sponge than rain gear. It repels nothing. It grabs and absorbs everything wet and cold. I'm soaked." The rain was as ceaseless as the happy complaining.

As the rain pelted the bunker's tarp roof, Hawkins muttered, "I used to like the sound of rain, but no more. Every time it rains from now on I'll probably remember Vietnam. Damn, there's just no escapin' the rain. It'll probably haunt me forever. Ain't no escapin' Vietnam."

Wiley searched for a warm and dry uniform, but nothing was dry in the ammo box in which he stored his personal items. "It's too musty and dark in here for anything to dry. We can't dry out anything because it's always moist and clammy," Wiley muttered in disgust as he resorted to the standby drying method. They often slept in wet uniforms to dry them with their body heat. It was wretchedly uncomfortable, but Vietnam was wickedly unpleasant.

The team braced for the rain and the cold with a degree of rejection, ceaseless and resolute rejection, to minimize or temporarily forget the miseries of the twin conspiring evils. Saturated wet clothes clinging to their bodies and bone chilling monsoon temperatures, however, were hard to minimize or forget. It was Con Thien, however, that was truly unforgettable.

"Payable's no heaven, but Con Thien's the real hell," Wiley sighed, glancing at his Bible.

"We've only been gone a few days, but it seems a lifetime," Hawkins moaned with fatigue.

"Yes, but everyday in Vietnam's a lifetime," Wiley replied, closing his Bible for sleeps.

"Yeah, everyday in Vietnam's a lifetime. But some days in Con Thien can seem like days or weeks of lifetimes," Corporal Thunder emphasized. "I just hope and pray we got more lifetimes than we got days in Vietnam." The team agreed and remembered, but then tried to forget.

"You know, I keep thinking about that steeple on the way up to Con Thien," Corporal Thunder recalled the next morning as they rummaged for Cs for breakfast, "and how out of place it seemed." The steeple seemed a harbinger of evil, a precursor of danger, to him.

But there was no response to the steeple comment, as Wiley noted, "It's another rainy cloud hidden sunrise, but it's a sunrise." Sunrises were Wiley's interest instead of steeples and Cs.

Corporal Thunder and the team managed a few housekeeping chores. They checked with supply for a case of C-Rations and refilled a five-gallon water can with decent water. Their main task, however, was to restock the bunker with grenades, flares, and ammo for all their weapons. "I think I'll write my folks a quick letter," Wiley mentioned. "It's been awhile and they're probably worrying." He pulled a notebook and pencil from his ammo box and began writing.

"Yeah, that's a good idea," Hawkins replied. "I should write more than I do, but it's just hard. If I tell'em where we been and what we're a doing they'll just worry. Hell, it scares me just to think 'bout where we been and what we're a doin' much less havin' to write about it."

"Yeah, it's not so much what we write, it's just that we write," Corporal Thunder urged. "When we write at least they know we're okay. There's not much I want to tell them about what we're doing and how we're living much less about all the dying. So, mostly I write about home and how much I miss them and love them. Whatever happens I want them to know that."

Unspoken was the thought that none knew what letter may be their last letter. It was a thought too morbid to discuss, but it inevitably crept into their thoughts.

The team, less Clary, who remained hospitalized in the rear, completed their tasks and letters and later saddled up for an afternoon patrol. While no patrols in Vietnam were truly routine, the patrol was uneventful with no enemy contact. It was another patrol in a never ending series of patrols, but as Wiley often commented, "A patrol that returns safe is always a good patrol."

"I like it when the days are kinda quiet and the patrols even quieter," Hawkins announced. The day and the night, however, became one of their worst and loudest nights in Vietnam.

Corporal Thunder, Wiley, and Hawkins slowly ambled toward their bunker. They were in no particular hurry because as Wiley noted, "We got nowhere particular to go. We got nothing in particular to do. The patrol's over and our next patrol isn't till tomorrow. We got nothing."

As the team settled into their bunker the shades of evening began to descend on Payable Hill. Corporal Thunder gazed westward across the valley as daylight began to fade. The picturesque Rockpile, Razorback, and Fishbowl dominated the view. The Corporal thought, *It's a beautiful sight, but the beauty masks the ugly horrors hidden in the lurking dense jungles.* The insidious dangers in the scenic brilliance of the landscape created a muted pallor to its breathtaking colors.

Corporal Thunder noticed a puff of gray smoke indicating an explosion outside Company L's perimeter in the Fishbowl almost two thousand meters across the valley. "I hope that's a Marine throwing a grenade out to the lines," he casually stated. "Throwing it to test it or the lot they're stockpiling." They were unconcerned. It was a common practice to occasionally test grenades. They saw the puff of gray smoke and seconds later heard the explosion.

"Yeah, I hope it's outgoin' and not incomin'," Hawkins confided. "It's happened a time or two since we been here the Fishbowl's been mortared. It's painful to have to sit and watch it."

As Corporal Thunder and his team continued to observe the Fishbowl and Lima Company the explosions intensified. "It ain't outgoin'. It's incomin'," Hawkins blurted, "and it's getting' heavier and heavier. Holy shit! I hope they're down and flat and okay."

The Fishbowl had experienced similar brief mortar attacks in the past. They began and ended rather quickly, but suddenly and unexpectedly the situation deviated strangely. Corporal Thunder was the first to recognize the variance from previous attacks and remarked, "Look, down in the valley, down east of Lima, down east of the river. Look right there where I'm pointing. I think I saw a puff of smoke. It looks like a mortar round impact. Did you see it?"

Wiley scanned the area intently and spoke first, "I think I see the smoke, but not the impact."

"Yeah, now there's two or three more and they're comin' this way," Hawkins yelled. "They must be shiftin' fires and walkin'em up the hill toward us."

"Incoming. Incoming," He shouted as loud as he could while running to the crest of the hill to alert the Marines on the opposite east side of Payable unable to view the western valley and the shift in fires.

Simultaneously, the identical alert came from Payable's east side, "Incoming. Incoming." It was the alert the Marines dreaded to hear. It was always terrifying. Mortars were always feared.

"Holy shit," Hawkins declared, "the NVA must be attacking both sides of Payable. They're doin' a coordinated attack. Let's get back to our bunker and get down fast."

Corporal Thunder's team was about twenty meters from their bunker when the incoming mortar impacts began edging upward on Payable Hill. They had maybe fifteen seconds to seek safety. As they bolted toward their bunker they noticed the new corpsman, Doc Henry, who had joined Company M that morning. Appearing confused and in panic as he searched for safety, he suddenly stumbled and fell.

"Doc, Doc," Corporal Thunder shouted. "You take this hole down this path about ten meters. It's closest. We'll run to our hole farther on. Just get down and get flat and just stay there. It's all you can do for now. Stay there until you hear the all clear." He watched the Doc till he was safe.

Corporal Thunder then sprinted to the team's bunker. Once safely in the bunker, he admitted, "I hope the Doc's okay. What bad luck to be in a mortar attack your first day here. He didn't seem to know quite where to go and what to do, but I put him in the closest and safest hole."

"Damn, they have us targeted now," Wiley moaned. "They're scoring direct hits all over."

"Yeah, and they don't seem to be lettin' up any either," Hawkins exclaimed.

"It'll probably be totally dark in about thirty minutes," Corporal Thunder estimated, "so let's be alert in case the NVA launches a ground attack. It's a good time and good situation for one."

"Great, that bit of bad news makes our bad situation even worse," Hawkins smiled.

Suddenly, despite the explosions and chaos, Corporal Thunder heard, "Ammo. We need 106 ammo up here on top." He ignored it at first, but after the second shout he knew he had to act.

"Listen, it's the 106mm recoilless rifle team on top of Payable. They're calling for ammo," he remarked. "They need ammo for counter-mortar fires." He looked suspiciously at Hawkins.

"Yeah," Hawkins yelled as he looked squarely at Corporal Thunder, "but it don't seem nobody else's gettin'em any ammo." They both knowingly shrugged their shoulders.

They both knew what the other was suggesting simply because they knew one another so well. "Hawkins, you and me. We know where the 106 ammo bunker is. On three, let's go. Wiley, you stay here and guard the perimeter. We'll be back later."

Corporal Thunder counted three and he and Hawkins vaulted from the bunker and darted and dashed to the 106 ammo site about 30 meters along the slope. Payable was under a severe attack and in desperate need of counter fires. Desperation trumped death as they delivered 106 ammo.

Mortars impacted endlessly across Payable, but once they arrived at the ammo bunker they quickly pulled out a large wooden ammo crate with two 106mm rounds, with two rope handles, one on each end. The crates required two men to carry them. Corporal Thunder grabbed one end and Hawkins the other. As mortar rounds exploded, they locked onto the ammo crate with fierce determination while Hawkins muttered, "Jesus, whose lousy idea was this?"

Corporal Thunder and Hawkins paused briefly to gather their breath till Hawkins declared, "We'd rather be dodgin' just rain drops than mortars, but now we're dodgin' both. Let's go."

The two Marines burst forward up the slope with the heavy ammo crate. Bobbing and weaving along the muddy slope was challenging because of the heavy and precious payload, but they managed to awkwardly continue to lunge steadily upward and onward. Rope handles burned into their palms, but their pain was nothing compared to their fear.

As they approached the crest of the hill a thunderous explosion erupted about ten meters to their front. The crest of the hill absorbed most of the blast, but shock waves tumbled them backwards violently and shrapnel ripped savagely into them with excruciating and numbing pain.

Corporal Thunder lay twisted and tangled in the mud and blood for either seconds or minutes. He was either briefly dazed or unconscious. All sense of time and awareness escaped him, as he told Hawkins, "I seem to be floating. I can't focus. I can't seem to see or feel nothing."

Hawkins had been crumbled under the power of the blast. Heaved upward then hurled downward into the soggy earth he lay in agony. The pain was tolerable because he was numb to it from the concussion of the blast and the force of his body slamming into the earth.

Hawkins admitted to Corporal Thunder, "I've taken roundhouse punches, but nothin' like this. But I ain't dying here. I ain't dyin' today. Not here. Not like this. Not dyin' now."

Hawkins was the first to shake his head clear and revive himself. He crawled to Corporal Thunder and implored, "Corporal Thunder, you okay? You okay?" But okay was relative.

Feigning a smile, a weak one, the Corporal groaned, "Never been better. You?"

Then they simply held one another's hand. The firm hand clasp spoke volumes, more than any words they shared. Corporal Thunder then stated, "Seriously, I don't know how I am. I'm afraid to move. I don't know if I can move. But the worst is I can't see out of my right eye."

"Yeah, I know what you mean," Hawkins responded, "but I think it's mostly soreness or stiffness from the blast and blood from the shrapnel. Once I start movin' it seems I can move little by little, but it hurts. We gotta stretch it out. I don't think nothin's broke. It's like boxing and some guy just punched the livin' shit outta me. I'm just numb and achy."

The NVA mortar attack continued in full force, but they were oblivious to it. Talking and assessing their wounds were now their priority. Partially dazed, maybe temporarily unconscious, they were both together in a faraway world of their own.

Hawkins rolled over slightly to check Corporal Thunder's wounds, especially his right eye because he said he couldn't see from that eye. The rain and mortars were steady and incessant.

"I ain't no Doc, but it looks like you mostly got mud and blood in your eye from splattered mud and shrapnel wounds up above your eye. Here, let me wipe away some dirt and bleeding and let me know if you can see any better," Hawkins guessed.

Corporal Thunder grimaced, "That's a lot better. Damn, I was scared I was blind in my eye."

Once they determined the shrapnel wounds were bloody but minor, they collected themselves and completed their mission of delivering 106 rounds to the recoilless rifle team. Their wounds and the weather slowed them, but they fought their pains and the rains. Returning for second and third crates, they were delivering the third when the NVA mortar attack abruptly ended.

"It's 'bout time," Hawkins shouted. "I can't run another step. I'm down for the count as far as runnin' goes. I ain't throwin' in the towel, but you'll have to prop me up for the next round."

The final glimmers of light dissolved as Corporal Thunder and Hawkins lay breathless and motionless. They had depleted every ounce of their physical and emotional energy. They lay silent. They lay spent. They had nothing left in them. But upon remembering Wiley, they bolted up in unison with everything they had and charged to the bunker and Wiley.

The bunker was in total disarray. It was too dark to conduct a full and complete assessment of the damage, but it appeared a mortar round impacted the front left corner of the bunker.

Corporal Thunder inspected the bunker and noted the mortar impact on the outside bottom of the sandbags. "It looks like the sandbags took most of the blast, but that's too damn close."

"But where the hell's Wiley?" Hawkins quickly implored. "Where's Wiley?"

Instantly, they were terrified. "Let's get our flashlights," Corporal Thunder directed. "To hell with night or light discipline. The NVA already know where we are. They already found us. They already lit us up. We have to find Wiley."

The moment Hawkins crawled into the bunker he cringed and hesitated. "I think I found Wiley," Hawkins whispered. "I think I just stepped on him."

Corporal Thunder was the first to shine his light down and into the far right front corner of the bunker. Wiley lay looking upward with a blank stare on his face. He was motionless. His eyes were wide open and he was bleeding from his nose, probably bleeding from his ears, too. But the darkness obscured other signs of bleeding. The smell of smoldering powder hung heavy.

Reluctantly, they thought Wiley was dead. He was nonresponsive to their lights and sounds. Corporal Thunder then bent down to check his pulse and smiled, "I got a pulse."

"Corpsman up. Corpsman up," Hawkins shouted. "We need a corpsman over here."

Corporal Thunder ordered, "Hawkins, go find a doc and get him here fast."

Hawkins soared from the bunker and disappeared into the darkness. He was back with a corpsman in less than a minute.

"Doc, I got a pulse and he's breathing, I think," Corporal Thunder announced, "but he's not moving a muscle or blinking from the light or responding."

"Here, let me down there to check him out," Doc Sam Lynn said as he slithered into the tight confines of the bunker's trench. Splotches of dark mud and bright blood were everywhere.

Doc Lynn examined Wiley quickly before pulling a small bottle from his medical kit, his Unit One. He opened the bottle and placed it under Wiley's nose. It smelled rank. Wiley snorted and shook his head. Slowly, he gained awareness as Doc Lynn sat with him.

"Wiley, you sit right here for a few minutes and don't move," Doc Lynn ordered.

"Doc, I ain't got nowhere to go. I'm staying right here," Wiley replied. "I can't move."

"Good, because I have to check out your teammates," Doc Lynn explained.

Doc Lynn then examined and treated Corporal Thunder and Hawkins. After cleaning and bandaging their wounds he advised them, "Nothing more you need or I can do tonight, but in the morning report to the Battalion Aid Station (BAS) and they'll check you out further. They'll probably send you to the rear if you need more treatment, but that will be up to them."

The Doc then checked Wiley one last time and told him the same before ordering them all, "Monitor one another during the night. If you get really bad headaches or start bleeding, or whatever, just call me. Now, I have to go and treat lots of others up and down the perimeter."

Doc Lynn's final words reminded Corporal Thunder of the new corpsman who he had directed to a hole at the beginning of the attack. He shouted his name, but heard no response.

Corporal Thunder advised Wiley and Hawkins, "You two wait here. I know where Doc Henry is and I'll go get him. He's probably scared. It's his first mortar attack. He's just scared."

The Corporal tracked the trail up to the hole he had guided Doc Henry toward. "Doc. Doc," he hollered. The only sounds he heard were those of the wounded and the docs who were treating them. The sounds came from virtually every bunker on Payable. It had been a devastating mortar attack, but the extent of the damage and the number dead and wounded would not be known until morning and sunrise. It would be a long night of worrying and searching the area.

Corporal Thunder was becoming frustrated. He subconsciously thought Doc Henry might be hiding or afraid to emerge from the hole or worse. It was an irrepressible thought. He shined his light and located the hole and he was suddenly appalled and sickened. Doc Henry, on his first day on Payable, his first day in combat, had sustained a direct hit from a mortar round.

Corporal Thunder quickly stumbled back before moving forward again. The mortar had hit at the base of Doc Henry's head and neck and right shoulder. The scattered remnants of his brains were all that remained of his head and scull. His right arm was severed from his body and lay outside the hole from the blast. Blood had soaked in the mud and pooled in the corner of the hole. It was so gruesome Corporal Thunder turned and stepped away once again to gather himself. Death hurts more when the dead and dying are known personally.

After placing the Doc's corpse and body parts in a poncho and preparing him for medevac, Corporal Thunder somberly returned to the team bunker. Wiley innocently asked, "What took you so long? How's Doc Henry?"

"The Doc's dead," he answered. There was simply nothing else he could or wanted to say. Devastated he repeated, "He's dead." Wiley and Hawkins understood. They gave him time to collect himself by remaining silent. They were lost in their respective thoughts of the brutality of the NVA mortar attack and the horrors of the damage and deaths.

But eventually they talked and shared their thoughts because they always talked and shared their thoughts. It was part of their survival.

Corporal Thunder began, "I should've never left Doc Henry alone. I should've never directed him to that hole. I should've had him come with us. He died alone. He died because of me. I directed and pointed him to the hole. The hole that became his grave."

Wiley and Hawkins were dismayed and anxious to comfort and console Corporal Thunder.

"Yeah, but you put him in the closest hole. He was safe while we were still runnin' to ours," Hawkins exclaimed. "He was down and flat first. You took care of him first and then yourself."

"We're never alone," Wiley added. "God's always with us. You and Hawkins left me here while you delivered the 106 rounds. I was fine. God was with me. Think about it that way."

"Yeah, it's like we've said a thousand times," Hawkins conceded, "survivin' mortar attacks is a matter of fate. We can only get down and get flat and pray like hell, but if one comes in our hole, well, there's nothin' we can do. It's war. It's just fate. It happens no matter what we do. We just have to move on."

"You're right, but it hurts. We hardly knew him, but it hurts," Corporal Thunder confessed.

"I started to yell for one of you to come help me, but I didn't want the other to be alone. Not now. Not with us being as messed up as we are," the Corporal admitted.

"But then I thought there's no need in you seeing the ugliness of it all," he continued. "No need for you to see it at all. It was ugly."

"Yeah, this whole day, everyday in Vietnam, is ugly and scary," Hawkins injected. "It's just Vietnam. It's one long scary horror movie, but we're the lead actors in this damn scary movie."

"Wiley and Hawkins, you two try to sleep. I'm too upset for sleeps," Corporal Thunder finally sighed to conclude the soulful discussion.

It had been a harsh and monstrous day and night. They were soaked and chilled to the bone from the monsoons. Shivering and shuddering from the cold and wetness, as well as the forlorn and foreboding dark fear, their fears embraced them as never before. The depth and breadth of their fears startled them. This scared them even more. Numb to the core of their every nerve and muscle from sheer exhaustion, they were hungry and thirsty but they hardly noticed. They were bloodied and bruised and ached from multiple pains, but they hardly cared. It was their hearts and souls that tortured them the most...*this they cared about and this they noticed.*

Hawkins, the testiest and feistiest, the most relentless and resilient, finally spoke with a sense of rare melancholy. "This is the first time I'm thinkin' I might die. I'm fightin' like hell to live, but I'm thinkin' it's gonna be harder to live and easier to die in this shithole of a cesspool."

Corporal Thunder and Wiley were temporarily stunned. Hawkins was always joking, but now he was genuinely serious. It distressed them because the team always told Hawkins he was "just too damn ornery to die." The team thrived on his energy and passion for fighting...*and living.*

Hawkins' talk of dying was grave. It was as grim a challenge as the team had ever encountered. The raw silence ripped into them with unexpected force and unsuspected serenity. It was minutes before anyone spoke; before anyone knew what to say.

"Hawkins, think of your mother for a few minutes," Wiley finally exclaimed. "Your mother never once gave up, never once quit. Your mother's the true fighter in your family and blessed you with your sense of fighting. You can't die because it would break your mother's heart."

While Hawkins dwelled on Wiley's encouragement, Corporal Thunder added, "Hawkins, we're all going to live because we're all going to help one another live through this damn war. We're all in this together. We'll all do what we have to do to live day-by-day until the day we go home. We'll just take it a day at a time. We survived today. We'll survive tomorrow."

The Corporal paused before he continued, "We have to fight to believe this. I can't promise any of us we'll live, but I can damn sure guarantee if one of us dies then a part of the rest of us dies, too. I can also promise if one of us dies there will always be a part of them that lives in those who survive. None of us are dying so long as one of us lives. We'll always live in spirit."

Corporal Thunder and Wiley remained silent. They both thought they should say more, but neither knew what else to say. Wiley had appealed to Hawkins' love for his mother and family. Corporal Thunder had talked of his Indian heritage and belief in the Great Spirit.

"It's hard as hell to have to just get down during these damn mortar attacks," Hawkins finally asserted. "It's hard havin' no enemy to shoot at or attack and just havin' to wait out the mortars. It's even harder to get outta the safety of the bunker to deliver ammo, but at least we're doin' somethin' besides just lyin' down and takin' incomin'. Ain't no easy choices in war. They're all hard, but I'd rather go out dyin' good than livin' bad.

"Wiley, I remember you talkin' 'bout good and bad in the south and all the evil and prejudices you faced. There's evil in the world just like there's evil in Vietnam," Hawkins confessed, "but like your dad said, we gotta beat the evil with the good. Sometimes it seems hopeless 'cause there's so much evil and that makes hopelessness worse than evil. When all you got is no hope; all you got is nothin'. If you ain't got nothin' to live for, you'll die for anythin'. But we got somethin' to hope for and somethin' to live for. I ain't dyin' for nothin'. Maybe I'll die in this shithole, but it'll be for somethin'. I'm hoping I don't die, but if I do it's for you and for freedoms. That's somethin' to fight for." He then smiled and paused remembering his mama.

"Yeah, but I better live or my mama will probably beat me half to death," Hawkins eventually softly laughed in the dark. "Besides, it's hard for me to think about littl' ole puny lily pink ass me livin' in big black ass Wiley. So I ain't givin' up. I ain't givin' in. I'm goin' on."

Hawkins was back from the dead, back with the living. Wiley shouted, "Hallelujah! Hawkins has arisen. Hawkins is resurrected. Glory to Hawkins." He laughed and hugged Hawkins tightly.

"Damn, if we can't laugh about this war," Hawkins declared, "we'll always be cryin' about it. I'd rather laugh than cry," as he almost fainted from Wiley's powerfully smothering hug.

"Death is part of the life we're living," Wiley concluded. "We're living with death most every day in this war, but we're living. War's mixed up and confusing. It's dirty and nasty and ugly, but it's also noble and pure and true if it's for freedom and family and peace."

Yeah, freedom's priceless, Hawkins' thought, *but damned if it don't cost a lot, too.*

In the darkness, Hawkins finally whispered, "Thanks, Corporal Thunder and Wiley. Thanks." Hawkins never knew if they heard his thanks because he heard no reply. He thought maybe they were asleep or maybe he whispered too softly. Whether they heard him or not he knew they understood. The team's thoughts and thanks were often felt without ever having been spoken. It was a silent and unspoken language they shared in the team.

Early the next morning Corporal Thunder reminded them, "We better pack up and move down to the BAS so they can check us out. The doc said to get down there early."

"Yeah, he said we might get a ticket to the rear for more treatment, too," Hawkins beamed.

Corporal Thunder and his team checked out with the Lieutenant and slowly trudged to the aid station. "Wow! Look at that line," Wiley gasped. "It looks like maybe forty Payable Marines were hit last night. The NVA got us bad last night." The scene was utterly depressing.

Corporal Thunder hesitated before pointing to the dead Marines stacked neatly by the tent and said, "Damn, look at that. It must be twenty to twenty-five dead. There's so many dead that we ran out of body bags and just had to wrap some of the dead in ponchos." Wiley instinctively prayed and Hawkins respectfully made the sign of the cross.

"Yeah, and there's a lot more wounded that look a lot worse than us. Damn, I thought we'd been hit fairly bad, but we're lucky," Corporal Thunder noted.

"Look, there's Clary," Wiley excitedly yelled as he pointed down the hill.

Clary heard Wiley's yell, scanned the Marines assembled in the area, finally located Corporal Thunder, and immediately sprinted toward them. "Can't tell you how good it is to see you," Clary exclaimed. "I was in the battalion's rear Casualty Tent last night when the reports started coming in about the mortar attack and all the dead and wounded. I was worried."

"Whoa, what are you doing out here? How'd you get here?" Corporal Thunder asked.

"Well, the battalion arranged a truck convoy to come out this morning for the dead and wounded. I went over to the Dong Ha hospital last night with the First Sergeant to see if any of the emergency or serious helo medevacs were any of you," Clary replied. "I didn't find any of you, but the First Sergeant said to keep praying that you weren't dead because the company was still accounting for everyone. Damn, it was a long night of worrying and waiting."

"So, you just hitched a ride out here just to see if I was dead?" Hawkins smiled.

"Well, I wanted to be next in line with Corporal Thunder's sister," Clary grinned. "You know, just in case the NVA thought it best to terminate your ass."

Corporal Thunder, Wiley, Clary, and Hawkins playfully hugged and badgered one another as if they had been apart for months. It had been only days, but it seemed like years. The war and combat and their life and death experiences had no clocks and no calendars. Time and days merged and meandered into the future at their own pace, but abruptly stopped at deaths.

Corporal Thunder surveyed the area and situation and proposed, "You know, I was looking forward to maybe a day or two break in the rear at Dong Ha because of our wounds. But looking at most of these wounded makes me know ours are minor compared to them."

"So, you're hintin' at what I'm thinkin' you're hintin'?" Hawkins hinted.

"Well, I'm saying I think I'll just stay, especially since Clary is now back," Corporal Thunder stated, "but, Wiley, you and Hawkins can go back if they want."

"Yeah, the only reason I was goin' back was to kick Clary's ass and tell him his ole cheap ass wounds and Purple Heart ain't worth shit, ain't worth as much as the expensive wounds of mine and the Heart I'm gonna get," Hawkins laughed. "Besides, he's here now and I can kick his ass right here and right now. No need to go back now."

"Well, I'm sure not going back by my lonesome," Wiley confessed. "I'm staying, too."

"Okay, it's settled," Clary teasingly smiled. "You guys stay, but I never checked out of the rear. I'll have to go back for at least one more night to check out. I'll see you in a day or two."

"Like hell you're goin' back," Hawkins frowned. "You're here and you're stayin' here. Right Corporal Thunder?"

Corporal Thunder stared pensively and replied, "Well, I suppose we could check Clary into the company here and it'll radio the First Sergeant to check Clary out of the rear there. That'll probably work. Just so everyone knows where everyone is. Just so everyone's accounted for."

Corporal Thunder, Wiley, and Hawkins had been looking forward to a day or more in the rear...or anywhere to escape the front. They feigned sadness as they ambled back up the hill, but there was more gladness than sadness. They were too glad to all be together again to be too sad.

Corporal Thunder reported to the Lieutenant once they were back on Payable. "Sir, the aid station said Wiley, Hawkins, and me weren't wounded that bad and we probably should stay here now, but to check in tomorrow to have our wounds looked at again," he explained as he fabricated the truth ever so slightly and maybe totally.

"Sir, by the way, PFC Clary is back, but the company needs to radio the First Sergeant to officially check him out of the rear," Corporal Thunder added.

The Lieutenant glanced quizzically and curiously at Corporal Thunder speculating how Clary was back so soon without checking out of the rear. But he remembered Corporal Thunder and his interrogation with Lieutenant Colonel David. He concluded it best to neither ask nor question.

"Okay," Lieutenant Abrahams stated, "but report to sick bay tomorrow for a checkup."

"Yes, Sir," Corporal Thunder replied and wheeled to walk back to the bunker. The team was together again. The brief separation, however, was a prelude to future separations. But for now they were together again. Staying together, however, became more and more challenging.

CHAPTER 9

Rocket Blasts & Drug Busts

We're killing to survive and to live. You learn to kill real fast or you'll be dead real fast. It's just the way the war is.

—Marine Lance Corporal Aaron Wiley

Corporal Thunder returned to the bunker from a leader's meeting and reported, "Tomorrow, for the first time since we're been up north, the platoon is going on a patrol. With a larger platoon we can go farther and deeper into the jungles than with a smaller squad." He awaited a reaction, but the team was mentally processing the news while reloading ammo into magazines.

The Corporal paused momentarily. "It'll be an all day patrol. We'll depart Payable before sunrise and return about sunset." Clary stirred a canteen cup of hot chocolate to warm them while glancing across the valley. The bunker was dreary. It was a cool morning of misty rain and erratic breezes. *Patrols are patrols, big or small, new or old, first or last,* he thought.

"The Lieutenant's coordinating on the exact route and distance, but he's fairly sure we'll be patrolling up north of the Razorback," he added and asked, "Any questions?"

Hawkins was always ready with a question, "Why're we going farther and deeper into the valley? Ain't we gettin' kinda close to the DMZ?" He glanced nervously north toward the DMZ.

"That's a good question," Corporal Thunder noted. "The intelligence folks think the NVA are bringing more supplies into this area and suspect a buildup somewhere in our area."

"Yeah, I ain't too smart and I ain't no intelligence type," Hawkins growled, "but I could've told'em that weeks ago. Hell, we been gettin' blasted ten ways from Sunday for weeks now. That takes ammo and NVA. That don't take much intelligence or thinking. I figured it out. Maybe I should transfer to the intelligence section," as he completed loading his shotgun bandoleer.

Clary considered agreeing it takes virtually no intelligence or thinking if Hawkins could figure it out, but decided to let it pass. Hawkins' rarely thought before he talked. It was Hawkins.

"You're right," Wiley admitted, "but let's find them and maybe stop some of these attacks. Let's at least find the ammo and blow it." Wiley loaded his last M14 magazine and sighed as he tamped the base end to seat the rounds tightly into the magazine.

"Wiley, you've described the mission of the patrol," Corporal Thunder stated. "Locate any NVA camps in the area and destroy them and any ammo. That's it, pure and simple. Thanks."

Corporal Thunder was proud of Wiley's leadership. He was confident Wiley would become an outstanding Team Leader, but first he hoped to keep Wiley with the team as long as possible.

The team was a little zany at times and at others a little zealous, but that was what made it good. It was fast developing a reputation as the best team in the company. This could help keep it together or hurt it by distributing its skill to other teams in need of such experience and expertise.

The platoon departed the base camp before sunrise the next morning. Clary whispered to Hawkins, "We're moving pretty steady and it's not daylight yet." By daylight they were soaked from the monsoon and exertion of heavy packs as they ascended ever deeper into the treacherous mountains and enveloping jungle. They were becoming more alert and more apprehensive, too.

Hawkins led the platoon to one of the area's five river crossing sites and cautioned, "When you cross the river hold your rifles above your heads because the water's swift and chest high."

After the platoon crossed the river Clary muttered, "We're no wetter now than we were before we crossed." The monsoon rains had them perpetually drenched and chilled as the patrol continued its northern advance past the Razorback and then veered northwest deeper into the valley before turning to follow a ridgeline west.

The team slowed and became cautious as it patrolled farther north than they had ever before advanced. Hawkins and Clary paused to listen intently and scanned the valley from a break in the dense jungle. One faced north and the other south. Then one faced east and the other west. They looked and listened. "I don't hear or see anything," Clary said, "You?"

Hawkins said, "Nothin'."

No more than ten minutes later, Clary whispered, "Wow. We got something now. I can only see part of it, but it's huge. It's camouflaged pretty good, too. I was actually in it before I saw it." At first, the camp excited Clary. It excited all of them. Then their excitement became anxiety.

Corporal Thunder low crawled forward with his team. They quickly and carefully assessed the camp for ten minutes. "Jesus, we're lucky no one's home. This'll hold a battalion or maybe a regiment or more," Hawkins exclaimed. Wiley gasped silently as an adrenalin rush jolted him.

"We better call the Lieutenant up before we go farther," Wiley suggested. "He needs to see this." Corporal Thunder agreed and passed the word back down the line to ask the Lieutenant to come forward. As he arrived and viewed the camp, the Lieutenant rotated 360 degrees to suspiciously assess the situation. Visibly awed, but equally apprehensive, he smiled then frowned.

"Damn, this is exactly what we're looking for, but wait here while I pass orders to the platoon," Lieutenant Abrahams cautioned. "Third squad, you're now in the rear of the patrol. Spread out and hold your position and alert me if you detect any enemy coming into the valley," the Lieutenant radioed the third squad. "First squad, you're now second in the formation and I've been with you. I'm now with Sergeant Swede and the second squad and we're going down into the valley to take a closer look at the camp," he ordered. "I want you to move up and replace the second squad here on the ridgeline and provide over watch as we drop down into the camp and valley." He also radioed battalion a brief Situation Report as well as coordinated six "On Call" artillery missions north and west of the NVA camp.

The three squads maneuvered simultaneously. As Corporal Thunder's team led the second squad and the Lieutenant into the camp they were visibly astounded. "This has to be a major camp or staging base for NVA units moving south," Lieutenant Abrahams whispered and ordered, "Sergeant Hedquist, take your squad and take a good count of the number of bunkers."

"Sir, we counted over four hundred two-to-four man bunkers," Sergeant Hedquist later reported to the Lieutenant, "and maybe twenty ammo bunkers. We also saw six larger bunkers or maybe command posts." The Lieutenant mentally calculated the bunker numbers to unit sizes.

"Okay, I'm a little uneasy because if this camp was occupied we'd be out-numbered twenty to one or more," Lieutenant Abrahams admitted. "Let's turn around and smartly start our move back to Payable. We've accomplished our mission." Hearts, every heart, raced a little faster.

The platoon quickly reorganized and reversed course for the patrol's return to Payable. It was past dark before the platoon wound its way back home. It was raining, but it had rained all day.

Corporal Thunder and his team huddled in their bunker while attempting to dry out and gain a degree of warmth against the howling winds and torrential rains. Hawkins stripped off his soggy socks and rung them out as best he could. Then he let them soak in his helmet full of rain water before rinsing and ringing them out again. His feet were pink from the cold and wrinkled and shriveled from the constant wetness. The bunker began to reek from wet wool socks and filthy unwashed feet. The stench, however, blended with the multiple foul smells of the bunker.

"Damn, Hawkins, can't you do that someplace else," Clary complained teasingly.

"Jesus, Clary, just pardon the hell out of me," Hawkins muttered. "Let me go to my suite and do this in private. Oh, wait. I forgot. I don't got a suite."

"But that's okay, I'll go to the deep sink in the four-car garage to wash my socks," Hawkins railed. "Oops. Forgot again. Our bunker don't have no garage either."

"Guess I'll have to use the laundry room," he rubbed it in. "Wait, we don't got one."

"If we had a bathroom or washer and dryer or maids quarters," he wailed and asked, "I guess I could go there, but we ain't got any of those either. You get the picture, Clary?

"All we got is this one room bunker that barely holds all of us at one time," Hawkins goaded.

The team laughed in an uproar as it considered its miseries. Finally, Corporal Thunder suggested, "Hawkins is right. Maybe we should all wash our socks and wash and dry our feet."

The team then did laundry and took a field bath as best they could, but it was an awkward struggle as they tossed and turned in such a confined space while dashing into and out of the rain. After air dying, they dressed in dirty and wet uniforms and prepared for night watches. As they checked their weapons and ate their Cs they talked. They talked as they always talked.

"I'd like to have blown that camp to bits." Hawkins mumbled, "But I'm likin' the way the Lieutenant thinks. Let's wait till there's hundreds of 'em in there and then blast 'em all to hell."

The following morning after reveille, Corporal Thunder received the word from Sergeant Hedquist to report with him to Lieutenant Abrahams. He wolfed down the last of his C-Ration.

"Oops, what the hell ya do now?" Hawkins teased. "You havin' to report to the Lieutenant ain't usually nothin' but bad news. Yep, just like Con Thien. Bad news."

"Well, it's probably something you did and I have to explain to get you out of trouble," the Corporal sighed. "Seems you're what most of my talks with the Lieutenant are about."

After Corporal Thunder departed, Wiley asked no one in particular, "Why does Corporal Thunder seem to always be asked to go with Sergeant Hedquist to see the Lieutenant?"

"I think it's because he's sort of like the senior Fire Team Leader," Clary guessed.

"Another part is that Sergeant Hedquist is from Kansas and it's close to Oklahoma. They have lots in common about farming and ranching and hunting and fishing," Hawkins alleged. "The two are good friends and trust one another. Sergeant Hedquist is from a Swedish town in Kansas, too. I think it's called Lindsborg. That's why he likes to be called Swede. But if they're so close I wonder why Corporal Thunder never calls him Sergeant Swede? Everyone else does."

Wiley, Hawkins, and Clary were contemplating one another's thoughts when Corporal Thunder quickly splashed back into the muddy bunker and ordered, "Okay, gather round."

"First, we gotta question for you," Hawkins interrupted. "You and Sergeant Hedquist are close, but why don't you ever call him Sergeant Swede?"

"Well, he's senior to me and I respect him and his rank," Corporal Thunder mentioned as he was caught off guard and searched for a good answer. "We have team nicknames, but we rarely use them. It's like we agreed. We'll save our Socrates, Baby Brute, and Little Italy for special times or special occasions."

"Yeah, we have nicknames. We all have one but you," Wiley commented. "Why not you?"

"Well, usually some idiot calls me Chief or Injun or Tonto," Corporal Thunder smiled, "and I'm not having any part of that. Besides, I just like Corporal and my name. I'm proud of both."

Wiley, Clary, and Hawkins understood. It had never occurred to them to call him anything but Corporal Thunder. It was just who he was and what he was. To them he was simply Corporal Thunder.

"Okay, but Sergeant Hedquist seems to like the nickname Swede," Clary explained.

"Well, out of courtesy I'll ask him," Corporal Thunder agreed, "but wait for my cue. Once I call him Sergeant Swede, then we'll all call him that."

"Okay, but first we got somethin' for you," Hawkins smiled devilishly. "The other day we was talkin' nicknames for you and Clary suggested Pocahontas." Hawkins fought to stifle a grin.

"Hawkins, that's pure bullshit," Clary quickly rebutted. "You're just lying like a dog. You're just wanting to start something, but I'm not buying into that horseshit."

"But Wiley had another opinion," Hawkins added ignoring Clary. "He suggested Geronimo 'cause you're Indian and always warpathing. We decided against it because we couldn't spell it."

"My God, there you go again," Wiley quickly entered the fray. "You sure have a fertile imagination. Besides, what does spelling it have to do with saying it? We're talking not writing."

"Yeah, Hawkins has a fertile imagination and more," Corporal Thunder finally entered the conversation to defend himself. "He just has fertilizer on the brain. You can interpret that as shit for brains if you want. I'll leave that to you." He punched Hawkins on the thigh in jest.

"Okay, hold on," Hawkins laughed, "before this gets nasty just remember I was the one that negotiated a compromise for the best nickname. Since Corporal Thunder loves cowboys, which we remember from our talk about poking cows, I suggested we call him Mad Cow or Insane Bovine, which Colonel David immediately agreed to after the machete whirling thing.

"But then Wiley remembered Corporal Thunder prefers horsemen to cowboy and suggested we call him Crazy Horse or Phony Pony," Hawkins grinned. "But Clary said Crazy Horse was already taken and we couldn't use it and he was too old to be called a pony. So, we let it ride."

"Well, let's just let it ride forever," Corporal Thunder laughed. "Now you know why I'm not too fond of nicknames." He shrugged and gave Hawkins a playful punch on the shoulder.

"Okay, I think I had news for us before we got sidetracked with nicknames," Corporal Thunder smiled. "The Lieutenant's ordering Wiley and me to report to the docs in the rear at Dong Ha for further evaluation for our wounds," Corporal Thunder continued. "Doc Lynn reported us for not checking in at the Payable Aid Station the other day."

"I told the Lieutenant we're fine, but he said we have to go," Corporal Thunder explained.

"The Doc says I got to see the eye doctor and Wiley has to see the ear doctor," he explained. "We got to see specialists and they're both in Dong Ha. It's precautionary, but it has to be done."

"Yeah, well did the Lieutenant forget about me?" Hawkins inquired. "You know I took shrapnel and got banged up pretty good the other night, too. What about me?"

"The Lieutenant says you're indispensable. He needs you in case the NVA attack," Corporal Thunder replied. "You're too indispensible to the Lieutenant," as he winked at Wiley and Clary.

"Bullshit, that's bullshit," Hawkins suspiciously groaned. "Hell, the Marine Corps ain't never considered me indispensable. Far from it. They treat me like I'm disposable. They wipe the ass of Vietnam with me everyday and just throw me away into the shitcan called Con Thien or Payable or whatever. Ain't that a helluva deal? Indispensable my ass. How 'bout disposable?"

Corporal Thunder remained silent while Hawkins ranted and raved before he interrupted, "Seriously, the Lieutenant said all three of us have to go back to Dong Ha today for medical reasons. But he said to let Hawkins hang out and dry for awhile before telling him."

"Yeah, well, I suspect that's bullshit, too, but I'll take it up with the Lieutenant later," Hawkins declared, "after our vacation in Dong Ha. Now, I'm packin' for the rear."

Corporal Thunder addressed Clary. "Clary, I asked if you could go with us, but the Lieutenant said the platoon needs all the help it can get for patrols and night perimeter watches."

"You all go and don't worry about me. I'll be fine," Clary replied. "Besides, you all deserve a break even if it's for one day and night. I had my break. Take yours. Take care and be safe."

They grinned every kilometer of the truck ride to Dong Ha. They hoped and dreamed it would be a brief respite from the field and combat. Their dreams, however, became nightmares.

The Company M First Sergeant, First Sergeant Sharp, collected and delivered Corporal Thunder, Wiley, and Hawkins to the field hospital at Dong Ha upon their arrival in the rear area base camp. The three Marines reported back to the Mike Company office tent by mid-afternoon.

"Well, we got some free time for the first time in months," Wiley announced. "No worries, no patrols, no watches, no listening posts, no ambushes." The three Marines settled into the Casual Tent, which was the temporary quarters for those rotating to and from the front.

"Yeah, no nothin'. Not a damn thing to do for a whole evenin'. Nothin'," Hawkins grinned.

"The best part is the peace of mind; rest and peace," Corporal Thunder wistfully commented.

"The First Sergeant said we each get two beers if we want two," Hawkins confided, "and I told 'em I'll take my two right after chow. Beer call's right after chow. That's something to do."

"Well, we have about an hour before chow," Corporal Thunder estimated, "and I'm going to lay right here on this cot in this warm tent and drift off to a deep sleep. Wake me for chow."

"Yeah, and later we'll get hot showers," Wiley added. "We got cots and showers for the first time in about four or five months." A tremor of excitement created huge smiles on their faces.

"And two cold beers," Hawkins reminded them. "Remember the beers. Don't forget 'em."

In time, it was silent as they simply fell asleep while talking. Physically exhausted, but warm and dry for the first time in months, they slept peacefully for the first time in ages.

"Chow call and beer call," First Sergeant Sharp yelled to wake the Casual Tent Marines.

Corporal Thunder and his team woke slowly and departed quickly for the chow hall.

"Now let's don't rush eating," Wiley pleaded. "Let's just take our time and enjoy the meal. We have nowhere else to go after dinner, so let's just take our time."

"Yeah, well, I got somewhere to go and it's to beer call," Hawkins reminded them.

"Praise the Lord," Wiley gasped as they walked the chow line. "We got rice with chili con carne and green beans and toasted bread. Look, we also got peanut butter and strawberry jelly."

"You won't believe this," Corporal Thunder almost shouted. "Chocolate cake. Peaches, too."

"Man, I ain't had real Bug Juice in ages," Hawkins announced, "and its grape, too, my favorite. Look, we got ice, too." Bug Juice was the affectionate name Marines called Kool Aid.

The ambiance of the muddy dirt floor, tent canvas walls, and dangling 100-watt light bulbs as well as the cuisine of rice and chili con carne and various desserts would never rival either a five-star restaurant or a home cooked meal with family. In Vietnam and the constant diet of C- Rations, however, the basics of the chow hall were delights and delicacies to the Marines.

Corporal Thunder's team passed through the chow line like kids. They were young men dirty and bloodied from combat and hardened by too many recent disasters and deaths. But they were softened by the simple pleasures of a decent meal in a dry and warm tent. Briefly, they reverted to the innocence and excitement of the young kids they once were but would never again be.

They walked to their chow hall wooden benches and tables with a renewed vigor and gait. "Look, we even get to sit on benches instead of stand in the rain or sit in the mud," Wiley intoned. They had missed the simple pleasures of a bench or chair or table.

As they sat they heard distant wails from the Dong Ha airfield sirens. "What the hell's that?" Hawkins asked suspiciously as the eerie sound rose and fell from its circular rotations.

"Incoming. Incoming." First Sergeant Sharp urgently shouted as he burst into the mess tent, "Everyone to the bunkers."

The chow hall was cleared in seconds. The Marines scattered and were quickly and safely in bunkers. Seconds before the chow hall had hungry Marines and full trays of food on the tables, but it was suddenly an abandoned and empty ghost town. The laughter and joy of moments ago were replaced by stark silence, except for the lonesome wail of the siren. As the siren screeched, they awaited the incoming. Waiting was usually the worst, but this time thoughts of the food trays on the chow hall tables were worse than worst.

The incoming initially impacted the Dong Ha airfield over a thousand meters away. The most lucrative targets were at the airfield with aircraft and fuel dumps and ammo bunkers.

"Yeah, not much of value over this way," Wiley whispered. "Ain't much here but us."

"Ain't much here my ass," Hawkins retorted. "I'm here and that's much to me. That's a whole lotta much to me. It's me and I'm about as much as it gets to me."

"Well, you know what I mean," Wiley apologized, "the high value lucrative military targets are at the airfield." Hawkins loved to fluster Wiley.

At first, the explosions were distant and harmless, but the rumblings and reverberations became thunderous and deafening. "Okay, brace yourself," Corporal Thunder yelled, "they're coming this way and they're coming hard and fast." The Marines recoiled with every tremor. They held tight to one another to mask their trembling. The incoming impacted with incredible violence and the scent and sounds of fear ebbed and flowed ever more potent and pungent.

"Okay! Who farted?" Hawkins teased, "or was that a NVA dud?" The Marines laughed to mask their fears. The devastation continued for minutes, for lifetimes. Then it was eerily quiet.

The Marines emerged from their dank bunkers into the black night to witness dark sadness and heartbreak, but the worst was yet to come. The night temporarily shielded them from the worst, but they sensed it hover above them and then slowly but forcefully descend upon them.

"Over here, we need a working party over here," First Sergeant Sharp yelled, "we need help at the BAS tent." The Battalion Air Station tent had taken two or three direct hits. It was razed and shredded beyond recognition and nothing remained but splintered rubble…*and death.*

Corporal Thunder, Wiley, and Hawkins carefully but quickly burrowed into the rubble in search of wounded to extricate from the shards of splintered wood and the twisted and mangled metal. Nothing could have prepared them, however, for what they eventually discovered.

The remainder of the night the Marines searched the trench line as they became bathed in blood and stained from remnants of mushy flesh and shattered bone fragments. Hawkins gagged from the soft wet feel of human flesh and the breathtakingly nauseous smells of death.

The rain and the cold became worse, but no one noticed. Afterwards, about midnight, First Sergeant Sharp announced, "Well, the best I can tell for now, at least until daylight when we search again, I have seven dog tags of the dead. I can't believe it, but four are Navy Corpsmen. We got lots more wounded, too. Let's call it a night and check it out again in the morning."

After their dreadful duty, Corporal Thunder, Wiley, and Hawkins strolled back to the Casual Tent. The team was bitterly disappointed. All they had hoped for was a quiet and dry overnight stay in the rear with a good meal and a warm shower and two beers for Hawkins.

Instead, it was another tragic day in Vietnam. Once back in their tent they were relatively quiet. "Let's not talk tonight," Wiley suggested. They always talked, but tonight they passed on talking. It was too demoralizing to talk. So, they took turns showering blood away underneath a 55-gallon barrel with a gravity hose. Later they slept. Hawkins slept dreaming of two beers.

Within minutes, however, they awoke to loud stumbling in the Casual Tent. "Please, hold it down so we can sleep," Corporal Thunder sleepily asked. The racket continued despite a second request.

"Yeah, who the hell are you to tell anyone to be quiet?" the stranger finally quipped.

Corporal Thunder's grogginess disappeared instantly as he bolted from the cot and swiftly confronted the unknown Marine. "I'll tell you who I am. I'm telling you to be quiet and get to sleep or I'll damn sure put you to sleep." Quiet Indian deference was transformed into defiant rage.

"Now, who the hell are you?" Corporal Thunder asked in soft measured but forceful tones.

The Marine staggered and virtually spat, "Lance Corporal Rogers, if it's any of your business."

"Well, Rogers, you just made it my business," Corporal Thunder replied as he thrust a precise and powerful forearm shiver into Rogers' chest and propelled him tumbling head over heels while crashing into four empty cots.

Rogers staggered up, but was immediately restrained by Hawkins holding one arm and shoulder and Wiley the other. They had been poised to intervene should Corporal Thunder erupt.

Hawkins later confessed, "Hell, Corporal Thunder, we were protecting you from you, from your own fury. We weren't protecting Rogers."

While restrained, Rogers' slurred, "What'd you do that for?" The strong odor of alcohol permeated the area. Hawkins suspiciously and angrily wondered how Rogers had found any beers.

"You been drinking beers? You have more than two?" Corporal Thunder asked.

"Yeah, I've been drinking a few beers. I probably had more than two," Rogers mumbled. "If it's any of your business, which it isn't." Hawkins was now furious. He could have cared less about Rogers' noise, but Rogers' maybe drinking his beers was beyond forgiveness.

Corporal Thunder immediately cocked to deliver another forearm shiver, but Wiley abruptly stepped between Corporal Thunder and Rogers to block it and exclaimed, "Rogers is just flat drunk. Let Hawkins and me talk to him and get him to bed before he gets all of us in trouble."

"Okay, but ask him why he's drunk and clean while we got bloody and sober," he agreed.

"We'll take care of it," Wiley answered, "we'll take him outside to splash a little water on his face and sober him up with fresh air. We'll take care of it. Hawkins and me, we know what to do."

Wiley and Hawkins escorted a belligerent and reluctant Rogers out the backside of the Casual Tent. Hawkins spoke slowly and softly, "Rogers, you listen and you listen good. We ain't out here in the cold drizzlin' shit to protect your ass because you don't deserve protectin'. We're protectin' Corporal Thunder. We're out here gettin' wet and freezin' our asses off because if we'da left you in there a minute more, there wouldn't be too much more to you. Least nothin' worth a damn."

"Yeah. Yeah." Rogers sputtered, "What the hell's that supposed to mean to me."

Hawkins wheeled and powered an upper cut into Rogers' gut. Every ounce of air burst from Rogers' lungs as he dropped to his knees and gasped for air between bouts of vomiting.

Hawkins placed a boot in his back and pushed forward hard as he thought about Rogers drinking his beers.

Rogers' slumped forward and lay in his vomit. The sight was disgusting. The smell was worse.

Wiley reached down and grabbed Rogers by his back collar to avoid the vomit and lifted Rogers up as if he were light as a feather. But Rogers was at least six feet and two hundred pounds, which caused him to realize whoever was thrusting him about so easily and casually was stout and sturdy.

"Rogers, I told you to listen. You interrupt me again and I'll beat you down into a pile of shit. So far you've shown me you're dumber than dirt, so that won't be too far or too hard," Hawkins growled. "Life's pretty hard here in Vietnam, but it's a lot harder if you're dumb. So far you're makin' it pretty easy for me to kick your ass while you're just makin' it harder for yourself.

"You better listen better because this is what it means to you," he continued. "Corporal Thunder is an Osage Indian and sometimes he's just down right wild and savage. I seen him with my own eyes. I seen him cut off a NVA soldiers arm and head with his machete. I seen him attack runnin' scared enemies with his machete swirlin' in the wind just like he was on the warpath, too.

"Corporal Thunder believes in two things. First, is accomplishin' the mission. Second, is protectin' his Marines," Hawkins explained, "and he knows no fear when it comes to both of those. You step in the way of those two beliefs and it'll cost you. Maybe it'll cost you your life."

"What do you mean by that?" Rogers mockingly asked.

Hawkins delivered another powerful gut punch that once again dropped Rogers to his knees struggling to breathe. As Rogers bent over, Hawkins then powered a stunning rabbit punch into the base of his neck and shoulders. Rogers thought he was alert the second time, but Hawkins' boxing skills were too fast and too furious. Rogers never saw the fist until he felt its force. Then he felt virtually nothing as the pain overwhelmed him.

"Rogers, you're even dumber than I thought. I told you to listen. Now listen and don't talk," Hawkins shrugged. "Now, this is what it means. I'm from Boston, the North End. I'm Italian and I'm Mafia. I know drugs when I smell 'em and I know you been doin' more than beers. You been dopin'. You been weedin'. We don't do dopin' or weedin' here. So far, Corporal Thunder just knows you been drinkin', but if he finds out you're drugin' you're a dead man. *Dead!*

"I know you had a few beers, but I know you had drugs, too," he continued. "I know the streets and I know users. I know by your wild eyes. I know by how your nostrils flare. I know by how your eyes are unsteady before settlin' down after you look here or there. I know by how your hands are nervously movin' and how you're standin' and shiftin' your body. I know you're dopin' now and I'll know it when you weed again. But there better not be dopin' or weedin' ever again.

"Okay, maybe you're new, but you better learn this fast or you'll die faster or you'll die slower. I ain't decided, yet," Hawkins explained. "We depend upon one another out here. This war's horrible and we been seein' death every day. We have to fight hard to help one another survive, but when you're stoned you can't help yourself much less your teammates. In fact, it's worse, because we have to help you when you don't deserve helpin' and that may cost us our lives. You just become a burden to all of us.

"I love Corporal Thunder like a brother and I won't ever let him get into trouble. Not if I can help it," Hawkins proclaimed, "especially over a dope head like you. That's why I'll kill you myself if you ever use drugs here again. If I ever smell or catch you with weed, you're dead. Maybe it'll be a gunshot on patrol or a grenade because that shit just happens in war.

"Now, you can do what you want and I'll do what I want. I'll do what I have to do. It's now up to you," Hawkins threatened, "but you better think 'bout what I'm sayin' and you better think hard. If anyone at all uses drugs out on the lines I'm comin' to you first to see what you know about it. Then, I'll do what has to be done. You better make sure it stops, if it's happening, or it'll be your ass and theirs. Got it?"

This time, Rogers simply nodded his head and said absolutely nothing.

"One last word, if you ever take my beers while I'm helpin' dead and wounded Marines on a workin' party, Marines who depend on me, well, I'll just kill you for fun," Hawkins concluded.

Hawkins then pummeled Rogers with three rapid-fire gut busters. Rogers again slammed into the mud breathless and gasping for air. Hawkins roughly rolled Rogers over with his boot as he lay flat on his back gazing up. He pressed the heel of his boot deep into Rogers' gut to further prevent his breathing. Rogers' eyes rolled upward and locked before Hawkins released the pressure. Now there was blatant fear in Rogers' eyes. He said nothing, not this time. Hawkins said nothing either as he casually turned and sauntered back into the tent.

Wiley waited a moment while Rogers considered the veracity of Hawkins' threats. "You better believe what Hawkins is telling you. He's Catholic." As if religion had anything to do with the threats. "Hawkins is kind of insane and Italian, too. He loves a fight. He's either your best friend or worst enemy. Right now, he's your worst enemy. You don't need more enemies here in Vietnam," which had everything to do with the situation Rogers was now in.

Rogers rolled over slightly and looked up at Wiley, who appeared positively monstrous. "Here, let me help you," Wiley extended a hand in sympathy. Wiley pulled Rogers up with uncanny ease.

"I'm Lance Corporal Wiley and what Hawkins said about Corporal Thunder is true, but I don't have to tell you because you'll learn," Wiley asserted. "Just ask around yourself.

"In our fire team there's nothing we won't do for the other," Wiley continued, "that means killing if we have to. Besides, killing's mostly what we do out here. We're killing to survive and to live. You learn to kill real fast or you'll be dead real fast. It's just the way the war is.

"Yeah, Hawkins is Italian, and I'm not too sure about the Mafia part," Wiley sighed, "but none of us doubt it too much after seeing him fight. He's really protective of all of us. We all protect one another. We're like a little Mafia family in Vietnam and you know how the Mafia feels about protecting the family. You won't doubt it either after you see him in combat. He's a little crazy, but the war makes all of us a little crazy. Sometimes, we just do crazy things because war is crazy."

Wiley spoke softly and caringly with Rogers to gain Rogers' confidence. Rogers began to believe Wiley was maybe the only caring and sane one of the three Marines.

"I don't have too much more to say because I think you're beginning to understand. Please, understand in the field, especially in combat, we depend on everyone to be alert and ready," Wiley reported. "We know we can't be alert and ready if we're high on weed and dope. Weed and dope is as much an enemy in combat as the NVA. We don't tolerate drugs and druggies out here.

"I know Hawkins said he'd kill you to protect Corporal Thunder from killing you. I know he would, too," Wiley continued, "but you need to know I'll kill you first to protect both of them from having to kill you. I won't gut you with a knife or machete off a body part so you'll bleed to death because some might think Corporal Thunder was involved. I won't shoot you or grenade you because some might think Hawkins did it.

"No, I'd never do that, but what I'll do is bear hug you and squeeze you till you can't breathe and there'll be no marks and no wounds," Wiley concluded. "They'll just think you had a heart attack or you just stressed out and suffocated from the fear. Out here that'll be all there is to that."

Wiley then took a quick step forward and without a word unfurled his massively folded arms and violently and viciously bear-hugged Rogers. Wiley clutched Rogers with such hydraulic force he was unable to so much as wiggle. His breath expired quickly. Wiley then tossed him aside roughly into a shallow watery depression and waited for Rogers to gasp for air and recover and regain his senses. Wiley then went to take another shower to wash off the vomit before re-entering the tent. Rogers lay in the wet mud in mortal fear while struggling to breathe. Moments later, he slipped quietly into the tent and there was silence as the Marines finally slept. It was silent at last.

CHAPTER 10

Marine Birthdays
& Arc Lights

Life comes at you hard and fast in Vietnam. Death comes at you harder and faster.

—Marine Lance Corporal Aaron Wiley

Hawkins moaned the next morning at reveille. "Damn, it was a down and dirty night. We got nothin' we dreamed of. No chow. No beers. No good sleeps. Nothin'. We just got a lot of nothin'."

"Sadly," Wiley corrected. "We got a lot of killing. Nothing but killing and dying."

"We thought it'd be safer here," Corporal Thunder mumbled, "but it's as deadly here in the rear as up front in the field. Nowhere's safe. Nowhere." The three momentarily stretched in their cots before they began packing and preparing for their return to the front.

Later, First Sergeant Sharp stumbled into the auxiliary mess tent recovering from a sleepless night as the Marines were completing a breakfast of powered eggs and bacon. He informed them, "Saddle up and move down to motor transport. The truck convoy's leaving for the front in ten."

Corporal Thunder, Wiley, and Hawkins strolled toward motor transport at a leisurely pace. They did their best to ignore the piles of debris and trash from last night's rocket attack, but the damage was present everywhere. As they trudged the littered path, First Sergeant Sharp intercepted them, "Thanks for your help with the working party last night. I know it was grisly and gross, but you're better at that than my rear area Marines. They're not as used to the deaths as much as you infantry Marines.

"I know you deserved more than damn rocket attacks, especially after all your time in the field," the First Sergeant continued, "but it was just not to be. Not this time. Maybe next time."

The First Sergeant and Corporal Thunder's team walked and talked slowly toward the truck convoy. At motor transport the First Sergeant took roll call to confirm all were present who were reporting forward. He then quietly and abruptly pulled Corporal Thunder's team and Rogers aside.

"First Sergeant's don't become First Sergeants by not knowing their Marines. By not knowing what the hell's going on, especially what's going on in every damn tent here in my rear area," First Sergeant Sharp growled. "I heard scuttlebutt you four had a little row last night and I hope it's over. You got me? It better be over." Glaring sternly at each of the four Marines he shrugged and placed his hands on his hips in the traditional drill instructor stance of absolute obedience.

Corporal Thunder hoped Hawkins would remain quiet and quickly responded, "Yes, First Sergeant, we had a little row over noise, but it's all settled now." Wiley sighed in relief.

"Well, it damn well better be. But I heard it was a little more than noise," First Sergeant Sharp scoffed, "and I want that settled, too." He stared at them defiantly. They stood uncomfortably.

It was apparent someone in the Casual Tent reported the confrontation over drugs. First Sergeant Sharp never mentioned drugs, but he peered directly into Wiley's and Hawkins' eyes and challenged them by repeating, "You understand me? I want it settled. You do what you have to do, but settle it." He then glared at Rogers and repeated, "I want it settled." He said no more.

"We'll settle it if it needs settling," Wiley assured the First Sergeant. "We'll do what we have to do." He, too, then glanced at Rogers. He, too, then said no more, but he nodded at Hawkins.

Rogers never said a word, but it was clear to Rogers the First Sergeant was endorsing Wiley's and Hawkins' solution to the issue that needed settling. He became decidedly more uncomfortable.

"Lock and load and put your weapons on semi-automatic," Corporal Thunder ordered the new Marines boarding the trucks. Then he turned to Wiley and asked, "What was that all about?"

Wiley and Hawkins suspected Corporal Thunder was unaware of the drug issue and thought it best it remain so for now. They were confident the consequences would be severe for Rogers. Instead, Wiley stated, "First Sergeant thought Rogers had too many beers last night. He talked to us about it while you were shaving this morning. He asked us to watch him. We'll watch him."

Corporal Thunder glanced toward Rogers, but Rogers turned away and climbed aboard the truck for the convoy to the front. "Damn, you can get killed anywhere in this damn war," Hawkins loudly groaned. "Front. Rear. Mountains. Jungles. Rice paddies. Patrols. Bunkers. You can get killed anywhere at anytime for somethin' or for nothin'. Ain't Vietnam the livin' and dyin' shits?"

While Hawkins was neither directly nor indirectly addressing Rogers, he left it open for him to interpret his veiled threat. Rogers dwelled on it until the convoy arrived at Payable. Corporal Thunder, Wiley, and Hawkins considered the dreams of the rear they had dreamed yesterday and how those dreams had become nightmares last night. No respite from death. Death followed them from here to there, to anywhere and to everywhere. "After all," Wiley concluded, "it's Vietnam."

The truck convoy arrived at India Company's base camp at the intersection of the Highway 9 Bridge and the Cua Viet River about noon. Wiley ordered the new Marines, "Okay, clear your weapons and put them on safe for now."

The India Company Gunnery Sergeant met the convoy and ordered, "I want all the India and Lima Marines over here. I'll get you India Marines assigned to your platoons. Later today you Lima Marines will report to your company at the Fishbowl."

The new Marines, over twenty, apprehensively assembled in the direction the Gunny indicated. "Spread out, one round will get you all," the Gunny yelled. The Marines dispersed.

The Gunnery Sergeant walked toward Corporal Thunder and observed, "Corporal, it looks like you're the senior Marine. You going to take the other twenty or so up to Payable?"

"Yes, Gunny," Corporal Thunder answered, "I'll organize them and take them up."

The Gunny then frowned and asked, "We heard it was a bad night in the battalion rear."

"Yes, Gunny, it was bad," Corporal Thunder sighed. "It was just something you don't expect in the rear. Not in Dong Ha. Not anywhere."

"Yeah, but nowhere is safe in this damn war," the Gunny replied.

"You better get these new Marines ready and take them up the hill," the Gunny motioned to Corporal Thunder, "but give me about ten minutes to alert battalion and Mike and Kilo that you're on the way up. I'll also loan you a radio so you can check in with your company while on your patrol up the hill. I'll preset the radio frequencies for you, too. It's Mike, right?"

"Thanks, Gunny, and, yes, it's Mike," he replied. "Thanks for your help."

Corporal Thunder assembled the twenty-two new and nervous Payable Marines and informed them, "Okay, this will be your first Vietnam patrol. It's only a few thousand meters up this hill to the battalion Headquarters Company and Mike and Kilo companies. It's a pretty secure area. The battalion has three separate base camps in this area, but no place is really secure or safe out here. So gather round and listen up, but keep spread out."

The Corporal announced this would be their first real combat patrol, which immediately gained their attention. Wiley noticed the anxiety level increased dramatically and confided, "Life comes at you hard and fast in Vietnam. Death comes at you harder and faster. You just have to be ready. Just listen up. We'll all be fine."

Hawkins noted the softer side of Wiley and smiled. Hawkins said nothing. He only glared.

"There are about three different and good and pretty safe trials up the mountain. We'll take the one I believe is the safest. It's the longest, but the safest. We'll take the eastern trail because it gets us into the jungle fastest," Corporal Thunder briefed and pointed up the mountain.

The Gunny returned with the radio and the Corporal ordered, "Wiley, check out the radio and alert Mike Company." Wiley radioed Mike they were en route with new Payable Marines.

Corporal Thunder issued the new Marines a modified patrol order. It was simple and straightforward, but he made it more understandable to them when he summarized, "Hawkins will take point with those seven Marines in the first section. I'll be in the middle section with these seven Marines. Wiley will be in the rear section with the radio and those eight Marines." He pointed to the Marines to form them into three teams.

The teams briefly discussed tactical actions on contact and immediate action drills. Pointing to the map and terrain, so they understood where they were and where they would be once in the jungle, Corporal Thunder explained, "It's always critical you have good situation and terrain awareness. Always know where you are and what's going on."

"Okay, extract your magazine and then re-insert it into your weapon. Keep it on safe until we get outside the India Company wire. Then, we'll pass the word to lock and load. Then, you'll chamber a round and put your weapons on semi-automatic," Corporal Thunder ordered.

Corporal Thunder, Wiley, and Hawkins watched the Marines carefully. The Corporal then commanded, "Let's move out and let's keep about two to three meters between you and the Marine to your front and rear. Remember to alternate your weapons port and starboard and pointed outboard. Stay spread out, too. Let's go. Hawkins, you take point. Let's get moving."

The team's patrol to Payable proceeded without incident. While it advanced slowly and steadily, Corporal Thunder halted about every three hundred meters. While Wiley radioed the company their position, Corporal Thunder gathered the new Marines to talk tactics and acquaint them with the jungle and mountain terrain. He was always teaching, but he asked Hawkins to help with the teaching. Hawkins loved to talk and he was learning to teach, too.

Corporal Thunder had consciously assigned Rogers to his section. He purposefully appeared to forget and distance himself from the incident the night before and take an interest in Rogers. After every halt and brief class, Corporal Thunder asked, "Okay, any questions or concerns?"

"Yes, Corporal," Rogers asked, "how often do we go on patrol?" Rodgers distanced himself from last night's altercation, too. He was genuinely interested in learning patrolling techniques.

"That's a good question, Rogers," Corporal Thunder replied. "We go on patrol most every day or night. Usually we call the night ones ambushes, but not always. Most of our patrols are squad level, but we sometimes do platoon and larger patrols, too. It just depends on our orders and our missions. We patrol all the time. It's what we do. We patrol almost daily."

The patrol up the mountain arrived at Payable Hill later that afternoon. As the new Marines were met by their company Gunnery Sergeants for escort to their respective companies and bunkers, Corporal Thunder approached Rogers. "We okay now? We good? You let me know if you need any help or if there's anything you want to know."

Rogers smiled and thankfully responded, "We're okay. We're fine. Thanks for the talks coming up the hill. We're all scared, but you really calmed us down and helped us focus."

Corporal Thunder nodded and held out his hand. They shook hands, but exchanged no additional words. Corporal Thunder wheeled to report to his bunker and his team. Rogers stood staring at him until he disappeared. Rogers acknowledged he had a bad start in the battalion, in Mike, but he had no one to blame but himself. He never imagined Corporal Thunder, Wiley, and Hawkins would be so severe toward drugs, but he was beginning to understand.

Clary was on patrol when the team returned, but they reunited at the bunker a few hours later. Clary frowned and sighed, "I heard you had a blast in the rear."

"Blast my ass," Hawkins hollered, "the only ones blastin' in the rear was the damn NVA. Yeah, they were blastin' Dong Ha to hell and back. Blastin' my beers, too."

"We did nothing, not one thing, we wanted to do or planned to do," Wiley frowned, "but the same ole same ole we always do. We dodged rockets and we pulled bodies from the wreckage."

"Yeah, I was worried all night. The First Sergeant radioed the Captain the dead and wounded list this morning. The Lieutenant told me you were okay, but it was a long night not knowing."

"Yeah, tell me about a long night," Hawkins groaned, "but it was longer for the wounded and forever for the dead. I'm bettin' we're survivin', but it's a damn crap shoot and the dice just keep on rollin' and crappin' on us." Hawkins mockingly tossed two malaria pills as if shooting craps.

Corporal Thunder, Wiley, Hawkins, and Clary were relieved to be together again. It was good to be back in their bunker, despite the dank and dark wetness and aromas. Talking late into the evening, Hawkins was the most animated and demonstrative in describing their Dong Ha adventure. But neither he nor Wiley mentioned the drug incident with Rogers. Hoping it was no longer an issue, they would share that news with Clary later.

Hawkins mentioned, however, about a thousand times, "I had my name on two cool beers and got to drink none of them. The NVA's gonna pay for that someday. Gonna pay big time."

Later, Wiley confided to Clary during listening post duty, "When we told you about our Dong Ha trip we mostly talked about goofy stuff because all the other was too gory; too hurtful. God, I'm glad you weren't with us and didn't have to pull all those body parts from the trench. I don't know how Corporal Thunder reached in there in the darkness and did what he did."

Wiley paused to collect himself and continued, "I know Corporal Thunder's a hunter. I remember his talking about gutting and dressing deer and game in the woods back home. It was probably just like that. The killed were just opened up and torn apart with blood everywhere and insides and body parts dripping and scattered all over. It was the worst I've ever seen. I'm glad you didn't have to see it and didn't have to be part of it. It was really bad. It was the worst."

With his eyes shut, Wiley shuddered to erase the disgusting visions of badly butchered bodies and streams of crimson blood drenching those destined for death. The visions persisted.

The Dong Ha rear visit escapade, however, faded in time. Later in the week, while hunched over heat tabs to warm their Cs and protecting them from the drizzling rain, Corporal Thunder asked, "Do you know what day it is?"

Hawkins blurted, "It's today. It's the day after yesterday. It's the day before tomorrow. It's today." In Vietnam, in the war, everyday was virtually just another day of patrols and misery. One day was invariably only another day with no specific distinction. Days were simply days.

"Well, we don't have much need to know the day or date, but I know it's about the second week in November," Wiley finally answered.

"Yep, right. It's 9 November. You win the contest and prize," Corporal Thunder announced.

"You didn't say nothin' 'bout a prize," Hawkins complained, wiping crumbs from his lips.

"Well, you didn't ask," Corporal Thunder laughed, "but there's a prize and it's a C-Ration can of ham and lima beans. Wiley, you win first prize in the contest."

"Jesus, if that's the first place prize I sure as hell don't want second," Hawkins countered. "Fact is, don't want the first place prize either. That ain't no prize. That's pork and poots in a can. Some prize that is."

Ham and lima beans was the one C-Ration meal all Marines loved to hate. Hawkins was fond of proclaiming, "If you ain't never had ham and lima beans, for breakfast, from a can, cold, with the rain dripping into it from the thick jungle canopy monsoon rains above, while fighting off the leeches from the jungle mud below, well, you ain't never had a real Marine infantry breakfast." Ham and lima beans seemed to characterize the worst of the worst of the Cs and the war.

"Okay, seriously, it's 9 November and tomorrow is 10 November and the Marine Corps Birthday," the Corporal announced. "Whether you're in combat or garrison or aboard ship or stateside or overseas," he remarked, "Marines do something special for the Marine Birthday."

"Well, tomorrow will be our first Marine Corps Birthday in combat," Wiley commented. "I wonder if we'll celebrate it and how?"

"Well, let's celebrate it the best we can," Clary stated. "I bet tomorrow we'll be asked the date of the Marine Corps Birthday and other important facts about the Corps."

"Ain't no Marine not knowing that," Hawkins confided. "It's 10 November 1775 and it was by an act of the Continental Congress. It's the law." While never too thrilled with tests, Hawkins loved competition. He joined all in for the Corps history quizzes.

"Now, where was the Marine Corps founded?" Hawkins asked.

"It was founded in Philadelphia at Tun Tavern. The right place to recruit the first Marines was from a bar and we been recruiting from bars ever since," Clary bragged.

Corporal Thunder, Wiley, Hawkins, and Clary then proceeded to ask questions and recite answers for the next hour or so. Clary asked, ""What's the Marine motto?"

"It's Semper Fidelis or Semper Fi," Hawkins replied, "and that's Latin for Always Faithful. Betcha didn't know I speak Latin?"

"What's the emblem of the Marine Corps?" Wiley asked as he covered the emblem stenciled on his uniform over his heart with his huge powerful hand.

"It's the eagle, globe, and anchor," Corporal Thunder answered, "The eagle stands for our nation. The globe stands for our worldwide service. The anchor stands for our naval heritage."

The four Marines shared questions and answers, trivia and facts, and legends and lore of Marine Corps history, well into the night. They were proud to be Marines and pleased with the surprise the next day. It was the Marine Corps Birthday, 10 November. The cooks in the Dong Ha rear baked birthday cakes all night and trucked them to the field for brief company and platoon level birthday ceremonies. They were simple ceremonies, but they were appreciated.

"It's a cake and peaches holiday," Wiley exclaimed. Despite the miseries of Vietnam, it was a day of merriment for the Marines. But quickly they returned to the war and to the patrols that defined them and their existence. Word of a new and special patrol later excited them.

"You remember the huge NVA camp we located on that platoon patrol with the Lieutenant a few weeks ago?" Corporal Thunder asked at reveille the next morning while sharpening his machete. "The Lieutenant seems to believe division wants to do something about it. He thinks they're planning and coordinating when and how to do it."

"Well, why not sooner rather than later?" Wiley asked.

"It's mostly to confirm that when it's attacked the NVA are in it," Corporal Thunder replied. "We want to destroy the camp, but it'd be better for us to destroy it with lots of NVA in it, too."

Two days later, Corporal Thunder returned from a briefing and announced, "Gather round. Listen up. The day after tomorrow we'll depart on a squad reinforced patrol with Sergeant Swede. We'll depart at 0300 and proceed northeast and then north. Then our mission is to conduct surveillance on the valley up north across and into the valley to the west where the NVA camp is."

"When you say our mission is to conduct surveillance, what does that mean?" Wiley inquired as he readjusted the straps on his pack and laid it on the bunker's sandbags to dry in the sun.

"Well, first it means we avoid contact. We go in like a recon team and we go in silently and secretly. We avoid detection of any type," Corporal Thunder replied.

Corporal Thunder laid his map on the ground and oriented it with the terrain. He traced the general route and surveillance site on the map with his K-Bar before he remembered, "It'll be about a four day mission. The hard part's getting there undetected. The easy part's hiding, sitting, and watching. Least we hope it's easy."

Lieutenant Abrahams officially briefed the patrol later that day and emphasized, "Remember, if you see anything report it, but don't engage it unless you're in real danger or it's a life or death situation. It's a surveillance mission and not a combat patrol."

"The best part is, if you observe a major NVA force in the camp then an Arc Light mission will destroy it. We report it and within twenty-four hours the Air Force will Arc Light it," the Lieutenant added, "The Air Force will be standing by for your confirmation of the target."

"What's an Arc Light mission?" Wiley innocently asked.

"It's Air Force B-52's flying out of Guam with thirty tons of bombs per plane. They say its iron bombing old style and just tears and wears the hell out of the target," the Lieutenant answered. "Bombs cover an area of several football fields or more per bomber, maybe a whole grid square on the map, and maybe two or four or more bombers fly the mission together."

Hawkins mentally calculated to himself, "Jesus, that's about sixty 1,000 pounders per bomber or a hundred and twenty 500 pounders. That'll be something to see and hear and feel."

The surveillance mission was launched at 0300 the following day. In the late afternoon they were on the eastern slope of the mountain ridge east of the valley and NVA camp. It advanced up the ridge hidden from any western observation before halting and crossing to the crest with views into the target valley.

Sergeant Swede dispatched a team to recon a surveillance site and four Marines crawled to the crest and disappeared. The team returned thirty minutes later to guide the squad to the site.

It was now dusk with sufficient light to move and to establish their team and individual positions as well as sufficient darkness to ensure they could do so without detection. Sergeant Swede ordered one team to the north and one to the south along the slope for flank security. Attached Marines from Weapons Platoon were assigned to rear security on the eastern slope.

"Corporal Thunder, you and your team will be with me in the center," Sergeant Swede exclaimed. By darkness, the squad was in its surveillance site and began its mission. It began to rain harder and the winds surged stronger. The bad weather was a blessing and curse. The torrential rains and cloud cover concealed their positions, but made them miserable, too.

"Damn, this is boring," Hawkins complained the afternoon of the first day. "I'm more comfortable patrolling than just lounging around." Whispering occasionally, they became more immobile and soundless as time passed. They waited and watched in abject monotony.

Rotating the binoculars among themselves, they stared through the lenses for about twenty minutes before their vision strained and boredom overwhelmed them. Then they passed the binoculars on and napped or escaped into their own thoughts and dreams.

In the early morning darkness of the second day, the team on the northern flank observed and reported a small group of NVA soldiers. "They're spread out, but I think it's about four or six," the team radioed Sergeant Swede. "*Finally, we got some action,*" Clary thought.

Within minutes the team on the southern flank glimpsed another small group of soldiers coming from the west and then turning north. "We got movement in the south. It looks like about six NVA moving north toward the valley with the camp," the team also radioed Sergeant Swede.

Sergeant Swede and Corporal Thunder focused on the valley and soon the soldiers from the north and south converged at the entrance and both turned west and disappeared into the valley.

"Maybe scouts. Maybe recon. Maybe advance or forward elements. Maybe teams to check out and secure the area for a larger force," Corporal Thunder whispered to Sergeant Swede.

The squad was energized. The dull duty of hours and hours of surveillance and observing quickly transitioned into excitement. The exhilaration, however, was temporary. "The rest of the day I saw nothing," Clary later confided, "I saw absolutely nothing."

It was disheartening, but that evening interest was again aroused as the squad observed four or five flickers of light and lingering glows from the valley and camp. "It's hard to tell if it's a match or cigarette or a small campfire or flashlight," Wiley hinted, "but something's definitely going on. Someone's definitely still in there. But we haven't seen much yet. Not a big force."

The following day the squad's initial enthusiasm slowly dissipated. "Damn, I'm hoping we see something soon," Hawkins confessed. But the third day passed with no NVA sightings. The monotony again overwhelmed them. "I ain't seein' nothin'," Hawkins railed.

"Damn, this is getting awfully depressing," Clary sighed, "sitting here doing nothing but looking for the enemy and seeing much of nothing. Maybe they aren't coming."

Later that night, Corporal Thunder exclaimed, "There. See them? It's those flashes and lights again. Those we saw yesterday must still be there. Maybe they're the advance force like we thought. Maybe they're preparing for the main force. Maybe they're waiting on the main force."

It was minimal activity, but it was activity. The squad continued its mission with renewed interest. *It don't take much out here to get you excited,* Wiley thought and frowned while fighting the rain and cold, *but sometimes it gets too exciting.*

The furor over the lights quickly faded as the night darkened. Once again it was dark beyond dark. The night wore on into boredom beyond boredom. Their misery was as dark as the darkness; however, their misery was never boring. It was brutal and they bore it constantly.

An hour or so before sunrise, Corporal Thunder felt someone lightly shake his shoulder. He was quickly awake. "Look in the valley toward the NVA camp," Wiley whispered. "See all those flickers of light. Lots more lights than last night, too. Maybe the big force is now there."

Corporal Thunder thought for a few seconds before he estimated, "Damn, maybe the main force came in under the cover of darkness and rain late last night. Maybe that's them."

Sergeant Swede called the team leaders to his position to discuss the appearance of increased enemy activity in the valley and said, "None of us are really sure. We only see what we see and no one sees anymore than that. We'll just have to wait and see what we see."

The dawn of a new day, their fourth day at the surveillance site, however, began a promising day for their mission. "Look, it's hard to see in the dark and morning fog, but I can see streaks of smoke coming from the enemy camp," Clary was the first to observe.

Sergeant Swede and Corporal Thunder discussed the situation. Later, Corporal Thunder debriefed Wiley, Hawkins, and Clary. "We agreed we think there's a large force in the camp, but we agreed to watch another night and day just to make sure. We just got to make sure."

After a day of no new sightings, a few hours after sunset, Hawkins excitedly declared, "Jesus, look toward the camp now. Look. There's a shit pot full more lights or cigarettes or fires than last night. That's one busy place tonight."

Throughout the night occasional flashes and flickers of light flowed from the enemy camp tucked into the valley jungles. Sergeant Swede and Corporal Thunder now agreed a large NVA force was in the camp. Sergeant Swede radioed the report to the company. An hour later the company confirmed the battalion was coordinating the Arc Light for tomorrow night at 2100.

Smiles unseen in the darkness erupted on the faces of the team. The miseries of the monsoon rains and the cold wetness evaporated. The Marines reflected on what would occur within the next thirty-six hours. The expectations of their mission were close to becoming reality. They had, however, a long night and day to persevere before they could proclaim success.

The Marines observed the valley and NVA camp site hidden in the jungle throughout the day and into the final night. Sergeant Swede reported every two hours, "NVA holding fast. Target confirmed."

At sunset the following day the Marines prepared to evacuate the surveillance site and commence the long patrol back to Payable and home. They had exhausted their C-Rations and for the last two days existed on one meal a day. The main concern, however, was their radio batteries. They were down to their last battery and they used it sparingly.

Wiley smiled, "Well, the B-52 Arc Light mission is a go and we're a go, too. We're going home. It doesn't get any better." He slung his pack on his back and checked his weapon.

"Yeah, but I wanna see the bombs burstin' and shit flyin'," Hawkins grinned.

Carefully and cautiously the patrol moved out. The jungle was thick and the mud slippery. Darkness was encompassing and embracing them with its black despair and danger, but the mission was progressing well. It was proceeding toward its finale. It was approaching success.

The patrol wearily, as well as with renewed energy, tracked south for about two hours. It purposefully followed a route to enable it to continue to observe the entrance to the valley with the NVA base camp as long as possible. Yet, there was a secondary reason for the route. "I want to be in a position to watch the B-52 bombs blast the NVA," Clary grinned.

Suddenly, brilliantly blazing flashes burst to illuminate the valley with reds and whites and yellows. Luminous bright reflections ricocheted from the earth to the low clouds and back endlessly. Fractions of a second later, thundering booms reverberated the length and breadth of the valley and beyond. The sights and sounds were blinding and deafening. The earth trembled.

"Damn, we're probably two or maybe three thousand meters away and the concussions from the blasts just knocked me to my knees," Wiley explained as he stood and wiped mud from his uniform and rubbed his knees.

Corporal Thunder exclaimed, "The best part is it appears right on target. I heard an officer say some kind of radars guide the B-52's to the target. They guided them right in, too."

While the mission's success was inspiring, it was temporary. The squad was exhausted physically, but fulfilled emotionally. Once in their base camp the team, minus Hawkins, ambled toward its bunker overwhelmed with fatigue and emotion.

Hawkins remained behind to regale the platoon with endless tales of the dangers and triumphs of the surveillance mission. They, too, despite the distance, had heard and felt the Arc Light's reign of terror. While a few Marines suspected a few exaggerations, none denied Hawkins' passion for storytelling. But either exhaustion or his excessive tales eventually overwhelmed the listeners and Hawkins slowly strode toward the team's bunker.

While Hawkins loved his stories, they had an ulterior motive for him, too. Wilson's letter of months before had introduced him to the disinterest in the war on the home front and he was committed to avoiding any adverse influences from such disinterest. Whether from the perils of daily patrols or the traumas of thirteen month tours, the team sensed talking was an antidote for decompression and preservation.

"We need to talk it out. Talking together and with others after our patrols helps us get over the ugly and nasty things we see and do and have to deal with," Corporal Thunder confided to the team after a particularly gruesome patrol experience, "because holding on to them only messes up and dirties our minds. So, flush out the bad and keep the good memories."

The cumulative effects of such terrorizing and dehumanizing experiences could eventually create depression, but frequent talks, according to Hawkins, "Helps me cleanse my mind and scrub the bad memories away as fast as possible. I gotta get my mind right or it'll go wrong on me." So, the four team members talked to decompress as well as preserve their sanity, despite Clary's allegation, "Hawkins, I doubt you have much sanity to preserve." Hawkins frowned before playfully throwing a ham and lima beans C-rat at Clary.

Another motive for the post-patrol talks was the team's acceptance over time that upon returning home there would be no ticker-tape parades, no recognition ceremonies, no welcome home events, and no appreciation for the sacrifices they were enduring…except from family and friends. So, they shared their talks and stories with those with whom they shared their sacrifices because they knew and they understood and they cared. While many came to feel alienated by a country to which they pledged their allegiance, they came to sense it was nothing personal. Instead, it was simply the politics and proselytizing of the Vietnam War. Nonetheless, it hurt them and hurt them bad. The talks simply helped them decompress and preserve a degree of emotional stability in the insanity of the war.

While squaring away the bunker and preparing for sleeps, the team talked briefly. Clary began with a reference to the recently completed surveillance mission. "Sometimes, this war and our patrols are nothing but boring and totally monotonous. Other times, they're frantic and chaotic. This last one was one of those boring ones for us, but pretty chaotic for the NVA in the camp we blew all to hell." He peered north up the valley and smiled as he observed smoldering smoke hours after the Arc Light mission.

"Yeah, but I'll take the boredom over the chaos," Wiley admitted, "especially if it means no killings and no deaths."

"Jesus, most people think when you're in war you're in combat and fightin' all the time," Hawkins confessed. "It's boring more times than it's exciting, but when it's exciting it's really exciting and it makes it seem like it's mostly exciting when it's really mostly boring." Hawkins seemed to have a unique method for explaining his theories and philosophies and arriving at his deductions and conclusions. Once the team figured him out they figured he made sense, but they often had to think long and hard to figure out what he was saying.

"Well, I'll make it unanimous. I'll vote for the boredom, too," Corporal Thunder agreed. "But what I'd really rather vote for is to end this war. Yep, I'll take the boredom of peace over the chaos of war."

The team nodded in agreement. They were good with that. They were good with peace.

After a few hours of "sleeps" they awoke about mid-afternoon to receive a warning order for another new and different mission. The tragedies of the forthcoming mission truly obliterated most all the fond memories of the successful but boring surveillance and B-52 Arc Light mission. Later, while struggling with the sadness, the Marines would accept it as simply another part of war. It was simply Vietnam. Fond memories were fleeting and soft. Sad ones loitered long and hard.

CHAPTER 11

The Razorback & Shakespeare

Nothing comes easy in Vietnam, except dying. Everything comes hard in war, especially living.

—Marine Private First Class Brad Clary

Clouds and mist dominated the sky the next day. The morning sun flirted briefly with the team to hail their B-52 mission's glowing success. Quickly, however, a morning monsoon deluge dampened their spirits. The wet cold dashed their hopes for a simple dry and warm day or half day or hour. "Nothing comes easy in Vietnam, except dying. Everything comes hard in war, especially living," Clary exclaimed after a bunker breakfast of Cs. "Nothing. Zero. Zilch. Not even a little sun or a little warmth." The steady cascading sheets of rain and howling winds symbolized the darkness and despair of war. The war's slaughter and the weather's onslaughts were increasingly demoralizing.

"Yeah, you'd think that's not too much to ask for," Hawkins growled, "but askin' and gettin' is kinda pointless in Vietnam. It's pointless except when you ask for nothin' because then you get a whole lot of it. A whole lotta nothin' is about everythin' we get. It's the only thing we get. We get a lotta nothin' and not much of anythin'. We get nothin' as somethin' and we get it like it's everythin'."

The team glanced quizzically at Hawkins with expressions of bewilderment laced with agreement. No one knew exactly what he had said, but they accepted it as part of their plight. Sometimes, nothing made sense in war, which Hawkins was consistently ready and willingly to prove with either his philosophies or opinions. Often, he made more sense than the war.

Corporal Thunder stood and stretched to excuse himself to attend a meeting. Returning to the team bunker he later announced, "Okay, gather round for an update. We have another new and different warning order for a new and different mission.

"We've been doing mostly squad level patrols and missions, except for the battalion minus operation to Con Thien. Plus, the platoon patrol up north of the Razorback when we discovered the empty NVA camp," he reminded his team. "Now we have another type or size mission.

"In a few days we're going to do a company level operation with about two hundred Marines in the field," the Corporal explained. "The company and battalion are coordinating the details now. We'll be launching the operation soon. First we'll head north up the valley along side the Razorback and river and then circle and go counter clockwise around the Razorback."

"We going up to check out the Arc Light damage to the NVA camp?" Wiley excitedly asked.

"No, the division is having a recon team do a post-strike analysis and report," the Corporal replied, "but I wish we were. We saw it before. I'd like to see it after."

"Yes, me too, because I heard it'll probably look just like the moon. There'll be craters and more craters everywhere," Clary added. "Least that's what I understand."

"Craters, hell. I'd like to see a piss pot full of dead NVA. That's what I wanna see," Hawkins declared. "To hell with any moon craters. I wanna see critters. Dead NVA critters."

"Okay. Let's focus on the mission for a few minutes and then you can talk about cowboys and nicknames and craters and critters and whatever you want," Corporal Thunder smiled.

"The mountains and valley jungles west of the battalion's current positions are high and deep," he explained, "and the division and regiment seem to think our presence here and the B-52 strike may cause the NVA to create more camps out there. Now that we're here, we're pushing them farther west. Later, we'll probably go out there to keep pushing them farther back.

"Battalion thinks the Razorback patrol is the first phase in operations to eventually take us farther west. We may conduct operations out toward Khe Sanh in the spring or sooner," Corporal Thunder surmised. "Anyway, that's what the Captain and Lieutenant seem to think." Although it remained unspoken for now, the team suspected they were preordained for Khe Sanh.

"It appears the operation will be planned for three to four days," he informed the team. "The exact start day is uncertain for now because they're hoping for a weather forecast with better weather."

"Damn, that sounds like a good idea to me. If we wait for good weather we may never do another patrol again till next spring or summer when the monsoons end," Hawkins groaned.

"Well, it's not exactly that," the Corporal frowned. "It's because we need good weather for aviation support. The western side of the Razor-back is hard for artillery to hit. The high ridges and terrain restrict certain targets. There's bad angles of fire in some places."

"Yeah, now that makes perfect sense. The pilots fly only in good weather, but we're out here sloshing in the mud and crap every day," Hawkin's grinned.

"Well, some aircraft can bomb at night and in bad weather with radars and sensors and whatever," Corporal Thunder explained, "but close air support missions usually need good weather and visibility so pilots can identify and confirm targets."

"Yeah, close means we'll be close to where they're bombin', too. I sure as hell hope they do confirm targets," Hawkins expounded, "'cause I ain't wantin' to be a friendly fire casualty."

"Well, I heard there's no such thing as friendly fire," Clary announced. "Rounds don't care if you're enemy or friendly. They don't discriminate. They're equal opportunity killers."

"Thanks for that little bit of enlightened horseshit, Clary. You're always just cheering up my day," Hawkins retorted, "with your indiscriminate and insane proclamations." The two grinned.

The day before the company operation launched, Corporal Thunder reported unexpected news to the team during a night bunker talk. "The division's approved a reporter accompanying us on the operation," he sighed. "The Captain and Lieutenant decided he'll be attached to us."

"What's that really mean for us?" Wiley asked as he glanced around for the team's reaction.

"It means we're to provide security for him and help him during the operation," Corporal Thunder frowned. "We'll help him with any equipment requests and combat questions."

"You mean such things as digging in each night and cooking Cs," Wiley asked.

"Yes, whatever he needs," he answered, "but he won't be armed."

"Captain Garvin and Lieutenant Abrahams said we're responsible for him and we better damn sure take good care of him," he emphasized. "It's just part of our mission."

The afternoon before the operation the reporter, Mr. Dan Robbins, reported to battalion and was escorted to Corporal Thunder's team. *He looks a little scared,* Wiley thought.

The team welcomed the reporter and equipped him with what the Marines referred to as 782-Gear, which included a web belt with suspenders, canteens for water, a pack, a helmet, an entrenching tool, flak jacket, and similar items for the field.

Corporal Thunder asked Hawkins and Clary to brief Mr. Robbins on survival techniques in the jungle and combat. "Make sure you dig a good hole every night for protection from enemy fires," Hawkins began, "and sleep and eat when you can. On patrol we always stay spread out. Keep about six to ten feet between you and the Marine to your front and rear."

Hawkins thought about discussing patrol tactics and immediate action drills with Mr. Robbins, but eventually decided otherwise because he thought they might confuse or scare him. Instead, he simply said, "If you hear rifle fire or any explosions or anyone holler incoming, you just get down. Just get down as fast and as flat as you can. Then, stay there until we come for you or let you know it's okay to get up." The reporter's eyes widened and his coloration disappeared.

In the early morning darkness, Company M departed its positions on Payable Hill for the Razorback patrol. The three rifle platoons and one weapons platoon moved out slowly. The first platoon was the lead, then second platoon, and last the third platoon was rear security. Weapons platoon machine guns and rocket launchers were mostly attached to the three rifle platoons.

The patrol began badly according to the second platoon Marines. They believed it was more secure to depart from the east instead of west side of Payable. This would have had them in the jungle faster and concealed from view longer, especially from any NVA in the valley or western mountains. "Be patient and positive," Lieutenant Abrahams explained to the platoon, "the first platoon was tasked to take the lead and decided on this west side of the hill. Later, maybe we can influence the route of advance a little more." The team understood the Lieutenant's predicament.

Hawkins was less polite and respectful in discussing the matter with Corporal Thunder. "This is dumb as dirt. It's more. It's dangerous. We're too exposed. It may seem it's the shortest way to get up toward the northern end of the Razorback, but it's the hardest and takes the most time."

"You're right and the Lieutenant knows it," the Corporal whispered to Hawkins, "but for now we follow orders. Maybe the Lieutenant can change things later with the Captain."

The first indication of agitation was when the patrol ground to a halt. The early advance was sporadic at best, but now it was at a complete standstill. Patience wore thin; then thinner.

Corporal Thunder had briefed his team in advance, "It takes a company of over 200 longer to get unwound and moving than it does a squad of 16 or 18. It's like an accordion. It's got to get stretched out. Then it'll move. Don't get frustrated. Just relax. It takes time."

But after an hour of no movement, Corporal Thunder and Sergeant Swede located the Lieutenant along the trail to ask about the lengthy delay, "Sir, do you know what the delay is?"

"I'm not sure, but I heard on the radio the river's deep and swift. They're building rope bridges to ferry Marines, packs, and gear across. I guess it's taking longer than they thought," the Lieutenant estimated.

"Sir, Sergeant Swede and I know this river and area well. We believe there's a better way to get across the river," the Corporal offered. "We've had no problems crossing the river before."

Lieutenant Abrahams considered his comment about a better river crossing site. "Let's the three of us move forward to the river to check on the delay," he shrugged.

Lieutenant Abrahams, Sergeant Swede, and Corporal Thunder advanced along the trail guarded by dispersed Marines. They arrived at the river and were astounded. "Damn, this little rope bridge ferry and river crossing is more a circus cluster than combat. What the hell are they thinking? What the hell are they doing?" Lieutenant Abrahams groaned in frustration.

The first platoon was crossing at the deepest and swiftest site on the river. Corporal Thunder thought, *They couldn't have picked a worse spot to cross.* The water was over the heads of the Marines and so swift they were building rope bridges to keep from being swept away down river.

"This is insane," the Lieutenant whispered. *It's unnecessary*, Corporal Thunder thought.

Sergeant Swede and Corporal Thunder were in total agreement, but said nothing. This was an officer issue and they understood the situation had to be resolved professionally and delicately. The officers had to make the final decision. As enlisted Marines they could maybe at best only influence it. They accepted they had to be careful and respectful.

It soon became apparent Captain Garvin was frustrated and impatient, too. The Lieutenant noted the frustration from afar while observing the rope bridge construction. He concluded it was safe and smart to talk about the situation and an alternative.

"You say you know a better place to cross the river?" Lieutenant Abrahams asked.

"Yes, Sir, you want us to show you?" Corporal Thunder answered. "It's close and it's safe."

The Lieutenant nodded and replied, "Okay, show me."

Corporal Thunder led the Lieutenant and a small security team north upstream about 150 meters. They remained on the east side of the river. "Look, it's a natural ford from the splintered and fallen Razorback boulders and rocks," Corporal Thunder exclaimed and pointed. "The river's flowing generally from north to south with the Razorback there on the west and we're here on the east."

Corporal Thunder then waded across the natural ford to the west side of the river. It was no more than thigh to waist deep. The water was swift from the monsoon rains, but no ropes were necessary. No ropes were needed to stabilize those crossing or help them maintain their footing. Reversing his course, the Corporal effortlessly splashed back across to the east bank with ease.

Lieutenant Abrahams peered back down the river at the first platoon Marines struggling to cross the river. Corporal Thunder smiled and considered what Hawkins might do if he were here. Hawkins would cross at the ford to the west side of the river, stroll down the river to the frustrated rope bridge Marines and shout, "You can screw around here all day if you want with your fancy rope bridge contraption, but you can tip toe across this river in one-tenth the time and trouble if you go north about 150 meters." Political correctness was never Hawkins' strong suit.

Corporal Thunder understood, however, this would have embarrassed the first platoon leader and maybe the Captain, too. He decided to explain the river to the Lieutenant to possibly grant him more time to decide upon a resolution or his actions.

"Lieutenant, the first platoon picked a bad spot. The river flows straight and true here for over 2,000 meters. It slows some at the ford," Corporal Thunder noted as he pointed at the ford.

"But look at the crossing site first platoon selected. The river bends and when rivers bend the outer bend is the deepest and the water races the fastest. It's like playing crack the whip when we were little kids with a rope. Those at one end of the rope are flying. Those on the anchor end are barely moving," Corporal Thunder explained and smiled remembering his sister, Bright Star, yelping and racing with glee at the whip end of the rope.

"Plus, where the water flows the fastest, there's more current and turbulence and the water carves into the bank and bottom and erodes it and makes it the deepest part of the turn and river," Corporal Thunder continued. "It's the worst or hardest place to try to cross."

"How do you know all this?' the Lieutenant asked.

"Well, Sir, my dad loves to hunt and fish and we hunted and fished all over Oklahoma. My dad taught me a lot about the land and earth and rivers. We hunted in all types of fields and woods and forests. We fished in all kinds of lakes and rivers and streams," he reminisced. "My dad taught me how to read the rivers and the land."

"Well, that makes a lot of sense. What else does the land and river tell you?" he asked.

"Sir, if we cross to the west side of the river we'll have a very narrow and dangerous trail we'll have to follow up north," Corporal Thunder replied. "Sergeant Swede and I have done it a few times, but now we avoid it. We never take this trail now."

"Why?" he asked.

"Sir, if the NVA are on the Razorback they'll be looking down on us. They got the high ground. That's one reason, but the main reason is the trail is too narrow. The NVA can hold us up too easy. We'd be in single file unable to deploy on line and put more fire on him," he explained, "and another reason is we're pretty much in the open here. It's rocky and has fewer trees and scattered jungle to cover or hide us. It's just a bad and hard trail. We're too exposed."

"Now, look at the other side of the river. Look at the east side. There's more space to deploy Marines. We don't have to walk in a single file. We can spread out. Plus, by moving into the tree line we're in the jungle and concealed better," the Corporal concluded.

The Lieutenant was momentarily pensive before he spoke, "You know, I think I need to talk with the Captain. First, I need to talk to him about aborting this ferry fiasco and wading across the ford. Second, I'll talk about staying on the east side of the river and moving north in better terrain. Is that about it or do we need to mention anything else?" the Lieutenant asked.

Sergeant Swede and Corporal Thunder replied in unison, "No, Sir, that's about it."

"If we stay on the east are there good river crossing sites up north?" the Lieutenant asked.

"Yes, Sir, there's a number of good options and as good as this ford here," Corporal Thunder replied. "Sergeant Swede and I know the area pretty good." Months of patrolling the area had created a sense of familiarity with the terrain for the Sergeant and Corporal and the Lieutenant accepted that they knew the terrain better than him because of this.

"Okay. Well, I'll go talk with the Captain, but I'll have to be careful," then he frowned, "because I don't want to appear to be a know-it-all and make them think the crossing and western advance are stupid." The two enlisted Marines understood the sensitivities of the situation, but smiled at the "stupid" reference.

Corporal Thunder thought it best to remain silent and resist stating his belief that both the crossing and western idea were dumb and unsafe ones. In fact, he confessed to himself, *They were tactically insane ideas.* But he withheld his thoughts. He was confident in the Lieutenant.

Nonetheless, he sighed, *This is one time I wish Hawkins was with us. He would have no reservations toward ranting about the insanity of the crossing and western advance. I know Hawkins is respectful, but he has no qualms about challenging bureaucratic blunders. Hawkins is intolerant of stupidity and bad tactics.*

While Corporal Thunder was momentarily lost in his thoughts, Sergeant Swede replied, "Yes, Sir, and good luck with the Captain."

The three Marines then strolled back to the river crossing site. "Sir, we're going to rejoin our squad and team," Sergeant Swede reported, "but radio us if we can help."

"Okay, I'll update the platoon once there's a decision," the Lieutenant nodded and edged toward the Captain. Sergeant Swede and the Corporal ambled back up the trial to their squad.

Corporal Thunder remarked, "Well, we discussed what we believed needed discussing. Now, the officers will have to decide what they have to decide."

Sergeant Swede agreed with a nod, but said nothing. He was often quieter than the Corporal.

Lieutenant Abrahams radioed for Sergeant Swede and Corporal Thunder to report to his position about twenty minutes later. "Well, I'll spare you all the bloody details of our talk, but the Captain compromised. We'll cross the river at the ford, but move north west of the river."

"Crossing at the ford was just too logical. It was a no-brainer once I walked the Captain up to the ford and he saw it," Lieutenant Abrahams briefed. "But the first platoon commander argued and convinced the Captain to stay with his western side of the river advance."

"We understand, Sir," Corporal Thunder shrugged, "if the Captain had decided to stay on the east side we wouldn't even have to cross at the ford. It would've made first platoon look worse."

"The worst part is we've wasted a lot of time for nothing," the Lieutenant injected. "We're behind schedule and we haven't even hardly started this patrol. We're almost a day behind and it's only the first day."

Corporal Thunder updated his team and Hawkins immediately groaned, "Hell, first platoon will fiddle and flounder taking down the rope ferry. It'll most likely be another hour before we get movin' again. Hell, I'm takin' another nap." Hawkins was never adverse to a combat nap.

"Wake up, Hawkins," Clary grinned. "You nailed it. It's been almost an hour, but we're about ready to move. It's late afternoon and we've been stuck here damn near all day."

"Well, it's a bad start, but maybe it'll get better," Wiley hinted as the team's eternal optimist.

"Yeah, better. Yeah, right," Hawkins moaned as the team's eternal pessimist. "Things just always get better and right in Vietnam." They stumbled to their feet and strapped on their packs.

"Okay, everyone up. Get focused," Corporal Thunder announced. "Saddle up. Let's move."

Mike Company then crossed the river at the ford. It took less than an hour. But it took most of the wasted day for only about 30 of 200 Marines to cross at the rope bridge ferry site.

It was then late, too late to advance, and the company prepared defensive positions for the night. The terrain and the darkness virtually prohibited movement at night. "Well, now we're just bunched up and strung out on this narrow trail between the Razorback's jagged rocks and the river," Wiley muttered, "and we don't have a perimeter and don't have much of a defense for the night." They slept fitfully. The first day fiascos were a bad omen for the patrol. Nothing had gone right.

The trek north the second day was agonizingly slow. "Now we'll be lucky to hit the end of the Razorback by tonight," Clary noted. "Then we'll be maybe two days behind."

"Let's hope it don't make much difference," Hawkins grinned and mumbled with concern, "but while we're fiddlin' and fartin' around here it gives the NVA more time to come outta the western mountains and jungles and maybe attack us or ambush us on the west side of the Razorback." Hawkins was never shy about voicing what they were all thinking.

The day's advance was consistently slow and never steady. It never developed a rhythm. Always out of tune, it was a frustrating day of starts and stops. Monotony and boredom made the advance tedious and tiring. It was a long day, however, the night was about to become longer. The war was waiting. It was always waiting.

The lead platoon, first platoon, veered west at the northern rim of the Razorback. The steep cliffs of the Razorback were between 100 and 200 meters high. Rocky and rugged, with generously dense foliage, maneuvering was challenging, but the narrow trail began to broaden and the landscape became more open at the northern end. Visibility was still limited because of the thick vegetation, but the Marines could disperse and advance on line or in multiple columns instead of one single file. Spreading out and dispersing were now priorities.

Corporal Thunder's team was cautious and anticipated enemy contact after turning the corner of the northern rim of the Razorback. They crouched below the tall thick willowing grass to conceal themselves. The enemy contact, however, came sooner than expected and from a larger enemy force than anticipated. It was what they had most feared and more, but they were ready.

Violent explosions from rocket propelled and hand grenades shattered the quietness of the jungle twilight. Rifle and machine gun fires erupted viciously. *Damn, I knew our delay was going to cost us,* Clary thought to himself. He was correct. The delay provided time for the NVA to mobilize a larger force from the western mountains and ambush the company. Quickly, realizing it was time to fight, the Marines steeled themselves for a hard and bitter battle.

Instantly, it was total chaos. Ambushes were always chaotic. "We have to learn to be familiar with chaos and then to deal with it. It's disorganized, but we'll learn to live in as well as function in it," Corporal Thunder often lectured the team. But the killing zone was the worst, which was precisely where they were located. Now, fighting through it was their mission and challenge.

Yeah, it's either learn and function or be stupid and die, Hawkins immediately thought as he remembered Corporal Thunder's talk, *and today I ain't being stupid and I ain't dyin'.*

Instantly, they were returning fire and maneuvering. The first few minutes of a firefight were critical. Corporal Thunder yelled above the din to Wiley, "Wiley, fire like hell. We gotta gain fire superiority to slow and then break this ambush. Keep hammering them or they'll nail us."

The lead platoon, first platoon, charged forward and then veered south to escape the killing zone and align itself with the Razorback. *Yeah, it's important the first platoon clear the northern edge so us other platoons can advance,* Hawkins theorized, *or the NVA'll create a bottleneck or obstacle for us and that'll keep the second and third platoons from comin' up to the fight. We gotta help first platoon clear a path. We gotta fight through this killing zone. We gotta punch on and get though it.* His thoughts came as fast and as furious as the battle.

Once the first platoon cleared the northern edge of the Razorback it laid down a base of fire to distract the enemy. The fires also limited the effectiveness of the enemy fire. "Okay, now let's move forward and take the fight to them," Corporal Thunder shouted. Then other second platoon squads and teams advanced and the Marines began to counter the effects of the ambush, but the situation was tenuous. Now it was critical to continue the advance and pull the third platoon up and into the fight, too. The company needed more firepower and manpower to overcome the ambush. Marines kneeled to fire then stretched forward into prone positions for protection and rolled either to their right or left to avoid enemy detection and fires as best as they could. They repeated the process as they advanced forward body length by body length.

The second platoon attacked straight into the killing zone of the ambush. Corporal Thunder charged into the killing area to protect the wounded. He groaned while pulling them off into low spots while firing steadily at the enemy. Meanwhile, Wiley covered him with suppressing fires.

Corporal Thunder noticed Sergeant Swede take an AK47 round to the chest and called for a corpsman. "Doc, take care of him. Don't let him die," he pleaded. He then attacked firing into the killing zone to recover other wounded and pulled them into ravines or concealed areas. His actions confused the NVA and the second and third platoons slowly advanced.

"I saw Corporal Thunder rush into the area countless times," Wiley exclaimed later as they reloaded magazines. "He'd throw a grenade and time his charge so the explosion covered him. It was risky as hell."

Hawkins and Clary similarly became a two-man killing machine. Time after time, they charged and attacked relentlessly. Hawkins fired while he zigged and zagged forward. Clary covered him with M79 fires and grenades. Then Clary fired and darted and dashed forward while Hawkins covered him with suppressing fires. They repeatedly attacked in tandem without hesitation and with total trust in one another.

"We were all desperate, but Hawkins was just damn devious. I think the NVA thought he was insane. Hawkins penetrated their ambush line," Clary later confessed as they reviewed the engagement. "He kept attacking. They just couldn't stop him. Finally, they just broke and ran. Then Hawkins ran after them. You had to see it to believe it." Hawkins had been inspired by Corporal Thunder's actions at Con Thien. Despite having no machete, he waved his K-Bar.

"What Clary said is true," Wiley later noted, "but he's too modest. Clary was right there with Hawkins every step of every charge. One fired and one rushed forward. Then the other fired and the other charged forward. Together they covered one another until the NVA folded."

"Wiley was the patient and steady one," Corporal Thunder later admitted as they analyzed the battle. "He knew most of us would act a little wild and crazy, but he knew we had to in that situation. You just have to be a little wild and weird to survive. Wiley patiently got into a position so he could overlook all of us. Once we had fire superiority, he fired slow and steady kill shots."

As the second platoon anchored the center, the first platoon moved to the south or left. Later, the third platoon cleared the rim of the Razorback and attacked west or right along the river. Corporal Thunder then passed the word down the line for situational awareness. "The third platoon's moving to our north or right and beginning to flank the enemy. We got the center."

Corporal Thunder shouted a war yell as the NVA initiated a retreat into the darkness. It was eerie, especially the following silence. "Jesus, it just seems we're fighting ghosts," Hawkins complained. "We hardly ever see the NVA for the dense jungle. We just see muzzle blasts. We just have to kinda feel our way to them. Then they run and disappear before we get to them."

"Yeah, that's their tactics," Corporal Thunder agreed. "They hide and ambush us, usually about dark, when they have all the advantages. They'll stay and fight only if they're kicking our ass, but the moment we get the momentum and start taking the fight to them they retreat and disappear into the jungle. It seems they don't really care about winning these little fights. They just care about harassing and frustrating us. Hawkins is right. It's like fighting phantom ghosts."

Once the NVA retreated the initial chaos was none too soon transformed into a semblance of order. The company and its units performed as well-trained teams. Corporal Thunder, Wiley, Clary, and Hawkins were only one of numerous fire teams and collectively they came together in victory.

"In combat, there are a lot of separate and independent actions," Corporal Thunder reminded his team after the battle waned and they reviewed if further, "because a lot of times one man or one team can't see the whole battlefield. We're sometimes scattered doing different types of actions over different types of terrain. We see only part of it and we take care of our part. We trust others to take care of their parts. We all have our parts and our roles and our duties."

Corporal Thunder emphasized, "It's critical for each of us to do our part and play our role."

Hawkins' response surprised them. They had come to expect Hawkins' surprises, but never his quoting Shakespeare, "All the world's a stage, And all the men and women merely players: They have their exits and their entrances; And one man in his time plays many parts."

"We're kinda like Shakespeare's *As You Like It* players," Hawkins continued. "We all come and go on the battlefield stage. Sometimes we play many parts and take different actions. Sometimes we attack and others we defend. Sometimes we charge and others we cover. Sometimes we play by rigid rules, others by impromptu scripts. We all play many parts, but we all play as a cast and a team." Hawkins then began to nonchalantly reload his magazines with ammo.

Corporal Thunder, Wiley, and Clary stared at Hawkins in total disbelief. Clary eventually spoke for them all. "Hawkins! You and Shakespeare? What are we to think now? We're thinking you're more than we first thought. There's more to you than we think or less to you than you want us to think," he philosophized as he adjusted the sights of his M79 grenade launcher.

"Ain't we all. Ain't we all," Hawkins simply replied. "We're all who we want others to think we are, but we can all be a lot different when we want to be." Hawkins never mentioned the quote was from his sister, Maria. She loved literature and shared that love with her brother. He shared the love with the team, but he never told them he had learned the quote a few weeks ago from one of his sister's letters. Hawkins was content to let them believe he was a literary genius.

While Corporal Thunder, Wiley, and Clary pondered Hawkins' remarks, Hawkins concluded, "Jesus, we've all made our grand entrances into the shithole of a stage called Vietnam. Now I just pray we can make our safe exits. No curtain call. No applause from the crowd. Just get us back home alive. That's the only exit we're wantin'. We're just wantin' to survive." Hawkins was a master at transitioning from grand literature to gutter language within seconds.

It was now dark and silent. The intense emotions of courage from the battle now transitioned to abject fear. A major NVA force was somewhere close in the darkness. They all sensed it and knew it. Corporal Thunder urged, "Dig in deep tonight. Be extra alert. It'll be a long night."

"I got Mr. Robbins dug in. He's good for now, but it's been a bad day for him," Clary said.

It was truly a long and fearful night, but at the time none realized how long and fearful it would be. Yet, it was simply another day and another night and another battle. Tonight or tomorrow they would fight again. It was what they did. They did it again and again. They did it over and over. It was what they did to survive. They fought today to survive today. They would fight again tomorrow to survive tomorrow. It was war.

CHAPTER 12

Love & Body Counts

Ain't no good days in Vietnam, except for the days you survive.

—Marine Private First Class Dominic Hawkins

The battle and daylight faded into night, but darkness and fear flourished. The fight was over—*for now*, but the location and intentions of the enemy were unknown. While preparing for a night fight, they prayed it never came because the uncertainty of night fights was unnerving. Hawkins calmed his nerves by reloading his M14 rifle magazines with ammunition. Clary again re-checked the sights on his M79 grenade launcher. Wiley read a scripture from his Bible in the final rays of twilight. Corporal Thunder sharpened his machete. Wiley thought as he listened to Corporal Thunder sharpen his machete, *He's either going to sharpen it to a nub or wear away the whetstone. Don't know which will disappear first.* Biding their time and collecting their thoughts, no one wanted to think too much about the coming night.

"Jesus, these damn firefights startle us when they start, but then they're almost over before we know it," Hawkins proclaimed. "But sometimes a thirty minute battle seems like either seconds or sometimes like a lifetime. It's just hard to tell. We just fight 'em till they're over."

"The company's requesting an emergency resupply of ammo." Corporal Thunder nodded in agreement and then informed the team, "It should be here within the hour. Maybe less. It'll be an external load, one with a sling under the helo, but we'll get ammo." He asked for an ammo check from the team, but he was confident they were all low on ammo. They were, too.

"Oh, one last word as we start digging in," Corporal Thunder added. "The company's setting up an assembly area for all the dead and wounded, but it'll be tomorrow before we can medevac them. Helos can't land here in this thick jungle. We'll move to a helo zone early tomorrow for our medevacs.

"Wiley, you're in charge," he unexpectedly announced after digging his position. "I'm going over to the area where the wounded are and check on Sergeant Swede.

"Oh, just thought of something," Corporal Thunder remembered. "Where's the reporter?"

Wiley, Hawkins, and Clary glanced at one another and shrugged indicating their uncertainty.

"Jesus, ain't seem him since the fight ended, but I know he's dug in," Hawkins replied guiltily. "He's probably okay. Probably just scared. Probably just holed up in his hole."

"Don't worry," Wiley said. "We'll check on him. Tell the Sergeant we're praying for him."

Corporal Thunder spun and sprinted toward the company command post and assembly area for the wounded. He located Sergeant Swede, but he was gravely wounded and barely breathing.

"I'm pretty sure one of his lungs has collapsed. That's why we have him laying on his side," Doc Lynn informed the Corporal. "He's in bad shape. It'll be touch and go for him. Chest wounds are nasty ones. We'll get him out as fast as we can, but it'll be tomorrow."

Corporal Thunder kneeled and comforted Sergeant Swede. He dug a hole to place him in for safety, but thought, *I hope this is not his grave.* He then prayed a silent prayer and held his hand gently. Sergeant Swede's grip was listless, his breathing was faint and labored, his eyes clamped shut in pain, and he spoke no words. The Corporal sensed, however, he was conserving all his energy to fight for his survival.

The helo with the emergency ammo resupply arrived on station while Corporal Thunder was with Sergeant Swede. It was a disaster. He later briefed his team when he returned to coordinate with them. "The helo tried to hover in the wind and rain and darkness. It was staying somewhat steady, but then a burst of fire from outside the lines must have spooked the pilots. We're sure it was the NVA just firing at the helo to harass us. The NVA's either policing the battlefield for their wounded or preparing to attack or covering their retreat or maybe all of them. Whatever, there's still some enemy close and in the area." Shaking rain from his poncho he paused and groaned.

"The pilots then powered up to get the hell out of there. They released the sling with the ammo as the helo began taking off," he frowned. "Unfortunately, the heavy ammo crates scattered and landed all over the assembly area with the wounded. One crushed Rodriquez from first platoon. It was bad. The docs said Rodriquez's wounds were minor. He would've been fine, but the ammo crate crushed and killed him right on the spot. It was awful, but the crates missed Sergeant Swede. He's bad, but alive…for now.

"It seems most of the wounded and killed, maybe thirty or so, are from the first platoon. They were in the lead and first to contact the enemy. Our platoon has six of the wounded, but only two killed," Corporal Thunder concluded as he continually wiped rain from his cheeks.

"We located Mr. Robbins," Wiley reported. "He's fine, but he's really quiet. He's having a hard time with all this. The rain and cold and miseries are bad enough, but then the firefight kind of pushed him over the edge. He says he just wants to be alone for a few minutes."

"Okay, thanks for locating him and taking care of him," Corporal Thunder replied nodding at Hawkins. "But make sure he's dug in okay. Then let's begin our night watches and pray for Sergeant Swede. Let's pray for another sunrise, too." He smiled at Wiley as he referred to another sunrise. The sunrises and sunsets were becoming harder to come by…but the darkness was always with them in one form or another.

Mr. Robbins appeared from the blackness and asked, "You think I can hitch a ride with the medevac helos tomorrow? I overheard you talking about the medevacs. I'm ready to go back."

"Yes, I'm pretty sure we can do that. I'll let the company know so it can coordinate your return," Corporal Thunder advised the reporter as he glanced at his three team members. "I think we can get you out early." It was clear the reporter was done…undone or over-done or whatever done. Maybe not done with his writing, but he was done with the miseries and the war.

Mr. Robbins grimaced, "Thanks," and smiled gratefully. He walked back to continue digging his hole for the night. "He's digging a deep one," Hawkins quipped. "Really deep."

"I thought Mr. Robbins was going to stay for the entire operation?" Wiley later whispered.

"Me, too, but I guess he finished up faster than he thought. I'd write fast, too, if I had to put up with this bullshit. I'd be a speed writer. I'd write like hell," Hawkins immediately scoffed.

"Wiley, you're in charge tonight. You set up the night watches and fighting positions," Corporal Thunder suddenly ordered, "because I'm going back to make sure Sergeant Swede is okay. I'll help him though the night. You know where I am. Come get me if you need me."

The Corporal then groped in the darkness toward the wounded assembly area. After locating Sergeant Swede he again took the Sergeant's hand, but the response was weaker than before.

Corporal Thunder was no Indian Medicine Man, but had witnessed numerous Indian healing rituals. Convinced Sergeant Swede's severe chest wound required emergency and compassionate actions, he became desperate. Refusing to concede to fate for the Sergeant's survival, he carefully considered options as he struggled in his quest to help. Sergeant Swede sporadically labored to breath and coughed blood, which caused Corporal Thunder to feel helpless, yet motivated to act.

Corporal Thunder remembered his tribe's Medicine Man once told him, *You have to perform a ritual purification to cleanse the body of harmful spirits and dangers.*

The Indian Medicine Man emphasized to him and he remembered, *Indian medicine is part herbs, part spirituality, and part magic. It's part mind, part body, and part spirit.*

The Corporal considered, *Well, that's about all I remember from my tribal elder, but I have to do something. Sergeant Swede's dying. I have to do something. I can't just do nothing.*

I have no natural herbs, he paused and continued to ponder, *except for maybe my blood. It's about as natural a thing as I have. It's the only thing natural I have. It's pure, too.*

Corporal Thunder recalled the blood brother ceremonies of Indians. Aware they were part mystique and part myth, they were all he could think of to do for Sergeant Swede. Unsheathing his machete, he sliced an incision into the Sergeant's left palm and then his own palm. As the blood began to flow, he grasped Sergeant Swede's hand with his hand and held them together tightly. Chanting softly and praying silently to the Great

Spirit, he felt Sergeant Swede shiver from the wet cold. *Shivering's good*, he thought, *because it means he's still alive.*

Corporal Thunder lay beside him for warmth throughout the night. In the silent stillness of the mountainous jungle, Corporal Thunder softly uttered a rhythmic Indian chant. He decided, *I don't know what else to do except to be here with my friend. Maybe it's part spirit, part prayer, and part magic. Maybe it's none, but I'm going to be here and do this all night. It's all I know to do. It's what I have to do for Sergeant Swede. It's just what Marines do for one another.*

Clary periodically shook the rain from his poncho all night. Hawkins shuttered from the bone chilling wetness until morning. Wiley dozed but only from sheer fatigue and his sleeps were more exhausting than staying awake. The team was assaulted ceaselessly by the damp cold and rain…*and fear*. Wet and miserable as usual, they were virtually numb from chattering teeth and sore shoulders from uncontrollable shaking. It was a frustrating and fearful night.

Corporal Thunder's vigil with Sergeant Swede challenged him more emotionally than physically, but he was thankful the Sergeant was alive as the night wore on. Repeatedly appealing to the Great Spirit on the Sergeant's behalf, he peered toward the heavens and prayed in the dark quiet night. Pleading with God to bless and comfort Sergeant Swede, his skyward gaze never wavered despite the rains drenching his face and blurring his vision. Oblivious to the rain, he was aware only of his severely wounded and possibly dying friend.

As Wiley approached in the early morning darkness, Corporal Thunder glanced up and smiled, "Wiley, he's still alive. It's hard breathing and it's faint, but he's breathing."

"We've been praying, too," Wiley nodded, "but now we got to get ready to move out. What you want us to do?" Wiley stood bent over from the wretched conditions…bent but unbroken.

"I'm staying with Sergeant Swede," Corporal Thunder replied, "but I need the team's help in carrying him to the medevac zone. Round up Hawkins and Clary and let them know we're carrying the Sergeant to the medevac area. Then meet me here. Oh, don't forget the reporter."

Wiley, Hawkins, and Clary met with Corporal Thunder minutes later. The Corporal stated, "We have to prepare a poncho litter to transport

Sergeant Swede to the medevac zone. We're all out of combat litters. We got too many killed and wounded." These few words alone indicated the seriousness of their plight. No more combat litters meant too many casualties.

The team was tired, dirty, wet, cold, hungry, and thirsty. Dipping and digging deep into their reservoir of will and strength, they fought their fears and their loneliness as well as the miseries of the battlefield and the war. Enduring incredible challenges, they were sacrificing daily. Yet, while experiencing the worst life had yet presented them, they were thankful to be alive. They had prayed throughout the night for life so that today they would be alive to do it all over again. Now, it was today. Now, it was time to do it all again.

"The Lieutenant's ordered us to saddle up to move about fifteen hundred meters to the southwest to a small clearing. The company wants to use it to medevac the dead and wounded," Wiley announced from the radio transmissions he was monitoring. Corporal Thunder nodded.

The company policed the area and prepared to advance with the team's second platoon as the lead platoon. Lieutenant Abrahams cautioned, "Let's advance slow and steady and remember we're carrying a lot of dead and wounded. It'll take longer because we have to be careful with the wounded." Lifting and carrying Sergeant Swede, the team struggled forward step by step.

"It's seems the NVA returned back to the mountains in the west," the lead and point notified Lieutenant Abrahams once they were on the move, "because so far we've made no sightings."

"Roger," the Lieutenant succinctly replied, "but be alert. The NVA'll know the clearing is there, too. We'll have to be cautious as we approach. Watch for mines and booby traps, too."

Throughout the 1,500 meter advance, Corporal Thunder, Wiley, Hawkins, and Clary each grabbed one corner of the poncho and improvised litter carrying Sergeant Swede. It was a strenuous and slow process for them. Sergeant Swede was, as Hawkins often declared, "A monster of a man. Hell, he makes three of me. Whata they feed'em in Sweden or Kansas anyway? Must be all that Kansas beef and corn and wheat."

"Yep, the Sergeant's from Kansas," Clary reminded Hawkins. "He ain't missed too many meals that's for sure." The team smiled as they protested and protected their precious cargo.

"Jesus, that helps explain his extra plus extra and large plus large everything. Hell, I could use his boots as my sleepin' bag and his jacket as my tent," Hawkins exaggerated and struggled.

"Damn, that's about the tenth time we've slipped and dropped a corner of the poncho," Clary exclaimed. "It's wet and the trail's rugged. The poncho's slippery and we're tired." By now, their rough hands were nonetheless becoming raw from grabbing and tugging on the slippery poncho.

"Yes, but every time we drop him it sort of jolts him. He opens his eyes and whispers that he's sorry we have to carry him," Wiley extolled. "Imagine that, he's hurting all over and fighting for his life, but he's apologizing for his wound and saying he's sorry we have to carry him."

Sergeant Swede then closed his eyes and strained to breathe. He had spoken his last words of the agonizingly painful trudge to the landing zone. Closer to death than he had ever been in his life, he was fighting harder for life than he had ever fought, too. Corporal Thunder and his team were fighting with him; however, his survival now depended on prayer and fate.

Approaching the landing zone mid-to-late morning, the company became cautious. Upon arrival, a defensive perimeter was established and they prepared to receive supplies as well as evacuate the dead and wounded. While performing multiple duties they remained alert to danger.

"While we're here," Corporal Thunder reported to his team, "our platoon's first squad is assigned part of the perimeter security duty. The third squad's assigned housekeeping duties to clean their weapons, clean up from the mud and blood from yesterday, and eat Cs. Our squad will tend to the wounded and killed and prepare them for medevac. We'll later rotate these duties so everyone can do what they have to do." He then devoted his attention to Sergeant Swede.

As the Corporal's team and squad performed their duties with the wounded, Mr. Robbins, the reporter, who had been distant and quiet all morning, walked up to their location. Corporal Thunder noted he was still visibly shaken, literally demoralized, from the chaos and killings as well as the brutality and bloodshed from the night before. The miseries of the monsoons and damp cold only exacerbated his despair. His morale was shattered. His motivation was shredded. He was disheveled and distraught. As Hawkins quietly alleged, "He's done. Flat ass done."

It's been over twelve hours since the firefight, but it obviously remains an emotional trauma to him, Clary thought as he observed him. He agreed with Hawkins, "Yep, he's done for sure."

The reporter ambled toward the team hunched over and dejected. Frustrated and flustered, Mr. Robbins spoke distressingly to Corporal Thunder and the team, "I wouldn't do what you Marines do for all the money in the world." The reporter shook his head in disbelief and wonder as he repeated, "Not for all the money in the world." But it was more than his head that shook. His entire body trembled. The wet cold and the hot fear combined to cause uncontrollable twitching. He attempted to gather himself, but failed. Shrugging in utter defeat, he glanced down and away.

Hawkins glared up from tending one of the wounded and growled, "Hell, neither would we. Neither would we," as if to question who the hell would do what they were doing for money.

"There's not enough money in the world to pay us to do what we do," Clary added. "There's just not enough," as if to question what gold and treasures would be enough.

Corporal Thunder then expressed, "We do what we do because we're Marines. It's our duty. It's our mission." He paused and continued, "It's just what Marines do."

Finally, Wiley stood erect with his towering frame and massive body, with his ragged uniform bloodied and muddied from the battlefield and nature, and with his deep bass voice he spoke ever so softly and reverently and respectfully, "We do it for love. We do it because we love one another as Marines."

Mr. Maxwell opened his mouth to speak, but no sounds and no words were heard. Hawkins later claimed, "The reporter had talked forever for the past three days or so. Sometimes, he talked to interview Marines and Docs. Sometimes, he talked because he was so scared and nervous. Mostly, he just talked to talk. He could sure talk, but then he couldn't talk. Couldn't say nothin'."

Now there were no words. No words at all. It was total silence. Possibly because he was so humbled, or maybe because he was so overwhelmed by the simplicity and sincerity of the Marines' comments, Clary later concluded, "The reporter simply turned and walked away toward the helicopter and disappeared." He was done and then he was gone.

The truth was there was nothing more to say. There was nothing more anyone could say. The four Marines in the team had said it all. They had said all that needed to be said.

There was simply nothing to add to the care and love they shared for one another. "Nothing. Zero. Zilch," Corporal Thunder would later conclude as they prepared to move on.

In one of their bunker talks Clary later reflected, "At the time, it probably seemed strange to some. Strange that in the midst of the death and destruction and the hatreds and angers of war that Wiley spoke the word 'Love'. But as we thought about it over time we understood 'Love' was the only word that could have or should have been spoken." It was that simple to them.

The miseries and the sacrifices faded with time. The battles and the challenges receded to the recesses of their memories. The love, however, endured. It was the love that sustained them. They lived in the love and the love lived in them. It overcame the hate and anger. It overcame the death and devastation of war. The love endured and conquered...*and survived.*

Mike Company completed the evacuation of its dead and wounded and accepted its resupply. The company command element ordered the platoons to remain in and strengthen their defensive positions and standby for further orders. Lieutenant Abrahams radioed the second platoon to, "Standby for a Frag Order. The Captain's coordinating with battalion now and we should know something soon." The continuation of the Razorback operation as initially planned was now temporarily on hold pending modifications.

Corporal Thunder passed the word and Hawkins asked, "What exactly's a Frag Order?"

"It's short for Fragmentary Order. A Frag Order more or less changes or modifies or updates our original order and gives us a new or updated order," the Corporal replied.

"You mean we could get an order to go west into the mountains to look for the NVA we just ran that way?" Hawkins asked. Hawkins had fought yesterday, but he was ready to fight today.

Corporal Thunder smiled and confessed, "It could be most anything, but I doubt that's what we'll be doing. We'll probably continue on south like planned or go back north. We could maybe later go west with a bigger force, maybe the battalion, but probably not now. We've been beat up too bad to be chasing a big force. Not now. Maybe later."

"While we're on standby, let's take a break," Wiley suggested. "We haven't slept or rested much the past three days. Let's get some sleeps while we can." Wiley flopped down cushioned by the lush jungle growth and tall grass to instantly lock into his sleeps.

Hawkins envied Wiley's ability to fall asleep with such ease and remarked, "Wiley takes the Infantryman's Creed to heart: 'We never sleep because we're sleepy. We sleep to keep from gettin' sleepy.' But that's kinda bullshit. We're always sleepy because we never get to sleep."

The team agreed and established a watch schedule and napped soundly for about an hour. "Okay, listen up," Corporal Thunder announced as he woke the team. "We got our new orders."

Once the team was awake and attentive, Corporal Thunder explained, "Battalion's ordered the company to more or less do an about face and reverse our course and then advance toward the north end of the Razorback. We won't go on south like originally planned, but go back north and then go east around the Razorback's northern end. Then we'll go back south to Payable."

"What's the mission?" Wiley asked curiously.

"Well, according to the Lieutenant, we're to sweep the area maybe a little farther to the west where the enemy retreated last night. But we're to mostly sweep toward the north and last night's ambush site. We just need to end up at the northern end of the Razorback so we can then head back to Payable," the Corporal continued. "The mission's to get back to our base camp safely."

"But what's the sweep all about?" Hawkins asked suspiciously.

"Well, that's the thing. We're supposed to do a body count of dead NVA," the Corporal frowned. "We have to do a good body count." It pained him to even mention body count.

"Body count? We gotta do a damn body count?" Hawkins moaned. "We gotta count the NVA dead bodies because some shithead in the

Pentagon thinks that's whata tell'em who won or lost the battle?" The body count issue, battle-by-battle, was becoming an anathema to the team.

"Yeah, somebody thinks that if you count the enemy dead and the friendly dead then you have a score. Then you can claim who won or who lost the ballgame," Clary observed. "I read that somewhere in some magazine. It's a new metric or calculus for the Pentagon. Now the statistics guys and analysts get to get in the game. Now they're keeping score on the game."

"Jesus, I hate to be the first to tell the Pentagon this, but this ain't no ballgame," Hawkins moaned. "This ain't no ballgame. This is a damn war. There's better ways to tell who's winning the war. We gotta just kick the shit outta'em til they surrender. Then we got a winner and loser."

"Well, you're right, Hawkins, but the Pentagon thinks one measuring stick for success is the body count numbers," Clary confided, "but most think that's just going to cause commanders to inflate the numbers to make their units look good. Then what kind of measuring stick is that?"

"Jesus, I gotta good idea what kinda measuring stick that is. They can stick it right up their Pentagon asses. That'll probably tickle them more than the body count numbers. Body count is plain bullshit," Hawkins declared as he rechecked his shotgun for the hundredth time.

"This article was saying that most past wars were kind of decided by what it called the geography and the political. I'm not too sure what the political really means, but the geography part was that the winner had to take and win territory," Clary asserted.

"Jesus, I don't know about the political either, but if it's our politicians against the NVA politicians we're in deep shit," Hawkins exclaimed. "But I'm all for lettin'em duke it out and lettin' me watch and then go home. Let's see how good the politicians can fight. I'll even count the knock outs to help keep score. That's one body count I'll be glad to do."

Hawkins paused briefly, but he was only warming up to the body count issue. "Now, to me the geography part is pretty simple. You don't own the land till you take it. 'Til you're on it. Then you gotta hold it. But we don't hold nothin'. We take it. We get on it. Then we get off it. We give it up. We're fightin' for a piece of land or terrain one day, but then we move on. Then we come back later and fight for it all over again. We ain't holdin' nothin' except our camps.

"Marines are killed or wounded each time we fight for it and then we just move on. How many Marines gotta die for something we ain't holdin' on to?" Hawkins continued, "If it's worth fightin' for why don't we hold on to it? This debatin' body count is exhaustin' me. Wiley, whata you think?" Hawkins finally asked after he had rambled and confused the team and himself.

"Well, it just seems senseless to me, too," Wiley replied. "It just seems to me that we value life more than the North Vietnamese. They'll just keep sending soldiers south to get killed and we'll just keep killing them. But the numbers killed don't mean much to them. They don't seem to much care how many are killed."

"Yeah, that's what I'ma sayin'," Hawkins agreed. "If body count ain't shit to the NVA, then why's the Pentagon morons so hung up on body count? The enemy don't care 'bout body count because they don't care how many's killed. They ain't countin'. They're just fightin' and dyin'."

"Gentlemen, I agree with you on this one," Corporal Thunder admitted, "but we have orders. We have a mission." He was as opposed to the body count as they were, but it was their mission.

"Okay, we'll do it cause it's a mission," Hawkins strongly agreed, "and if they want a damn body count, I'll give'em a count. But I'm countin' ten for every one NVA I see dead. I'll count ten 'cause Sergeant Swede is at least good for a ten to one count. Ain't no ten NVA I know that's worth one Sergeant Swede. Let me get at the countin'. I'm rarin' to count now."

Once the body count issue was resolved to Hawkins' satisfaction, Corporal Thunder rallied and focused the team. "The company has ordered two platoons forward on line for the sweep. One platoon and the command element will follow in trace as a reserve.

"Our platoon will take the right flank and third platoon will take the left flank. The first platoon, because it took the most casualties, will follow in trace and protect the command element," Corporal Thunder continued. "We'll be the right platoon and the guide platoon and aim in on the northern end of the Razorback. Once we get to the river north of the Razorback we'll cross the river and provide security while the rest of the company crosses after us. Then we'll veer east and later head south to Payable." He sketched the advance on his map with his machete as he briefed the team. They were all familiar with the terrain and now the route.

"By the way, Corporal Cozart is now the senior Corporal in our squad and is now the new squad leader to replace Sergeant Swede," Corporal Thunder announced. "Now, let's saddle up and get ready to move out. Remember, count dead NVA bodies, too. One of our missions is body count." He nodded at Hawkins as he emphasized the body count task, but he grinned, too.

While Corporal Thunder waited for the order from Lieutenant Abrahams to move out, he remembered. "One last word. The Captain has requested fixed-wing air support on station just in case the NVA try to attack out of the mountains and hit us on the left flank or rear. The jets won't be there all the time, but they'll be available. They'll be available for several Marine units operating down south from us and not just us."

It was an ominous announcement. At the time they were unaware how ominous it was, but they learned later. Now they were simply relieved the rain and clouds were lifting. The weather was improving. Corporal Thunder observed and relayed to Wiley, "Well, it looks like we might have a good day or at least a good weather day." They glanced upward toward the blue sky.

Wiley smiled and replied, "Yes, we could use a good day. We've had a few bad ones here recently. We need a good day. The weather's kind of nice, too."

It was a good weather day, but they had concluded months ago there were no good days in Vietnam. In time, it became a particularly bad day. It became one of their worst days in Vietnam. It caused Hawkins to later confide to the team after a company memorial service, "Ain't no good days in Vietnam, except for the days you survive."

CHAPTER 13

River Crossing & Friendly Fires

Well, we're back in our base camp bunker and this is the safest I've felt in too long. I feel like I just keep going to hell and back. This sure ain't heaven, but it'll do for now.

—Marine Lance Corporal Aaron Wiley

Hawkins and Clary were sloshing in the squishy mud and thrashing through the shoulder high thick grass conducting the body count for the team. Clary admitted to Hawkins, "It looks like the NVA may have come back in here last night to recover their dead. I don't see too many."

"Yeah, they probably snuck right in after we left. We didn't hold it and they just came in after we set our defensive lines. So, I'm just countin' big spots of blood, too," Hawkins groused. "I'm even countin' little spots of blood. I ain't too damn interested in counting dead bodies anyway. Ain't interested at all. But they want a count bad, they get a bad count."

"Well, the Pentagon seems really interested," Clary devilishly smiled knowing his remark would only irritate Hawkins and initiate yet another tirade of his bitching and complaining.

"Yeah, well, if the Pentagon's so damn interested in countin' dead bodies they can come here and count'em anytime. I'll make way for'em and they can take my spot in the countin' sweepstakes derby anytime they want," Hawkins growled…and counted. It was, as Corporal Thunder said, their mission and Hawkins understood their commitment to missions.

The movement toward the Razorback's north end and the river progressed steadily and without incident. "Ain't too may bodies to count and we seem to be moving a little faster," Hawkins shrugged. "Truth is, I ain't searching too hard for bodies to count. Just interested in gettin' the hell outta here safely. If they're dead, they're dead, and dead's good enough for me."

"Well, everyone's probably ready to get back to Payable Hill and home," Clary replied.

"Yeah, it ain't much, but its home for now," Hawkins smiled. "Ain't it funny how we call it home. It's a real shithole, but compared to the patrols it's a five-star hotel."

"Yeah, but I sure wish it had a five-star restaurant, too," Clary grinned. "I really miss good food. Hell, I'd love a plain ole hamburger and fries right now." Hawkins' stomach rumbled.

"Clary, don't torture me like that," Hawkins pleaded. "Talkin' 'bout good food is just the worst kinda talk for me." Hawkins thought of his mama's pasta specialties and beamed fondly.

Corporal Thunder and the team advanced alertly and cautiously. Attentive to the terrain and threat, they had learned to discern times to talk. Talking was moral support and helped them maintain focus. They talked for fun in the tedium of their task and to escape the drudgery. It was only occasionally the body count issue interrupted their talks.

As the company approached the northern rim of the Razorback and the river, Corporal Cozart's squad and Corporal Thunder's team assumed the point position in the platoon. The remaining company units began to slowly converge into one column for the river crossing.

Corporal Thunder briefly assembled his team to update it on the river crossing. "The Lieutenant just radioed and told us to select a good river crossing site. Then, we're to lead the platoon across and the Lieutenant will disperse us on the northern side of the river."

"Corporal Cozart's squad and us will secure the center section. First squad will take the left or west. Third squad will take the right or east. We'll all secure the far bank for the remainder of the company to cross." He concluded by asking, "Any questions?"

"The Lieutenant's passing the word to the Captain that our selecting the site, crossing the river, and establishing security will take some time," Corporal Thunder emphasized. "He also recommended to the Captain that the other units should hold their positions and later move up slowly so as not to all jam up in a cluster at the river crossing." He glanced to the western skyline and squinted to clear his vision for a distant view of the far mountains.

"We're vulnerable at river crossings because everyone always wants to rush up to the river, but the crossing slows us down," Lieutenant Abrahams noted. "Then we have a gaggle of people waiting to cross. It makes a good target." Corporal Thunder studied the western mountains again.

"Yes, Sir," Corporal Thunder acknowledged. "We'll move out now and secure the far bank as fast as we can." He motioned for Hawkins to proceed north to the river, but looked west again.

The Corporal and his team led the company to the river crossing. Hawkins and Clary waded into the river at three locations before selecting a good crossing site. The river was swift, but only about waist deep. Once on the far bank they signaled for the second platoon to cross the river. While the platoon established security on the north bank, the company passed the word for the remaining units to advance to the crossing site.

Corporal Thunder and his team were safely across the river and relieved the day and the patrol and mission were proceeding on schedule and without incident. But then it seemed, according to Wiley, *All hell's broke loose. I'm down and frozen in place. I gotta unfreeze fast, but right now I'm too scared to move.*

Thunderous explosions shattered the quiet still jungle. The force of the violent blasts was incredible. "The blast's knocked me to my knees," Clary yelled to the team to let them know he was okay as well as to hopefully hear their responses back to him. The concussion from the eruptions rippled through the dense jungle with unbelievable force. Trees waved to and fro and branches flapped wildly up and down. Stillness then returned, but there was no accompanying silence. Screams of agony were instantly heard from the direction of the river crossing.

"Jesus, what the hell's that?" Hawkins yelled as shock waves reverberated through the dense jungle as they immediately flung themselves flat into the tall grass, tangled vines, and soft mud.

It was unnerving. It was unexpected. Scared beyond scared, they immediately collected their wits. "The blasts and screams seem to be coming from the direction of the river crossing, but they're blasts and screams like I've never heard before," Corporal Thunder assessed and shared with the team within seconds as they collected themselves in the terrifying jungle.

"At first, I thought it musta been a booby trap at the river, but ain't no booby trap I ever seen or heard that powerful," Hawkins frantically confessed. "Beside booby traps are mostly down south with the VC and not up north with the NVA."

"Yeah, at first I thought it was maybe a mortar attack," Clary added as they reviewed the incident, "but it was much stronger and louder than mortars."

"Yeah, I'm probably a hundred meters away, but my ears will probably ring for days," Wiley reported as the blast's heat unfroze him, "I'm still sorta dazed and deafened by the blasts. This war's after my hearing." Fear had temporarily frozen him, but now fear motivated him.

Corporal Thunder quickly contacted Corporal Cozart for any update and any orders.

"The Lieutenant's as shocked and confused as we are," Corporal Thunder advised his team, "but he's asking all the squads to hold firm in their defensive positions while he takes Corporal Cozart and us to the river to see what the hell happened."

Corporal Thunder and his team rushed to Lieutenant Abraham's location back down the trail. Backtracking to the river crossing they thought to themselves what could have been so devastating. They prepared themselves for the worst, but they could never have remotely imagined the carnage that greeted them at the river crossing. *Damn, this is beyond imaginable*, Wiley thought.

The destruction on the south bank of the river was horrific. Within seconds, the Corporal recognized the smoldering and suffocating scents and sights of ugly death. "Whatever it was it was more powerful than anything we've ever encountered," Corporal Thunder shouted amid the chaos, but at the time he had no idea what had caused the violent blasts.

Wiley quickly noticed the company command element in the center of the blast area. He recognized the upper half of the executive officer's body on the muddy shore with its lower half in the water. Wiley sloshed to his location and grabbed his arms to pull him from the water, but there was no bottom half. Gagging, he yelled to Clary, "He's been blown apart. The bottom half's floating down the river."

Corporal Thunder ran to a face down casualty and slowly turned him over to treat him. He immediately grimaced and dropped to his knees. It was the company radio operator, Phillips, who was due to rotate home in about two weeks in time for Christmas. As a short-timer, Phillips was exempt from the patrol, but he insisted he wanted to make one final patrol, especially with the company command group, which was usually the safest location in most patrols. But now he was dead. His body was literally shredded by the force of the blast and multiple shrapnel gorges in his bloodied upper torso. He was one of Corporal Thunder's best friends outside the team. His death deeply saddened the Corporal, but there was no time for sadness. He had to move on.

Lieutenant Abrahams noticed the Captain was hurt bad and immediately radioed the platoons on the south side of the river, "The NVA probably booby trapped the river crossing site. They might be preparing to attack us during all the chaos and confusion. Be alert and defend hard while we clear up this mess at the river. We have multiple casualties."

"It's a good time for the NVA to attack because we're divided on both sides of the river and the command element's decimated," Corporal Thunder yelled to his team. "Plus, we got all the wounded and killed to treat and medevac. We have to work fast. Be alert."

The Lieutenant's initiating emergency helo medevacs and the third platoon's converging on the crossing site to begin treating the wounded and caring for the dead, Corporal Thunder noted. Confusion reigned as they tended to the repulsive duty of recovering the dead and wounded. Concurrently, they defended against an attack. Although extremely vulnerable, they controlled their fears while sharing an unspoken sense of hopelessness and helplessness and determination.

"The river's only about ten meters wide, but it's fairly swift. I'm seeing body parts drifting down the river," Corporal Thunder updated his team. "The Lieutenant's ordering our fire team to stay on the south bank to begin helping the wounded and preparing them for medevac."

Chaos was evident, but order was slowly established. The tasks were monumental and the circumstances dire. The Marines checked their emotions and fear, however, and began to do what had to be done. Gravely wounded, possibly dying, the Company Commander lay crumpled on the river bank. Lieutenant Abrahams took charge of the company and medevac coordination. Corporal Thunder took charge of preparing the dead and the wounded for medevac.

"The hardest part is recovering the dead and stacking them as neatly as we can along the muddy bank," Wiley shouted to Clary. "It hurts so bad because the Captain died while a corpsman was treating him and the First Lieutenant Executive Officer's dead form just being cut into at the waist. The Company Gunny is hardly recognizable and most of the Senior Corpsmen in the command element are dead or dying. Phillips is dead, too. It's the worst I've ever seen. It's a lot worse than the mortar and rocket attack on the rear in Dong Ha or Con Thien or Payable. They were horrible, but this is worse. It'll be even worse if the enemy attacks."

"Jesus, we're back to countin' dead bodies, but it's our own Marines and Navy Corpsmen dead we're countin'," Hawkins sighed. "I kinda just stopped countin' at eighteen dead. I ain't countin' no more. I'll just help with the wounded 'cause I know even more are wounded."

Corporal Thunder quickly saw Doc Roman lying in the mud on the river bank and pointed to him. Wiley noticed and called for Clary and Hawkins. "Over here. We got Doc Roman. He needs us." Doc Roman was the Senior Corpsman in the company and the only corpsman of four in the command element still alive.

"Yeah, but he needs more than us," Hawkins exclaimed as the first on the scene. "Doc Roman's legs are severed at the knees and he's only got two bleeding stumps for legs. It's gross. Prepare yourself because it's bad," he whispered as the others arrived.

Corporal Thunder took charge and asked, "Doc Roman, what can we do for you?"

The doc groaned, "Stay with me," and motioned the team to drag the wounded to him.

"Doc Roman's gotta be in shock. He knows he has maybe only minutes to live," Clary whispered to Hawkins. "But he's a corpsman and he knows what he has to do, too."

First, Doc Roman applied tourniquets to his legs and then scooped up wet mud from the river bank and plastered it on his bloody stumps to stop the bleeding as best he could, Corporal Thunder thought. *The doc's in shock but knows he has to be calm. I don't know how he's doing it, but he is. How do you think of that? Plastering your own stumps with mud knowing you're probably dying. He's fighting to live because it's what he knows he has to do.*

As Wiley, Hawkins, and Clary carried or dragged the wounded to Doc Roman, the doc softly whispered instructions to Corporal Thunder, who then passed to his team. "Bandage that wound. Splint that broken bone.

Put a tourniquet on that bloody stump." It was heartbreaking duty, but the team devoted itself to it.

"It's another mission," Corporal Thunder sighed, "but a mission of mercy instead of killing."

"Yeah, I ain't too good at some of it, but the doc's patient explanations are guiding and helping," Hawkins asserted, "but damned if it ain't the most grisly damn thing I've ever had to do. God bless Navy Corpsmen. They do it all the time."

"I think the hardest part for the doc is to tell me to lay one of the wounded aside because he's maybe too far gone and not likely to live," Wiley shrugged, "and then to go get another one who maybe has a better chance of making it. That has to be hard. Deciding who lives."

The team treated and cared for the wounded for about an hour before Lieutenant Abrahams yelled, "Medevac helos inbound."

"Damn, we got no landing zone," Wiley observed. "What're we going to do to medevac the wounded?"

Corporal Thunder ordered Clary, "Maybe the Lieutenant's already thought of it, but tell him to radio the CH-46 helo pilots to just hover over the river with their back ramps down and low enough to the water for us to lift the wounded up and into the helos. We'll mark the location."

"The pilots know it's risky," Hawkins admitted to Wiley, "but they know we're in a soup sandwich. This is the only clearing we got. I'll mark the zone with a purple smoke grenade."

It was challenging at first, but the pilots eventually developed a plan and decided how best to hover and hold steady over the river to perform the medevacs. Minutes later, Corporal Thunder smiled to Wiley, "It was hard as hell for them at first, but they just kept trying. They finally figured out the best way to do it and then just did it. Great piloting. Great skills."

As the pilots hovered over the river, Corporal Thunder ordered, "Okay, Wiley, this is where we need you. You're the biggest and strongest and you'll have to do most of the final heavy lifting. We'll carry the wounded and dead out to you and Clary at this rocky shoal sticking out of the water. Clary will steady you and help you while you lift the dead and wounded up to the helo tailgate. It should work. It better work. It's got to work."

"Wiley's great," Lieutenant Abrahams admitted to his radioman as he watched. "He's damn strong and just keeps lifting and lifting. I bet he bench presses over four hundred pounds. The others are doing a helluva job, too, fighting the swift river and horrible task."

It took most of the afternoon to complete the medevacs and then prepare for continuing the mission. The Lieutenant eventually radioed the company's radio operators to pass the final casualty numbers, "It's twenty-three killed and eighteen wounded and ten helo medevac loads."

"Damn, after yesterday's bad numbers these are even worse," Wiley remarked with a sigh.

"Yeah, but I bet Doc Roman saved a lot of wounded. He was probably the last one to die, but he saved a good number of lives before he died," Clary stated with respect.

"Jesus, can you imagine if the NVA had of attacked?" Hawkins exclaimed. "We were all pretty busy with carin' for the dead and treatin' the wounded. Can you imagine if we'da had fight on our hands, too? We were really messed up there for awhile. Jesus, we was lucky."

The clouds collected and roared in as sunset approached. It rained harder. Cold wetness embraced them again. The miseries in Vietnam were the miseries of war and they were always only seconds or minutes away. One tragic event after another assaulted them. They were in no position, however, to relax or rest. Any sorrow or grieving the loss of friends, of Marines, of corpsmen, would have to wait. To the contrary, with the casualties the company had sustained, it was imperative to return to Payable Hill at the earliest. They were vulnerable and they knew it.

Lieutenant Abrahams requested Staff Sergeant Antoine and Corporal Thunder report to his temporary position at the river bank. Once they both reported, the Lieutenant announced, "Staff Sergeant Antoine, you take charge of second platoon because I'm now the senior man in the company. I'll be the acting company commander for our return to Payable."

Lieutenant Abrahams paused while they reflected on the gravity of the situation before he asked, "Corporal Thunder, it's probably less than an hour before total darkness. How long do you think it'll take us to move the company back to Payable?"

"Sir, if we take the east side of the river it'll be faster and safer, but in the dark it'll still take us about six hours," Corporal Thunder replied. "If we make good time we may be able to get to Payable by about midnight or so."

"Okay, Corporal, you take your team and rejoin the squad on the north side of the river. Let all the squad leaders know what's happening and to standby." Lieutenant Abrahams then ordered, "Staff Sergeant Antoine, you stay here with me and we'll meet with the other platoon commanders and coordinate our return to Payable.

"Corporal Thunder, it'll probably take us about thirty minutes for the units on the south side of the river to organize. Then it'll take time to cross the river. The crossing should take less than an hour, too. But be ready to move out smartly when you get the word from Staff Sergeant Antoine," Lieutenant Abrahams explained. They all looked at one another fully comprehending their vulnerable, almost desperate, situation. Their expressions, however, were emotionless. Corporal Thunder thought, *It's gut check time. Night's coming. Maybe the NV's coming, too.*

"Yes, Sir," Corporal Thunder replied. He then turned to cross the river and alert his team and the second platoon squad leaders. The situation was dire, but now they had a plan and orders. A mission always focused and motivated them while presenting them with actions to perform.

Lieutenant Abrahams briefed the platoon leaders and together they coordinated plans for the return to Payable. It took time for word to filter down the chain of command, but the company was on the move by the time darkness blanketed the jungle. They slid quickly into the darkness.

The monsoons became steadier and stronger. The cold became penetratingly colder. Howling north winds screeched erratically and eerily. Hawkins shuddered once and steadied himself. The weather could hardly have been worse, but Hawkins declared, "No sane person, except us, 'cause we ain't too sane, would be movin' on a night like tonight. The NVA'll be hunkered down dry and warm somewhere. We'll probably be the only ones out in this mess, but that's good for us." Hawkins was learning no matter how bad it was to consider the good.

"Well, that's just the way I like it," Wiley countered. "It'll be damn hard to see us or hear us or find us in this weather." Wiley quickly paused for a silent prayer.

"At least somethin's in our favor," Clary sighed, "but we still got a long patrol ahead of us. There's not much good and a lot of bad for us here in these jungles." Clary simply paused to sigh and collect himself before sauntering toward Hawkins.

"Jesus, Clary, we got you and me leadin' us back and we're the best there is," Hawkins boasted. "So, let's just do what we do and take us home. We're good." Hawkins neither paused nor prayed nor pined. Instead, he shouldered his pack and prepared himself for point.

Corporal Thunder proposed, "Okay, Hawkins and Clary, let's go home. Take us in and keep us moving with no stops. We stop at night as tired as we are somebody's going to fall asleep on the trail and we'll never see them to know it in this darkness. We're all just so damn exhausted to halt. We're walking zombies. Just keep us moving. No stops. None. Zero. Zilch."

The trail to Payable was treacherous; however, Corporal Thunder and his team knew it well despite the darkness. They knew it better than the NVA. The patrolling skills they had acquired from months of patrolling in the area were invaluable. It was what Corporal Thunder had taught them about the terrain and how to read the valleys and the streams and the land, however, that helped them the most. Hawkins grinned as he thought of Clary and himself as street and surf boys now comfortable as well as proficient in the jungles and mountains. "Life's strange," he said to Clary.

Clary simply nodded and thought, *We're as unlikely a pair as there is.* They had a sixth sense for the land, the darkness, the weather...and each other. Negotiating the dark and stormy trails as much by feel, fortitude, and faith as they did by their patrolling skills, they moved out and on with assurance and confidence. *We're Corporal Thunder trained*, Hawkins confidently thought.

"We're moving pretty steady considering the conditions and the fatigue," Wiley noted to the Corporal hours later. After another hour or so, the Lieutenant radioed Wiley to ask how much longer before they reached Payable. Maps and compasses were always useful tools of their trade. Now, however, in the coal black night it was their gut feel for the land that was most meaningful.

Corporal Thunder received the request from Wiley and without stopping passed it to Clary and Hawkins. "The Lieutenant wants to know how much longer before Payable. I'm estimating about two hours. What's your estimate? Is two hours good? Is two about right?"

Hawkins and Clary briefly consulted and confirmed without stopping, "Yeah, two's about right. Two's fine." Quickening the pace slightly, they bowed hard into the mountains and rain.

Corporal Thunder passed the word back to Wiley. Wiley succinctly radioed Lieutenant Abrahams, "Two hours." They were familiar with the trail and location despite the darkness.

The Lieutenant radioed Wiley about an hour later, "I'm coordinating with battalion now to fire 81mm mortar illumination rounds for about the last 1,000 meters of our patrol. The illum rounds will help us guide in on Payable in all this darkness for the final part of the patrol. I'm passing the word so everyone knows."

The patrol silently and stalwartly strengthened itself collectively for the final surge home to Payable. The Marines leaned forward and braved the pelting stings from the howling rains. The individual physical and psychological capabilities of the Marines were beginning to falter. Their resolve as a unit, as a team, however, remained resolute. The patrol strained hard to stretch deep into its heart and soul to maintain its forward momentum. It was one agonizing thrust forward. Then two. Then another. They became numb as sensations faltered into utter exhaustion.

"Toward the end it's one step at a time. It's one foot in front of the other. Let's just keep going forward. We're running on empty, but we're running," Corporal Thunder conceded to the team as they prepared for the final push knowing if they stopped they would never start again.

Then the illumination flares started popping and the light lifted the spirits of the company. Now, moving more and more confidently, most every step was nonetheless painful.

Mike Company arrived on Payable about 0030. It was raining. It was cold. It was miserable. Yet, no one seemed to notice. They were beyond fatigue, but they were alive and home. Hawkins shouldered his weapon. Clary unbuckled his helmet. Wiley unstrapped his radio. Corporal Thunder inserted his machete into its scabbard. The company, what remained of it, was home again and relatively safe. Thoughts drifted, however, to the many they had lost, who were no longer with them, who had failed to survive the patrol and the past four days. It was four days that seemed a lifetime. Unfortunately, it was a lifetime for some; for too many.

"Well, we're back in our base camp bunker and this is the safest I've felt in too long," Wiley announced. "I feel like I just keep going to hell and back. This sure ain't heaven, but it'll do for now."

"Jesus, I ain't hardly slept but maybe a couple hours a day for the last four days," Hawkins groaned, "and when I did it was for maybe minutes at a time. I'm just beat to hell."

"We're all so tired we're just making it on fumes," Corporal Thunder remarked. "I just don't have much left in me. Not much at all."

No one spoke as the company traipsed into the camp. Speaking required energy and they had virtually none. After the last Marine entered, Lieutenant Abrahams confided to Corporal Thunder and his team, "Good job. Good pace. We made it. Now, get some rest. We'll talk tomorrow."

"Yes, Sir," Corporal Thunder replied. The Lieutenant and the team turned slowly and trudged wearily to their respective bunkers. The team locked arms to steady one another as they staggered to their bunker. "Jesus, anyone lookin' will think we're drunk," Hawkins grinned as visions of a beer or two vaulted into his dreams.

Within minutes, Corporal Thunder and his team settled into their bunker. Once relatively comfortable, Hawkins asked, "You think it's possible to be too damn tired to sleep?"

Despite their exhaustion they were still wide awake. "Yeah, I think it's possible. It seems my body is asleep, but my mind's just racing," Clary answered, "and the cold wet's bothering me most. It's the cold wet that makes it hard to sleep, but maybe my mind is wet, too."

Wiley agreed with a simple grunt and muttered, "Too tired to talk. Saving my energy for sleeps. Just trying to shut down my mind. I'm remembering too much of what I want to forget."

"I can't sleep either. I'll just take the first watch. You sleep," Corporal Thunder groaned.

It seemed an eternity, but the team eventually slept. In the morning, however, Hawkins ranted, "Most everything in this shithole called Vietnam seems an eternity, but when I sleeps it seems like just a brief instant. Damned if I don't wish my tour would pass as fast as my sleeps. Hell, I'da been home yesterday."

As they sat huddled in their bunker, the team slowly opened Cs for breakfast. They were starving, but first they needed warmth. Clary dutifully made coffee and hot chocolate as Wiley opened four meal cans of Cs. Hawkins wrestled with the cheese and crackers or canned cakes as

Corporal Thunder filled their canteens with water from their five-gallon water can.

"Jesus, ain't this a helluva way to start our day," Hawkins lamented. "Cs are ruining me."

"Yep, it's not the Ritz or home cooking," Wiley shared, "but we're together and we're surviving." He uttered a brief breakfast prayer, but the Cs were as horrible as ever. Prayer never seemed to improve Cs. Maybe they were, in fact, the devil's food as Hawkins often swore.

Corporal Thunder's team momentarily reflected on yesterday and the past few days. They remembered the multiple devastating battles and numerous wounded and killed. It seemed an eternity; an everlasting series of enemy engagements and tragedies. In reality, however, it was only four days, but it was four days of hell. It was also, for far too many, their last four days alive. Hopefully, they were now in heaven where they could no longer be touched by the hell of the war. The war, however, relentlessly reached out and touched the survivors.

They were sad for the losses, but they were glad to be alive. Such emotions were one of the sad anomalies of the war. Sometimes they felt guilty for feeling glad and being alive, but it was better than feeling sad and being dead. It was war. They felt glad simply because they were alive.

One of their most cherished memories from the patrol, however, was Wiley's softly and sincerely spoken, "We do what we do for love." It was a love they shared and lived daily, but they had never been as aware of it as they were now. The team had lost its innocence and the only life they had previously known, but it had gained an appreciation and respect for the love they shared and the love that sustained them.

CHAPTER 14

Christmas & Cease Fires

Don't talk to me about those ceasefires. We're the only ones not firin'. Jesus, we cease and they fire. How 'bout that? The NVA's a firin' and we're a ceasin'. Ain't that a helluva ceasefire? Wait'll I tell the Pentagon about their ceasefire.

—Marine Private First Class Dominic Hawkins

The morning sun was rising as they ate breakfast, but Wiley was too fatigued to comment on another sunrise. He did, however, gaze on it with a smile and promptly sat on a row of sandbags. The team had no patrol today and it was a fairly leisurely morning. Wiley said, "We've done what needs to be done for now. Tonight we have an ambush. Then we'll ambush. Now there's nothing." It was a day to recover from the exhausting past four days on patrol.

"At first, doing nothing was frustrating," complained Clary, "but now doing nothing's often better than something or anything. I'm either preparing for a patrol, on a patrol, or recovering from a patrol. The something I'm always doing is patrolling. Nothing is good at times."

"Let's just do our housekeeping duties and get ourselves squared away. Let's just round up some Cs, clean weapons, and maybe wash some uniforms as best we can," Corporal Thunder advised the team, "but nap when you can, too. Get rested up. Take a nap. Get some sleeps."

In the early morning sun, Hawkins removed his utility tops and bottoms. He stood in his skivvies and boots, which were filthy, while he inspected every inch of his utilities. Clary asked and instantly regretted, "What are you doing half naked? Why are you checking your uniform?"

"I'm inspecting for one square inch, just one, that's clean. But every damn inch is soiled with mud or blood or whatever," Hawkins frowned. "Maybe I'll just wash it today since we got sun."

The word was passed for Corporal Thunder to report to Lieutenant Abrahams. "Wiley, I have to go see the Lieutenant. You're in charge. I'll be back as soon as I can. I'll update us then."

Later, the team's exhaustion overwhelmed them. In the midst of cleaning weapons and squaring away the bunker, Wiley, Hawkins, and Clary virtually passed out cold. Sleep finally subdued them and they slept a good and restful sleep exactly where they had paused.

Corporal Thunder returned to the bunker an hour later and noticed the team sleeping. His news would wait. Sleep was what they now needed most. He was reluctant to wake Hawkins from the child-like fetal position he had adopted on a poncho laid over sandbags. He had taken off his boots to wash his socks as well as his uniform and skivvies. He was naked as a jaybird. Corporal Thunder quickly glanced away thinking, *This mental picture of a naked Hawkins will haunt me forever.* Smiling, he wished he had a camera. It was not exactly a Kodak moment, but it was a bribery one. It was a cool December day and the warmth of the sun was refreshing.

It was mid-afternoon before the team awoke. Once awake, Corporal Thunder announced, "The Lieutenant passed word. Some is good and some is bad. It's just the way it is in Vietnam."

"First, is the best news. As tragic as it was for Doc Roman, the doctors at Delta Med in Dong Ha said eight of the seriously wounded he helped treat yesterday will survive because of his actions at the river crossing," the Corporal announced.

"We've seen lots of battlefield courage, but we've seen just as much compassion. Doc Roman displayed more courage and compassion than I've ever seen," Clary exclaimed.

It was silent for an extended time before anyone spoke. They were lost in thought.

"Second, is the good news. The Lieutenant will be the acting company commander until a new one's assigned. The company lost a lot of Marines the past few days." Corporal Thunder continued, "but the battalion's coordinating replacements with the division now.

"It may be the Lieutenant becomes the company commander, but no one knows right now," he stated. "Anyway, the company will reorganize once the replacements start reporting in. The reorganization will be based on the ranks of the replacements."

"Jesus, I think this is headin' to you tellin' us we may be split up into other teams," Hawkins blurted. He stretched and shrugged his shoulders. Hawkins sat up while rubbing his temples. He was easing into a late afternoon reveille while easing out of his nudity and into a clean uniform.

"Well, to be honest, it may happen because there's now a lot of experience and skills in this team that might be needed in other teams," Corporal Thunder replied. "The company just lost a lot of good Marines and docs. We lost too many officers and small unit leaders, too.

"But the Lieutenant told me later he'll do his best to keep us together. He knows we're good. He knows he can trust us," he continued. "He said he can't make any promises, but he really wants to keep us together if he can. But he says he wants us to help build up the other teams. He wants us to be a good example for the new teams to be formed."

"Well, I hope the Lieutenant keeps the company," Wiley responded, "because a new Captain who doesn't know us just might split us up. He may look at the ranks and amount of time we have in Vietnam and send us here or there or anywhere or everywhere."

"Okay, let's don't worry about it. There's nothing we can do about it," Corporal Thunder admonished. "Let's keep doing good and see what happens. I'll do my best to keep us a team."

"Hell, if that's the good news I don't know if I wanta hear the bad news," Hawkins muttered. "Us maybe splittin' up ain't exactly givin' me a warm fuzzy cozy feelin'."

"Yeah, you're right," Corporal Thunder responded, "but at least the Lieutenant will do his best. If a new Captain comes in the Lieutenant may become the executive officer or come back to the platoon and that'll be good for the platoon and us, too."

"Okay, you and Wiley are eternal optimists," Hawkins chided, "but I sure hope you're right. I don't want us to be split apart." Hawkins was momentarily consumed by break-up thoughts.

"The worst part is we have so damn much to worry about and now we have to worry about this," Clary finally stated. "I really hope we stay together." Clary was equally disturbed by a possible split-up of the team. Despite the first sunny day in ages, they were consumed by gloom.

"Well, that's the company reorganization news," Corporal Thunder frowned and hesitated. "Now for the bad news and this is really bad, but we all need to know about it because rumors will really be flying according to the Lieutenant. The Lieutenant said he doesn't know all the details yet, but he told us what the battalion knows for now."

Corporal Thunder inhaled and exhaled before continuing, "I don't know how else to say it but to just say it. So, here goes. The explosion at the river crossing yesterday that killed and wounded so many was bombs from a Marine aircraft. It was friendly fire. It was our bombs."

Hesitating even longer, he finally added, "It was most likely two or more five hundred pound bombs, which is why it was so powerful. It was an accident, but a horrible one.

"The division's initiating an investigation with the air wing, but that'll take time," Corporal Thunder asserted to complete the update as quickly as possible, "but it won't change nothing."

"Jesus, it was friendly fire from one of our Marine pilots. Hard to understand how that could happen," Hawkins mumbled. "Survivin' this war is just a lotta luck and just a lotta fate."

"It's takes a lot of prayers, too," Wiley added. "A whole lot of prayers."

"Yeah, the Lieutenant called it the 'Fog of War.' He said it was probably because of miscommunication or miscalculation, but it happens sometimes," Corporal Thunder explained.

"The Lieutenant later said the pilot may have been supporting us the day before and dropping bombs in the area," he remarked. "He said he thought the pilot probably remembered we were going south so when he saw a unit going north he might have thought it was the NVA. He didn't know we'd turned around to go north.

"The truth is no one knows for sure until the investigation is done," the Corporal conceded. "So, let's stop guessing and stop the rumors. Let's just pray it doesn't happen again."

"Let's pray for the pilot, too," Wiley requested, "because I'm sure he never wanted it to happen. Now he'll have to live with it. That'll be hard. It'd be hard for any of us."

Hawkins started to speak and the team cringed. They expected a typical Hawkins tirade, but Hawkins spoke slowly and softly, "Jesus, Wiley, you're right. I feel bad for the pilot. He didn't mean to do it. It was just an accident. Good people are doing a lotta good, but sometimes bad just happens to the good. Bad just up and kicks us square in the ass. It's a bad part of this bad war."

Unknown to them, the friendly fire incident unnerved their parents. Although the media stories usually avoided mentioning specific units, their parents knew from their letters home the general location in which they were operating. More than one mother monitored the unit's location with maps and articles they clipped from newspapers and magazines. Parents of those in war also suffer. They suffer in unique ways and their sacrifices are beyond belief.

The friendly fire incident investigation was conducted and completed a month or so later. Corporal Thunder and his team, however, never heard the results. "What happens just happens. Let's just move on," Corporal Thunder recommended, which was what they did. The investigation report was released, but by then they were moving on. They were always moving on. It was what they did. It was what they did to survive. They moved on.

Although the company sustained serious personnel losses, its patrolling missions remained constant. Instead of a lighter schedule of patrols due to the killed and wounded, those surviving simply carried a heavier load. The patrol schedule intensified until new replacements arrived. As the Christmas holiday approached, however, replacements were unlikely until later in January. The replacement delays were disheartening. The patrols were demanding.

"Ain't this gonna be one helluva Christmas," Hawkins predicted in an evening bunker talk. "Ain't this war the shits." The team glanced around the bunker's dirt and darkness and agreed.

"Yeah, Santa's coming to town soon, but I'm not expecting any presents," Clary admitted.

"Well, we may get an unexpected present," Corporal Thunder smiled.

The team immediately focused on Corporal Thunder. "If I get nothin' it'll be more than I'm expectin'," Hawkins moaned. "But what's this about an unexpected somethin'?"

"Well, evidently there's been articles in the newspapers back home about the U.S. and North Vietnamese governments talking about a cease-fire during the holidays," Corporal Thunder stated. "The Lieutenant talked about it at a meeting today and said they've been negotiating about it for awhile."

"Damn, what's to negotiate?" Wiley asked in a tone of bewilderment. "Who'd oppose a ceasefire? Who'd be against stopping the killings."

"Well, it seems the U.S. and maybe the North Vietnamese are talking about a 72-hour truce or ceasefire for Christmas and New Year's and a six or seven day halt for TET, the Chinese New Year," Corporal Thunder continued. "But the South Vietnamese favors shorter ceasefires."

"Jesus, they can't seem to agree on nothin'," Hawkins injected. "Just can't agree on much but for us to keep shootin' one another. There won't be no real truce or ceasefire until one of us has had enough of the killin'. We ain't quite there yet because we just keep on a killin'."

"It seems neither side trusts the other much," the Corporal finally added. "The NVA thinks we'll use the ceasefire to our advantage and we think they'll do the same."

"How's that," Wiley asked as he knocked caked mud off his boots.

"Think it hell. Think it my ass. I know for a fact the NVA will use it to their advantage," Hawkins accused. "Ain't no doubt in my military mind 'bout that." Hawkins was shying away from Wiley to avoid the blast range of the mud clumps Wiley was hurling in every direction. Hawkins' afternoon combat bath was about to be undone by Wiley.

Corporal Thunder attempted to refocus the talk and answered, "Well, each side claims the other will maybe stop shooting, but they'll move troops and supplies to just get ready to start the fighting back up. They'll just use the time to do what they want without fear of any attacks from the ground or air. The Lieutenant called it a whole lot of political and propaganda posturing."

By now Hawkins was barely listening as he dodged Wiley's flinging mud. "Wiley, I take one bath a month and you're trying to dirty me all up before I feel like a human again."

"Well, maybe I just want to see your scrawny ass all naked again," Wiley grinned. "Just want you to take another bath so you won't forget how to bathe. Just want to see your lily pink ass."

Hawkins thought about a rebuttal, but in seconds the team was in tears laughing.

A few days later Lieutenant Abrahams informed the company a one-day ceasefire was agreed to for Christmas and New Year's and a three day ceasefire for TET.

"How come Jesus and Christians gets only 24 hours for Christmas," Hawkins asked, "and Buddha and the Buddhists get 72 hours for TET? Ain't nothin' fair in war, even in ceasefires.

"Oh, well, it ain't much, but it's more than nothin' and less than somethin'," Hawkins grinned. "A one-day stand down from patrols is fine with me. It's better than no days."

"Maybe so," Clary admonished, "but as you'd say, Hawkins, there ain't nothin' free in Vietnam. It'll cost us something. You wait. I bet it costs us something."

"I bet you're right. I bet it costs us something. The NVA are setting us up big time," Corporal Thunder predicted. "As much as I want one, it's just hard for me to trust the ceasefires."

Corporal Thunder and his team's ceasefire predictions proved correct. The ceasefires were fragile and fraudulent interludes to the war. After each ceasefire the war briefly intensified. The ceasefires were violated, but virtually no one predicted the blatant disregard North Vietnam demonstrated in the TET ceasefire in 1968. The result was the TET Offensive of 1968, which literally doomed the war for the United States.

The TET 1968 ceasefire cost the United States the war. It was a battlefield victory for the United States and South Vietnamese. It was, however, a media and propaganda victory for the North Vietnamese. In time the battlefield victories were far less important than the media and propaganda victories. The war became stranger than they could have ever imagined.

As they concluded the ceasefire talks, Hawkins huddled over a small heat tab and warmed his hands with his hot canteen cup. "Damned if life ain't becoming one long, rainy, cold, miserable patrol," Hawkins asserted and grinned. "We just keep a patrollin' and a patrollin', but I snuck in a nap in the sun today while it was out. Just needed to dry out. It was kinda cool, but the sun felt good. I did it combat style so's I wouldn't have a bikini sun tan line." The Marines smiled while attempting to avoid any mental picture of Hawkins in a bikini.

The Marines' patrols continued. The monsoon rains persisted. The cold dampness endured. The miseries intensified. Two days before Christmas, Corporal Thunder sharpened his machete while reminding the team, "In two days, just in case you forgot, it'll be Christmas." He sat on a bunker sandbag in the misty drizzle as he glanced north up the valley. It was too warm to snow, but so cool he tightened his collar for warmth while humming Elvis' *Blue Christmas* song.

"Yeah, in case you forgot, remember I'm trying to forget Christmas," Hawkins quipped. He was occupied with repairing a broken pack strap. This year Christmas was broken for him, too.

"Okay, Scrooge, but remember the ceasefire." Corporal Thunder smiled. "The Lieutenant says some of us can take the resupply convoy back to the rear for a break on Christmas Eve," he slyly grinned. "The Lieutenant also has a request or a duty for us."

"Yeah, here it comes. Somebody gets to go to the rear and somebody gets to do an extra duty," Hawkins lamented. "Ain't Vietnam just one good deal and one good duty after another?"

"Seriously, this is a good duty and a good deal," Corporal Thunder insisted. "Here's the deal. The Lieutenant wants us who go to the rear to go over to Delta Med and check on the platoon casualties. Now how hard is that? Some of us gets to check on Sergeant Swede and others."

"Who you thinking should go?" Wiley asked curiously looking up from his scripture reading.

"Well, the Lieutenant more or less asked me to stay to help Corporal Cozart. You know Corporal Cozart's pretty new to our platoon and Vietnam," Corporal Thunder answered.

"So, Clary and me think you and Hawkins should go," he persisted. "You're the assistant team leader and the Lieutenant likes the idea of you and Hawkins going instead of two PFC's. Besides, Hawkins will need a little adult supervision."

"You sure you don't want to go?" Wiley asked as he folded his pocket Bible.

"I'm sure. The company is kind of short on small unit leaders and experience right now. I think the Lieutenant will feel more comfortable if I stayed," the Corporal responded.

"Well, I'm not really into babysitting Hawkins for a day," Wiley grinned, "but I guess somebody has to do it." He was eager to spend a night in the rear; to escape the front for a day.

"Okay, that settles that," Corporal Thunder shrugged. "You'll go in early on Christmas Eve day and return later on Christmas Day. That's a Christmas gift. There's a Santa after all."

"Yeah, well I just hope we don't get mortared and rocketed like we did the last time we were in Dong Ha," Hawkins groused. "That'll just be my luck. Hope there's no Christmas Grinch."

"You shouldn't," Corporal Thunder replied. "Remember the holiday ceasefire?"

"Jesus, you're not thinkin' I'm trustin' the NVA are you?" Hawkins frowned. "They're the Christmas grinches for sure. They're probably waiting to put coal in my stocking.

"By the way, is the 24-hour ceasefire on Christmas Eve or Christmas Day?" Hawkins added. "When does it start and when does it end?"

Corporal Thunder smiled, "I'm not sure, but I think Christmas day. You might find out."

"Damn, that's comfortin'," Hawkins nodded. "That's just comfortin' as all hell."

"We have one other topic to talk about," Corporal Thunder mentioned. "Remember when we talked about asking for information about this war? Remember we wanted to write to ask our parents or someone who might help us try to learn about limited war?

"I'm starting to receive some stuff and I hope you are, too," he said before anyone answered.

"Yeah, my dad's sent me several letters and small packages from professors he works with at the university," Clary confirmed. "I'm saving them for when we start our talks on the war."

Hawkins added, "Yeah, I'm getting stuff, too. I'm ready to start learning and maybe help."

"My dad's collected and mailed some information, too," Wiley reported. "It may help."

"Okay, that's just what I wanted to know. That's what I was hoping," Corporal Thunder said. "Let's review it and plan on talking about it after the holidays. It's just been so busy lately we haven't had time, but let's make time in January." Understanding the war remained a team goal.

On Christmas Eve, Wiley and Hawkins visited the Dong Ha rear. They joked they were traveling for the holidays on a holiday excursion.

What they witnessed in Dong Ha, however, was anything but a holiday. It was anything but an excursion.

Hawkins later declared, "It was an exorcism of sorts."

What they witnessed became a soulful part of them forever. It was neither spiritual nor blasphemous. It was simply another acquaintance with the brutality and the finality of death. A death they were struggling to avoid, but a death that constantly shadowed and haunted them. Their dealings with death, however, only intensified their gritty determination to survive.

Wiley and Hawkins arrived at the Mike Company rear mid-morning Christmas Eve. First Sergeant Sharp greeted them and had his driver standing by to take them to Delta Med.

The jeep ride to Delta Med was only minutes. What Wiley and Hawkins witnessed, however, would remain with them for an eternity. They would remember it throughout their lives. It was as depressing as it was inspiring. It was as casual as it was intense. It was a reawakening to the vitality of the human spirit. It was a rebellion against the irrevocable consequences of death. It was a morning of contradictions and contrasts as well as affirmations and conformations.

The brutality of the battlefield had acquainted them with death; it had prepared them for death. So Wiley and Hawkins were initially unfazed by what they saw. They learned, however, death was a mysterious phenomenon the living confront with enduring defiance. They learned the will to live dissolves only with death. Until then, the human spirit and human will fight with incredible courage and compassion. While they sensed this in battle, the fullness of their beliefs could only be validated by the emptiness of death itself. Today, death emptied them.

Wiley and Hawkins agreed to defer sharing their thoughts about what they observed until they were reunited with Corporal Thunder and Clary. They simply had to emotionally process their sightings with their sentiments. They simply needed time to think solitarily before talking collectively. They needed the team because it was too surreal for only the two of them.

Returning to the Mike Company area after their hospital visit, Wiley and Hawkins were overwhelmed with the visit. They shared diverse thoughts, but their most challenging thought was to think of the night as Christmas Eve. It was simply the most impossible and improbable thought imaginable. The reality was, however, it actually was Christmas Eve. Tomorrow, it was Christmas Day, but there was no joy or enthusiasm for the holiday. "It's just another joyless day in Vietnam," Wiley frowned, "but there's joy in surviving. Let's take that joy and hold on to it."

Hawkins expressed it best or worst, "Ain't this the shits. The war and death are replacin' Christmas and the birth as our holiday thoughts. It's the damnedest holidays I've ever had."

After a night to recover from their hospital visit, Wiley declared the next morning, "I'm not letting the NVA and this war spoil Christmas. I'm going to think good thoughts and be thankful."

Hawkins smiled and added, "Wiley, you just won't let all the bad keep you from feeling good. Today I'm with you. Let's make the best of it and be thankful we're okay."

Once Corporal Thunder, Wiley, Hawkins, and Clary were reunited in their bunker later that evening, Corporal Thunder asked, "Well, how was the visit to Delta Med and the rear?"

Wiley and Hawkins glanced at one another in doubt as to where and how to begin. Wiley finally spoke, "Sergeant Swede's been medevaced to Da Nang. The First Sergeant doesn't know if he'll make it. His chest wound is bad and he needs treatment not available in Dong Ha."

"Yeah, the First Sergeant says he had to transfer his records," Hawkins added. "It may be hard now to track him in the evacuation pipeline, as he called it, but he'll do his best for us."

"We saw Rogers, too," Wiley reported. "You remember the new Marine we met in the rear."

"Yeah, I remember," Corporal Thunder remarked, "He went to first platoon, right?"

"Yep, first platoon," Hawkins continued, "he took an AK47 round in the right shoulder, but he'll be okay in a month or so. He'll be back." Wiley and Hawkins then paused in seriousness.

"Wiley and me saw things we wished we'd never seen," Hawkins finally admitted.

Clary started to ask, "What?" but quickly decided to wait while they collected themselves.

"As we were arriving at Delta Med they began clanging of an ole 105mm artillery casing," Wiley began. "At first we thought it was incoming, but the corpsman was yelling 'inbound'."

"Yeah, we didn't quite know what the hell that meant," Hawkins confessed, "but we learned it was inbound emergency medevac helos with wounded Marines and not incoming rockets."

"Yeah, and these were really bad cases, too," Wiley sighed remembering the corpsmen quickly unloading the casualties from the helos and racing them into the hospital. "One Marine on a stretcher had his trousers stripped off and tied around his stomach to hold in his intestines from a gut wound. He was bleeding awful and stuffing his guts back toward his stomach."

"Jesus, it looked like one of those Bouncin' Betty mines that's buried in the ground, but when you step on it the damn thing pops up about waist or shoulder high before it explodes," Hawkins exclaimed. "Damn, it tore the Marine apart. It was a basketball-size gut wound."

"He had to be in shock and a lot of pain," Wiley added, "but he was doing his best to hold his guts in with his hands and keep them from falling out any more. It was really gory and nasty."

"He was fightin' to live." Hawkins declared. "You talk about the will to live. You have a gut wound like that you gotta know you're probably gonna die, but he was fightin' to live.

"Jesus, I guess we learned the stupid ass truce musta been only for Christmas day, because it was Christmas Eve and the NVA were getting' in their last killin's before the ceasefire," Hawkins proclaimed. "Ceasefire my ass. Ask those wounded Marines about a ceasefire."

"We saw another Marine who'd stepped on a mine or something," Wiley continued, "because one foot was so mangled and bandaged we couldn't see how bad the wounds were. But the other foot was missing all the toes and front part of the foot. It was just a heel and a stump."

"Yeah, but the Marine was pissed off," Hawkins shrugged. "He was probably in shock and the doc's had maybe morphined him up to ease the pain, but the Marine kept trying to get off the stretcher. He kept saying he needed to get back to his buddies to help'em kick some NVA asses. He was madder than hell and they finally had to tie him down to keep him down."

"I been in lotta fights. I been knocked down lotta times, but I wouldn't wanta ever have to fight that Marine," Hawkins paused before continuing. "Ain't nobody keepin' him down. Ain't nobody. He'll just keep comin' till either you was down and didn't get up or till he was dead. He'll probably live, but livin'll never be the same for him."

Silence descended as the Marines reflected on the sights and thoughts Wiley and Hawkins were expressing. "Corporal Thunder, you and Clary could never begin to picture the scenes we saw. Don't even try because we don't want you to ever have to see them," Hawkins lamented. "It was bad enough Wiley and me saw them. We're sorry to tell you, but we gotta talk to someone."

Corporal Thunder laid his hand on Hawkins' shoulder and softly squeezed, "It's okay."

The team slowly glanced at one another in an expression of support and understanding. It was Christmas and they were the only family they had with whom to share this special day of days.

"A lot of those Marines probably died," Wiley guessed. "It has to be terrible to die on Christmas. Think about the dads and moms and families who'll be notified over the holidays that their son was killed on Christmas. Others might live, but their bodies will be broken and their minds shattered forever. The holidays will never be the same. There'll always be the sadness." It was a somber and solemn thought. Families ravaged at Christmas...*forever.*

"We saw something else that made us mad as hell at first, but it was kind of funny, too," Wiley allowed the mood to settle before shifting to another subject. He was dubious about sharing it, but felt compelled to divulge it. "As we watched we sort of understood what was happening and why. It was funny in a really sad way." What they witnessed underscored the complexity of war and death and the simplicity of death and dying; of surviving and living.

"Jesus, we were leavin' the hospital after checking on our wounded and seeing all those emergency medevacs. Then we saw something we thought we'd never see," Hawkins continued.

"We were walking out the side of the hospital to find the vehicle and we came to the outdoor morgue. We got kinda lost in the hospital and went out the wrong exit, but I hope I never get to know it too good, especially the morgue," Wiley added. "It was just big ole metal conex boxes or containers, but they seemed refrigerated for dead bodies. They were crude and rusty boxes, too."

"Anyway, one Corpsman was sorta taking a role call or muster of the dead. He'd call a name, 'Smith', for example, and the other Corpsman would answer 'here'," Hawkins frowned. "He'd answer like he was a puppet or ventriloquist for the dead. It seemed to me at first that they were mocking the dead and making fun of the killed." Hawkins' fists clinched as he remembered the absurdity of the scene. Meanwhile, Wiley patted the Bible in his pocket for reassurance that there was a God and that God was good despite man's evil killing.

"They were like playing Dean Martin and Jerry Lewis or maybe Abbott and Costello. They were playing off one another and joking around," Hawkins disgustedly proclaimed. "It was like a little theater comedy routine with the poor dead as stage props."

"Hawkins started to confront the corpsmen, but I held out my arm to hold him back," Wiley continued, "and told him we should just watch for a minute or so. Well, we learned what they were doing was serious, but that it had to be seriously depressing work."

"Yeah, if I had to do what they were doing it'd drive me crazy." Hawkins intervened. "They weren't making a joke of the dead. They were just trying to forget how terrible it was what they was doing. They were trying to survive this damn war in their own damn way. We all just gotta find our own ways to survive the ugliness."

"After each roll call they'd go into the metal container and bring out a dead body on a stretcher," Wiley added. "The corpsmen would then lay the dead body on a long piece of corrugated sheet metal. It was just metal siding like our chicken house roof back in Mississippi."

"The sheet metal plank sat on two old wooden saw horses. Once the body was laid out, they cut off the uniform and boots and the body was naked. Then you could really see the wounds and all the torn and bloodied mess," Hawkins flinched involuntarily.

"But then they'd do the damnedest thing," Wiley continued. "There was a fifty-five gallon barrel on about an eight-foot wooden platform built from two-by-four lumber. At the bottom of the barrel was a garden hose. Golly, we had better on the farm in Mississippi."

"One corpsman would release a clamp on the hose to let the water run by gravity. The other corpsman would wash off the mud and blood from the body. You'll never guess what they used to wash off the bodies," Hawkins frowned. "It was a damned ole toilet brush. You know, the kinds with the hard bristles for scrubbing. The blood and mess was dried and caked. It took hard scrubbing to clean them. They'd scrub those bodies clean with a toilet brush of all things."

"Yeah, it seemed awfully crude, but it worked. But don't ever look at the foot end of the corrugated metal. It was kind of elevated on one end at the head," Wiley nodded. "The blood and mud and maybe a few small body parts would fall into the grooves and just be washed away to the foot end. It was crude and sickening, but it worked, too.

"Once the bodies were cleaned, the corpsmen would respectfully place them in body bags and powder them good. Then they'd place them back in the metal containers," Wiley added. "Later, the corpsmen said they'd be shipped to Saigon for later transport back to the states."

"Then, I understood the muster or roll call thing. Jesus, you'd have to do something to maybe help you laugh or to distract you from the ugliness of handling dead bodies all day," Hawkins confessed. "I sure wouldn't wanna have to do that all day. Not any damned day."

"At the end, we decided it was an ugly duty, but the corpsmen were doing it as respectfully as they could under the circumstances," Wiley added.

"I respect them for doin' it, but I don't wanna ever do that duty," Hawkins sighed.

Wiley and Hawkins concluded their report. The team reminisced about it briefly, but it was too gruesome to talk about for too long. By then it was late. It was raining, but they barely noticed. It was always raining. It was cold, too, which they always noticed. They shivered and their trembling reminded them of the cold. Although miserable, Wiley's and Hawkins' account of their visit to Dong Ha and Delta Med convinced them how blessed they were to be alive. In their thoughts the purity of life trumped the pollution of death.

Christmas evening was anything but one of good tidings and good cheer, but it soon vanished into the dark night. Tomorrow, the holiday mirth and mysterious ceasefire would be in the past. Tomorrow, a patrol was in their future. Gradually, they remembered they were in Vietnam. They were confused as to how they could momentarily forget. Suddenly, they remembered they were in war. The war was hard to forget, too. The spirit of Christmas, however, was alive in them as they struggled to live their lives in the horrors and deaths of the war.

"Well, in less than a week we'll have another ceasefire and maybe another day of no patrols. It'll be another holiday," Wiley reminded the team as they prepared for watches and sleeps.

"Yeah, well, you just remind me the day before 'cause I'll be sheltering in my bunker all day. The NVA cheat on those ceasefires. I seen the proof, too. Don't talk to me about ceasefires. We're the only ones not firin'. Jesus, we cease and they fire. How 'bout that? The NVA's a firin' and we're a ceasin'. Ain't that a helluva ceasefire? Wait'll I tell the Pentagon about their ceasefire," Hawkins ranted.

A week later, New Year's Eve was celebrated and the ceasefire was again criticized. It was a new year; however, the old war persisted.

CHAPTER 15

New Year & Old War

It's just that everything's pretty easy or simple in theory or in books. But it's damn hard and just plain complicated on the battlefield. It's just hard as hell to take good theories and good words and fight a bad war with them.

—Marine Private First Class Brad Clary

"Well, it's a new year. It's 1967 and it's going to be a good year, too," Wiley exclaimed.

It was minutes after midnight in their Payable bunker. Depressingly dark and dank, it was nonetheless a holiday and the team had stayed awake to celebrate New Year's Eve together. C-Ration cakes and Bug Juice were the celebrations main fare. "Ain't this a helluva celebration," Hawkins proclaimed. "It's the worst New Year's Eve ever, but with the best ever friends.

"Yeah, it's a new year, but it's the same old Vietnam," he continued. "So, what's so good about that, Wiley? We're gonna be patrollin' everyday, too. You gonna tell me that's good, too?"

"What's good is we can finally say this is the year we're going home," Wiley replied. "This year we're going home. We've been waiting since last summer, waiting for about six months, for January. Now, it's January and it's our year to go home. We've made it to 1967. This summer we're going home." Simply mentioning "we're going home" caused the team to briefly suspend all talk. In the cold and musty bunker thoughts of home and family overcame them.

"Jesus, Wiley, we ain't even half way through our thirteen month tours and you're talking about going home," Hawkins groaned. "You must be half crazy." He lifted his canteen cup and toasted, "But, Wiley, I must be the other half of your crazy." Sipping Kool Aid, they smiled while Hawkins pretended it was intoxicating.

"Well, tell me you don't think about going home every single day," Wiley joked.

"Yep, you got me there," Hawkins shrugged. "I think about it everyday and twice on Sundays. Maybe I think about it so much I can't even count how many times I think about it."

It was a new year, but the old patrols. The January patrols continued as they had since the previous summer. The patrols were the unrelenting one constant in their lives. A new dimension to their patrols, however, was about to emerge.

Initially, Corporal Thunder, Wiley, Hawkins, and Clary were confused by the war, which caused them to become resolute in their quest to understand it. The journey was a torturous and complicated one, but they began with plain and simple questions during nightly bunker talks.

While cleaning weapons and conducting housekeeping duties later that week, Corporal Thunder called a team meeting to begin their war talks. Without much prelude, they simply began talks they would continue for months. The talks began innocently and partly because of the guilt of their misunderstanding. Initially, the talks were disjointed and disorganized, but that was Clary's plan. It was the plan his dad had suggested to him.

"Jesus, I just don't get it. How can a world superpower like us not just kick the ass of a backwater country like Vietnam?" Hawkins declared. "They got nowhere near any the military strength of us, but we fiddle and fart around and sort of hold back on using our power. It's just damn frustratin'." Hawkins was bitterly opposed to fighting less than one's best.

"Well, I agree," Clary observed. "It's hard for us to limit the use of our power in limited war, especially when we have so much. The enemy's not stopping us. We're stopping us."

"What does he really mean by limited war?" Wiley asked. "I just thought war was war. I didn't know there were other types." The complexities of war were confusing to the team.

"I thought the same," Clary confessed, "but my dad tells me there are total wars, wars of annihilation, wars of attrition, wars of deterrence, civil wars, insurgent wars, preemptive wars, and others I can't recall right now. There's lots of types of war with lots of different strategies and policies for each of them."

"Well, that's why we're asking for help," Corporal Thunder emphasized. "Fighting it's hard, but understanding it's just as hard or maybe even harder. It's hard and confusing." Shaking his head in bewilderment, he exhaled loudly.

"Jesus, I always thought that we'd just fight until one had enough of the beat downs and throwed in the towel to surrender or quit like in boxin'," Hawkins injected. "Then we'd have a winner and a loser. Then the war would be over." War was initially that simple to Hawkins.

"Yeah, but it seems nothing's ever over in war," the Corporal commented. "We mostly just take a break and come back to fighting again and again. It seems someone's always fighting someone about something."

Relatively unstructured and unsophisticated, the talks initially generated more questions and confusion than answers and clarity. Clary asked for a halt exclaiming, "Okay, what's happening is what my dad said would happen. He said we'd just charge off and throw out a lot of opinions and express our frustrations and accomplish nothing. Nothing except sort of let ourselves start to know this won't be easy.

"My dad told me to let us run with it at first and then reel us in," Clary admitted, "and then to explain to everyone two basic points for us to keep in mind during our talks. If we remember these two points, my dad says, it will help us have better talks and better understand war."

Nodding in agreement and for Clary to continue, the team sensed it had been a rough start and that they needed to improve their approach and format for expressing their thoughts.

"First, my dad says we need to understand one of Karl von Clausewitz's fundamental beliefs about war," Clary continued. "Clausewitz was an iconic theorist on war who wrote, *War is relatively simple in theory, but exceedingly complex in its execution.* I think the point is that if we try to make this easy we'll fail because it's going to be really hard. My dad also cautions us not to confuse theory with execution and that will really help us better understand both.

"Second, my dad says there are many intriguing moral dilemmas associated with war and that many of these are accentuated by limited war," Clary related. "He warns us not to get too hung up on the dilemmas now, but to keep them in mind as we talk and think about war.

"In summary," Clary concluded, "we need to always distinguish between the simple theories of war and its complex execution as well as gain an appreciation for the moral dilemmas of war."

It was these concerns and questions they delved into throughout January and the coming months. In their frequent bunker talks and during their patrol breaks, they shared thoughts on war. Although they never became political theorists, military strategists, or philosophical moralists, they began their journey to learn what they could about the war they were fighting.

"Clary's college professor dad is probably our best source of information and our best guide," Corporal Thunder admitted after their first bunker talk. "So, we'll sort of trust and depend on Clary to be our visiting professor. We'll listen and then talk." The team stared into the darkness wondering if they would ever understand the darkness of Vietnam.

Clary continued the team's quest for understanding in another January talk before their night watches by asserting, "I don't think I really know what the hell I'm doing. Corporal Thunder's asked us to team up to understand Vietnam. Truth is, I don't understand it any more than any of us, but I asked my dad for help." Clary was obviously apprehensive but willing.

They all appealed to Clary to persuade him to simply do his best and they would do their best. It was irascible Hawkins who was probably the most convincing. "Clary, you know me and how I feel about fightin' and this war. You know my thoughts and ideas about just squarin' off and just throwin' haymakers," Hawkins confided. "You know, too, that if my suggestions ever become Pentagon policies or the general's strategies that we'll probably be in World War III in a heartbeat. Jesus, listen to me and I'll have us in the next big one, a really big one, and really fast." Hawkins delivered a roundhouse punch into thin air and collapsed pretending a knockout.

"You know I only know one way to fight. Fight till the last man's standin'." Hawkins paused. "But I think I may be learnin' from what you're sayin' about limited war is that it's a type of war that you have to pull a few punches and maybe throw a few rounds. You have to do that to win because if you just pound someone you may win but you really lose. It's hard to understand how kickin' someone's ass really bad can come to no good, but I'm willin' to learn and understand."

"Okay, but understand I may sometimes just be a page ahead of you in the lecture book. Maybe sometimes a page behind the class outline," Clary confessed. "Hell, truth is, I don't have a book or outline. I just have letters and papers from my dad. If you have questions I probably won't know the answers, but maybe we can talk them through.

"Okay, let's start tonight with what my dad says is a good starting point," Clary noted as he read by flashlight from his dad's letter and papers. "It's important to understand that war is first and foremost more political than military. It involves diplomatic policies as well as military strategies. These sometimes competing interests must inevitably be reconciled and resolved.

"This complicates diplomacy and war and the prosecution of both." Clary paused to collect himself as he reviewed his dad's papers. "Nation's have a responsibility to peace and to freedom as well as to protect their interests and security. While diplomacy is the preferred action, war is sometimes necessary. It's sometimes more than necessary. It's a responsibility, especially if another nation wants to deny us freedom.

"If we want to be free and independent, we sometimes have to fight for them. Why? It's because throughout history there's always someone who wants to take away our freedoms and liberties or cause us harm," Clary continued. "We sometimes have a responsibility to those freedoms to fight for them. It's that or live in bondage or in slavery or controlled by someone. Maybe it's a king or a dictator or despot or someone who wants power over us."

"What do you mean when you say war is more political than military?" Wiley asked.

"My dad gave me two quotes that can maybe help explain," Clary answered as he referred to the literature his dad had provided him. "One is by an ancient Chinese warlord named Sun Tzu. In about 400 B.C., he wrote that war is of vital importance to the state. My dad told me to note that Sun Tzu didn't say war was vital to the military or the economy or the politicians or whoever or whatever."

Clary softly inhaled and exhaled while Corporal Thunder, Wiley, and Hawkins considered his Sun Tzu quote. He sensed them wrestling with the concept, but he nervously pressed forward.

"My dad's second quote is another one from Clausewitz," Clary exclaimed. "My dad says that Clausewitz is probably the classic theorist on war. Maybe his most renowned theory, according to my dad, is that the military is an instrument of policy and is therefore an extension of politics by other means. So, war is an extension or the continuation of politics.

"I think this means politicians decide if a nation goes to war and what the policies and political objectives are for the war," Clary added. "Then the generals develop the military strategies and tactics for achieving the political objectives. It seems kind of contrary to what I've always thought, but in war the political considerations are dominant and the military ones subservient."

"Jesus, I bet that's frustrating to the generals," Hawkins quipped, "but it's probably just as frustratin' to the politicians, too. Hell, it's a lot more frustratin' to us fightin' the war.

"I'm havin' a hard time, for example, understandin' when we were down south why that religious site and certain villages were off limits to us, especially when we kinda knew they weren't off limits to the VC," he explained. "It was a disadvantage to us and advantage to the VC.

"Don't they understand whenever they limit us or give us a disadvantage that there's consequences to us?" Hawkins continued. "Bad consequences. Dead's a pretty bad consequence. Yep, dead's pretty damn bad."

"I guess that's what limited war really means," Wiley responded. "There's just limitations on what we can and can't do. We had off limits areas down south? We had counter-battery restrictions at Con Thien. We just had to take it and it cost us Marines. Those were bad consequences and hard to understand."

"Yeah, and what about limitations on attacking or bombing major NVA base camps and supply and ammo sites in Cambodia, Laos, and North Vietnam?" Corporal Thunder declared. "It seems that sometimes we can't really strike the ones that'll hurt the enemy the most."

"Jesus, ain't that the truth The limitations are just one big kabuki dance. We just tip toe and lightly kabuki dance around targets we should be stomping to holy hell. We're dancin' this little ballet with soft slippers and the NVA is Texas two-stepping the hell out of us with clod hoppers," Hawkins groaned in a tirade. "The Pentagon and the politicians need to figure out if this is a real war or a phony kabuki dance. I'll fight like hell if it's a war. I'll dance like hell if it's a dance. But I ain't fightin' at a dance and I ain't dancin' at a fight. Let's call it what it is. Let's get on with it.

Fightin' or dancin'." Hawkins then danced a few jigs and threw a few jabs in exasperation.

"Hell, don't forget the ceasefires," he added as an afterthought. "The ceasefires are bullshit. We're the ones ceasin' and the NVA's the ones firin'. We're supposed to fight by the rules, but the NVA don't have no rules. We have limits, but they have none."

In a plain and simple and colorful talk, Clary guided the team to the central issues of limited war. While they were only beginning their study of war, they identified the key concerns of scholars and intellectuals and professionals. But they approached them as Marine infantrymen; as those who fought and died in the conundrum of limited war. "Theories and principles are good, but when they cause us fightin' to die they ain't so good. They're damned bad," Hawkins groaned.

Corporal Thunder identified one of their most challenging issues by declaring, "It's total war for us fighting in war because it's often life or death for us. It's total for us. Nothing's more total than death. It may be limited war for the politicians and generals, but it's total for us."

"Jesus, this is scorching my brain," Hawkins decried. "I'm thinkin' we're sacrificin' and sufferin' for limited war, but I'm thinkin' we shouldn't be so limited or restricted we fight from bad positions. It seems limited war sometimes makes war harder and harder for us to fight, but maybe it helps keep the war from becomin' a bigger and bigger or worse and worse war. Jesus, talk about a riddle. War's easy with words, but hard with weapons and harder with bad policies."

"Okay, I believe that's enough for tonight. That's enough for now," Clary remarked. "We're doing better. Let's take a break and think about our questions and issues for next time."

"These talks are better than I thought they'd be," Hawkins admitted. "I thought we'd mostly be complain' and bitchin' 'bout the war. I was thinkin' we'd get too much into questionin' the war. But good questions are good. They're helping us." He then paused before startling the team.

"In about 800 B. C., in *The Iliad*, Homer wrote: 'Our business in the field of fight is not to question, but to fight'," Hawkins said as he quoted Homer, "So, I was a thinkin' we should fight rather than question. We're here to fight and that's our business, but questions help us fight better. I'm now okay with the questions, but I still like the fightin' part best."

The team stared at Hawkins in complete bewilderment. "Hawkins is quoting Homer," Clary finally said in pure astonishment. "Hawkins and Homer in the same sentence are unbelievable."

"Yeah, first it's Shakespeare and now it's Homer," Wiley laughed and asked, "Who's it going to be next? Maybe the Pope. Maybe the Godfather."

Hawkins remained silent while noting the team was somewhat dumbfounded, which was the effect he wanted. Orneriness personified him and presenting an ole Italian, uneducated, poor boy persona, was fun for Hawkins. Yet, he was smarter than he wanted them to know, especially with his sister's help with famous quotes, which she mailed to him every month or so. Sometimes baffling and sometimes transparent, Hawkins was always mysterious to the team.

Homer and Shakespeare validated the baffling character of Hawkins and the war. Hawkins never revealed the mystery. His sister remained his secret scholar and his co-conspirator. She never knew how Hawkins used her quotes she mailed him, but she suspected the quotes would become part of his mystique. Maria knew her brother well.

"Okay, now we've really had a good night and it really is a good place to stop for now," Corporal Thunder pleaded. "We'll have Homer, I mean Hawkins, lead us next time."

Laughing the team ceased its talk and started preparing for their night activities. The thoughts and questions they discussed, however, became reoccurring ones until Clary resumed their talks days later. To ease the stress of their talk on war, the team played poker with M14 rounds as chips. Hawkins always won at poker. Clary was suspicious, but Wiley simply accepted Hawkins as a bona fide, but honest card shark…at least honest while playing with the team.

Meanwhile, they patrolled in the monsoons and the cold and the miseries of Vietnam and war. Curiously, they were warmed by their heated discussions on limited war and their attempts to understand it. Yet, the war remained foreign to them. The war was changing them; however, they were determined to change the war, too.

"Okay, gather round and listen up," Corporal Thunder announced as he slipped on the muddy hillside and fell into the bunker head first. The team huddled in the bunker as Hawkins was squeezed and forced closer to Clary by Corporal Thunder's acrobatic spill into the dark bunker.

"Hawkins, can't you give me a little space?" Clary urged jokingly.

"Jesus, pardon the hell outta me. Maybe I'll just set over on the sofa. Wait! We don't got a sofa. Okay, maybe the Lazy Boy. Oops! No Lazy Boy. Well, maybe the chaises lounge. Nope, don't got one of them either," Hawkins teased. "All we got's sandbags, ammo cans, helmets, and mud. Guess I'll just nuzzle up to ole Clary." Hawkins affectionately cozied up close to Clary.

Clary leaned over to kiss his forehead. Hawkins quickly gave Clary space...lots of space.

"Okay, you two can have your lover's quarrel later," Corporal Thunder smiled as they all laughed at Hawkins rubbing the kiss from his forehead, "but let's get serious for a minute."

"I'll begin at the top with personnel issues," he began. "Second Lieutenant Abrahams is getting promoted to First Lieutenant the first of February and will remain the company commander. That's good. It means we'll have a better chance of staying together.

"Staff Sergeant Antoine's also getting promoted in February," the Corporal continued. "He's receiving a battlefield commission to Second Lieutenant and will remain as our permanent platoon commander. That's good, too." The team was happy for him and truly respected him.

"Also, Corporal Cozart is on the new promotion list and he'll be promoted to Sergeant this spring sometime," he added, "and he'll remain our squad leader.

"Best is, we'll start receiving a lot of new Marines soon. Most are boot camp grads, but there'll be some Corporals and Sergeants to fill our vacancies," Corporal Thunder explained. "Since I'm a fairly new Corporal, I'll probably do most of my tour as a Corporal. That's good for me because I hope it means I'll stay with this team my whole tour, too.

"The company commander said now that the holidays are over we can expect to start receiving new Marines the middle of January into February," he continued, "and by March we should be at full strength and have our new Marines trained and ready for spring offensives.

"Oh, yeah, in addition to new troops, there's a rumor, a pretty good one, too, that we may be getting a new rifle sometime this spring," Corporal Thunder recalled. "We'll get more updates on the new rifle later. But that's what I know for now." He patted the stock of his M14 with true affection. Transferring to a new rifle would be disappointing for him and for the team.

"Since we expect to be back at good strength in February," Corporal Thunder added, "the First Sergeant will start coordinating our R & R or Rest & Relaxations, with us in a month or so. The word is once we have about six or seven months in country we're eligible."

"Well, I'm thinking of passing on R & R," Wiley announced. They all looked at Wiley in absolute astonishment. Except for those killed or wounded, R & R was about the only way, the best way, to escape Vietnam. It was a temporary escape, but it was an escape.

"Jesus, Wiley, are you crazy?" Hawkins asked. "The Marines will fly you free to Bangkok or Hawaii or Hong Kong or wherever you want to go on the list. It's a free week of girls and beers and just gettin' outta this shithole. I can't wait to get the hell outta here for a week."

"Well, I'm saving my money," Wiley replied, "because my dad wrote and told me our church was vandalized and robbed. It needs a new piano and repairs. I want to help my dad and church."

Corporal Thunder noted the vandalizing and robbing of the church disturbed Wiley and quickly injected, "Well, no one has to decide anything right now because the First Sergeant will get with us later in February to discuss R & R. We got time to think about it.

"Oh, by the way," he remembered, "Staff Sergeant Antoine will take R & R to Hawaii the first week in February to meet his wife. He'll probably get promoted first so he can surprise her with his new rank as a Second Lieutenant.

"Any questions?" Corporal Thunder paused briefly and asked.

"I ain't heard nothin' I particularly want to bitch about," Hawkins smiled. "So far you're doing okay by me. I like best the part about us staying together as long as possible. That's the best part of the news, but it's all good by me. I really liked the part about R & R, too. I'm ready for some beers and girls and no patrols and no incoming mortars...*and no killin's.*"

"What's this about spring offensives?" Clary inquired. "What exactly does that mean?"

"Good question and that's my next news," Corporal Thunder answered, "We got an Army 155mm self-propelled artillery battery, reinforced with some Marine 175mm howitzers, that's moving in with us. It'll be assigned positions near the road where India Company is now."

"When we gonna see them?" Hawkins asked. "And why?"

"We'll see them because all the units on Payable Hill are going to relocate down to the river and bridge to provide security for the Army and Marine artillery," Corporal Thunder replied. "Kilo, Mike, and H&S Company is relocating within the week. It'll be called Payable River."

"Jesus, a new Vietnam address is fine with me," Hawkins mumbled. "I ain't leaving the NVA no forwardin' address either."

"Yeah, we been on this hill too long," Clary added, "but the best part is we'll be close to the river and we'll have fresh water. When the weather turns a little warmer we can take a bath and wash our clothes whenever we want. India Company likes being close to the river."

"Seriously, another reason for the relocation is our battalion's Tactical Area of Responsibility is about to change some," Corporal Thunder reported. "We'll begin to operate more toward the west, more toward the high mountains, more toward Khe Sanh. The Lieutenant says we'll still secure this valley complex and occasionally operate at Con Thien, but we'll probably shift our attention to the west more and more.

"That's why the artillery's moving in with us. The artillery at Camp Carroll to the east of us can't range a lot of the new area out west where we'll be operating this spring," he added. "Now that the Army's here with us, we'll have artillery support deeper and farther into our area of operations." He laid his map on the bunker sandbags and pointed to the new western op area.

"So, we get the artillery so we can go deeper and farther into the most dangerous parts of Vietnam. We get to operate as close to the DMZ, the Vietnamese and Laotian boarders, and the NVA as possible," Hawkins retorted. "We get to advance to where the NVA is strongest and closest to its supply and ammo depots. We get to patrol where the NVA is most protected by its many sanctuaries and off-limit areas.

"Meanwhile, we get to go farther away from our supply lines and support systems," he surmised. "We get to go farther into their strengths and the farther we go the weaker we get. We get to go where we're the least protected and they're most protected."

Hawkins then reverted to Hawkins, "Ain't that a pisser? Ain't that the Marines?" The truth of Hawkins' pessimism was evident. They would be executing ever more dangerous patrols in ever more dangerous areas at ever greater distances.

Days later the team conducted another war talk. Clary began by summarizing the previous session. "The last time we talked a lot about the use of power, limitations, no fire zones, sanctuaries, ceasefires, and such," Clary outlined as he laid his notes and papers on the bunker sandbags he used as a lectern, "but we never really defined limited war."

"One of my dad's professor friends teaches Military History and gave my dad a brief paper that defines limited war," Clary commented. "One of the best is by a writer and statesman, Henry Kissinger. He defines limited war as one fought for specific political objectives, which tend to establish a relationship between the force employed and the goal to be attained. It's an attempt to damage the enemy's will, but not crush it. It's trying to make negotiations and peace more attractive than more fighting and more killing." He paused from his readings to glance at the team. The team glanced back with wide and wondering eyes.

"Jesus, what I don't understand though is how do we get someone to do what he don't wanna do?" Hawkins frowned. "How do we influence his will or negotiate a peace? It seems we'da tried that first. It probably didn't work then and that's why we're fightin' him in a war now. I sorta always thought that if the enemy didn't listen to words and talkin' then the best way to get the enemy to do what you want him to do is to beat the livin' shit outta him and force him to admit he's done or sit down and talk and negotiate with us to stop poundin' him. We gotta first fight'em and hit'em hard enough for them to want to do what we want them to do or they'll just keep doin' what they want and never do what we want'em to do." Hawkins gasped for breath as the team grappled in an attempt to figure out what Hawkins had just said.

"You're maybe right in one way, but maybe wrong in another," Corporal Thunder replied, "but we can't go around beating up those who disagrees with us or us with them."

"Seriously, it's just that everything's pretty easy or simple in theory or in books," Clary continued, "but it's damn hard and just plain complicated on the battlefield. It's just hard as hell to take good theories and good words and fight a bad war with them."

"They want us to fight, but not fight too hard. They want us to win, but make it so the enemy don't really lose. That makes it harder for us to win and easier for the enemy to resist," Wiley frowned. "The worst part is it makes it easier for the enemy to fight on because he knows we won't use all the force or power we could use. He knows we won't just crush him."

"Jesus, it's kinda like goin' in the boxin' ring with an opponent who knows you're gonna take a dive or hold punches," Hawkins mumbled, "if he knows you're gonna hold back it sorta encourages him knowin' you ain't really fightin' to really hurt him."

"Okay, good points, but we're now talking about the complexities of limited war," Clary acknowledged, "but we haven't yet talked about some of the issues that make limited war a better alternative than total war. I think this might be where considering some of the intriguing moral dilemmas of war might be useful. My dad's mailed me some papers on the dilemmas. Sometimes a total war just might make it worse or worse than worse. Let me read them over and next time I'll summarize them. Maybe it'll help clear up a little of the confusion we're in now."

"Good idea," Corporal Thunder agreed, "because now we just seem to be marking time and getting nowhere fast. The talking is good and we're letting out our frustrations, but we probably need to take a break."

"Jesus, yep, maybe we better just call a ceasefire and think about all this." Hawkins joked, "So, Wiley, you cease talkin' while I keepa thinkin'. Your talkin' inteferes with my thinkin'."

"Yeah, well, I usually talk so you can't think," Wiley joked. "When you think it worries me. Usually, your thinking just ends up bad for us. The less you think the more good we have."

Hawkins feigned a painful and hurtful countenance before he laughed and hugged Wiley. "Damn, you're bigger than a bull. I can't even reach half way around you. But you know what they say. The bigger they are the harder they fall."

"Well, you know I'm falling hard on you," Wiley retorted, "and I'll crush you like a bug."

"No fair, Wiley, you and me's fightin' a limited war and you gotta hold back some of the brute power of yours against little ole weak me," Hawkins smiled, "We gotta negotiate to settle any fightin' you're thinkin'."

"Okay, you fight a limited war and I'll fight a total war," Wiley conceded. "You're the little enemy and I'm the big one. So, I get to make the rules and I'm crushing you."

"Jesus, Wiley, I'ma thinkin' that's the war we're in now," Hawkins blurted. "We're fightin' a limited war and the NVA's fightin' a total war. But we're the big powerful ones and they're the little weak ones. Go figure. We let the little guys make the big rules. Ain't Vietnam something?"

Corporal Thunder laughed and instituted an immediate ceasefire. "We'll talk later, but now we have a night ambush patrol to get ready for."

Talking was over for now. Patrolling was beginning again. It was always one or the other. Day after day and night after night it was what they did. Rivulets of meandering rain slid down their backs as they shuddered from the ceaseless monsoons while exiting their bunker. It was miserably damp and dark and depressing inside the bunker, but worse outside it in the open.

Within minutes the brisk cool wetness began to slowly tingle and tighten to numb their fingers and toes before gradually spreading and navigating inward to envelop their feet and hands. Eventually, as it crept and seeped into veins and muscles, to extremities and torsos, it engulfed and embraced their bodies. Its grip firmly diluted and then forcefully extinguished any existing warmth. The onslaught raged and persisted. While they rarely surrendered to the cool wetness, they resigned themselves to it. There was no recourse and no relief because living with it everyday defied any pretense of its nonexistence. The cold shivering wetness simply became a constant and obnoxious part of their miseries.

Although less literary and scientific, Hawkins had probably characterized the weather and its weariness best the time he slipped on a sloppy trail and tumbled into a rocky and ragged ravine. He simply lost his balance from his tiresome and uncontrollable shaking, which caused his every muscle and fiber to relax and eventually reflexively fail. After a litany of profanities, he uttered in total exhaustion, "Damn, these cold temps and rain. They just keep fallin' down till they rise up and strangle my heart and suffocate my mind. But they ain't satisfied till they try to stomp on my soul and crush my spirit. Then they just try to kick me into the gutter and flush me down the sewer of this shithole of an outhouse called Vietnam." *My words exactly*, Clary thought, *that's what the wretched weather is doing to all of us. Hawkins nailed it.*

As he had picked himself up and pulled himself from the ravine, Hawkins had continued, "Yeah, the temps and rain can do all this, but they cain't keep me down. They might get me down, but I'm gettin' up and goin' on." Surrendering to the intolerable elements or the war was foreign to Hawkins. They could attack him relentlessly, but they could never defeat his will to fight and overcome them. It was an attitude the team adopted, too. They had no recourse.

"Yeah, the temps are probably never too awfully low, but when we live in them, eat in them, patrol in them, sleep in them, even piss and poop in them, well, then the temps and wetness just wear us down and out," Clary agreed to support Hawkins' bitterness toward the weather and war.

Corporal Thunder and Wiley always nodded agreement when Hawkins and Clary expressed their frustrations with the cold wetness. But they simply braved it, bore it, and moved on. When the team first arrived in Vietnam last summer the torrid tropical heat and humidity assaulted them. Now it was the cool wetness of the monsoon rains. It was always one or the other.

Wiley once attempted to mollify Hawkins' and Clary's discontent with the cool wet winter weather by reminding them of the hot humid summer when they first arrived in Vietnam. "Yeah, but remember how we'd sweat so much our utilities would be crusted with salt stains. The worst part, however, was the suffocating humidity that was so thick and clammy it seemed we felt all syrupy and slick all the time. It was like we were doused in a gooey mix of salty honey. It was a different kind of sticky wetness, especially when we could hardly ever bathe or wash off."

"What you sayin', Wiley, that I ain't never happy with the weather or this war or Vietnam?" Hawkins teased. "Well, I ain't and I like complainin' 'bout them."

While the weather was discomforting, the team was comforted by their friendships and their talks despite sensing they may never understand the war or the weather. At times, they were both for and against the war, but they always protested and despised the weather. They were doing their best. They were good with that. They were good at fighting, too, but Con Thien was their next fight and complaint. It was a bad fight. Yet, they made it a good fight; good fair fight.

~

CHAPTER 16

Good Actions
Defeat Bad Rules

"We're accomplishing our missions and we're doing our duties. We're caring for one another, too. Missions and Marines come first. There shouldn't be any rules or steeples that stop us from doing just that. None. Zero. Zilch."

—Marine Corporal Dark Pale Thunder

"We're relocating to the river and bridge and new home the day after tomorrow," Corporal Thunder announced two days later, "We need to start packing up and preparing for the move." Surveying the tired and worn bunker to assess what to take and what to trash, he had no remorse in relocating. It had been home for months, but now they were moving on…again.

"Well, it won't take long to pack because we don't have much to pack," Clary replied. "Most of what I own fits in my pack. What won't fit I'll wrap in a sandbag. Pretty simply move."

"Oh, yeah, we need to slit open all the sandbags and pour the dirt in our fighting position or bunker," Corporal Thunder remembered as they discussed various duties for the move. "We just need to police up the area and leave nothing behind the NVA could maybe use."

"Jesus, I have a good idea," Hawkins exclaimed. "Why don't we leave'em all our papers and letters on limited war. Hell, they might read'em and be as confused and screwed up as we are. Then, nobody'll know what the hell's really going on."

Eventually, Clary was unable to resist. "Hawkins, I have a better idea. Let's leave you behind. You'll talk the NVA to death or they'll surrender to escape your incessant ramblings."

"Clary, that's the strategy," Wiley agreed. "Let's leave Hawkins behind. He'll be our nuclear talker and atomic babbler. The NVA will never survive his talking. He's our secret weapon."

"Jesus, who needs friends with shitheads like you two?" Hawkins muttered with a pained expression. "Hell, I might pretend to desert and become a traitor to help the enemy. They'll probably have enough smarts to listen to me better than you guys and the Pentagon. I'll convince the NVA to do limited war things and they'll lose the war for sure. Then I'll be a hero."

"Okay, I know we're all becoming policy scholars and strategic experts, but right now we have a night patrol and a few jobs to do," Corporal Thunder interrupted and joked, "Let's do these few hard tasks first and then you can continue with the easy one of ending this war."

The team conducted its final two patrols from Payable Hill. While policing the area, despite their initial thoughts to leave Hawkins behind to brainwash the NVA, they decided to take him with them."

The hill had been home for over three months. They had fought for it, occupied it, owned it, and held it. Constant mortar attacks and deaths and casualties had plagued them. They were neither sad nor glad to bid farewell. They simply moved on. It was what they did. They moved on.

"Incoming. Incoming mortars. Incoming," Corporal Thunder shouted. The threat was relayed quickly throughout the platoon. Scrambling for cover Hawkins mumbled, "Damnit, we filled in our holes with our sand-bags. Now we gotta dig'em again. Ain't this the shits?"

Wiley and Hawkins burrowed into the side of the hill, but they were exposed without any fighting holes for better protection and it was too late to dig one. Hawkins smiled at Wiley and said, "Wiley, take off your helmet and put it over me. It's so big it'll be my steel dome and I'll be safe as all hell. I won't have to crawl into it. You just plop it on top of me."

Thankfully, the mortar attack was a brief one and the relocation was completed before dark. Within an hour of darkness, Corporal Thunder and his team settled into their new bunker. The same ole rain, same ole cold, and same ole miseries assaulted them in their new position. It was another location, but it was still Vietnam…still war.

After a week of patrols to acquaint themselves with their new western patrolling area the team continued its series of talks on war. The bunker was newer but muddier than the old one.

"Now, last time we got confused over why we just can't use all our power to solve all our problems," Clary noted, "and why some limitations are better than no limitations. Is that about right?" The team nodded in agreement as it recalled their previous talks.

"We finally sort of agreed we needed to stop and I'd review my dad's mailings and materials," Clary emphasized as he held up a stack of papers and two small pamphlets.

"One of the first items I discovered, just as we debated, is the thought that in limited war one of the true dilemmas is how much power to use. That's what the experts say and that's what we said. Another thought is that there is no purely military solution to limited war," Clary noted as Hawkins began rustling uncomfortably and started to speak.

"Okay, but there's more," Clary continued, "Some who know a lot more about all this than we do say the amount of force used is only one limiting factor and there are others."

"What others?" Wiley asked as he listened while precariously balancing on his helmet seat.

"Well, I think we've talked about some and some we haven't," Clary recalled

"I'm thinking out loud," Corporal Thunder injected, "but one of the letters my dad sent to me talks about probably the main reason for limiting the war. We support the South Vietnamese and the Soviet Union the North. We're both super powers and agreed we don't really want to fight one another because we don't want a nuclear war. So, we have to keep the war limited and not let it become bigger so it won't become nuclear."

"Yeah, that's probably one of the main reasons," Clary concurred. "So, we kind of agreed to keep most of the war, most of the time, in South Vietnam. We also agreed not to attack targets in other countries and to not strike the ports in the North where maybe Soviet resupply ships are. That's why there are sanctuaries and no strike zones and ceasefires and other limits."

"Well, now I remember one of my dad's letters talking about wanting to eliminate any escalation of the war," Wiley added, "and that's what all these limitations are for. They're to avoid any escalation to make sure, or to try to make sure, the war doesn't become bigger and maybe nuclear. That's a war none of us really want. That's a war no one wins."

"Jesus, this makes a little more sense to me now," Hawkins asserted, "and it reminds me of a little article my mama sent me. The article's now making more sense than when I first read it.

"Let me see if I can explain. You know my family's from Italy and Europe," Hawkins paused before he continued. "Well, the article was from an Italian newspaper and it was sayin' Europe is becomin' concerned, maybe anxious, about the United States fightin' a war in Asia. The concern is the Soviets are right next door to Europe and if America gets bogged down or too distracted in Asia the Soviets might take advantage and do something in Europe. If too many U.S. military forces are in Vietnam, maybe there won't be enough if Russia causes problems in Europe.

"You know, I think I'm beginnin' to learn a little about the big policies and strategies," Hawkins professed. "But, Clary, I'm still strugglin' with the dilemma you mentioned at the beginning. The dilemma is how much power to use. It seems we gotta use enough power to make the NVA know we're serious, but not so much power that the war goes too serious on us.

"It just seems to me right now we ain't using enough power to make 'em think we're serious. We're not makin' it as hard on them as we could or should. Yeah, we're keepin' the war limited for the big guys, but the little guys like us are sacrificin' and dealin' with the consequences of all that. The worst part of this is too many of us are dyin' when maybe more of us should be livin'. That's all I'm sayin'," Hawkins expounded. "There's the big picture and the little one. We gotta support the big picture for the politicians and generals, but they gotta support us as the little picture.

"Maybe we should use a little more power and squeeze 'em a little more to see what happens," Hawkins concluded. "Then, if that don't work and the war ain't gettin' bigger, we use a little more power and squeeze 'em a little more. We just keep doin' that till we get peace."

"Hawkins, I think you're right," Corporal Thunder agreed. "Somehow our country has to figure out what the right degree of force is. What the right balance is to protect us, but prevent the war from getting out of hand. I bet figuring that all out is really hard.

"To us fighting the war," the Corporal suggested, "it seems minimizing deaths and damage to the enemy just maximizes the possible deaths and damage to us. It's not that simple, however, because if that means fewer people are killed so more people live that's good. While that's bad for us, maybe it's good for our nation. It probably doesn't make much sense to us, however, because we're the ones maybe dying so others can live free."

"Yeah, we're fighting and dying and we're the minority," Clary injected, "It's always a few who fight and die for the many. In one of my dad's letters, for example, he wrote that it's often two to four percent, maybe less, of our population who fight in combat."

"You're kidding?" Wiley asked, "That seems awfully small. It's kind of like Jesus sacrificing his life for all of us. Jesus is the good shepherd protecting his flock and we're all his flock."

"Jesus, Wiley, I ain't never been compared to Jesus," Hawkins sighed, "but you're sorta right about the few protectin' and defendin' the many. Bad's always ready to harm good. We just gotta be good and ready to protect our freedoms and flock. Now we're good shepherds. Ain't war somethin'. Ain't we somethin'."

"Okay, I don't have anything else for tonight. I didn't have much to begin," Clary declared. "But it's been a good night. I wanted us to focus on one issue. Let's call it a night." Clary sensed this was a good point at which to stop...one with many hard but thoughtful issues to consider.

"Clary, you accomplished much more than you think," Corporal Thunder corrected. "Let's call it a good talk, a damn good talk. Let's think about all this. We'll talk more later, but now let's start our night watches and get some sleeps."

Corporal Thunder stood the midnight watch, but Wiley joined him about an hour into his duty. "I can't seem to sleep for thinking," Wiley pensively related to the Corporal, "especially about what you said about the few maybe dying so the many maybe live.

"As I wrestled with what you said I remembered one of the favorite songs we play in church several times a month," Wiley confessed. "It's *The Battle Hymn of the Republic*. I never thought about it this way, but one of the verses is, *As He died to make men holy, let us die to make men free*. While maybe there's not much holy about war, hopefully war's dying helps make men free and that's holy.

"I'm not wanting to die, none of us are, but none of those before us wanted to die either. Yet, they fought and died so we could be free," Wiley mused while glancing into the darkness.

"Wiley, you and me know about dying and freedom," Corporal Thunder somberly said to Wiley. "Your people were slaves to the white man and the white man considered my people savages. We had all the land and freedoms we could ever want and the white man had his, but the white man wanted our land and freedom, too. We simply wanted to roam the plains and prairies in a lifestyle we'd always known. In the Civil War, many died for your people's freedoms. In the Indian Wars, many of my people died only to lose our freedoms.

"Our land and freedoms were taken and many who survived were exiled to reservations or a different way of life," Corporal Thunder regretfully explained. "It seems the Indian Wars were total wars of annihilation or extinction for the white man because we Indians signed treaty after treaty and compromised our freedoms and lifestyles time after time only to have our treaties and lives broken. I don't know if you'd call that us fighting a limited war so we weren't crushed, but it seems it might have been. Yet, it didn't work. In time, neither the white man nor the Indian trusted one another and we both broke treaties and did wrong. That's why it's important we help do this war right and for right."

While the entire team shared a kindred spirit, from that night forward a unique and special bond was created and flourished between Corporal Thunder and Wiley. Brothers in arms aptly described them, but true brothers are who they truly became.

The next morning, the Corporal announced, "Gather round. Listen up. We've been patrolling west and south from our new location here, but now we're going back east to Con Thien."

Wiley, Hawkins, and Clary groaned in unison. "Jesus, they relocate us here to operate to the west and now they send us back east," Hawkins complained. "Cain't anybody make up their damn minds? Damned if I ain't feelin' like a yo-yo. Yo, Hawkins, go here. Yo, Hawkins, go there. I'm just a damn yo-yo."

"Okay, but remember I mentioned we'd probably go back to Con Thien a time or two," Corporal Thunder reminded the team. "We're centrally located and we can go in almost any direction. We're sitting on key real estate and we're protecting a lot of critical areas."

"Well, you're right," Wiley commented as the peacemaker, "but we hate Con Thien. It's ugly and nasty. Besides, the rules favor the NVA, especially us not being able to fire back."

"Yes, I know. It's a tough area, but the Marines have now established a permanent base camp at Con Thien and we're starting to build it up as a major fire base, too," the Corporal reported. "It's different now than when we were last there."

"How different?" Hawkins asked as he closed his eyes to remember it as it was.

"Well, there's plans to reinforce the fire base with parts of the Fourth and Ninth Marines and with artillery and heavy weapons. The infantry battalions will probably rotate in and out of Con Thien. I'm pretty sure they're adding more artillery, 106mm recoilless rifles, and even tanks," Corporal Thunder answered. "That's one of the reasons we're going back."

"We're not tankers or artillery," Wiley frowned, "what's that got to do with us?"

"Wiley, good question. It's exactly why we're going back," the Corporal replied. "Our mission is to protect the road from Cam Lo on Highway 9 north to Con Thien. Our mission is to secure the road so the artillery and heavy weapons can move safely into Con Thien."

"Oh, yeah, they'll be moving a lot of ordnance and supplies up, too," Corporal Thunder remembered. "Anyway, we'll be securing and protecting the road for all the convoys."

"So, we're not going into the fire base?" Clary asked. "We're just securing the road?"

"Right. Right now there's no plans for us to go into the base," Corporal Thunder answered. "We just secure the road, but you know how plans change."

"When we goin' and how long will we gonna be gone?" Hawkins asked.

"We'll start the mission the day after tomorrow and it'll probably last three to four days," Corporal Thunder answered. "If all goes well the Lieutenant says the transportation and supply types think they can move everything in three days. That's what they told the battalion.

"The Chinese TET holiday is coming up. I think it's like 9 February," he noted. "Anyway, the Marines at division want all the reinforcements and supplies in before TET."

"They suspect the NVA may try something either before or after TET?" Clary asked.

"Jesus, right before or right after? How about right during? We got another ceasefire a comin' or a goin'," Hawkins laughed. "We're a ceasin' and they're a firin'. By the way, we still can't fire counter-battery north into the NVA artillery even though they can fire at us?"

"As far as I know we can't do counter-battery fire now, but the company commander said the division's appealing that," Corporal Thunder replied.

"Appealin's better than nothing," Hawkins countered, "but I'm pleadin' and prayin'."

"Well, Hawkins, you might as well just piss in the wind, too," Clary smiled, "because that'll probably do just as much good. No one seems to listen to us. Instead, we're the ones pissed on."

"Well, God's listening and we better keep praying," Wiley declared. "The moment we stop praying we're in serious trouble. It's serious now, but it'll get more serious if we stop praying."

"You're right. I didn't mean it that way," Clary apologized. "It's just so damn frustrating at times. It seems everything's against us. We're just wanting fair rules, but the rules are unfair."

"Clary, that's okay. If they wanna play dirty, I'm the master at ugly and dirty," Hawkins asserted. "We'll show'em we can play by their rules, which is no rules. Zero. Zilch. None."

"Well, that wasn't a good brief by me," Corporal Thunder apologized, "but I hope you have some idea about the plan." He sensed he had lost control of the briefing to the team's ramblings.

"We're the ones should be apologizing," Wiley said defending Corporal Thunder. "We just kept asking questions and interrupting. I guess we got too excited about Con Thien."

Wiley glared rather sternly at Hawkins and Clary for confirmation as well as to subtlety suggest they apologize for the interruptions.

"Jesus, I started it by complaining," Hawkins admitted. "It's my fault."

"Yeah, well I was right there with you. Talking instead of listening," Clary confessed. "It's my fault, too."

"Thanks, but you have a right to ask questions and to get all the information you can," Corporal Thunder conceded. "Talking's what we do best, but listening's good, too.

"One point we didn't talk about is who's going on the operation," Corporal Thunder remembered. "It's just part of Headquarters Company and Mike and India Companies.

"Lima Company will continue to patrol from its base camp at the Fishbowl and Kilo Company will stay here to patrol and provide security for the artillery," he added.

The Con Thien operation commenced two days later. "We'll be patrolling to the operating area instead of riding trucks like before. All the trucks are staging in Dong Ha and loading supplies," Corporal Thunder briefed. "We'll depart before daylight and arrive later that afternoon. Then we'll secure the road before the convoys north begin the next day."

The battalion minus departed its base camp before sunrise and advanced toward the road to Con Thien patrolling through the mountains and jungles instead of the roads. An hour or so before noon Clary noted, "I've been noticing that ole steeple in the distance for the past hour. It just stands out. It just seems suspicious."

"I've been watching, too," Corporal Thunder admitted. "I can see it for over a thousand meters."

"Jesus, it can see us even farther. We've passed it before and we always got mortared," Hawkins declared. "I'm gonna be pissed if we get mortared again."

"You're going to be pissed?" Clary muttered. "I was the one got hit. Why're you pissed?

"I'm gonna be pissed if you get another tiny little metal scratch and get another Purple Heart," Hawkins laughed. "You getting' too many medals is gonna piss me off. I'm talking about medals and not metals, just in case you didn't catch what I was saying."

"Yeah, I caught it, but I wished I'd of missed it," Clary smiled, "just like I'm wishing I miss the next mortars."

"Yeah, let's wish that," Corporal Thunder agreed, "but before we came from the south on the road and later back down from the north on the road. This time we're coming from the west where there's no road. Maybe whoever's calling in the mortars mostly watches the road. Maybe we'll surprise them coming from the west. Maybe it'll take them longer to figure out we're here."

By mid-afternoon the battalion arrived at the road and halted to await orders. The team lay in a four-man circle to shelter themselves from the rain and wind and relax from the grueling hike.

Corporal Thunder later briefed his team, "Company M will stack up from south to north along the road from here toward Con Thien. It'll be first platoon up north, then second platoon in the middle, and third platoon here. Our platoon will be with company headquarters in the center. We'll spread out more than normal, but we'll have a lot of fire support on call and standing by. Plus, tanks will be leading the convoys to protect the road as the artillery and supplies move up.

"I asked Staff Sergeant Antoine to assign us an area east of the road closest to the steeple. It's less than a thousand meters from our night defensive position," he smiled to the team.

"Why'd you do that?" Wiley frowned. "That's awful close if there's enemy there."

"Yeah, it's close, but I'm kinda suspecting nothing happens at night. If it's an observation post it'll mostly be used in the day," Corporal Thunder explained. "Plus, looking at the map it seems they might come in from the east and go back that way to always avoid us."

"Yep, that's probably what I'd do," Hawkins agreed. "Just sneak in, hit us, and sneak out."

"So, what are you figuring or planning we should do?" Clary asked apprehensively.

"Well, I'm reasoning we could patrol over there tonight on our listening post and check it out," Corporal Thunder smiled. "Just check it out. That's it. Just check it out."

"Ain't it off limits? Ain't it a church steeple? Ain't that a religious site that we ain't supposed to mess with?" Hawkins smiled teasingly as he was beginning to sense the Corporal's plan.

"Maybe. Maybe. Maybe," Corporal Thunder answered to all three questions. "But if it's an observation post, maybe it ain't too religious. Maybe if war stuff's there, it ain't too spiritual. Besides, we're just checking it out. We ain't hurting nothing. Except Hawkins' got me hurting the English language by saying ain't so much."

"Hell, I'm for checkin' it out," Hawkins grinned. "Count me in. I'm good with checkin' it out."

Wiley and Clary agreed and Corporal Thunder shared his plan with the team and they agreed. Hawkins' mischievous grin all afternoon was a dead give away that something was up. Usually he had a good noncommittal poker face, but he could hardly contain himself.

Corporal Thunder had already coordinated with Corporal Cozart and volunteered his team for the two two-man listening posts in front of the platoons sector on the east side of the road. He had set that part of the plan in motion earlier that day. Later, the team huddled to finalize the plan.

"Once we finish digging in our permanent defensive positions," Corporal Thunder ordered, "let's get ready for our listening post duty." They quickly dug in and slowly waited.

Although they departed the platoon line for the listening posts as darkness descended, the silhouette of the steeple was clearly visible. "Hawkins, lead us straight to the steeple, but halt about a hundred meters from it," Corporal Thunder directed. "Then Wiley and Clary will dig in a listening post position, but you and me will go on to check out the steeple."

"Okay, this is a good spot for Wiley and Clary and the listening post," Corporal Thunder noted once they arrived at a good location. "It has good fields of observation and fire.

"Wiley, you and Clary dig in. Hawkins and me are going on," Corporal Thunder whispered. "Cover us, but listen and report to the platoon. Remember to report for both of us because we're supposed to be doing two listening posts."

Within minutes, Corporal Thunder and Hawkins were stealthily crawling toward the steeple. They rotated crawling a few meters, halting, listening, and crawling again. It took about an hour, but they arrived at the steeple undetected. While silently waiting and watching for another ten to fifteen minutes, they smiled in anticipation before cautiously advancing to the steeple.

"Look, a few flat grave markers just like down south," Corporal Thunder whispered.

"Jesus, probably just as fake and phony as the ones down south, too," Hawkins replied.

"Let's check them out, but be careful. They might be booby trapped. Check for trip wires," Corporal Thunder cautioned. "Go slow and be cautious. You take those over there. I'll take these. I'll check mine first while you watch and listen. Then I'll listen while you check yours."

Corporal Thunder paused, listened, then began carefully and slowing feeling around the edges of the markers for wires or suspicious touches. "I've checked four and found nothing suspicious. Crawl farther away. I'm going to try to lift or slide the lids," he warned Hawkins.

The first marker was too heavy to budge. "It's probably a grave," Corporal Thunder whispered to Hawkins. He then crawled to a second. It was heavy, too, but it slid to one side fairly easily. He pushed it hard with his legs while laying on his back and beneath in ammo crates were 82mm mortar rounds, small arms ammo, and hand grenades.

"Hawkins, I found what we're looking for. I found the explosives," the Corporal muttered quietly, "There's no AK47 rifles, but there's ammo. It's mostly mortars and hand grenades. Give me a few minutes and I'll check the others."

Continuing his search he discovered another cache of explosives, four AK47s, six 82mm mortar tubes, and reported, "Hawkins, I'll stand guard and listen while you search your graves."

Hawkins initiated a systematic search of his markers and discovered two were actual graves, but three contained similar caches of explosives. "I gotta lot of 82 mortar rounds, too, but a lot more hand grenades," Hawkins excitedly reported.

"Damned if we didn't hit the jackpot," Corporal Thunder whispered as they paused to consider what to do next. "Okay, Hawkins, this is what I want you to do. Go get Wiley and bring him here. We need his muscles. Tell Clary to come about halfway and stop and continue to report. Tell him to watch our flanks and we'll all go back to the listening post later."

Hawkins started to quickly turn and scamper to locate Wiley. Corporal Thunder grabbed him by the arm and added "Oh, I forgot. I'll wait inside the church or steeple. Join me there inside."

Hawkins shook his head silently and darted for Wiley. Meanwhile, the Corporal entered the church and began to inspect the steeple. It was rudimentary, but a wooden ladder led to a loft platform high into the steeple. The ladder led to a trap door. He pushed upward and held onto it as he climbed onto the enclosed platform. He thought, *Damn, you can see for miles from up here. It's dark, but you can see the mountains to the west and the horizons to the north and south. It's a great observation post.*

Corporal Thunder climbed down the ladder and waited silently for Hawkins to return with Wiley. Minutes later the two entered the building and he led them to the graves and caches. "Look, by the edge of the clearing. There's more grave markers," Hawkins whispered.

"Yeah, there's probably more caches, too, but we got enough to do what we got to do," Corporal Thunder replied. "We'll take care of those later."

"What we going to do?" Wiley asked carefully looking to and fro for anything suspicious.

"Well, we're going to booby trap the steeple," Corporal Thunder smiled. "I found trip wire in with the grenades. The NVA or VC or whoever is using it for booby traps. We'll do the same."

"I'm going up in the steeple and rigging the trap door for tripping when anyone pushes it open," Corporal Thunder explained. "While I'm doing that, you two carry about ten mortar rounds each and a hand full of grenades up to me."

"While you're working, one work and one watch," Corporal Thunder reminded them.

Corporal Thunder, Wiley, and Hawkins immediately began their respective tasks. In less than thirty minutes, Corporal Thunder had stacked the mortar rounds on the steeple platform and wired four separate grenades to explode when the trap door was pushed up and flipped over.

"Okay, now let's cover the graves and leave the area as close to possible just like we found it," Corporal Thunder whispered. "Then we'll see what happens."

After the graves area was policed and all signs of their presence concealed or covered, they returned to Clary and the listening post.

"Okay, let's get some sleep, but let's leave here before sunrise to report back to our squad," the Corporal muttered quietly. "If what happens is what I suspect might happen, we'll know how good a job we've done sometime tomorrow. We'll just have to wait for now. Take a nap."

"What do we suspect might happen?" Clary innocently asked.

"Well, if it's an observation post, tomorrow the VC or NVA or whoever will know we're on the road," Corporal Thunder answered. "Maybe they know we're here now, but they'll for sure know we're here tomorrow when all the convoys start running up and down this road."

"Jesus, that'll be too good a target for them to pass up," Hawkins smiled. "If they go into the steeple we gotta surprise for them. We gotta surprise funeral for them. Yep, it'll be a surprise and it'll be a funeral, too. They'll already be in a fake church. Killed in church. Praise the Lord."

"We found a cache of mortar rounds and grenades in the graves," Corporal Thunder added. "It was like down south. So, we stacked some of the ammo in the steeple and booby trapped it."

"If all goes as we plan," Corporal Thunder explained, "the hand grenades will explode and then the mortar rounds. It's what's called sympathetic detonation. One goes and it causes the others to go. It just ripples. It should be a pretty big blast, too."

"Jesus, sympathetic detonations," Hawkins laughed. "But they ain't gettin' no sympathy from us. They ain't getting nothin' but a good payback and shit pile of their own mortar rounds for using a church steeple against the rules. Yep, I'd call that killed by friendly fire."

Prior to sunrise the team closed their listening posts and Wiley radioed they were returning to the company lines. They were inside the lines and sleeping when the sun began to shine.

"Well, it's another sunrise. It looks like it's going to be a good day," Wiley rejoiced.

"Yep, Wiley, it's gonna be a good day," Hawkins agreed. "A good fine day for Vietnam."

Corporal Thunder, Wiley, Clary, and Hawkins were anxious with anticipation. They were eager to pass the word of their exploits from last night to other Marines. They knew, however, it had to remain a secret. If they were to become heroes, it had to remain their secret. If they were to become villains, it would be known by all, including the Pentagon. So, they waited in secrecy.

The convoys started rolling Marines and materials to Con Thien at mid-morning. The nondescript dirt road became a major highway. The convoys belched smoke and dust and fumes.

"Looks like they're running ten to twelve trucks at a time. Then thirty minutes later they're running another ten or twelve," Clary observed. "They're hurrying to get it done fast."

"Yep, they're staggering them in good intervals. But it's still busy as hell," Hawkins noted, "and it'll just get busier when the trucks start comin' back down from Con Thien."

Throughout the morning, Corporal Thunder and his team monitored the progress of the periodic convoys. They waited and watched with anticipation and with vigilance.

Thunderous explosions rocked the region about noon. Corporal Thunder glanced toward the steeple. "Damn, look at all that wood splintering and showering from the sky," Corporal Thunder shouted. A huge black plume of smoke drifted upward. Then debris floated downward. The steeple disintegrated and disappeared. Then it was strangely and deadly silent.

Wiley was monitoring the radio and informed the team, "The radio nets are alive with chatter. Higher headquarters is demanding immediate reports. There's lots of questions and requests for information. The transmissions are rapid fire and the radio traffic is nonstop."

Corporal Thunder and his team smiled and remained calm. They knew exactly what had happened, but they maintained silence. As Wiley listened to the radio he reported, "Mike Company told battalion it's closest to the explosion and that it'll check it out and report back.

"Now the company is tasking the second platoon to check it out," Wiley informed the team minutes later. "Standby. We'll probably get the word to assemble and move out any minute."

Minutes later Staff Sergeant Antoine and the platoon were on line and sweeping toward the explosion. Corporal Thunder cautioned, "Sort of lay back and let them figure it out without much help from us. We don't want to make them suspicious by us knowing too much."

"Yeah, Hawkins, just play stupid," Clary joked. "That shouldn't be too hard for you."

"Okay, I'll just do what you do," Hawkins joked back, "That'll be as stupid as all hell."

The team smiled as the platoon advanced and established a perimeter to surround the burning structure and steeple. Staff Sergeant Antoine led a small team forward to investigate.

Corporal Thunder overheard Staff Sergeant Antoine radio the company, "We got three VC killed. It looks like they were maybe getting ready to mortar us, but blowed themselves and the steeple all to hell. Nothing much left of anyone or anything."

Corporal Thunder was unable to hear the response from the company, but he soon learned what was ordered. "Okay, bring second squad in and let's check out the area closer," Staff Sergeant Antoine ordered. "The Lieutenant's ordered us to check out the area really good."

Corporal Thunder's team was careful while clandestinely guiding Marines from the second squad to the graves and caches. They cautiously drifted toward the graves and strolled near the four potential caches outside the small churchyard.

Corporal Thunder and his team remained in the background and shadows while the search intensified. When it was over, Staff Sergeant Antoine excitedly reported, "We've located a major cache of munitions." The company immediately passed the word to battalion and asked for instructions on the disposition of the enemy weapons and munitions.

Upon receiving guidance, Staff Sergeant Antoine ordered, "Corporal Cozart you lead the second squad back to the road and our security duties there. I'll wait here with the first and third squads. The battalion is sending an engineer team to blow all these weapons and ammo in place.

"Oh, yeah, I almost forgot. The battalion's sending some intelligence Marines, too. I think they're taking pictures and writing reports to verify the enemy was using the graves and the church illegally. We'll rejoin you later," Staff Sergeant Antoine remembered to tell his Marines.

The battalion's discovery of the major enemy munitions caches confirmed the enemy rules violations. Three dead enemy validated the illegalities. The incident at the church was closed and the operation concluded successfully. Division reported no further investigation or action required.

"The steeple's history," Corporal Thunder later noted.

"Dust to dust. Ashes to ashes," Hawkins added with a smile.

Days later, Corporal Thunder and his team led the battalion on its return home. As darkness approached the team settled into its bunker. A light but steady rain pelted them. It was cool, but not cold. It was miserable, but there was joy, too. Corporal Thunder and his team glanced at one another knowingly, but they never spoke to anyone about booby trapping the steeple.

Corporal Thunder simply declared, "We did what we did to accomplish the mission and to protect the convoys and the Marines. It was our duty and we did our duty. That's what we do. That's what Marines do. We're accomplishing our missions. We're caring for one another, too. Missions and Marines come first. There shouldn't be any rules or steeples that stop us from doing just that. None. Zero. Zilch."

In his stoic and succinct Indian manner Corporal Thunder summarized the team's actions in eliminating the steeple threat. Throughout the remainder of their tour the incident was never again mentioned. It was done. It was over. They were good with that. They were good with returning to Payable, too.

~

CHAPTER 17

Gamma Phi's and R & R

I suppose I just like complainin' 'bout war and Vietnam. Com-
plainin' 'bout war and Vietnam is easy 'cause there's lots to
complain 'bout, too.

—Marine Private First Class Dominic Hawkins

Corporal Thunder, Wiley, Clary, and Hawkins rummaged around
in their bunker as they attempted to gain a measure of space and
comfort in their too small quarters. Four Marines locating space in an
eight-by-eight foot bunker, which they had to crawl into because it was
too low for them to stand, was challenging. Usually, two sat and two
stood in the fighting hole trench at the front, except when they slept.
While sleeping, one was always on watch standing or sitting in the front
trench. Once they confirmed a space, as usual, they cleaned their weapons,
squared away their bunker, and ate their Cs.

"It's been a long, tiring day," Clary noted while massaging his sore
calves for warmth, "but it was kind of an easy operation, especially for
Con Thien." They were home at Payable River and Con Thien was again
a bad memory, but the memory of the steeple made it a good one, too.

"Jesus, it was almost an R & R or rest and relaxation type duty…with
no broads or booze," Hawkins observed while stowing gear. "We did no
patrollin' 'ceptin' to get there and get back."

Wiley coordinated the night watch schedule and reported, "Okay, it's
Clary, Hawkins, Corporal Thunder, and me. We got about an hour before
it starts. Clary, do you want to catch a few sleeps before your watch starts
at 2200? I'll wait up and wake you."

"Thanks, but I'll just start my watch now," Clary replied. "You guys
get your sleeps."

The bunker was silent within minutes. The team respected the too
infrequent quiet times they experienced in Vietnam. Clary cocked his
ears, but the night was quieter than quiet. It was eerily silent as he scanned

the darkness with blinking and steadily moving eyes and noted it was darker than it was on Payable Hill. *Down and deeper in the jungle by the river the noises and darkness are distinctly different than those up and higher in the mountains*, he thought.

The triple canopy foliage embraced and captured Clary and the jungle's night sounds and shadows. Clary thought it was almost too tranquil to sleep because the team was so accustomed to the intermittent sounds of war. Sounds of war were random, but they were comforting, too. The absences of such sounds were often dubious warnings. It was overwhelming fatigue; however, that most often aided their ability to sleep and the team was again beyond exhaustion.

Reveille came both sooner and later than expected. They savored the opportunity to sleep, but preferred daylight to darkness. "It's another sunrise," Wiley observed with a smile.

Corporal Thunder added, "The weather seems to be changing. Maybe it's finally improving after all the rain and cold we've had for three or four months. It seems we're still getting lots of rain, but we're getting some sunny and warmer days. It'll probably be hot and dry again in a month or so."

"Yeah, I ain't done complainin' 'bout that cause I had just about enough rain and cold," Hawkins groaned, "but once the hot and humid days are here again I'll be complainin' 'bout them, too. I suppose I just like complainin' 'bout war and Vietnam. Complainin' 'bout war and Vietnam is easy 'cause there's lots to complain 'bout, too."

"The company's having a mail call right after breakfast," Corporal Cozart informed Corporal Thunder as he strolled through the area. "The Gunny said you got a lot of mail and to send two of you." The team looked surprised with the news of a mail call that required two to carry it.

"Also, right after breakfast we're meeting with Second Lieutenant Antoine for tonight's patrol order," Corporal Cozart mentioned as an afterthought. "So, let's go together about 0800. By the way, we should all remember to congratulate him on his promotion. It happened yesterday."

"It's been a while since we've had mail," Clary noted, "we've been gone so much."

"Good, you and Hawkins get the mail. I'll get our patrol order," Corporal Thunder agreed. "Then we'll meet back here at the bunker. Wiley, you mind the bunker while we're gone."

Corporal Thunder was surprised when he returned to the bunker. His first response and reaction was to ask the team, "Okay, what are those goofy grins on your faces?"

Hawkins was unable to contain himself and simply pointed and said, "Look! Just look."

Corporal Thunder glanced where Hawkins pointed and saw three large bright orange nylon mail bags at the side of the bunker. It was a company's worth of mail for only the four of them.

Hawkins declared, "All three of'em are for you. Every damn one of'ems for you. Count'em. Three. I get two tiny lightweight letters and you get three heavyweight bags of stuff."

"Wow! Who's it from?" Corporal Thunder asked, both delighted and confused by three bags.

"Jesus, how the hell should we know," Hawkins groaned. "We ain't openin' and readin' your mail. Not unless you want us to," Hawkins added with a smile.

"Well, yeah, help me open the bags," Corporal Thunder replied.

"Damn, it's like a late Christmas," Clary exclaimed. "It's sodas, candies, chips and snacks."

"Yeah, and in this bag," Wiley announced gleefully, "we got writing notebooks and pens. Wow! We got *Playboy* and *Sports Illustrated* magazines, too. Plus, more drinks and snacks."

"They musta known we stink to high heavens," Hawkins admitted playfully, "because this one is full of soaps, toothpastes, shaving creams, and lots of bathroom kinda stuff. Thank goodness, it's also got some foot powders for our feets and lotions for our faces and hands. It's even got small boxes of soaps for washing our clothes."

"We're just like kids at Christmas," Corporal Thunder paused to declare before he asked, "but who's Santa Claus? Who's giving us these special gifts?"

"Okay, this may explain," Clary exclaimed as he pulled a letter from his bag addressed to Corporal Thunder and handed it to him.

Corporal Thunder quietly and slowly read the letter. Overwhelmed by his emotions and lost in his thoughts, he paused before summarizing it for the team.

"The letter is from my friend Bonnie in Bartlesville, Oklahoma," Corporal Thunder began. "We met in school. We went to different high schools, but our sports teams played one another. I also knew her from summer work at Phillips Petroleum and the oil fields. We stayed friends."

"Bonnie has two sisters, too, Sherry and Patrice," Corporal Thunder smiled. "They were all too good for me. They're all too good for you, too, Hawkins, so don't even ask about them."

Hawkins feigned pitiful hurt. "I weren't gonna ask, but why you teasin' me just talkin''bout'em? Just don't mention any girls. Let's not talk about girls. Just pass me the *Playboy*."

"Bonnie's mother is the best cook in Washington County. She always made all us kids feel special when we visited and was like a second mom to everyone," Corporal Thunder smiled. "Bonnie's now attending the University of Oklahoma. She's in a sorority called Gamma Phi Beta and her sorority sisters collected and donated all this to us." The team quickly surveyed the donated items and smiled, but they were still partially in shock.

Corporal Thunder paused again before he concluded, "The last paragraph of the letter reads: 'Thank you to you and your Marines. We appreciate your sacrifices for our country and our freedoms. We hope you are safe and soon have special homecomings with your families and loved ones. You're in our thoughts and prayers.' Then, it's signed by The Goo Phoo Boos. I think that's a funny nickname the Gamma Phi Beta's give themselves."

The team sat in stunned silence. Wiley spoke first, "The gifts are the nicest things anyone has done for us since we've been in Vietnam. They don't know us, yet they're nice to us. The gifts are special, but knowing they care is the best."

"I hope they know how much we appreciate all this and them," Clary agreed.

"Well, I'll write a thank you note," Corporal Thunder offered, "and we can all sign it. We can all write a brief note. That's what we'll do to let them know what this means to us."

The team laughed and joked as it counted its treasures from the Gamma Phi Beta sorority. While sorting through the mail bags, Wiley discovered a small shoe box with a stack of about fifty or so letters. Most were simply addressed "To a Marine," but one was specifically addressed to Corporal Thunder. He asked Wiley to distribute the Marine letters throughout the platoon so those who rarely received mail would have a nice letter from someone who cared.

While Wiley delivered the letters to the platoon commander for distribution to the platoon, the Corporal suddenly became quiet and smiled reading his surprise letter. Hawkins noticed his grin and teasingly asked, "Okay, who's your letter from?"

Although reluctant to discuss the letter, Corporal Thunder knew Hawkins would pester him until he answered. "It's from Sydney. She's a sorority friend of Bonnie's who I met on leave at the University of Oklahoma before coming to Vietnam."

"Yeah, well, it must be more than that because I ain't never seen you smile like that since we been in Vietnam," Hawkins joked. "She must be someone special."

"Yes, she's special; she's really special. One of the most special girls I've ever met, but she's someone else's special," the Corporal truthfully answered, hoping to end Hawkins' interrogation, "We simply met for lunch and talked. Sydney was very sophisticated and had a lot of class, but she was really kind and thoughtful and nice. She was stunningly beautiful, too. I learned she was adopted, like my mom, and like my mom she knew little about her real parents. I'm pretty sure, though, that she's Indian because she had such soft and smooth features and colors…and her favorite color was lavender. We had a nice talk and time together, but we knew I was soon leaving for Vietnam and this war. I'm surprised she remembered, but that's the kind of girl she is. Yes, she's special."

Corporal Thunder then glanced toward the western mountains deep in remembrances of Sydney's friendship. Hawkins thought of grilling him with more questions, but Clary silently signaled for him to ceasefire. Both sensed the Corporal's thoughtful mood and respectfully returned to their own activities. Clary returned to his mail from home and Hawkins his *Playboy*.

Corporal Thunder's memories of home were both sad and glad ones, but his thoughts eventually returned to Vietnam and he decided, "This is too much for just us. It's a bunch of great stuff, but we need to share it with the platoon. Let's make three stacks of goodies. We'll keep one for ourselves and second squad and we'll take a bag each to first and third squads."

"Yeah, we could just squirrel this away just for ourselves," Wiley agreed, "but we'd feel guilty about us having so much and the others nothing. Let's share. It's the Marine thing to do."

"Jesus, we could make all this last for a month," Hawkins confirmed, "but I'd rather share it, too. Let's do it before we change our minds, but I'm keeping the *Playboys* for now."

Corporal Thunder and the team divided up the treasures. They later loaded three bags and delivered them to Lieutenant Antoine to pass to the platoon's three squads.

"Well, it feels pretty good to play Santa Claus," Clary admitted. "It's a couple of months late for Christmas, but that's Vietnam and that's war. We just got to go with it as it comes."

The team nodded in agreement and for the first time in months had a drinks and snacks party while it read its mail. Hawkins giggled while reading a letter from Maria. It was a good morning. It was the best morning in months. Clary basked in the warmth of a sunny day and thought of California and beaches. They were free until their evening patrol. Wiley wrote a letter to his dad. Life was good. It took little to make life good in Vietnam. It took a lot to keep living, but only a little to make living good. They were living good as Corporal Thunder began their "thank you" letter to Bonnie and the Goo Phoo Boos. The good times were good, but sadly the good times never lasted. The good was always a lull. The bad was always lurking.

The team was determined, however, to make the good last as long as possible. Wiley read a letter from home while Hawkins scanned the *Playboy*. Corporal Thunder savored a Snickers candy bar and Clary sipped on a Pepsi. The team read its mail and clippings from home in silence. They were in a thoughtful mood while they snacked on the Gamma Phi Beta delights.

The care package snacks, one by one, bite by bite, sip by sip, reminded them that someone back home, some total strangers, cared. They were hardened to the brutalities of war, but they were soft and needed to know people cared.

As the team completed reading its letters and clippings from home they started to talk. "My friend Bonnie's a journalism major at the University of Oklahoma or OU for short. She works on the university newspaper and sent me some clippings," Corporal Thunder noted.

"One clipping is just a picture with college students protesting and demonstrating against the war. But the one I like best is a picture of a Marine reservist taking a sign from a protestor and whacking him over his head with his own peace symbol sign," he smiled. "The Marine must have hit him pretty hard because the protest guy's really bleeding and drenched in blood."

"Jesus, another casualty of the war," Hawkins laughed looking at the picture. "We got a peace symbol guy gettin' a little taste of fightin'. Can you imagine, bloodied by a peace symbol sign? That must be embarrassin'. I wonder if you can get Purple Heart from a peace symbol sign?"

Hawkins hurriedly added, "I read somewhere the peace symbol circle with the upside down 'Y' in it and an "I" represents a chicken track impression on a horse turd. Close your eyes and just picture that symbol. Course, the chicken and the turd kinda speak for themselves. Can you imagine supportin' such a sign that kinda says you're both a little chicken and big turd?"

Corporal Thunder, Wiley, and Clary laughed uncontrollably. They laughed when they could, which was infrequent, but laughter and Hawkins were their few reliefs from the war.

Wiley, Hawkins, and Clary admitted they had received news clippings, too. The clippings contained both concerns and confirmations for the Vietnam War. "My priest uncle sent me an article about three major areas of support for the Vietnam War," Hawkins said.

"He said the Congress, the Catholic Church, and the Chamber of Commerce all supported the war in the early days," he continued, "and that support represented politicians and governments, churches and religions, and businesses and workers in America. Unfortunately, he said the support's now beginning to erode."

"Yeah, my dad sent me a clipping about the country beginning to doubt the war, too" Clary noted, "At first over 60 percent of Americans favored the war and escalation, but later those percentages changed.

"My dad claims those are high percentages for a war, but two other clippings talk about support for the war starting to decline," Clary sighed. "First, we believe in the war, but now we're beginning to doubt it. It seems people's opinions about the war change, but their opinions about freedom stay the same. Don't they know sometimes we just have to fight for freedom?"

"Well, there's lots who believe in us, but it seems they don't say as much as the protesters," Wiley smiled. "I have a clipping here from my dad. It's a picture of a Natchez march."

Hawkins was quick to interrupt, "Jesus, Wiley, you people in Natchez love marchin'. You're always marchin'. First, it's the KKK whities marchin' against the blacks. Then, it's the blacks marchin' for Civil Rights. Now, it's probably blacks and whites marchin' against the war.

"Let's make a deal, Wiley," Hawkins suggested. "You get a job on the Natchez City Council. Then you can hire me as the Natchez Parade Permit and Demonstration Director. I'll sell parade permits right and left. We'll make fortunes much as you southerners like to march."

"Well, I don't know if Natchez is ready for a carpetbagger Bostonian Mafia Irish type," Wiley answered, "but come on down. We'll get you in politics. You're a natural politician."

"Jesus, on second thought, I might have to rethink that little proposition," Hawkins sighed. "I was thinkin' it was more like Mafia graft and corruption, but if it's more like politics I'm out."

Clary was unable to resist, "Damn, Hawkins, you better listen to Wiley. He said you'd be a natural politician and you would. There's more graft and corruption in politics than in the Mafia. You'd be a natural because you already got a head start on the graft and corruption part."

"Okay, let me get back to my clipping. We're getting off track here," Wiley remarked. "It's a picture of my brothers and sisters and other students marching, but they're marching to support the war. Can you believe that? They're marching for us not against us."

Wiley passed the clipping to the team. Corporal Thunder commented and asked, "Yep, they're protesting the protestors. Wiley, which ones are your brothers and sisters?"

Wiley pointed with pride. "Those. That's my littlest brother, but he's the biggest."

"Jesus, I thought you was huge, Wiley," Hawkins exclaimed in awe, "but he's monstrous."

"My dad says in his letter the war protestors made a mistake interrupting the march," Wiley continued, "because my brothers just started punching and kicking like our ole mule. The police let it go till the war protesters were beaten and bloodied good. Then they took them to jail."

"The best part is the caption, 'Brothers and Sisters Support and Defend Marine Brother in Vietnam'," Wiley smiled proudly. "They're fighting for us back in Natchez. How about that?"

Corporal Thunder, Hawkins, and Clary viewed the picture as Wiley passed it to them. They said nothing, but their thoughts and silence were understood by Wiley. Wiley was as proud of his brothers and sisters as they were of him. They all sensed it and they were all comforted by it, too. Someone caring was important to them.

"Jesus, people protestin' the war say war is good for nothin', but freedoms are somethin'," Hawkins smiled. "Maybe wars are good for nothin' but helpin' us be free in our American Revolution, for gettin' rid of slavery in our Civil War, and for kickin' the asses of lots of dictators and evil tyrants in two World Wars is somethin'. Maybe war's sometimes good for somethin'."

"Well, that's what my dad's saying the Bible says about war," Wiley continued. "We either fight for freedoms and peace or we let the bad or evil ones take them from us. Maybe we don't want to fight, but we want to be free. We'd rather fight than lose our freedoms."

"Jesus, if asked, I bet most people would say they hate war." Hawkins frowned. "I'd sure say I hate it. Hell, I bet I hate it more than most because I ain't exactly having the time of my life in this damn war. I gotta lotta reasons to hate war.

"But, if asked, I bet most people would say they love freedom, too." Hawkins smiled. "I'm for freedom. That's a no brainer. I'd rather be free than a slave to anyone or anything."

"The problem is, sometimes we cain't have one without the other. Sometimes we have to be willin' to fight a war to be free." Hawkins concluded. "Sometimes we have to love freedom more than we hate war."

"Well, that's one way to look at it," Wiley agreed. "It'd be best if countries could solve their problems with diplomacy, but history proves it doesn't always work. I wish it did, but it don't."

"Jesus, there just ain't nothin' easy about war," Hawkins declared, "but there's a lot of hard evil in the world. There's always been evil, too. That's why we just have to keep fightin' for good. We just have to keep fightin' for freedom and peace. We stop fightin' and we're done."

Corporal Thunder, Wiley, Hawkins, and Clary continued grappling to understand war. They were more than ever under no illusions the struggle would be quick and effortless. Learning how exhausting the tussle would actually become took time and thought. They were also beginning to sense, in early 1967, the erosion of public support for the Vietnam War.

Learning America's lack of public support for the war, however, created consequences for them. "When our people protest the war it's probably because none of us likes war. We sure as hell don't," Hawkins grumbled. "I hate war, but American's protestin' the war only makes it harder for us to win the peace they really want. But worst, it only makes it easier for the North Vietnamese to keep wearin' us down and keep on fightin'. Don't the protestors know they're makin' the war longer not shorter? They're makin' it harder for us and easier for the enemy. Maybe they ain't thought about it that way, but they're supportin' the enemy more than they're supportin' us. They're helpin' the enemy more than they're helpin' us."

This was part of the darker than dark thoughts that began to plague them more and more. It was the darkness they struggled to understand. Meanwhile, they patrolled and battled to survive, but too many were dying. More and more they heard dark rumors of Khe Sanh, too.

"Here from the river we've just been patrolling south and west to Ca Lu so far," Clary added, "but the road leads on out to Khe Sanh. I bet we go to Khe Sanh before too long. It's coming."

"Yeah, that's what Corporal Thunder mentioned a month or so ago," Hawkins sighed. "Khe Sanh's a comin'. We'll be goin' there before long. Yep, I bet so. Count on it."

Corporal Thunder and the team patrolled west and south of the river base camp in February and the first weeks of March. "Damn, I'm kinda likin' this new routine. We got a river to bathe in. We're gettin' better weather, too," Hawkins admitted. "Best of all we got R & R's a comin'."

One evening during a bunker talk, Wiley remarked, "Hawkins, you don't know where you want to go on R & R. First, it's Bangkok. Then, it's Hong Kong. Next, it's Tokyo. I don't know where it'll be next. Maybe the Philippines? Maybe Malaysia? I bet you don't even know."

"Not even don't I know, I don't give a damn," Hawkins smiled. "Just so long as it's outta this shithole. Just so they ain't no patrols and ain't no one tryin' to kill me. That's all I know."

"Well, wherever it is I hope it comes fast," Corporal Thunder grinned and teased. "You been talking about R & R ever since I mentioned it in January. Now I wish I'd waited to talk about it. You've been driving us crazy with all this talk about R & R."

Hawkins was undeterred. "Actually, I've been dreamin' a new dream for R & R. I've been dreamin' of a Midget Triple." Hawkins was again preparing to verbally ambush the team.

"What the hell is a Midget Triple?" Clary quickly asked before he considered the various possibilities. Imaging the possibilities, however, would have been impossible for him; for any of them. Thankfully, none of them were remotely possible of thinking Hawkins' thoughts.

"You know, I read about it in the *Playboy* from the sorority. It's where three people have sex together," Hawkins confidently replied. "Me and two tiny Asian girls. A Midget Triple."

"Hawkins, you idiot. That's not Midget Triple. That's a Menage a Trois," Clary corrected. "It's French for a sexual threesome."

"Jesus, Clary, that's what I said," Hawkins continued unfazed. "You guys are always sayin' I'm a midget. So, I'm gettin' me two little midget Asian girls and we're gonna have a party. I can damn well call it what I wanta call it. I'm callin' it a Midget Triple. I can't even say Menage a Trois. I ain't goin' to France. Don't talk France. I'm goin' to Singapore."

Corporal Thunder and Wiley quickly deduced this was a conversation it would be best for them to elude. Hawkins was once again verbally abusing Clary. "The problem is," Wiley mumbled, "Clary hasn't yet figured out Hawkins has outflanked him again."

"So, now it's Singapore. Well, you can go straight to hell for all I care," Clary smiled in exasperation once he concluded Hawkins had bested him with his idiocy, "because I'm going to Australia. You can have a Midget Six Pack for all I care."

"Clary, that's the best idea yet," Hawkins declared. "A Midget Six Pack. I'll just try that. If two girls and a Midget Triple are good, then six girls and a Midget Six Pack has to be better."

"They've been talking like this for a month," Corporal Thunder whispered to Wiley. "I'm glad the First Sergeant's coming out tomorrow morning to start the coordination for R & Rs."

Mid-morning the following day, First Sergeant Sharp visited the front to talk with Mike Company Marines about R & R. He drifted to the team's bunker about noon. The team had just returned from the river and bathing and washing laundry. Clothing was scattered about to dry. It was a pleasant day for Vietnam, despite the war. Clary thought, *At least Hawkins is not naked because the First Sergeant would probably walk on by and take his R & Rs with him.*

"You four all came last summer and you're all eligible for R & R now or whenever you want," First Sergeant Sharp began, "but it'll take me about two weeks to schedule you once you let me know where you want to go. I can't guarantee you your first choice, but give me three choices. I can guarantee you one of the three. Most get their first or second choice."

Corporal Thunder was the first to speak. "First Sergeant, I'm not taking R & R. I have a little sister who's graduating from high school this May. I want her to have nice prom and graduation dresses. I'm sending money to my mother to buy my sister dresses."

"You sure that's what you want to do?" First Sergeant Sharp asked questioningly.

"I've never been surer," the Corporal replied. "My sister deserves to graduate in style more than I need to get hammered with beer and laid by strange girls."

"Well, you're one helluva big brother," the First Sergeant conceded. "Maybe a little chaste and crazy, but a good brother. If you change your mind, just let me know. Okay, who's next?"

"First Sergeant, I want to pass on R & R, too," Wiley explained. "My dad's a part-time preacher and our local rural church was robbed and vandalized. I'm sending my R & R money to my dad to help with the repairs and buying new church needs. It needs a new piano."

"Damn, don't we have no sinners here?" First Sergeant Sharp smiled and asked in mock exasperation, "or are all of you my choir boys? Okay, next?"

"First Sergeant, I'm probably…" Hawkins began, but the First Sergeant quickly interrupted.

"Okay, now I know I got me a sinner and R & R taker," he laughed. "Hawkins, you've been talking about R & R since you arrived in Vietnam. You only get one. You can't have Corporal Thunder's and Wiley's, but you got one coming. Where you want to go?"

"I'm passin', too," Hawkins smiled. "I figure I'd blow two or three months pay on booze and broads. I'm savin', too. But I want you to help me get the paymaster to cut me a check for $200."

"This is the damnedest fire team I've ever seen," First Sergeant Sharp answered. "Yeah, I can get you a check. Who you want it made out to? You get me a name and I'll get you a check."

Hawkins glanced at Wiley and asked, "Wiley, what's your dad's name?"

"It's George Abraham Wiley," Wiley answered without thinking.

"Make the check out to George Abraham Wiley," Hawkins quickly told the First Sergeant.

Wiley then sensed what was occurring and asked, "Hawkins, what're you doing?"

"I'm helpin' you and your dad buy that new piano for your church," Hawkins beamed and answered casually, "You need a piano and I want to help. Besides, I've been a cussin' and killin' too much in this war. I need a lot of prayin' for me and I'm hopin' your dad will do me prayers."

"Hawkins, you been talking R & R for ages. It's been your dream for months. You got to go on R & R," Wiley pleaded. "My dad will pray for you here in Vietnam and on R & R, too. You need prayers for both, especially R & R. You been talking R & R forever and you got to go."

"Jesus, I been talkin' 'bout lotta things. Hell, I just talk to talk. Dreamin' 'bout R & R is probably just as good as goin'. I been a hundred times already in my dreams. Hell, I been on so many R & R's I don't need no more. I'm kinda tired of R & Rs," Hawkins blurted. "Besides, I talk to guys who've been and they say the worst part is havin' to come back to this war. It just ruins it. You just go back to the real world for a week of fun and girls and then you just have to come back for months of more Vietnam and more killin's. When I leave this shithole I wanna leave it for good. I ain't comin' back. I'll just be good and gone."

"But you got to go," Wiley begged again. Wiley was exasperated but overcome because he realized $200 was about two months base pay for Hawkins as a PFC.

"Wiley, I don't gotta go and don't make me get emotional," Hawkins mumbled. "I'm doin' what I wanna do. I'm doin' it 'cause your mama needs a piano to play and your sisters need a piano to sing with. I'm doin' it 'cause you're my friend. I'm doin' it 'cause we're teammates and brothers and family. Now I ain't sayin' no more 'bout this. It's done. It's over. Let's move on."

Wiley attempted to respond, but he was unable to speak. Finally, he stood, walked to Hawkins, stood towering over him, reached down, and lifted him up. He gave him a monster bear hug shaking him ever so tenderly and playfully. Hawkins' feet dangled and danced two feet off the ground. Wiley then shuffled back to his sandbag location and sat with his head bowed. He said nothing. He was overcome and speechless, but Corporal Thunder noticed tears in his eyes. Corporal Thunder placed an arm across his shoulder and gave Wiley a tender pat on his broad muscular back. Corporal Thunder thought, *I don't know which is stronger, Wiley's hard brute strength or his soft gentle compassion.*

Corporal Thunder muttered, "First Sergeant's right. This is the damnedest fire team ever."

"Well, you don't even have to ask who's next," Clary proclaimed to break the silence. "I'm not going anywhere either. I'm not going anywhere without the team going. I'm saving my money to buy my mother the nicest Mother's Day present ever. She deserves it. We all put our moms through a lot being here in Vietnam. She deserves a nice present. I'll wait till I get home in Southern California to take R & R. It's the best place in the world for R & R. I'll wait, too."

First Sergeant Sharp's countenance was one of stoned silence, "Marines, I don't know what to say. This is not what I expected." He shook his head in disbelief, but with respect, too.

"You don't have to say anything, First Sergeant," Corporal Thunder exclaimed. "We said what we wanted to say. We said what needed to be said. There's nothing else to say."

First Sergeant Sharp nodded his head in agreement, stood, and walked to the next bunker shaking his head. He knew there were no words to express what he had witnessed. No words at all. At least no words he knew.

Two patrols and one ambush later, First Sergeant Sharp passed a cryptic note from the Company M rear area to the company forward in the field.

The note simply read, "At earliest have Lance Corporal Wiley and PFC Hawkins report to the rear in Dong Ha. Need both for admin issue."

A day later Wiley and Hawkins boarded the mid-morning truck convoy for its return to Dong Ha. "I wonder why the First Sergeant wants to see us?" Wiley asked Hawkins.

"Damned if I know, but I ain't done nothin' I know of," Hawkins answered. "Nothin' at all. I been good. I ain't done nothin' wrong. Nothin' at all I know of." Guilt forever plagued Hawkins.

They were apprehensive and curious about why the First Sergeant was requesting them in the rear. Imagining a number of reasons, they sighed because none were too pleasant to imagine. They refused to even consider the steeple incident. Finally, Hawkins said, "Oh, well, it's the rear and a break. Can't be nothin' too bad. Can't be worse than the patrols and mortars here up front."

Awaiting them in the Dong Ha rear, however, was another battle. It was an old style brawl. It was the style and type of fight in which Hawkins excelled. It was a combat engagement like none other they would ever experience in Vietnam. It was, as Wiley later professed, "Awesome."

CHAPTER 18

~

Boots, Brawls, & Kabuki Dances

"The Pentagon and the politicians need to figure out if this is a real war or if this is a phony kabuki dance. I'll fight like hell if it's a war. I'll dance like hell if it's a dance. But I ain't fightin' at a dance and I ain't dancin' at a fight. Let's call it what it is and let's get on with it. Fightin' or dancin'. Either one is okay by me, but just let me know which one it is."

—Marine Private First Class Dominic Hawkins

Wiley and Hawkins arrived in Dong Ha and hesitatingly reported to First Sergeant Sharp as ordered. "I was hoping you'd be coming in today," First Sergeant Sharp welcomed them. "Now, Hawkins, let's go down to the paymaster and get you your check. You have to come in and sign for it in person." Wiley and Hawkins immediately smiled at one another in relief.

First Sergeant Sharp, Wiley, and Hawkins strolled to the battalion paymaster's tent. The First Sergeant had alerted the paymaster in advance and the check was ready. "Okay, here's the check and here's where you sign for it," the First Sergeant explained and pointed to a journal for Hawkins to sign. "I had it made for two hundred dollars and to George Abraham Wiley.

"Now, Wiley, you need to take the check to the post office right now and mail it," the First Sergeant recommended, "but first let's go the office and get you an envelope. You can write a quick letter to your dad, too. Then you can mail the letter with the check."

Wiley wrote his dad a letter and addressed the envelope. While inserting the letter and check into the envelope and sealing it, he asked, "Thanks, First Sergeant. Now what do we do?"

"I'll have the company driver take you to the Post Office. It's on the other side of the airfield," First Sergeant Sharp replied. "You can get a little insurance and mail it there."

"By the way, they have an All Hands Club for enlisted on the other side not too far from the Post Office," the First Sergeant smiled and hinted. "The driver can take you there for burgers and fries if you want. The club's run by the Army and it has pretty good food for Vietnam."

"Jesus, you kiddin', First Sergeant?" Hawkins blurted. "We ain't had no burgers and fries in ages. Damn right we're stoppin' in and eatin' the hell outta some good eats."

The First Sergeant smiled as the company driver departed with Wiley and Hawkins. He instinctively liked both Marines and alleged they reminded him of himself when he was a young enlisted Marine in World War II. Absent-mindedly, he remarked to the young admin Marines in the tent office, "Yes, Sir, those two are full of piss and vinegar. Talk about opposites attracting. They're quite a pair. This should be quite a day. Quite a day." The Marines smiled knowingly.

Wiley and Hawkins conducted their Post Office business as quick as possible and rushed to the All Hands Club for a late lunch. Unfortunately, their excitement quickly plummeted to depths of despair. Fortunately, it soared to heights of ecstasy even quicker. It was a priceless incident. It was Boston North End Italian Hawkins and Southern Black Natchez Wiley...men among boys.

Wiley and Hawkins entered the club and instantly the club manager confronted them, "Hey, Boy, you're black, but you just ain't quite black enough. Besides, lunch hours are over."

At first, Hawkins thought it was an ill attempt at racial humor and asked, "What'da you mean? What's this about Boy and black?" He was eager to rumble, but exercised patience.

"We have a dress code here and you two look like soup sandwiches," the club manager soldier scoffed. "Just look at those boots. They haven't been shined in months. They're dirty brown and they should be polished shiny black." The haughty attitude of the club manager was grating on Hawkins. It was his rear area disrespect for front line combat Marines, however, that inflamed Hawkins the most as he thought, *We ain't gonna put up with this rear area bullshit. Not damned now. Not damned ever. This shithead soldier probably ain't never seen warpathin' Marines. Since Corporal Thunder ain't here, I suppose I gotta have us a little powwow.* "You're kiddin'? Right? You're kiddin'?" Hawkins replied. Hawkins was about to explode, but first he wanted his burgers and fries. He was a volcano seething and waiting to erupt.

"What's to kid about? You two are absolutely filthy and you expect us to serve you two jarheads?" the club manager soldier affirmed. Wiley grabbed and released Hawkins' arm to both restrain him as well as confirm he was with him in whatever happened.

Hawkins slowly, deliberately, and meekly stepped two paces forward toward the offending soldier. His arms rested purposefully down and by his side. He avoided alerting the soldier or taking any actions to cause suspicions. Ambushing the soldier by surprise was his tactic. Revenge and retaliation were standing by. Hawkins simply wanted to address a few grievances with a fight. All else was now secondary to the fight…even the burgers and fries.

Presenting an appeasing or compromising attitude was a challenge for Hawkins. The meek role was contrary to Hawkins' beliefs, but he was after his burger and fries and Coke inheritance. Erroneously concluding Hawkins was too small and meek to be a threat, the club manager stared at him defiantly. Hawkins smiled with a whimper to falsely embolden the soldier club manager.

Hawkins slowly groveled toward the soldier, while his small bent over humbled approach caused the soldier to tower over him. Once he was close, arms reach close; he swiftly thrust his hand toward the soldier's crotch, grabbed a hand full of testicles, twisted forcefully, and declared, "Now listen you shithead soldier boy." The prologue was over; the play then began.

The soldier started to speak. Hawkins pulled downward and twisted his testicles firmly and scowled, "Listen, soldier boy. I said listen. You open your mouth to talk one more time and I'll rip your balls out and stuff 'em down your throat. You gonna gag on your balls right here and right now. Now shake your head, yes, you understand because if you open your mouth one more time to talk you ain't gonna ever have sex again. You got me?"

The soldier winced in abject agony and shook his head. "Good, you learn fast," Hawkins smiled. "Now, you seem to be a little offended by us dirtyin' up your clean little club here. We'll get to the dirtyin' part, but let me first tell you my friend don't deserve to be called no Boy."

The soldier was too afraid to speak and in too much pain to respond. Hawkins pulled and twisted harder and said, "So, before we go on with our little talk to get a few other things straight, you best apologize to my friend. It's okay for you to talk and apologize. You can say 'I'm sorry for calling you, Boy'. But that's all you gotta say. It's all you better say, too."

The soldier whimpered and apologized, "I'm sorry for calling you, Boy." He winced in pain.

Wiley wasn't quite sure what he should do or say, so he simply replied, "Apology accepted."

Hawkins glanced at Wiley and smiled. He then glared at the soldier and frowned, "We don't polish our boots black in the field, not in combat. We let'em get all scuffed and buffed brown and beige from the weather and the mud. It's kinda like a real natural camouflage. Course, you wouldn't know nothin' about that. You shitheads in the rear don't know nothin' 'bout the field, much less 'bout combat. These dirty muddy brown boots are our *Red Badge of Courage.*"

"You asshole rear area morons don't know a damn thing 'bout what it's like in this war. Hell, you probably ain't seen any killin' or any combat," Hawkins began to rant. "You just hole up here real safe in your damned little club and try to act and play all important and tough."

Hawkins pulled and twisted subconsciously as his anger rose. Realizing the soldier was about to pass out from the pain, he eased back and raved, "Yep, we're pretty filthy 'cause we ain't had too many chances to bathe. We probably stink like a crappy four-holer, too, but I'd rather stink like a combat Marine than smell like an Aqua Velva splashed fruity like you."

Wiley sensed Hawkins was close to seriously injuring the soldier and requested, "Hawkins, let's let him be. Let's just have our burgers and fries and drinks and be done with it."

Hawkins glanced at Wiley. Wiley's expression pleaded for compassion instead of revenge. Wiley noted, "I've been called 'Boy' before. Some don't know better. Let's eat and move on."

"Okay, but this is one soldier who better know better from now on," Hawkins insisted, "and I got a few more things to say before we enjoy a good meal."

"First, let's go over to the bar and order our food," Wiley hungrily implored.

The Company M driver suspected the situation was about to deteriorate and deteriorate rapidly. He quietly and quickly slipped out of the club and drove as fast as he could to report the situation to First Sergeant Sharp. Neither Wiley nor Hawkins noticed the driver disappear.

Wiley and Hawkins ambled toward the bar while the soldier shuffled along awkwardly. He retained a tight grip on the soldier's testicles as he followed them like a little tethered puppy.

Wiley and Hawkins ordered burgers and fries and Cokes from the Vietnamese girl tending bar. At first, she was hesitant to take their orders, but Hawkins glanced at the club manager and tugged and twisted slightly. The soldier said nothing, but he nodded his head in approval.

"One last thing soldier boy," Hawkins emphasized. "Yep, we're filthy and dirty. We don't shine our boots and we do stink like shit, but we're staying that way 'cause we don't wanta have no one ever think we're a rear area clean scented snooty moron like you. We don't wanna ever be mistook for a shithead like you. Not ever." Hawkins was rubbing it in now.

"These scruffy unshined dirty boots kinda distinguish us from turds like you," Hawkins railed, "and we don't wanta ever be confused for some dirt bag like you."

"Jesus, I almost forgot," Hawkins remembered. "Corpsmen and other Marines can call us Jarheads, but you call us that again and I'll twist your head off and shit in your damn skull. Then if I want any more shit outta you I'll squeeze your head. You gonna have shit for brains if you say that word again." The soldier grimaced in abject pain and nodded slowly.

The food and drinks came quickly. Hawkins released the soldier club manager and ordered, "Okay, stay behind the bar where I can see you." The soldier cowered and complied.

Wiley and Hawkins enjoyed their first burger and fries in over seven months. While Wiley and Hawkins focused on their meal the club manager whispered to the Vietnamese girl. The girl quickly disappeared, but minutes later she reappeared with six Army soldiers.

While devouring their meal, Wiley and Hawkins noticed a smile creep to the soldier's contorted face. "Somethin' funny, shithead?" Hawkins smiled back at the soldier.

"It's about to get funnier," the soldier frowned. "It's about payback time."

Hawkins slowly wheeled and noticed the six imposing soldiers. Hawkins' mood mellowed as his smile broke into a broad grin. Unfortunately, for the soldier club manager, he failed to notice Hawkins' broad grin of eager anticipation. He probably expected a frown of fear, but Hawkins was not into fear. Hawkins was into the fight. What the soldier failed to realize was that what was about to happen was exactly what Hawkins wanted to happen. Hawkins was more than ready for a fight. He wanted a fight and now he had the fight he wanted.

Hawkins leaped over the bar in one swift motion. "I knew the soldier would be slowed by the pain in his groin. I knew he was hurtin' bad and movin' slow. I just flattened my palm and trust up with the heel of my hand and caught him right below the nose. It was just a little love tap," Hawkins later explained to Corporal Thunder and Clary as he and Wiley recounted the fight.

"I hit him kinda easy so's not to push his nose bones up into his brain and kill'im," Hawkins alleged, "but hard enough so the blood would gush like a busted fire hydrant. There's so much blood from a hit like that. He was finished fightin' because all he was tryin' to do was stop the bleedin'. When you bleed like a stuck pig, it really bothers you. You just can't do much else. It scares you. He was bleedin' and he was scared. He was too scared to get angry, too."

Hawkins hollered to Wiley, "I'm learnin' this limited war bullshit. I coulda hurt'im bad or damned near killed him with that palm thrust, but I held back on the force."

"Well, now it's total war," Wiley yelled back. "It's six soldiers against us two Marines."

"Jesus, Wiley, that's just our kinda odds," Hawkins answered. "Now we don't have to hold back at all. We can just fight like livin' hell. We can fight for survival. It's a real street brawl."

"Yeah, that's exactly what we best do," Wiley frowned, as Hawkins started throwing bar stools and chairs across the deck at the soldiers' feet. He wondered why the hell Hawkins was throwing stuff until he noticed the soldiers tripping and falling all over the bar stools and chairs.

"They can't stand up. Can't keep their balance," Hawkins yelled. "Let's just bowl'em down.

"Jesus, Wiley, that's Boston Mafia tactics," Hawkins shouted. "First, you get'em down and then you keep'em down. Don't ever let'em up. Just pound'em down again and again. They'll stay down, too. It hurt likes hell to get your shins and knees clobbered. It just sorta makes you wanna hop around like a dancin' fool. You just gotta go down and rub'em."

While the soldiers struggled to rise up, Hawkins and Wiley simply delivered uppercut kicks to their guts and ribs as well as rabbit punches to the back of their heads. The soldiers were bloodied and battered almost beyond recognition, but the only marks on Wiley and Hawkins were bruised knuckles and sore arches from their punches and kicks.

"Well, it seems to be working," Wiley confirmed. "I don't see a one of them getting back to his feet. They're just hunkering down and hoping we'll be easy on them."

"Yeah, it was a helluva beat down," Hawkins later declared to Corporal Thunder and Clary, "until the Army Military Police arrived. The club manager musta called them. He was more of a rear area moron than I thought. He had a chance to get in a really good fight and he cowered out. What a shithead. Probably afraid of messing up his clean uniform. Probably scared of scuffing up his polished boots. Probably faint from losing so much blood from his nose, too."

The Army MPs quickly restored order. The six soldiers were lined up against one side of the wooden framed reinforced tent and Wiley and Hawkins on the other. "Okay, what the hell is happening here?" the Army Sergeant MP shouted, "What's this fight all about?"

The Army club manager hobbled around the bar and started to answer, "The two Marines..."

Instantly, the tent flap and screen door sprang open and First Sergeant Sharp burst into the club with his entourage and bellowed, "Okay, I heard you got them." He bounded into the club with such a commotion the Army club manager's words were immediately suspended. Seconds later, four Marine MP's bolted into the club with batons at the ready in their left hands and with their right hands on their holstered .45 caliber pistols. Menacingly hostile, the four Marines were eager to flaunt their MP authority in support of the First Sergeant.

First Sergeant Sharp marched angrily and quickly to the Army Sergeant MP, extended his hand in sincere friendship, smiled crookedly, shook the MP's hand, and profusely explained, "Thanks, Sergeant. I'm First Sergeant Sharp and these two Marines are my prisoners. Somehow they escaped this morning and we've been looking all over for them. They got a ton of legal charges and they'll probably end up in the brig. Thanks for capturing them for us."

The First Sergeant strolled to Hawkins with flair and for effect and grabbing the scruff of Hawkins's neck he bellowed, "You can't run fast or far enough for me not to catch you."

Wiley and Hawkins observed the discussion and maltreatment in total disbelief. "Jesus, at first I thought the First Sergeant had lost his mind," Hawkins later explained, "but eventually I kinda thought it was all an act. He had us going for awhile though. Damned if he ain't one helluva actor."

"Fast as hell, before the Army MP's could figure out what was happening," Wiley later explained, once back in their bunker with Corporal Thunder and Clary, "the First Sergeant ordered the Marine MP's to take us into custody and escort us to the battalion legal officer for Courts Martial proceedings."

"The Marine MP's grabbed us kinda forcefully, one on each of our arms, and got us to hell outta there as fast as they could," Hawkins asserted. "Hell, the Army MP's just couldn't keep up with the First Sergeant's talking and maneuvering. We was outta there in a flash. First Sergeant Sharp just took charge and took us outta there before they knew what was happenin'."

The Army club manager, bruised and befuddled, whined, "What about my nose and club?"

"Damn, breaking a little furniture and punching on a nose is the least of the charges against these two Marines," the First Sergeant responded. "Hell, I got them on a lot more serious charges. They're serious criminals and you'll have to get in line with your charges."

First Sergeant Sharp then wheeled toward the Army Sergeant MP. With the utmost of thanks and friendliness, he again acknowledged, "Thanks, again, for apprehending these two Marines. I'll take them from here, but if the club manager wants to prefer charges just have him fill out a charge sheet and send it over to me. I'll take care of it." The First

Sergeant stroked the Army MP Sergeant brilliantly with all the aplomb of a Senior Enlisted Marine to a Junior Enlisted Soldier.

Then, before the Army Sergeant MP could respond, First Sergeant Sharp did an about-face and walked briskly from the club. He paused briefly at the door and stared directly at the Army Sergeant MP one last time. "Thanks again, you Army MPs do good work. Damn good. I'll let your boss know you did good today." The Army MP nodded proudly and professionally. He was unsure exactly what had transpired, but he appreciated the profuse congratulations and thanks.

The three Jeep Marine convoy then sped to the other side of the Dong Ha airfield in a massive cloud of dust. Quickly, the jeeps crossed from the Army side of the field to the Marine side. Wiley and Hawkins sighed in relief, but they were confused. They rode in silence as they attempted to unravel their jumbled thoughts about the events in the Army club. Hawkins thought, *This is sure one damned strange war. Nothin' makes much sense. Not now, not ever. Nothin'.*

Hawkins whispered to Wiley, "Jesus, there ain't nothin' happenin' in Vietnam that makes much sense. Not much at all. Damn, I was there and I saw what just happened, but what really happened? I don't know what's happenin' now. Nothin' makes sense in this war. Nothin' at all."

The Marine convoy screeched to a halt in front of the Mike Company office tent in minutes. First Sergeant Sharp stretched his huge frame from the confining Jeep. Without glancing at them, but pointing at Wiley and Hawkins, he ordered the Marine MPs, "Escort them to my office."

Wiley and Hawkins became more confused. Once they centered themselves at attention in front of the First Sergeant's field desk they heard him growl, "Okay, what the hell happened?"

Wiley glanced at Hawkins and Hawkins then took the lead in explaining the incident at the club. Wiley and Hawkins both sensed this was no inquisition as First Sergeant Sharp began to smile as Hawkins recounted the scene in excruciatingly minute detail. Hawkins heaped more and more minutia into his story. The First Sergeant grinned even more as he soaked it all in.

With deep regret, Hawkins eventually concluded his laborious account of the incident. The First Sergeant regretted the conclusion of the account more than they would ever understand. The incident was over, it was discussed and dissected and debated, but it would be remembered and retold until it became Marine Corps Dong Ha folklore.

"Well, that's about what I thought and hoped would happen," First Sergeant Sharp roared.

Wiley and Hawkins stole quick glances of confusion at one another. "What do you mean, First Sergeant?" Wiley asked innocently.

"Yeah, well, that damn Army club manager has been harassing Marines every time we go over there," First Sergeant Sharp grumbled. "He's always pissing and moaning about Marines this and about Marines that. He just doesn't like Marines. We more or less have to take it because they got the only club."

"Jesus, he's gonna hate us now," Hawkins exclaimed. "We gave him a few more reasons."

"Well, that's what I was hoping. I know you two. I know how you handled Rogers and the drugs a few months ago. I knew you'd handle the Army asshole, too," First Sergeant Sharp continued. "I know what happens around here even if you young Marines sometimes think I don't. First Sergeant's are supposed to know what the hell's going on. I know.

"But I know I had to be careful about how to handle the club situation," he confessed. "I couldn't get too involved, especially with my rank and seniority. I have to get along with all the tenants in the rear area, especially the Army. The Army gives us really good support and we need it. It's not the Army. The Army's good to us; real good. We get a lot of good stuff from the Army we can't get from the Marines. They got a good supply system and they share with us.

"Most rear area types provide super support to the frontline troops, but some just think they're too good for the infantry," Wiley and Hawkins remained silent as the First Sergeant vented. "Hell, sometimes most all of us pull rear area duty for one reason or another, which makes us respect those on the front more. The Army club soldier, however, is one of those who looks down on the combat types and doesn't know what it's like up front. He's an asshole.

"You two remind me of me when I was a young enlisted Marine. I know I maybe set you up, but I figured you'd figure out how to take care of the Army club manager," the First Sergeant beamed. "Damned if I wasn't right. You took care of him. I bet he thinks twice before he tries to shit on one of us Marines again.

"Then he has the nerve to threaten to file charges," First Sergeant Sharp laughed. "I hope he does. I hope he holds his breath until I process them, too. He'll just suffocate on his own hot air."

"Jesus, you mean you kinda thought we'd be harassed. You sorta thought we'd take on the club manager?" Hawkins smiled.

"Thought, hell, I bet my ass you would. Was I right?" First Sergeant Sharp howled, "Damn, son, I'm no First Sergeant for nothing. I mentioned the burgers and fries knowing you couldn't resist. Then I had my driver watch over you and come get me if you got in trouble. Hell, we were standing by all the time. We were just hoping and waiting for the action to begin.

"I had my two admin clerks and two supply Marines standing by, too," First Sergeant Sharp laughed. "I had my supply Marines appropriate a few extra MP shoulder brassards from the Army to make them look real official, too. What do you think? Don't they look like MPs?"

The Marines in the office could no longer contain themselves. The office erupted in hoots and hollers of uproarious laughter. The typically gruff and grumpy character of First Sergeants evaporated. First Sergeant Sharp laughed until tears streamed from his eyes and proclaimed, "I got to have you two come back more often. I got a few more problems for you to fix."

"Jesus, I got more problem fixin' time than you got problems," Hawkins smiled, "just call us anytime, but you got to call all four of us. You got to call in Corporal Thunder and Clary, too. They're real good at fixin' problems."

"Well, if we miss a few patrols that'll probably be okay, too," Wiley said, "but I don't think the Army club will be a problem anymore. Call us if it does. I really like those burgers and fries."

"Yeah, and I kinda like kicking the shit outta asshole Army club managers who don't have no respect for field and fightin' Marines," Hawkins muttered. "Just let us know if he ain't learned what he shoulda learned. We'll come back. We'll come back hard, too."

"Well, I'm working with the Navy to get us a Marine and Navy Club on this side of the airfield," First Sergeant Sharp replied, "and I'm hoping it's sooner rather than later."

"Does that mean Marines won't have to go there because we'll have a club?" Wiley asked.

"What that means," Hawkins interrupted, "is that we'll just go over there for R & R."

Wiley looked inquisitively at Hawkins and asked, "What do you mean, R & R?"

"Jesus, Wiley, we'll just go over for R & R. We'll go over there just for fun, just to pound the piss outta a few disrespectful rear area soldiers ever now and then," Hawkins giggled. "The front line Army soldiers will probably appreciate our help and join in the fightin', too. Bet they don't really like rear area shitheads either. We'll have a few fights for fun. Just a little R & R. Yeah, we'll just have us in-country R & R. Instead of foolin' with girls in some flop house, we'll be fightin' rear area morons. It'll probably be just as much fun and it'll damn sure be cheaper."

The ceaseless chatter continued until the First Sergeant declared, "Let's go to the beer tent and have a beer or two. I owe you two a few beers. I got sodas, too. It's a little early for beer call, but let's just have a few for the helluva it. I'm buying."

While sharing beers, Hawkins asked, "What if the Army club manager makes out charges?"

"Well, son, I was a rifleman just like you for a lot more years than I've been a First Sergeant. I'm better with a rifle than I am with a typewriter and the paperwork," First Sergeant Sharp grinned. "Sometimes I lose paperwork in the shit can. It just disappears. It's how I deal with useless crap. Don't worry about no charges. Let's just worry about another beer. You up for another?" The rest of the day and night was a blur to Hawkins.

Corporal Thunder and Clary were on an afternoon patrol when Wiley and Hawkins returned to their bunker and base camp later the next day. "Thankfully, we have nothing to do with our squad on patrol," Wiley said. Wiley and Hawkins were asleep in minutes while attempting to mitigate the effects of Hawkins' lingering hangover and the near sleepless night.

Later, as the sun surrendered to the mountains and jungles, the team was together again and Clary said, "Okay, let's have Wiley and Hawkins tell us about their trip to the rear."

Hawkins immediately transitioned into his storytelling mode. He loved a good story, but he loved telling one more. Wiley conceded most of the storytelling to Hawkins because he knew it would be futile for him to attempt to interrupt with much more than a few passing comments. Hawkins' arms flailed wildly and his spontaneous gestures were raucous. He was as dangerous at telling stories as he was fighting. Wiley had to duck a time or two, but the dark bunker glowed.

Hawkins entertained the team for over an hour and told the story with extreme gusto. He exaggerated a time or two, but he was always careful to ask, "Ain't that right, Wiley?"

Launching back into his story before Wiley had an opportunity to confirm or deny the rendition with either a nod of his head or word of agreement, Hawkins attacked the story relentlessly. Hawkins was fast and free with his words, but equally compelling and captivating.

Once Hawkins completed his storytelling, the team repeated portions of it for another hour. The repetitions created as much laughter as the original…and even more exaggerations.

The dark and silent night passed without incident and the team woke to an early reveille. Corporal Thunder attended a morning briefing and returned to the team bunker. "Okay, gather round and listen up," he asked. The team sat on sandbags to enjoy the morning sun.

"Yep, we're up and listening. If we had anywhere to go we'd go," Hawkins complained.

"Yeah, I know. It's force of habit," he replied. "Besides, you kind of expect it. It gives you something to bitch about. Not that you're ever lacking for something to bitch about."

Hawkins smiled and nodded in agreement. He said nothing, but he cradled his head tenderly.

"Okay, remember I mentioned a couple of months ago something about a new rifle?" the Corporal reminded the team. "Well, it's about to happen."

"Why a new rifle?" Clary frowned. "I like the M14. I like the one we have now."

"Well, we like the M14 best," Corporal Thunder continued, "but there's complaints it's too heavy, not good in jungles, uncontrollable in full-automatic, and we can't carry enough ammo."

"Who's complainin'?" Hawkins asked softly and answered, "Some moron who ain't carried a rifle in these mountains and jungles. Probably some gun maker wantin' to sell us a new rifle."

"When we gonna get it?" Wiley asked as he mixed Hawkins a C-Ration Kool Aid.

"We start getting classes on it next week. The last weeks in March we'll get instructors teaching us about the weapon," Corporal Thunder answered. "Then we'll do familiarization and battle sight zero firing. Then, on 1 April, we'll officially transition to the M16."

"Wow, that's pretty fast," Wiley noted. "Hope that's enough time"

"Jesus, that's April Fool's Day. Hope it ain't a bad joke," Hawkins frowned. "That's sorta a bad sign."

After the introductory training sessions the team talked about the new M16 in its nightly bunker talk. They caressed their M14s. The clutched the M16s with disdain.

"Well, the M16 sure isn't the M14," Corporal Thunder began. "I'm praying this is not a mistake, but it sure don't seem right to me. Yeah, it's light, but it just seems it's plastic and tin."

"Plastic and tin, my ass," Hawkins complained. "It's a piece of shit. I got turds stronger than that damn M16. Hell, it's a toy gun. It ain't no rifle. G.I. Joe could probably fart down the barrel and punch rounds out harder. His farts would probably be more powerful, too."

"Well, I like the hard steel and polished wood stock of the M14 a lot better," Wiley agreed. "It just feels like a weapon. It's strong and sturdy and dependable. It just feels strong."

"Jesus, did you notice how small the M16 rounds are?" Hawkins asked. "They're 5.56mm and the M14 is 7.62mm. They're a lot smaller round."

"But remember the instructor said the 5.56 tends to fragment on impact and that causes larger and more serious wounds than the 7.62," Clary commented. "I'm not saying I like the M16, but that's what the instructor claims is a good feature of the M16."

"Jesus, the instructor kept saying one of the main advantages was the M16 is lighter. Maybe three or four pounds lighter." Hawkins asserted, "What the hell they think we are out here? They think we're weaklings? They think we can't carry a ten pound M14? Hell, I'd rather carry a heavyweight weapon than a featherweight one. If you can't carry a ten pound weapon, then damnit, maybe you shouldn't be out here. They think we're a bunch of girly and frilly sissies?"

"I agree," Clary noted, "but if the ammo's lighter we can carry more of it."

"Jesus, Clary, it's lighter 'cause it's smaller," Hawkins retorted. "I wanna jack the NVA up with big rounds that'll knock'em down and keep'em down. I don't want no little tiny lightweight type rounds. The bigger the better as far as I'm concerned. I'll carry the bigger heavier ammo."

"It's just disappointing because we like the M14," Corporal Thunder exclaimed, "but let's hope for the best. Besides, there's not much we can do about it. Not much at all."

"Well, I'm wondering why we're getting a new weapon now," Wiley wondered. "Why right in the middle of our tours? Why right in the middle of a war? Can't they wait?"

"My concern is we haven't really tested the M16 and the M16 hasn't really tested us," Clary alleged. "At least not in combat. But I sure hope someone's tested it really good and hard."

"Jesus, you can bet they tested it," Hawkins agreed and asked. "They probably tested it in some fancy lab, but did they test it in all the ugly, dirty, and filthy places we're in every day?"

The Marines railed about the transition from the M14 to the M16 rifle, but they agreed to do their best with the new rifle. Reluctantly, they agreed it was a functional weapon with potential. Unfortunately, the new M16 would malfunction in their first major crisis with it and most of their concerns and suspicions would be confirmed. The team's complaints were prophetic. The M16's defects and deficiencies contributed to tragic consequences and numerous deaths within the month. In the company's most courageous and defining and iconic battle of the Vietnam War, the M16 was their most unexpected and worst enemy.

Hawkins later summarized it best. "We're the world's most powerful and richest nation, but somehow we bought a weak and bad weapon that even the poorest ghetto would reject."

Later in the week the team conducted one of its final talks on war. Clary summarized past talks and concluded, "We've been talking about starting and fighting a war and maybe now we need to talk about ending a war."

"Jesus, that's a helluva novel idea," Hawkins interrupted. "Who the hell's gonna ever start a war without thinkin' about how to end it? That's dumber than dirt. Hell, I'm a PFC and I can tell you the endin' is more important than the beginin' of a war."

"Well, I agree, fighting to end the war is important," Corporal Thunder added. "It helps you decide how you're going to fight it and how hard you're willing to fight it to end it right."

"But that seems our problem with Vietnam," Clary asserted. "We don't seem to know how we really want the war to end. If we don't really know how we want to end it, it's hard to know how hard to fight it. We just don't seem to know what it's really worth to us."

"You'd think with all the practice we have with war," Wiley exclaimed, "we'd be better at war, but wars are never easy and neat. They're always hard and messy. They're hardly ever what you think they'll be and never what you want them to be. We seem to do the fighting good, but the politicking bad."

"Jesus, I hope they hurry and figure this one out fast," Hawkins mumbled, "because if they ain't wantin' to end this right, then us dyin' for it is just wrong."

"It's too easy to kill people and too hard to kill a war," Clary asserted. "People die and war lives. It's hard to figure it all out."

"The Pentagon and the politicians need to figure out if this is a real war or if this is a phony kabuki dance," Hawkins, as he repeatedly declared, again philosophized, "I'll fight like hell if it's a war. I'll dance like hell if it's a dance. But I ain't fightin' at a dance and I ain't dancin' at a fight. Let's call it what it is and let's get on with it. Fightin' or dancin'. Either one is okay by me, but let me know which one it is."

Hawkins, irreverent and irascible Hawkins, usually fought tenaciously to have the last thought and final word on almost every subject the team discussed. Tonight, however, Wiley, the team's conscience, was determined to speak last on the subject of starting and stopping wars. "It's too easy to get into a bad war and too hard to get a good peace," Wiley succinctly summarized the team's talk about the start and end of war. "War's easy; peace is hard."

Wiley's focus on peace essentially concluded the talk on starting and finishing wars. The team realized victory was never necessarily the true objective of war, but only the means to achieve the ultimate objective, which was peace…a just and free peace for all. Wiley repeated, "War's easy; peace's hard," before taking his rifle and starting his night watch in the silence that descended upon the bunker. But before taps and their sleeps, Hawkins independently decided to introduce one final talk to have the last word that he thought Wiley almost stole from him.

Suddenly, with no warning, Hawkins philosophized, "Sometimes, I love the fightin', but hate we gotta do it. Other times, I hate the fightin', but love we gotta do it." He smiled slyly and said no more. Silence dominated for an extended period of time as he waited for a response.

Wiley shrugged his shoulders and shook his head in a bemused but perplexed manner. Corporal Thunder glanced at Hawkins in exasperation at the confounding and challenging nature of his riddles. Clary simply scowled and scolded him, "Hawkins, there you go again. You poop in the punch and goad us into sipping on your stupid sayings. Do you know, do you have any idea, what the hell you're saying because it makes no sense to any of us?"

"I ain't sure. Maybe I'm sayin' somethin'. Maybe I'm sayin' nothin'," Hawkins ruefully admitted, "but I know I don't know much more 'bout what I'm sayin' than I know 'bout the way we're fightin' this war. Most times none of it makes much sense, but I gotta say what I'm sayin' and thinkin' to help me make sense of it and help me figure it all out." It was then quieter than quiet. It was too quiet.

Corporal Thunder attempted to speak, but Hawkins signaled him to wait as he paused before continuing, "I'm just prayin' that the fightin' is for right and good and that it makes sense to someone somewhere because I know some fightin' is wrong and bad and that makes no sense to anyone."

As a deeper and prolonged silence blanketed the bunker the team began to thoughtfully consider the sense they were searching for in the fighting and in the war. In time, a sense of understanding began to creep into their consciousness. It took hard thinking, but thinking and understanding was better than no thinking and no understanding.

"I know all this talkin' and thinkin' is hurtin' our brains," Hawkins finally surmised, "but I'm hopin' it's healin' our hearts. Gettin' our hearts right is what's right 'bout all our talkin' and thinkin'. We gotta do right by this war and this war's gotta do right by us."

Slowly the dark night seemed darker than dark, but it was a dark that was part of the team's journey toward the light. It was another one of the team's dark forays into more of something about which they knew much of nothing. They knew Con Thien, however, and they were about to be introduced to Khe Sanh. In both of these their hearts came to know the worst of the war.

CHAPTER 19

Khe Sanh's Tumultuous Beginning

"Days of eluding death and embracing life."

—Marine Corporal Dark Pale Thunder

The first week in April, Corporal Thunder briefed the team. "Tomorrow we're going back to Con Thien. It's kind of strange. Our mission's simply to man the defensive perimeters. We'll be doing no patrols. The Con Thien units will do all the patrolling just so they can get out of the bunkers and in the field for ten days. They need a break from the trenches and bombardments."

Wiley, Clary, and Hawkins nodded, but no one replied. They were lounging on sandbags reading letters from home from the morning mail call. Reading letters from home was more important to them than complaining about Con Thien...at least for the moment.

The battalion command element and two companies deployed to Con Thien the next day. It was an uneventful patrol to the fire base, except for the tension while approaching the location of the now destroyed steeple. This time, unlike all previous times, there were no attacks from the steeple or NVA mortars simply because there was no steeple. Smiling knowingly, the team advanced and passed the steeple ruins without incident. Hawkins pantomimed an explosion with his hands and a whistling sound with his lips and then turned away in disgust.

The battalion's arrival at Con Thien, however, was cause for anything but cheer. Clary immediately exclaimed, "It's just an ugly, barren, and filthy wasteland of trenches, bunkers, and craters. It's littered with shell casings, vehicle hulls, and dried or muddy rutted trails. It reeks of death, desolation, and despair. This is the end of the earth." He kicked a pile of debris in disgust.

"It's ten days of livin' nightmares," Hawkins mumbled to Wiley as the team settled into their Con Thien bunker, "and ten days of dyin' dreams," as he viewed the tired and torn landscape.

"Yeah," Wiley agreed. "No one comes here to live, but a lot come here to die. This place is not too good for living and too bad a place for dying," he shuddered while jettisoning his heavy pack and stretching to relieve tight muscles. Rubbing his aching shoulders, he yawned.

Thankfully, for the Marines at Con Thien, a month later, in May 1967, the politicians and Pentagon rescinded the restrictions on Marines engaging the NVA in the southern part of the DMZ with counter-battery fires. It was tacit recognition that the NVA were violating the rules and attacking Marine forces from the DMZ. The recognition and rescission, however, were too late for Corporal Thunder, Wiley, Clary, and Hawkins. The war for the team was over before the rules were rescinded. The war for the team was abruptly over in late April 1967 at Khe Sanh. Con Thien and Khe Sanh were their twin nemeses.

Con Thien's bombardments were sometimes sporadic and sometimes sustained. They were always something, but never anything one expected. Con Thien was sometimes anything, but it was always nothing if not unpredictable and chaotic. It was unrelenting and unrepentant. It challenged you. It confounded you. It consumed you. It was a perfect prelude to Khe Sanh.

Wiley described it as "days of living hell," after the last night's bombardments.

"Days of dyin' hell," was Hawkins' counter as they assisted in medevacing casualties.

Clary declared it, "days of living and dying a little each day," as he defiantly shrugged.

"Days of eluding death and embracing life," was Corporal Thunder's summation.

The Siege of Con Thien became the scourge of all who graced its vile red dust and filthy clay mud as well as its ugly scars created by as many as 1,200 rounds of NVA rockets per day. "Jesus, that's about a rocket a minute all damn day and night long," Hawkins calculated.

Con Thien was horrific, but it paled compared to Khe Sanh. Hell became indistinguishable and inconsequential based on pain and suffering. Hell was simply hell. To define it in degrees was dubious at best and insane at worst.

"There ain't no words, no pictures, no nothin' that can help anyone know or feel the evil of combat or war," Hawkins philosophized after a bitter Con Thien rocket and mortar barrage. "It's just so bad and nasty you want to forget it. You don't want to remember it 'cause you don't want it in your mind. You gotta get rid of its nasty filth and wash it out and tear it up and outta your thoughts and memories."

In an attempt to escape the somber morbid talk of hell, Corporal Thunder joked, "Hawkins, you better pray you're in heaven before the devil knows your dead."

Hawkins stared blankly into the dark night before finally concluding, "War is hell. Hell is war. I'm doin'em both right here, right now. When my time comes I can say I done been there and done done that. I ain't doin' hell again. Ain't doin' no second tour in hell."

Con Thien's hell drifted into the team's past, but Khe Sanh's hell was its future. Khe Sanh was their fate and destiny. Khe Sanh was next. After Khe Sanh, however, there was nothing for them...nothing but the fiercest battle of their life…*the battle to survive.*

Corporal Thunder, Wiley, Hawkins, and Clary were only remotely aware of what awaited them in Khe Sanh. The psychological trauma of Con Thien was discouraging and depressing, but demoralizing was closer to the truth. It was relieving and reassuring, however, to evade it and to escape it... *to escape it alive.* They escaped Con Thien, however, only to be challenged by Khe Sanh. Khe Sanh was inescapable.

The team was bitter about Con Thien, but Hawkins was the most vitriolic as they patrolled home to Payable, "You gotta hate Con Thien. You gotta hate the damn stupid rules that don't let us use counter-battery fires to fire back. You gotta hate just havin' to take the bombardments and the killings. It's just not fair," Hawkins concluded. "You gotta think we'd have a better plan."

The day following the Con Thien operation was a rather pleasant one for the team. It was a respite from their normal patrols, but it was also a prelude to a pending major operation. The team relaxed, but strangely they sensed a premonition of unequaled and unsurpassed brutal and ruthless death. The premonition became their last experience with war. It was the end for them. It was their fate. The war would come crashing down on them at Khe Sanh. Today, however, they appreciated life.

After reveille, Corporal Thunder was summoned to meet with Lieutenant Antoine. The meeting included briefings regarding preliminary plans for combat operations at Khe Sanh. It was an extensive brief and Corporal Thunder wrote notes furiously in his green notebook.

"Okay, gather round," Corporal Thunder announced as he returned to the bunker from his briefing. "We have updates and information on a new mission." Wiley, Hawkins, and Clary had been bathing in the river. They were still wet, but drying in the afternoon sun and breeze.

The team neither smiled nor frowned. They simply gathered round. Hawkins sensed the seriousness in Corporal Thunder's voice. Wiley recognized his solemn attitude. Clary observed his seasoned confidence. They all respected his somber thoughtfulness.

Wiley, Hawkins, and Clary assembled and Corporal Thunder began his update. "Mostly what I have is information and intelligence reports on why we're going. It's mostly just the situation part of a standard five paragraph order. We'll get the operational details later today or probably tomorrow at the latest. But it's going to happen fast. We're going to Khe Sanh soon.

"A huge battle is going on at Khe Sanh. It's been raging for a few days and a number of different Marine battalions are fighting to secure mountains they call 861, 881 South, and 881 North," he continued. "The Marines are fighting hard, but the NVA's fighting hard, too. We're going in to continue the fight. It seems both sides have temporarily withdrawn or suspended the fighting, but we're all just waiting to start it up again.

"Intelligence reports claim the NVA are attempting a build-up in the area. They want to establish fire bases in the mountains to launch a major offensive against the Khe Sanh fire base in the valley," the Corporal outlined. "One of the officer's said the NVA intent seems to be to inflict a crushing and embarrassing defeat on the Marines at Khe Sanh. It's similar to what they did to France in 1954. The French were defeated and that war was over.

"I don't know much of anything about it, but the officer said that was part of the Indochina War. The French were defeated at a place call Dien Bien Phu. The North Vietnamese Army hauled artillery high in the mountains and blasted a French camp in the valley." Corporal Thunder added, "The officer said it seems the NVA are trying to do the same to us at Khe Sanh. He said it's critical that we stop them and hold the hills." Hawkins listened while mixing a canteen of Kool Aid. Wiley and Clary munched on C-Ration peanut butter and crackers.

"When you think we'll get the orders with all the details of the operation?" Wiley asked.

"Soon," he estimated, "because it's a major emergency. It's a battle we have to win. I don't know how much it'll cost us, but we'll win it. We have to win it, but it'll cost us.

"By the way, we should all write a letter home," Corporal Thunder concluded. "It may be awhile before we can write again. Let's write a nice letter home." The simple request punctuated the brutality that awaited them at Khe Sanh. Corporal Thunder's premonition validated it.

The soon proved to be sooner than originally thought. The cost eventually proved higher than any of them could have ever dared imagine.

Chaos reigned as word spread as wildfire regarding the pending deployment to Khe Sanh. By afternoon the word was reality, but the greater reality was they were deploying the next morning. The Khe Sanh battle was becoming fierce and desperate. It was a dark beacon beckoning them into the firestorm and inferno it would become. Its soaring heat would first embrace them, then engulf them, while searing their souls and scaring their memories with indescribable suffering. Although hardened to war, Khe Sanh became like the blacksmith's forge in which they were melted and sledgehammered and reshaped, but only after enduring intense heat, the iron anvil, and the bludgeoning and melding and painful blows. They entered Khe Sanh as one person; they exited as another. They were reborn, but first they had to die.

"Mike and Kilo companies and part of the Battalion Command Element are deploying to Khe Sanh early tomorrow morning," Corporal Thunder summarized his team's final brief. "India and Lima companies will stay here to patrol and defend this area and protect the artillery.

"At 0600 tomorrow morning, we'll cross the river to a HLZ or helicopter landing zone near the southern end of the Razorback. We'll be heloed into the vicinity of Hill 861," Corporal Thunder explained as he laid out his maps and pointed to various locations on the maps.

"The plan now is for Kilo to attack and secure Hill 861 tomorrow and then the next day Mike will attack and secure 881 South," Corporal Thunder explained as he again pointed to the map. "That's a quick overview and it'll get us started. They're coordinating more details now. Meanwhile, let's get our gear ready. Let's get lots of ammo." He later took a break to sharpen his machete, which was always razor sharp. But working the blade calmed and focused him.

Corporal Thunder then issued team orders. "Wiley, check with Sergeant Cozart and see if he wants us to have a radio since we'll probably be point. Clary, you get us enough C-Rats for three days for all of us. Hawkins, you take care of getting us all the M16 ammo we need. Get lots of M79, .45, and shotgun ammo, too. Also, see if you can scrounge up some extra M16 magazines."

"How long we gonna be there?" Clary asked as he cleaned and reassembled his M16.

"As long as it takes," Corporal Thunder answered. "I don't mean to be a smart ass, but we'll be there till the mountains are secure. A battalion officer said they're flying in a larger force for Khe Sanh and expect to have it in place within days. Once it's settled and ready to establish defenses and the mountains secured, we'll be relieved and come back here to our base camp. It could be days or weeks, but probably only days. The division wants this done and done fast."

"Jesus, you told us we'd probably go out to Khe Sanh one day," Hawkins noted. "Now we're goin'. It'll just be another patrol and another operation." This became a tragic understatement.

"Yeah, but this one sounds more urgent. It sounds more critical, too," Clary grimaced. "This one could really be something big." Clary had no conception; no one had any conception, of the magnitude and criticality of Khe Sanh. It was a seismic shift in their tomorrows.

At that time, it was beyond the team's perception to appreciate the significance of the battle on the war and on their lives. It became known in the annals of Marine Corps history as the First Battle of Khe Sanh or the Battle for Hill 881 South or The Hill Fights. To Corporal Thunder and his team, however, Khe Sanh simply became the worst day of their lives.

In Vietnam, combat infantrymen confronted death almost daily, but they rarely talked about dying. Instead, they mostly talked about living. Talking of living, however, invariably evoked thoughts of dying.

"Ain't it kinda strange that what's worth fightin' and livin' for is also worth fightin' and dyin' for." Hawkins surmised. "There just ain't nothin' simple and clear in this war.

"We wanna live, but we're willin' to die for the right somethin' so we ain't dying for the wrong nothin'. I ain't doubtin' what we're fightin' for. I'm believin' in it," Hawkins groaned, "but I wish our people were believin', too."

In time, a quiet thoughtfulness roared as Corporal Thunder, Wiley, Hawkins, and Clary considered Hawkins' thoughts about living and dying. In the coming days they would remember the talk and it would inspire them to incredible feats of courage and compassion. Now, however, it was time for watches and sleeps as a silent stillness overcame the bunker.

The team slept fitfully and fatefully that night. Corporal Thunder pondered his responsibility to the team and its survival. Wiley woke repeatedly because of both nervous excitement and calm fears. Hawkins resigned himself to eager as well as indifferent anticipation toward the coming fight. Clary sensed Khe Sanh would be distinguished by its devastation. They could have never known, however, how extraordinarily devastating it would be.

The team's pre-dawn reveille was met with a mixture of both relief and anxiety. As the team saddled up, Corporal Thunder shared good news. "Lieutenant Antoine told us his wife is expecting their first child. While on R & R to Hawaii in February, he surprised her with the news of his promotion. This week, she surprised him with a letter about they're expecting a baby girl.

"I'd have told you earlier, but wanted to pass the good news now to help start Khe Sanh off as a good operation," he concluded. The talk of a birth counterbalanced the death to come.

"That's great news," Wiley stated. "He'll be a great dad. I bet he's excited." The team chatted mindlessly to relieve its anxieties as it prepared to advance to the helo landing zone.

"Waitin' to fight is the worst parta fightin'," Hawkins fidgeted and confessed at the HLZ.

"Waiting is bad, but getting hit is the worst," Clary mumbled as he checked his M79 for the hundredth time. Repetitive actions soothed their nerves as they sought to clear their minds of unthinkable thoughts.

"Jesus, Clary, I don't aim on gettin' hit. I aim on doin' the hittin'," Hawkins replied.

The HLZ banter continued until Wiley announced, "I'm monitoring the radio. Helos are inbound." They expected the warning, but it jolted them nonetheless as their resolve stiffened.

The Corporal ordered, "Saddle up and let's move out. We're in helo team four. Let's get our helo team organized and ready." Reassuringly patting the machete at his side while disconcertedly shouldering his M16, he adopted his stoic countenance. The beginning of the end was beginning.

The CH-46 helicopters landed and loaded the Marines and then launched quickly for Khe Sanh. The urgency of the operation was evident in all that transpired throughout the day. The more distant their actions from Khe Sanh the more chaotic they were. The closer they came to Khe Sanh the calmer they were. "It's time to lock and load," Hawkins smiled. "It's time again."

The business of war required emotional involvement as well as emotional detachment. Corporal Thunder thought, *It's time for careful and deliberate thoughts and actions.* Meanwhile, Hawkins mentally prepared himself for anything and everything. Clary thought, *A sense of calm primes us for unknown chaos.* Wiley forced himself to be calm because he realized the later chaos would propel him to rage.

The helos landed at the zone near Hill 861 and the Marines disembarked quickly. The units understood their orders and their actions confirmed it. As helo engines roared the pilots throttled them for takeoff power. Then the helos disappeared and the Marines were alone and it was quiet. It was too quiet, but the quiet was a good quiet. The Corporal immediately observed the zone was cold, which was decidedly better than a hot one. *At least there's no incoming and no enemy contacts,* he thought.

Hawkins assumed point for the company to lead the battalion toward Hill 861. Corporal Thunder had pre-briefed Hawkins, "Wait for no orders. Once we're on the ground just get your bearings and aim in on 861 and move out. We got to get everyone out of the HLZ as fast as we can. Just take off. Let's pull them out of the zone and not wait for them to push us out. Let's move out fast. Lieutenant Antoine will radio everyone to follow. They know to follow."

Hawkins oriented his map and compass with the terrain and swiftly moved out. The battalion minus quickly followed. The team had talked Khe Sanh for months. Now the team was there. It was Khe Sanh day one for them, but Khe Sanh for them will be over by day two. The war would then be over for them, too, but first there was hard fighting to do. They fought hard one last time.

The terrain was mountainous, but the jungle was mostly tall scrub grass and trees with no canopy. "The visibility's good," Wiley noted, "which is kind of bad. If we can see, they can see." The trio of mountains, 861, 881 South, and 881 North, dominated the northern landscape and hovered over them as preying vultures. A sense of death seemed to dominate the area.

"Jesus, this is one time I like being short," Hawkins smiled. "The grass and scrub are mostly taller than me." The high mountains were ominous and waiting. So, too, was the NVA.

Corporal Thunder passed the word to Hawkins, "Hold up about a thousand meters from 861. The Lieutenant is checking with battalion about prep fires on the hill before Kilo Company attacks. Hold up and take a break, but spread out and stay down and stay concealed in the grass."

Later, Wiley passed the word from radio traffic he was monitoring. "The battalion's planning artillery and air strikes on 861. Kilo will pass through us to assembly areas closer to 861. Then Kilo will attack and Mike will deploy to the west of 861 toward 881 South. We'll dig in there and prepare for the attack on 881 South tomorrow. Kilo will hold 861."

"Take a break, but be alert. Do a 50-50 watch. Rest because it'll probably be a long night," Corporal Thunder urged. "Get a nap when and while you can. But first dig in and be alert."

Corporal Thunder crouched and crawled back down the column to talk with Sergeant Cozart and the Lieutenant. He reappeared later and passed to the team, "It'll be awhile, but once the air and artillery strikes begin we're to start moving out. We'll advance under the cover of the fires."

Once the fires began, Wiley passed the word from the Lieutenant's radio call, "Okay, let's move out." Hawkins and Clary were already on the move.

The thunderous explosions from the supporting arms fires were strong and steady for about thirty minutes. Then they became sporadic as Kilo Company began its ascent up 861.

Wiley learned from radio traffic that Kilo's advance up 861 was littered with dead and rotting NVA bodies. He passed to Corporal Thunder, "The close quarters fighting was fierce and Kilo's reporting hundreds of fighting positions and bunkers all over the hill. The NVA's been digging and working these hills hard. The killings have been hard, too. But now the enemy's gone and Kilo's advance is with virtually no contact." *They may be gone from 861, but they're probably waiting for us on 881 South,* Corporal Thunder thought. Meanwhile, Mike Company closed to a point midway between 861 and 881 to prepare for tomorrow's attack on 881 South.

"Yeah, the NVA are defending hard. They must really want these hills," Clary added.

"Well, if they worked 861 hard I hate to think how hard they worked the other hills. The other hills and the hill we're attacking and securing tomorrow. Hill 881 South is more important to them. They're higher and have better views over the valley," Wiley noted. "I'm thinking tomorrow will be hard and bad. Maybe the hardest and the worst of all."

The day was rather uneventful and Hill 861 was secured by sunset without significant enemy contact. The hard fighting had been days before. "Let's set the night watches and get some sleep. Let's get ready for tomorrow," Corporal Thunder urged. "Let's do our two hours in this order: Wiley, me, Hawkins, Clary." The Corporal simply wanted the team to cease the negative talk.

Corporal Thunder had the midnight to 0200 watch and thought, *I thought the NVA would've hit us with something by now. It's probably a bad sign they're not fighting us tonight. They're probably preparing hard for tomorrow. They're probably digging in deeper and saving all their ammo to fight us tomorrow. Yep, it's a bad sign. Tomorrow'll be bad.*

But he shared none of these thoughts with the team, except to warn them to be especially alert and prepared for 881 South. He was reluctant for them to be thinking of the fear. He wanted them to be thinking of the fight. Yet, he knew that fear was part of the fight.

"It's too quiet," Corporal Thunder whispered to Hawkins as he woke him for his 0200 watch.

"Yeah, well, I'd rather it be too quiet than too loud from incoming," Hawkins groggily replied as he awoke and shook the slumber from his mind and body. "Quiet's okay by me."

Corporal Thunder and Hawkins talked briefly until the Corporal was confident Hawkins was awake and alert for his watch. He then slept a worried sleep as he continued to have concerns about tomorrow. The uneasy feelings were difficult to suppress.

The battalion reveille was before dawn. Kilo Company minus defended 861 while Mike Company, a platoon from Kilo, and the battalion command element advanced west toward 881 South. "The two hills are separated by only about two to three thousand kilometers," Corporal Thunder estimated to Hawkins, "and the Lieutenant says we're to halt about half way between them and await further orders."

Once the team arrived at the half way point it halted. The team waited while the battalion command element briefed the company commanders on the 881S attack order. "We might as well set up a temporary defense and get comfortable," Corporal Thunder whispered, "because the company commanders will have to brief the platoon commanders. Then they'll have to brief the squad leaders. Then we'll get the word. Then later we'll move on to 881."

Talking to force their fears to the recesses of their consciousness, the team checked their weapons and ammo magazines. This time, however, the fears were challenging to subdue. The fears were immediately below the surface and waiting to be released. They kept rising in the silence. So, the team kept talking as they halted and awaited orders while glancing at 881.

Corporal Thunder was later called to meet with the platoon commander. The team realized the ascent up Hill 881 South was to begin soon. They waited silently with their own thoughts.

"Okay, gather round," Corporal Thunder whispered as he crawled toward them. "The battalion's already coordinated the prep fires on the hill. They should begin any time. Then we'll get the word to start our attack up 881. As we advance to the base of the hill, we'll be moving while the fires are still going. But once we start up the hill, the prep fires will shift to the top and north side of the hill. Once we approach the top, the supporting arms fires will be lifted. That's the situation for our move from here to the base of the hill and our advance to the top.

"Once we're at the base we'll climb up 881 as quickly and as tactically as possible. It's probably going to be steep and slippery in places, but we just got to keep moving," Corporal Thunder emphasized. "Once we reach the crest of the mountain our platoon will veer to the right and first platoon to the left. We'll both then sweep north on line and secure the mountain.

"The company command element and the third platoon and the Kilo Company platoon will remain at the base of the mountain as a reserve." Corporal Thunder reported, "Plus, Kilo Company's holding 861 and can maybe reinforce us if we need it."

The coordinated air strikes and artillery bombardments on 881 South began minutes later. The first and second platoons with attached weapons saddled up and prepared to advance. The word was passed and the team led the two platoons reinforced up 881 South.

"Jesus, it sounds so simple. Okay, mount up and move out. Okay, climb the hill and secure it. It just sounds so damn simple," Hawkins whispered to Clary, "but it ain't simple at all. It's hard as hell. The enemy makes it harder. On a map it looks easy. Grease pins and symbols and arrows on a map are easy. On the ground and in the mud and blood it's damn hard. The killin' is easier for us now, but livin' just keeps gettin' harder. Ain't war somethin'?"

"Not much is easy in war," Clary agreed, "but this is probably going to be harder than most. Yet, it's what we do. We've been doing it for months. We'll just keep doing it till we go home. It's just what we've been doing again and again. We're infantry."

Hawkins nodded his agreement and wheeled to take the point. Hawkins and Clary then led the two platoons reinforced on the advance up 881 South. Previous airstrikes with napalm and 500 pound bombs had scorched the hill and created numerous craters. Artillery barrages had stripped the vegetation and unearthed trees. The landscape was ominous; the terrain dangerous. It was ugly, but it was about to become uglier.

"Damn, the goin's gettin' tougher and tougher," Hawkins groaned to Clary as he struggled with his footing and balance on the steep and slippery terrain. "It's just steep angles in spots and we gotta kinda pull our way up by the roots and tree branches and clumps of grass." Hawkins slipped and slid about six feet before he caught himself and pulled himself forward.

Clary caught his breath and agreed as he wiped sweat from his forehead. "Yep, it's slow going, but we're getting there. I thought we'd have made enemy contact by now. Now I'm wondering where they are." The fifty plus pound pack straps dug deep into their shoulders as they strained and struggled to climb the rugged terrain. Breaths became harder and deeper.

"Yeah, well, we probably ain't gonna have to wonder much longer," Hawkins replied. "We're almost to the crest. Let's stop here and pass the word for Corporal Thunder to come up."

Corporal Thunder slithered up on his belly to consult with Hawkins. Hawkins explained and asked, "We're almost to the crest. I figure about another twenty or thirty meters or so. You wanta go with me and recon it and get the lay of the land before we just pop up and we're there?"

"Thanks. Yeah, good idea. Let's crawl forward far enough to get a good look at the top and the terrain, but let's stay low and in the grass and brush," Corporal Thunder cautiously replied.

Corporal Thunder and Hawkins crawled forward and conducted a recon of the top of 881 South. The two then wiggled back down to Wiley's position and asked him to radio Lieutenant Antoine to ask him to come forward to talk.

Lieutenant Antoine arrived within minutes and Corporal Thunder reported, "The top's fairly flat, but it looks like there's a lot of craters and trees blasted down. The area's fairly open, but most is covered in waist high grass and brush. The area is maybe fifty to sixty meters wide and long, maybe more, but it's not exactly a circle or square. The edges are uneven and there's taller trees and thicker foliage around the perimeter, too. It's maybe half a football field. Maybe more."

"In the center of the area is something that looks like stacked logs, but we couldn't tell for sure. It's just kinda strange and silent, but it gives you an uneasy feeling," Hawkins added. "It just don't seem right, but we saw nothin' wrong."

"We thought you might want to have the first platoon come on up on the left kinda side by side with us," Corporal Thunder whispered. "Then, instead of just half the force being at the top, we'll all be advancing at the same time with second veering to the right and first veering to the left. That way we got more manpower and firepower going for us."

"Yes, that's what I was thinking, too," Lieutenant Antoine replied. "I'll pass that word to first platoon. Then, when it moves up beside you, let me know. Once we're all in position I'll radio the company and let it know we're going over the top."

In about thirty minutes the two reinforced platoons were in position, side by side, and the Lieutenant radioed both units to attack. Corporal

Thunder's team led the move to the crest of the hill. It was then and there Hill 881 South became the most fateful day of their lives.

It was strangely and eerily silent. It was a warm day, but not hot. It was a cloudy day, but not overcast. It was a dry day, but the earth was damp from the morning dew. It was simply another day. It was, however, another day unlike any other day. It was Hill 881 South. It was Khe Sanh.

"No matter how good the day is now, every day in Vietnam seems to have bad. But every day is a good day for living," Wiley whispered to the team, "which means there's no good day for dying...only bad days." Then he prayed for a good day, but the devil intervened.

The two platoons veered to the right and to the left, respectively, and advanced on line for about twenty meters. At that point, both units were crouching low and moving north and forward in the high grass and underbrush. They were, however, unknowingly exposed and vulnerable.

The NVA were dug in deep and waiting patiently and silently. They had preregistered supporting arms fires and their rockets and mortars were on alert and ready to fire. Rocket propelled grenades and machine guns prepared to saturate multiple fields of fire with devastatingly accurate salvos. Marines advanced into the killing zone while the enemy waited with them in the sights of their weapons. They waited until the Marines were exposed and most vulnerable. Once again the NVA were unseen phantoms and ghosts who would have to be hunted down, dug out, exposed...and killed. As the Marines advanced into the killing zone the NVA attacked. The battle then began. The killing quickly followed.

The silence was shattered by explosions from rocket-propelled and hand grenades as well as machine gun and rifle fire. Concurrently, enemy artillery and 82mm mortars began impacting the NVA killing zone. "Well, the fight's on," Corporal Thunder shouted to his team, but the fight was instantly over before it ever began for far too many Marines. It was a fight for sheer and utter survival.

CHAPTER 20

Khe Sanh's NVA Ambush

*We want to live today, we have to kill NVA fast. We want to
survive this war, we have to kill more NVA faster. It's that
simple. We have to kill more and more and kill faster and faster.*

—Marine Private First Class Brad Clary

As Corporal Thunder's team crossed the crest of Hill 881 South
the NVA launched a ferocious fusillade of devastating fire from
concealed positions and an extensive bunker system. The enemy had
preregistered indirect fires on virtually every foot of the mountain top.
"Ain't this a helluva way to start the day," Hawkins yelled to Clary primarily to let him know he was alive as well as to vent his frustration…
and his fear.

"Yeah, let's pray it doesn't get worse," Clary hollered in response.
While neither then thought it remotely possible, they later realized the
worst was yet to come. It was 30 April 1967 and it became the worst
day of their lives. It was a day they would remember forever. Forever for
many, however, would last only a few more seconds or minutes or hours.
Many would never see another sunset or sunrise as the hill became a
graveyard for most of them that day.

Corporal Thunder quickly assessed the situation and shouted, "We're
surrounded. We're in the middle of the damn killing zone. We got casualties everywhere. We got to fight our way out of this fast." He fired
and maneuvered forward to further evaluate the situation realizing he
had stated the obvious to those fighting to survive. Inching forward on
his stomach, he sensed anyone above two or three feet high became an
instant target. He scrunched lower as enemy rounds whistled overhead
at an alarming rate of fire. Halting for safety was sensible, but stubbornly
he moved on. *I'm done with careful,* he thought, *I'm not into careless, but
too careful is worse than too careless right now.* The Corporal, as always,
moved on aggressively and courageously.

Attacking slowly at first, however, was best. Too many Marines were immediately hit and wounded or killed. Those not hit were about to be hit. Those not yet dead were about to die. The numerically superior NVA were overpowering them with overwhelming firepower. Fighting fast and hard the NVA pressed on relentlessly while the Marines sluggishly struggled to overcome the initial onslaught, recover, and counterattack. It was slow and tenuous at best; tragic at worst.

"This ain't gonna be easy," Hawkins screamed to Clary. Yet, they were incapable of remotely understanding how hard it would be. If they had known they may have abandoned the hill, but they were Marines and that was no option. It was the hardest fight of their lives, but fighting their fears was as hard as fighting the NVA. Hawkins thought, *It's gut check time. It's that or it's checkout time,* as a sense of desperation pummeled them as never before.

"Yeah, anyone who tries to look up or move forward becomes a target," Clary responded while hugging the earth, "Snipers and machine guns are everywhere, not to mention incoming mortars and RPGs. Fires are coming from every direction." The enemy was everywhere, but nowhere. They were wicked phantom ghosts and the battle began wretchedly for the Marines.

Wiley attempted to radio Lieutenant Antoine, but received no response. He knew his general location and low crawled to it. The Lieutenant was severely wounded and Wiley exclaimed, "Sir, hold on. Just hold on. I'll get a corpsman." Wiley immediately prayed briefly for the Lieutenant.

The Lieutenant attempted to speak, but nothing was heard but gargling sounds. He had sustained serious neck and chest wound from shrapnel. The ripped open and gapping wounds were bleeding profusely as he struggled to breathe and talk. He failed at both and a dark fear emerged in his eyes. His eyes rolled upward and locked as he painfully stared into oblivion…*into eternity.*

"Corpsman! Corpsman up," Wiley shouted. Yelling at times so they would know one another was alive and for situational awareness aided them in overcoming the confusion and chaos.

Corporal Thunder heard Wiley's plea and quickly crawled to him. He arrived as Doc Lynn bounded on site and kneeled low. "Doc, how's he look?" Corporal Thunder asked breathlessly.

"He's bad. We got to stop the bleeding. We got to get him breathing, too," Doc Lynn answered. "Here, I have to do an emergency tracheotomy. I'm going to cut a small incision in his throat below his Adam's apple. Then I'll hold it open while you insert the bottom half of this ballpoint pen into his throat so he can breathe. It's like a little tube. It's a field expedient. It won't bleed much from the incision, but there's a lot of blood from the shrapnel. Get some combat bandages and stop the bleeding. Starting the breathing and stopping the bleeding are our priorities."

"Okay," the Corporal replied. He had heard of emergency field, or combat "traches," as the corpsmen often called them, but he never thought he would have to actually assist in one.

Doc Lynn cut Lieutenant Antoine's throat and Corporal Thunder inserted the pen. Blood from the tracheotomy was minimal. The wounds were extensive, however, as blood gushed and gagged the Lieutenant. Holding the Lieutenant in his arms tenderly as warm blood flowed freely onto his hands and arms and lap, Corporal Thunder sighed. The blood was hauntingly warm, but the Lieutenant hideously cold.

Lieutenant Antoine motioned Corporal Thunder to bend down and he whispered two words: "Wife. Daughter." The Lieutenant then convulsed once and was dead. Corporal Thunder had no time to respond, but he nodded his head in understanding and squeezed Lieutenant Antoine's hand as his farewell. As a former enlisted Marine and Staff Sergeant, who had earned a battlefield commission, the Lieutenant was loved and respected throughout the platoon. He was one of them. They were part of him. Now he was gone. A part of them was gone, too.

Corporal Thunder reflected on his Indian heritage and sensed the Lieutenant's spirit battle briefly for life, but then surrender reluctantly to death. He felt his spirit ascend the hell of 881 South and drift toward the heavens. Praying quietly to the Great Spirit, he wiped a tear from his eyes. The Corporal then confronted the evil and the devils and the hell of 881.

"Damn this war," Corporal Thunder muttered to Wiley. "Our Lieutenant's dead. He has a wife he'll never see again. He has a daughter he'll never ever see. Damn this war."

Immediately, right then and right there, Corporal Thunder promised himself he would one day write Lieutenant Antoine's wife, now widow, a condolence letter. He realized he had neither the words nor skills to write the letter he truly wanted to write. Every sentence and every phrase and every word would be a struggle for him, but he would write them. While he knew he would neither understand her anger nor anguish, neither her love nor loss, he knew he would write her. Writing her was what he had to do...what he would do.

Corporal Thunder was confident he would never receive a response and he never expected one. He was convinced she would be as much at a loss for words as he was. They would both in their own way mourn the death of someone special to them. Their respective mourning's, however, would be decidedly different and difficult. It was death. It was war. It was Vietnam. Nothing he would write or she would feel would alter the death or the war. Wiping glistening glints from his eyes he steeled his nerves and fortitude for the battle ahead. The battle had become personal...*very personal as tears flowed in his heart.*

Lieutenant Antoine's death touched Corporal Thunder as no other. Instantly, he collected himself and ordered Wiley, "The NVA targeted the Lieutenant and his radio operator. They must have seen the radios and antennas and blasted away. The radios are destroyed and the Lieutenant and his radio operator are dead. You and your radio are now the platoon's link to the company and supporting arms fires. Take over and let the company know what's happened. They've probably heard all the explosions and they'll know something's happened. Just update them every now and then when you can. But mostly you just have to take charge up here and let us all know what all the others are doing. Help keep us working together. Just work for us and with us.

"Wiley, the damn NVA have this area all preregistered for fires. They have us cold right now. They're just slaughtering us with small arms fires, RPGs, and mortars and rockets," the Corporal announced in frustration. "We have to get our own incoming coming in here fast. We need you to do that. You got to get the supporting arms coordinated and firing.

"It looks like we're on our own, too," Corporal Thunder shook his head as he looked back toward Hill 861. "The NVA are engaging the rest of our battalion on 861. They're getting hit hard with artillery and rockets. They got their own fight. I doubt they'll be able to get here in time to help us. We got to fight this one ourselves. We got to fight it all alone."

Corporal Thunder then paused and continued, "Wiley, what I want you to do is call in artillery and airstrikes on 881 South. Keep our strikes on the north part of 881 South. Ask the battalion to do the same for 881 North, but all over 881 North. Tell them you got 881 South and they got 881 North. We've talked about calling for fires. We talked about it in bunker talks. You've had lessons. We've practiced. Now you got to do it. You know how. Now do it."

Corporal Thunder's calm but beseeching tone confided to Wiley the gravity of the situation and Wiley's role in overcoming the horrific quandary they were in. Wiley knew unequivocally his role was critical and he responded accordingly.

"If the company starts asking too many questions and interfering with your requests for fire support, well, just tune them out and say their transmissions are garbled," Corporal Thunder hurriedly continued. "Tell them we lost damned near every radio up here and we need yours almost exclusively for supporting arms. Supporting arms fires is the priority.

"They'll probably ask you, for example, for situation reports and for damn body counts and for information like that. Just tell them we're still counting. Or just tell them any ole number. Hell, no one cares what the number is. They just want a number. Damn, just give them a number. It's not like they'll come up here to check if it's right. It's stuff like that you have to ignore. You'll know what to do. Just do it," the Corporal again repeated to Wiley and reemphasized for him to simply take charge and coordinate the supporting arms fires. The Corporal sensed he was rambling and repeating himself, but he was also formulating his plan of action for the team. As rapid-fire thoughts and words assaulted him, his plan began to take shape.

"Wiley, find a good position over there near the tree line," Corporal Thunder suggested and pointed. "Then I'll know where you are. I'm going to find Hawkins and Clary and we'll get our defenses set and our counterattack going. We'll check in with you in about an hour or when we can. You settle in and get the supporting arms fires coming in fast. Remember, you got 881 South. Tell battalion to take 881 North. Call in all the fires you can. Okay, I'm going now."

Corporal Thunder wheeled and zigged and zagged in the direction he last saw Hawkins and Clary. Wiley rumbled to the location Corporal Thunder identified for him as the NVA fires intensified. Responding furiously, the Marines started to crawl forward, slowly, inch by inch. They were, however, too disorganized to launch a counterattack. They were simply fighting to survive. First, they had to defend before they could attack. Then, they had to stop the dying to keep on living. Finally, they had to counterattack…those still living would counterattack.

Corporal Thunder located Hawkins and Clary near the eastern tree line and updated them. "Lieutenant Antoine and his radio operator are dead. Wiley's going to call in supporting arms fires. Wiley's going to be located over there somewhere," as he pointed to the tree line. "We got to get organized so we can counterattack. It's that or it's over. We're done unless we do it.

"Let's do what we have to do. Let's meet over there in about an hour. We'll update one each so we can work together. Then Wiley can update the company," he requested in choppy staccato sentences. "That way we can all know what the other is doing. Wiley'll be our point of contact."

Corporal Thunder then asked, "Okay, Hawkins, what's your situation over here?"

"It's hard to tell 'cause so much shit's happenin'. But the NVA's dug in deep and there's more fightin' holes and bunkers than I ever seen. I ain't seen but a few of them, but I know there's lots more. I ain't seen too many NVA either. They're like ghosts, but I'm seein' and hearin' muzzle flashes. That's how I'm findin'em and zeroin' in on them." Hawkins answered.

"Plus, I'm pretty sure they got snipers up in the trees around the perimeter. Damn, they just seem to be pickin' us off. We gotta stay low in the grass, but they're firing so many rounds it's like they're just mowing the grass so they can see us," Hawkins added. "We got us a shit sandwich here. It's nasty. Then, to make it worse, the rockets and mortars just keep a comin'."

"Okay, Hawkins. Now, Clary, what've you seen?" Corporal Thunder quickly inquired.

"Well, I talked with one of the corpsmen who'd just come from the first platoon and it's as bad on the left and center," Clary began. "There's dead and wounded everywhere. The first platoon commander and platoon sergeant are dead and a lot of the NCOs. They just got a bunch of enlisted like us and a lot of them have only been in country a few months or so."

"Okay, we just got to rally everyone," Corporal Thunder declared. "We'll just do our best to make sure everyone has a task and does it, but mostly we just got to start finding and killing the NVA. Right now they're just kicking butt and killing us. We got to start attacking and killing and killing and attacking. We got to keep killing them till they're all killed or we're all killed.

"Hawkins, work the right flank and tree line. Hunt down the snipers. Start blasting those bunkers with automatic weapons, which is probably all of them," he ordered. "While you're working the right, Hawkins, I'll be working the left and doing the same.

"Clary, you get Marines in the middle to start working together. Get them firing and get them advancing. Just get some firing while some are advancing. Then get the ones firing to advancing and the ones advancing to firing. Just keep them covering one another with fires and advancing toward the enemy." Corporal Thunder sighed. He knew he was repeating himself, but his rapid thoughts were racing ever faster. They had to act fast. Speed was essential. They had to gain the momentum. It was either act fast and live or act slow and die.

"Okay, let's go do it. We all need to find us small teams to work with, too. We better do it fast. It's either that or the NVA are going to kill us all. We got the fight of our life and we got to make sure the enemy starts dying. We want to live we have to make sure the NVA starts dying," Corporal Thunder repeated and concluded.

"We want to live today, we have to kill NVA fast," Clary gasped. "We want to survive this war, we have to kill more NVA faster. It's that simple. We have to kill more and more and kill faster and faster. It'll be hard because that's what the NVA's attempting to do to us, but we ain't here because we thought it'd be easy." It was probably as much a sports pep talk to himself from his athletic days as it was a firebrand speech to the team, but Clary was preparing himself psychologically for the most and fastest killing of his life.

"Jesus, I ain't dyin' on this shit pile called 881," Hawkins muttered. "I just ain't dyin' today. Not here. Not now." Hawkins was now in his fighting mode and committed to killing, too.

Corporal Thunder, Hawkins, and Clary turned and sprinted to their respective areas and tasks. As they darted away, dirt and dust erupted from NVA small arms rounds nipping at their heels. They ran faster and darted quicker as flying debris from NVA rounds gained on them.

Corporal Thunder bolted to the left tree line as enemy rounds spewed splintered earth in his wake. Firing as he crawled, darting as he rushed, he maneuvered until he arrived at the tree line. Noticing a Marine firing he asked, "Can you give me a quick SitRep or Situation Report"

Continuing to fire, the Marine looked over toward Corporal Thunder. "Yeah, we got NVA everywhere. We don't exactly know where they are, but it don't matter. They're everywhere."

"Where's your team leader?" Corporal Thunder asked while straightening his helmet.

"He's dead," the Marine replied as he flinched from a close round. "Most here are dead."

It was then Corporal Thunder recognized the Marine. "You're Rogers, aren't you?"

"Yes, I'm surviving thanks to you," Rogers replied as he recognized Corporal Thunder.

"Well, I'm not doing that much over here. Least not yet, but together we're going to get a lot of something going," he smiled. "I'm going to work this tree line. You're going to get a few Marines together and fire and maneuver forward with me. Let's just work as a team. Got it?"

"Yes, I'll do it," Rogers answered and asked, "but will they listen to me?"

"Take charge. They'll listen. They'll do it if they want to live," the Corporal reassured him. "Tell them that's what we have to do to survive. I'll come back to check, too. Tell them that."

"Okay, I'm going now. You got anything before I go?" Corporal Thunder asked.

"Only one problem, other than the NVA," Rogers answered. "It's these damn M16s. They're malfunctioning a lot. They're just not firing right. The fight's bad, but the M16s are worse."

"Okay, I'll check it out and do what I can," he replied, "but for now collect up M16s and ammo from the dead. Just use whatever you can find. Use whatever works."

Corporal Thunder repeated his instructions to four or five other Marines as he fired and maneuvered toward the left tree line. The Marine line began to slowly hold; then began to steadily creep forward. It was inch by inch, however, it was forward.

As the Corporal fired and maneuvered along the line he encountered an unusually high number of dead and wounded. He noticed a corpsman treating a wounded Marine and asked, "Doc, how you doing over here? What can I do to help?"

"We ain't doing good," the corpsman replied. "We got lots of casualties. We got to get them off this hill and get them treated. The NVA's targeting the wounded. We got to evacuate them."

"Okay, we'll work on it. You keep working on the wounded. I'll get something going to get the wounded off the hill," Corporal Thunder promised. "It'll take me awhile, but I'll get to it."

The Corporal then charged to the far left flank and immediately detected NVA snipers high in the trees as Hawkins had warned. Motioning two Marines to come to him, he formed a hunter-killer team. Once they joined him, he ordered, "Okay, we're going to take out a few snipers. Look up and over there," Corporal Thunder directed and pointed with his rifle.

"It's a sniper. I'm going to maneuver over in this direction to outflank him. You fire at him to distract him and then duck down and roll over and hide the best you can," he continued. "Keep doing that until I take him out. Then we'll look for another one. Let's flush out a few so we can move forward. Let's work together as a little hunter-killer team. You with me on this?"

The Marines nodded, grateful to have someone in charge and a plan of action. They began to coordinate their firing with Corporal Thunder's maneuvering to outflank the NVA sniper. In minutes, the NVA was dead. They inched forward and located another sniper and repeated the process and killed another sniper. Corporal Thunder and his two Marines quickly established a system and routine as the left flank began to steady and hold.

As Corporal Thunder advanced to a third sniper, a volley of fire erupted from a camouflaged bunker. AK47 rounds slammed into his left shoulder and forearm. The force of the rounds twisted him violently and then spun him backward and down. Razor sharp and ragged scrub grass sliced his face. His left arm burned as if torched by fire. Lying still, he gathered himself.

Corporal Thunder prayed his new Marine partners observed the enemy bunker and thought, *I hope they fire on the bunker. If they can distract the bunker maybe I can flank it and take it out.*

As if on cue, the two Marines laid down suppressive fire at the bunker. They alternated firing and maneuvering to engage and distract the enemy in the bunker. While the enemy focused on the two Marines, Corporal Thunder focused on flanking the bunker.

The Corporal then painfully but quickly crawled to within a few meters of the bunker. He noticed a small aperture in the side. He pulled two pins from two grenades. Timing his grenade toss with the two Marines firing on the bunker he tossed two perfect strikes. Two rapid grenade blasts neutralized the bunker.

The Corporal charged the bunker, lowered his shoulder, and burst in it with his M16 on full automatic. Two NVA were dead and two were wounded and stunned from the grenades. One of the stunned NVA was gunned down by Corporal Thunder's M16 as the NVA scurried to fire at him. It was then, however, his M16 jammed. In a critical moment, it jammed. It simply failed. It quit. But Corporal Thunder quickly drew his machete and plunged it into the second NVA. It was a devastating gut thrust and the NVA bunker was now an NVA tomb.

Remembering Rogers talking of excessive M16 malfunctions, Corporal Thunder winced. Now he understood more fully as he collected the NVA AK47's and as much ammo as he could carry. He bolted out of the bunker and returned to his two new Marine teammates.

"Okay, great job. You did great. I was hoping you'd know to keep firing on the bunker so I could flank it. That's great teamwork," he exclaimed. "Now I got to go check on other Marines, but you keep doing what we just did. You got it. You know what to do. You take care of holding this left flank. You have to hold it up at all costs. It's that or we go down. So, just hold it up."

Corporal Thunder wheeled to go and remembered, "We got M16s jamming on us all over the line. Yours may be okay. Keep firing them, but if they jam here's some AK47s and some ammo. We haven't had any lessons on firing them, but you'll figure them out. They're just rifles and most fire pretty much the same. Don't worry about the safety and semi-automatic fire. Just load them up and fire like hell. Just go full automatic. Kill them with their own damn rifles. You can do that can't you?"

"Okay, but what about your shoulder and arm?" the Marines asked as they noted the stream of blood soaking the Corporal's sagging left arm as well as his unusual tolerance for pain.

"It's not much. It hurts, but it's okay. There's lots more wounded lots worse," Corporal Thunder admitted. "I'll have a corpsman check it later, but help me put a battle dressing on it for now to stop the bleeding. Then, you just keep fighting." He bandaged his wound with their help and then whirled and sprinted toward Wiley's position. The Marines, bolstered by Corporal Thunder's actions and refusal to bend to his pain, reengaged in battle on the left flank fight.

Corporal Thunder's wounds reminded him that casualties needed to be evacuated from the hill. They must be evacuated or they would die on the hill. *The wounded had to be extracted from the killing zone*, he repeated over and over. As he searched for Wiley, he noticed PFC Cord lying wounded from multiple shrapnel wounds. *Maybe they're from mortars or RPGs*, he thought.

"Cord, I know you're not exactly okay, but are you okay?" Corporal Thunder asked. "We got a job needs doing and we need you to do it." He immediately realized it was a dumb ass question and request, but it was a relative one. No one on the hill was okay, but if you were alive you were more okay than most. If you were dead or wounded, you were in the majority. If you were alive, you were in the minority. Alive, despite wounds, was okay...*for now.*

"Yeah, I'm okay. I'm just damn tired. It's just hard work. We're working hard to hold the lines and move forward little by little." Cord frowned.

"But we just have to keep charging here and then there to escape the NVA fires. At the same time, we have to find good weapons because ours are so bad. I think we're losing the fight right now. It's wearing on us all."

"Yeah, I know. It's a damn mess, but we got to keep fighting," Corporal Thunder replied. "I got a job for you as important as the fighting. Maybe I don't have the right to ask you, but I got to ask you. It's maybe more dangerous than the fighting. We got to get the wounded off the hill. We got to get them out of here. Most are helpless and the NVA are just zeroing in on them. They're targeting the helpless wounded. They're killing the wounded.

"We need you to evacuate the wounded to a site on the back side of the hill. It's over there where we came up. Get the wounded there. Then medevac teams will take them on down the hill," Corporal Thunder pointed and summarized, "It's their only chance to make it out alive."

Corporal Thunder realized, as did Cord, that Cord would have to repeatedly expose himself to enemy fire by combat carrying the wounded to the evacuation site. Lifting and shouldering heavy wounded and sprinting them to the evac site would be excruciatingly exhausting. It would be exceedingly dangerous, too. The NVA would do their best to stop Cord and the evacuations. They would do their best to kill Cord. Then they would continue killing the helpless wounded.

"Yep, okay, I'll do it," Cord agreed without hesitation, "but I kind of hate going back away from the enemy when we're trying to move forward toward him."

"Yeah well, you don't have to worry about that none," Corporal Thunder smiled. "The enemy is everywhere. He's to our front and back. He's on both sides and all around. But we're going up and on and over and through this damn hill and take him down.

"So, find another Marine to help you. One carries a wounded. One covers with fires," Corporal Thunder urged. "Just work as a team. Cover one another. Figure it out and do it."

Corporal Thunder and Cord nodded to one another and gathered themselves. Both then charged off to do what had to be done. Fatigue and fear had to be overcome.

"Cord was wounded twice while evacuating the casualties and ordered from the hill because of his wounds," Doc Lynn told Wiley later while he was lying in the wounded assembly area at the bottom of the hill, "but Cord refused any medevac until the fighting was done; until the last wounded was evacuated. Later, he collapsed and had to be evacuated himself." Throughout the fight, Cord evacuated the wounded to the rear with the utmost compassion. Then he mercilessly attacked forward with incredible courage to locate another wounded while maneuvering and firing and killing.

While Corporal Thunder was coordinating the protection of the left flank, Hawkins was initiating similar actions on the right flank. Populated with numerous trails that crisscrossed the right flank, the area was a virtual maze. It was a horrendously dangerous maze, too.

Hawkins estimated the NVA probably made the trails for a reason. Halting at an intersection of multiple trails, he crawled off into a fighting hole with good fields of fire and vision over most of them. He reloaded his M16. Waiting and watching, he steeled himself for killing. *Okay, now I'm the ghost who's gonna spook a few NVA*, Hawkins smiled.

Within minutes, two NVA soldiers charged forward to roll up the right flank. Hawkins aimed and fired and killed both. Seconds later, two more attacked forward and Hawkins again killed them both. *Damn, these idiots are dumber than dirt*, Hawkins grinned.

Realizing this was probably an attack route for the NVA, he deduced more would come and come quickly. He concluded he would probably eventually be discovered or overwhelmed, but he confirmed four more kills before he noticed the enemy stop attacking down the trails. *Yep, they finally got smart*, Hawkins guessed, *but some were dumb and now dead.* He then moved on.

Pressing deeper into the tree line and thicker foliage, Hawkins was now taking the fight to the enemy and searching for NVA bunkers. Confident the earth and log NVA bunkers were well fortified, Hawkins advanced deliberately but determinedly. He learned they were low or recessed and dug into the ground and well-camouflaged, too. Concluding they were most likely mutually supporting, he believed the key was to locate one to help lead him to others.

Hawkins crawled lower on the slope of the mountain. The lower or rear approach helped him avoid fire from mutually supporting bunkers.

At the same time, he knew it was lonely work behind the enemy line. Waiting and listening, he moved alone and parallel along the tree line.

Minutes later Hawkins heard the sounds of machine gun fire. Crawling slowly upward to the back entrance to a NVA bunker, he pulled pins from two grenades and lobbed them into the bunker. He charged forward before the smoke and dust cleared. Busting into the bunker with his M16 blazing at full automatic, he kneeled and waited and listened. Although choking from the smoke and smell of death, he smiled. He both loved and loathed the fighting…the killing.

While Hawkins waited and listened, an NVA soldier emerged from an adjacent supporting bunker. Hawkins tracked his movements through the bunker's front aperture. The enemy soldier darted toward Hawkins and the destroyed bunker to check on his comrades. Hawkins greeted the NVAs entrance into the bunker with a shotgun blast. The flechette rounds with their razor sharp points and fins tore ghastly holes in the NVA. The rounds tumbled on impact and ripped into body flesh mercilessly. No other NVA came to check on comrades or assess the damage.

Biding his time while the adjoining bunker was preoccupied with fires into the killing zone to its front, Hawkins rigged the bunker with enemy grenades for destruction. Should any NVA check later, a surprise waited them. He withdrew from the booby-trapped bunker to maneuver to the adjoining bunker. Repeating his tactics he attacked and destroyed another bunker.

While inside a third bunker, he again paused with all his senses on high alert. This time he observed two snipers in trees to the rear of the NVA line of defense. He killed one with his M16, but then it jammed. Furiously shattering the M16 by violently smashing it against the bunker's log supports, he killed another with a captured AK47. It took him three shots to set the AK47 sights right and calibrate his fire, but his third shot was true. *At least the AKs work*, he thought.

Hawkins concluded he was able to move relatively undetected by coming from the rear. He also surmised the NVA were more preoccupied with firing into the killing zone to their front. Analyzing the bunkers were fairly unprotected to attacks from the rear, Hawkins destroyed two more bunkers and killed six more NVA before he decided to reverse course and check in with Wiley. He estimated the Marines had mounted a defense, but now they needed to counterattack.

Scampering to Wiley's location an RPG round slammed into the ground as Hawkins emerged from the tree line. It impacted about 10 or 15 meters to his rear. He suspected he heard it launched and then whistling in his direction. Diving to protect himself helped, but he was hit with shrapnel in his right buttocks, leg, and shoulder. Grimacing in pain, he then smiled knowing Clary, *will harass the hell out of me for an ass wound.*

Hawkins suffered immediate pain, but crawled instantly back toward the tree line and cover. Noticing a wounded Marine being treated by a corpsman, he hollered, "Doc, can you check me out when you're done with him?" Hawkins wiggled into a depression for cover and safety.

The corpsman rushed over minutes later and while bandaging Hawkins he explained, "You have some bad wounds. They're more than superficial, but they're not too deep. It looks like there's no major muscle tears. I got the bleeding covered for now, but you'll need to watch it. It's so damn bad up here and we're so outgunned you better just keep fighting for now."

"Doc, you're my kinda corpsman. Thanks for fixin' me up. Patch me up and pitch me back in the fight," Hawkins replied. "Ain't nobody gonna keep me outta this fight. Ain't nobody. I got killin's to do. Lots of killin's." Hawkins then hobbled off skirting the tree line and low crawling to locate Wiley.

Corporal Thunder and Hawkins were now concurrently searching for Wiley to coordinate with him and Clary. As they crouched and scooted low in the blistering fires and ravaged battlefield, they prayed the others were alive and surviving. They were relatively uncertain about the actions and progress of one another. Consumed by their own fight and fate, they nonetheless worried about the team. It took time for them to reunite and meet and talk and prepare to continue the fight. They were anxious to share updates, but learning the fate of one another was their major concern. At that moment, they were unsure who lived and who died. They simply knew too many were dying.

CHAPTER 21

Khe Sanh's Marine Counterattack

Our M16 rifles are killing more of us than the NVA.

—Marine Private First Class Kenny Cider

While Corporal Thunder was fighting on Khe Sanh's 881 South's left flank and Hawkins on the right flank, Clary was rallying the center and Wiley the rear. Wiley, however, was primarily coordinating and calling in supporting arms fires and the rear security was a secondary action. The individual actions of the divided and separated team members were a collective effort, but one with individual and independent actions. They were alone, but they were together, too.

Clary quickly noticed too many Marines gathered at the fallen trees and logs near the top and center of the hill. It became obvious the NVA had positioned them there on purpose. Observing it was the only such barricade in the area, he sensed it was false protection. Preregistered NVA fires from mortars and machineguns were saturating the area. The epicenter of the killing zone, the log barricade was a trap. It was the deadliest real estate on the hill. Clary acted quickly.

The logs were a natural barricade for concealment as well as for firing M-60 machine guns. While protecting the Marines and helping elevate the machine guns for better fields of fire, the height of the mangled logs also caused the weapons and gunners to be more exposed. Clary witnessed two gunners sequentially commence firing and instantly take enemy kill shots to their heads and chests. It was virtually suicidal. Rushing to the machine guns to propose an alternate course of action, Clary was intuitively aware that teamwork was essential.

As Clary darted and dodged toward the machine gun, he was too late to save a third gunner. In a death defying act, PFC Murphy, the assistant gunner for one of the guns, leaped up to commence firing. Murphy almost certainly knew he would be accurately targeted, but he also unquestionably knew his fellow Marines were in desperate need of suppressive fires. It was suicidal, but it was sacrificial, too. It was as courageous as it was crucial to the Marines halting the NVA assaults and organizing for a counterattack. Murphy knew it, but accepted the risks.

The Marine advance was at a virtual standstill. Fire superiority was maintained by the NVA and the enemy mortars and rockets as well as machine gun and rifle fires were devastating. It was a perilous situation for the Marines on 881 South. It was a time of utmost fear, but it was no time for the fainthearted. It was a time for boldness or the Marines would be banished from the hill. It was a living hell; however, it was a dying hell, too.

Murphy valiantly commenced firing and instantly the NVA zeroed in on him. Struck and shattered by the force of blasts from an intense and incredible burst of enemy automatic weapons and RPG fire, he bravely held himself upright by tightening his grip on his machine gun. His right jaw was transformed into a bloody and pulverized and exposed open wound. Twisted in agony, his face exploded and roughly half of it virtually disappeared. Murphy reflexively fired two more bursts from his M-60, however, before the sustained enemy volleys propelled him backward and downward. Murphy was down, but the Marines were up. Murphy's courageous actions lifted the spirits of the Marine line and they were now emboldened to attack and advance.

Clary rushed to Murphy and dove beside him about the time a corpsman was wrapping a tight bandage around his face and jaw. Blood and splinters of jaw bone splattered everywhere. Broken and jagged teeth were exposed and littered the area. It was a gruesome scene and Clary glanced away to distance himself from the bludgeoned wound before collecting himself.

Clary attempted to briefly console Murphy. "Damn, Murph, I've read about Marines jumping on grenades to save fellow Marines and later awarded the Medal of Honor. It's just a death-defying act of bravery. The way you jumped up on the machine gun is the same. It was a death-defying act. Your suppressive fires helped save us. Now we're going to fight to save you."

Murphy's shattered face was contorted and he convulsed as he attempted to speak. Slurring his words, because speaking without a jaw and with his face shot to a jagged hell was virtually impossible, he pointed with his hand to his jaw. Murphy sighed with a glint in his eye for the corpsman to loosen the bandage. "Damn Doc, you trying to choke me to death. The bandage is a noose. I can't breathe." Murphy was near death, but he was joking with the Doc.

Close to death Murphy was nonetheless awkwardly smiling through the blood and bandages with a sense of humor that lent a little comedy to their serious situation. *The damnedest things happen in combat,* Clary thought as he returned to the serious business of fighting.

"Who's in charge here?" Clary asked as he bolted to the logs and the machine guns.

"All our leaders are killed or wounded. We're just fighting and doing our best to stay alive, but the M16s ain't helping us much. They're killing us," PFC Cider solemnly answered.

"Okay. Well, you're doing a good job, but we got to get organized. Listen up. Let's get some teams working together," Clary ordered the Marines. "All we got to do is work as teams and we'll be fine. Let's just take charge of this hill and charge forward.

"First, let's move these machine guns. These logs are just a damn target or bull's eye for the NVA. Then, let's spread out and get on line," Clary urged. "After that, we'll start firing and maneuvering. We have to move forward. We have to just keep shooting and scooting forward."

One of the Marines exclaimed, "The shooting part is getting harder because our rifles keep jamming. They ain't worth shit. They're dog shit. Some of us are taking our cleaning rods to punch rounds out of the barrels. The rounds get stuck in the barrels. Shell casings won't eject either. Shells get stuck in the chamber. The ejection system is bad."

"Our M16 rifles are killing more of us than the NVA," Cider reemphasized. Virtually defying death, he rose up and fired toward the enemy. He would rather fight than bitch and moan.

"Yeah, and the damned rifle's not ejecting rounds right and it fouls up the bolt. It just keeps jamming up and not ejecting rounds. It's just junk," another Marine complained.

"Damn, the magazines are bad, too," yet another Marine groaned. "The edges bend too easy. Then the rounds don't feed into the rifle right." He threw the empty magazine toward the NVA in disgust. The M16 was an indignity that plagued them, but they persevered despite it.

Clary listened attentively. He remembered Corporal Thunder's talk about complaining Marines being happy Marines. After allowing the Marines to complain and vent frustrations, he declared in agreement, "Well, that's what I'm hearing up and down the line. It seems once we fire a lot of rounds and really work the weapon hard, it just gives out. It just quits."

"But we can't quit," Clary paused and confessed. "We quit and we're done. We quit and we're dead. We just have to keep going. We have to work together with whatever works."

"We need to collect all the M16s we can from our dead and use them. Use anything we can find. Use them till they quit. Then find others that work. Keep collecting ammo, too," Clary exclaimed. "Use AK47s. They're working fine. As we move forward, start collecting and using AK47s. We're collecting some now and we'll collect more because we're going to kill more NVA. The AK47s are working best. Just kill the NVA and take their weapons."

Clary pointed to Cider, "You put a team together and spread out to the left on line. Hold your position until we're all in position and ready. You're in charge of the left." Cider took charge with a vengeance. The left flank held and later attacked. Cider led it.

Clary pointed to another Marine and asked, "You with the machine guns?"

"Yeah," the Marine answered as he inserted a belt of ammo in his machine gun.

"Okay, good. We need you. You take all your guns and take them off these logs. Then put your teams together as best you can. Then have them ready for suppressive fires so the rest of us can move forward," Clary appealed. "But keep the guns separated and keep them working together. Fire one and then the other. Alternate firing. You know what to do."

Clary glanced at another Marine and asked, "You with the 3.5 rockets?"

"Yes, we got four tubes with us or what's left of us," the Marine shrugged.

"Good. That's really good. Spread yourselves out along the line and be ready to fire," Clary ordered. "We'll just all get on line and get ready to do a little counterattacking."

Clary repeated similar instructions to the Marines along the line. He created impromptu teams and designated team leaders and duties. Once the almost twenty Marines were organized, Clary ordered, "I have an M79 grenade launcher. Once we're all in position, I'll start firing. That'll be the signal for all of us to start firing and maneuvering forward. Any questions?"

"How far we supposed to advance?" one Marine asked.

"Well, for now let's just advance about ten meters. That'll be tough enough for now. Just ten meters. Just enough to get us out of this damn killing zone and push the NVA back a little and make them worry we're not done. Just enough to let them know we're coming after them."

Clary paused and then added, "Once we advance and move out of this killing zone, just hold the line. I'll go coordinate with our forward observers for artillery and air support. We'll have them blast the tree line and NVA bunkers before we take another ten meters. Then we'll make the last advance into the tree line. Then we'll take this hill. Then we'll own it and hold it."

Clary's reorganization plans and duties were passed fast and furiously. Time was at a premium. He waited while the Marines and teams assumed their positions. He then fired his M79 to launch the counterattack. They began crawling more than charging, but it was a start. The Marine line held and then advanced. It was the beginning of the counterattack.

Clary overheard one of the machine gun crew Marines remark, "Damn, now we're really together. Now we're firing. I bet the NVA thought we was done. But we ain't close to done. We're just getting started."

Once Clary sensed the Marines were firing and maneuvering and advancing, he collected himself and dashed toward Wiley's position. He took no more than four steps and an AK47 round pierced the rear left side of his helmet. The round spun around the inside of his helmet and scalp and exited at the right front. The rounds velocity slowed, but metal fragments ripped into his scalp, forehead, and cheek as it spun wildly downward and exited his helmet.

Clary crashed hard to the hard ground with an awkward thud. He lay dazed. His thoughts were jumbled. His head throbbed. Blood drained into his eyes. He had a hard time clearing his thoughts and his vision, both from the blood and the throbbing…as well as the fear.

Clary realized, however, he had to report to Wiley. He knew the supporting arms fires were crucial to the Marines he had organized for the counterattack. He understood they were now fighting for every inch of their advance. He knew he had to move on for them to move on. His mind whirled uncontrollably, but he remembered he had to coordinate with the team. He fought thoughts of dying. He knew he was fighting to live, but he trembled with the knowledge that his severe head wound was affecting his mind and body. His thoughts swirled erratically. He knew he was fighting to avoid dying; fighting for his survival and the survival of the Marines on the hill, too. Fighting to control his thoughts, however, became his main fight. His mind whirled.

Clary recognized his mind was racing uncontrollably. He knew his thoughts were totally and terribly and utterly scattered, but he gathered and collected himself. He knew he had to move on. He knew that much. Surviving was moving on. He moved on.

Corporal Thunder and Hawkins were moving on, too. Independently, but simultaneously, Corporal Thunder, Hawkins, and Clary were moving to locate Wiley. None knew if the other was alive, but all knew they had to locate Wiley. They prayed Wiley was alive. They prayed they were all alive. The situation was perilous, but they knew they would surely perish without meeting and coordinating with one another. Clary's singular goal was to locate Wiley; to locate Wiley alive. Hopefully, Wiley was alive. Clary's mind continued to race wildly and his thoughts spun repeatedly.

While Corporal Thunder was fighting on the left flank, Hawkins on the right flank, and Clary in the center, Wiley was simply fighting to stay alive. Wiley had taken charge of the radio, but radios and crew served weapons were prime targets of the NVA.

Wiley had lumbered toward the tree line Corporal Thunder had pointed out to him as their meeting area, but as he approached multiple RPG rounds exploded immediately to his rear. The powerful blasts bowled him over and tumbled him into a bomb crater. The force of the blasts and their heaving him into the crater probably saved his life. He lay in defilade, but could hear rounds zinging overhead. The whistling and whining rounds splattered dirt and debris. Wiley hunkered down and laid flat. Motionless at first, he slowly regained consciousness.

Wiley thought, *I have to check the radio. It has to be okay. We have to have a good radio or we're doomed. We're done. We need it for artillery and air. We need it to keep us working together. We just need it.* His thoughts were rapid and ragged, but he slowly regained his senses. The radio was critical to survival and he protected it caringly and courageously.

Once Wiley confirmed the radio was okay, he checked himself. Doc Lynn saw Wiley tossed into the crater and later rushed to his aid. "Wiley, let me check you out."

Doc Lynn inspected Wiley and discovered deep and gory gashes in his back and legs from the shrapnel. He shouted, "Wiley, I'm cutting off most of your jacket and bandaging you up. You have some bad cuts. I'll fix them as best I can, but it's only temporary. I just want to stop the bleeding for now. We'll get you better care later."

"Thanks, Doc," Wiley replied. "I got a lot to do. I got to get to doing it, too."

"Okay, but you better stay here in this crater. We got dead and wounded scattered all over the battlefield," Doc Lynn replied. "As soon as I can get some help and get it going, I'm going to start bringing the wounded here to this area. They'll be safer here than in that killing zone." Later, the first wounded Marine began to be transported to Wiley and the crater.

"Corpsman. Corpsman up," rang out from a wounded Marine. Doc Lynn heard the call and charged over the crest of the crater and disappeared. Instantly, the crater came under attack with rounds tearing into the crater's berm and rocks and shards exploding wildly in every direction. Wiley thought, *the crater's becoming a NVA killing zone. The whole hilltop is a killing zone.*

Crawling carefully to the top edge of the crater to check on Doc Lynn, Wiley located the doc. He observed the doc desperately tugging and dragging a wounded Marine toward the crater and safety. "Doc, let me help," Wiley shouted as he slowly and agonizingly slithered from the crater. Wiley was instantly hit with an AK47 round in his right hip and he tumbled backward into the crater. Moments later, Doc Lynn dragged the wounded Marine into the crater with Wiley, who lay quiet and still. He was writhing in pain, but he endured it in silence. He was either too proud or too shocked to reveal his pain, but his blood splattered and shattered body and uniform more than confirmed his plight. Drifting into and out of consciousness, Wiley was fading fast.

"Wiley, we need you on the radio. We don't need you getting yourself killed. Like I said, you stay here and do what you're supposed to do," Doc Lynn scolded. "We'll take care of the killed and wounded. You take care of us with the radio and supporting arms fires."

Wiley writhed in excruciating pain while Doc Lynn checked him out again. "Wiley, you got a nasty flesh wound, but I don't think nothing vital has been hit. Damn, look at that. The round went in your hip, but exited out your thigh. Damn, those rounds tumble and do strange things in our bodies," Doc Lynn exclaimed as he bandaged Wiley again.

"Okay, I'm going back out," Doc Lynn warned, "but you stay down and do what you're supposed to do. You got it? Get the supporting fires going."

Nodding his head, Wiley hurt so bad he could barely talk. He knew he was now unable to walk, too. He knew he would have to do what Doc Lynn told him. Finally, Wiley simply sighed, "Doc, I know what I have to do. I'll do it." Wiley and the radio were crucial. Without the radio there would be no supporting arms coordination. Without supporting arms they had virtually no chance at surviving. Wiley realized that now more than ever as he and the radio became a team.

Doc Lynn disappeared again, but seconds later an NVA tossed a ChiCom grenade into the crater. The wounded Marine yelled, "Grenade," and Wiley instinctively rolled over to shield the Marine from the blast with his body and the radio. Intuitively he realized he was jeopardizing the radio, but instinct motivated him to protect the wounded Marine.

Thankfully, the radio was encased in his pack and the padding absorbed most of the blast. Wiley immediately checked the radio. It was damaged, but okay. The wounded Marine was fine, too. Wiley, however, was again showered with more shrapnel. He thought, *I'm becoming a sieve.* He had holes in his body from head to foot. The blood matted, crusted, and glistened from the sweat and sun. He was bleeding profusely and faint from the fatigue of battling his wounds.

Wiley realized the crater was too dangerous. He thought, *The NVA know about this crater, too. They probably figured we'd take advantage of its concealment and protection. Then, once we were wounded and kind of helpless with a lot of us in here, they'd just start targeting us with rifles and grenades and whatever.*

Fear propelled Wiley into action. First, he established radio contact with the company and updated their situation and initiated artillery and air strikes. Once he began his supporting arms requests and coordination, Wiley struggled out the backside of the crater. He helped drag the wounded Marine with him because the crater was now too dangerous. It was its own killing zone. He had to move on, but every small move was punctuated by large pain. Then, in a blinding flash from nowhere, Wiley remembered the farm's stubborn mule Blackjack. Wiley stubbornly plowed forward.

"We got to get out of here and get over there," Wiley groaned in pain and pointed. "We'll drag ourselves over near where we came up the hill. We'll be safer there." Both Marines knew, however, that safer was relative because there was no safety on the hill that day.

Once Wiley was securely in the new and safer position, he shimmied to the crest of the hill. He was now in a better position to observe and control supporting arms fires and he was safer, too. As ordered by Corporal Thunder, Wiley parceled out the 881 North fires to the battalion. In addition, he now had a 0-1 Bird Dog aircraft on station with an Airborne Forward Air Controller (FAC) for coordinating air and artillery on 881 South.

It was then Wiley understood exactly what Corporal Thunder had intended. With a team of professionals to help coordinate the supporting arms fires, he was relieved. The mental pressure dissipated and he could focus exclusively on 881 South and staying alive, but he smiled, *I'm not doing too good with this staying alive part.*

Wiley was back to functioning and monitoring the radio traffic and it was a timely return. He overheard an air strike mission and immediately checked the coordinates on his map. "Damn, the coordinates are dead center on our hill. They're right in the middle of our forward positions. They're targeting 881 South. They're targeting us," Wiley yelled to his wounded comrade.

Wiley was unsure how to stop or abort the mission, but he improvised. He was unfamiliar with the correct terminology, but he recalled Corporal Thunder ordering him to do whatever had to be done. He had memorized the Forward Air Controller's (FAC) call sign and immediately entered the radio net and declared, "You got to stop the strikes on 881 South. Those coordinates are on friendlies. There's NVA there, too, but it's mostly Marines. We're in a close fight. It's close combat, but you got to cancel the mission."

The FAC recognized the urgency of the request to abort and immediately the battalion operations fires team entered the radio net to confirm the abort. Wiley initiated an abort that could have been disastrous for the Marines. The Airborne FAC confirmed the abort and relayed, "We're shifting all air strikes to 881 North for now. We'll standby for 881 South.

We'll attack 881 South only upon your requests. Good job, Marine. Hang on down there. We'll cover you from up here."

Wiley breathed a massive sigh of relief, but the deep breath caused deep pain. He reflexively froze to lessen the pain, which nonetheless persisted. Although severely wounded, Wiley was reinvigorated by his multiple duties. *Damn, I just have to keep hanging on,* Wiley thought, *I have to hang on till sunset. Later, we'll take care of sunrise tomorrow. One day at a time.*

Exhausted and bleeding from multiple wounds, Wiley lay in the tall grass. He transmitted and monitored radio calls to keep from drifting into unconsciousness or, worse, death. Fighting to remain alert and to defy death were major battles for him, but they were helping to keep him alive. He was, however, mostly hoping and praying for Corporal Thunder, Hawkins, and Clary to join him. Alone and scared, he prayed for life. He was as scared of never seeing his team again, however, as he was of dying. Wiley was lonely for the team.

Wiley remembered Hawkins' declaration, *It's a lot harder to live in Vietnam. It's a lot easier to die in Vietnam.* Then he steeled himself for the harder option of living. Life had always been hard for Wiley. Nothing had ever been easy for him. *I'm not taking the easy way now,* Wiley whispered to himself. *I know hard and I got to be as hard as ever to survive.*

Wiley's thoughts drifted as he waited for Corporal Thunder, Hawkins, and Clary to locate him. Bleeding from multiple wounds, he was fighting to avoid shifting into unconsciousness or worse. His strongest and surest battle, however, was to coordinate the supporting arms fires for the Marines under attack and preparing to counterattack.

At this point in the battle for 881 South, more Marines were dead or wounded than were alive. Wiley fought to remain among the living, but he drifted further from life and closer to death. Continuing to float and fade, his faith and fear challenged him. It was somewhat inevitable considering the severity of his multiple wounds that Wiley's eyes would eventually close and he then lay motionless. Now, he waited in peace for Corporal Thunder, Hawkins, and Clary. He waited for what seemed an eternity. To him it was an eternity, but it was peace, too. It was peace in the midst of war. In the midst of the hell of 881 South, Wiley thought he glimpsed heaven. His last thoughts were of his dad and family as he drifted into a sense of relief beyond the world he had always known and into one beyond his comprehension.

Chapter 22

Khe Sanh's Initial Tragedy

Hawkins, sorry. The platoon looked everywhere for Corporal Thunder. They couldn't find him. He's not there. He's dead or blown up or the NVA captured him. He's gone. He's just not there.

—Marine First Lieutenant Thomas Abrahams

"Wiley! Wiley, are you okay?" Corporal Thunder asked as the first to arrive at Wiley's position, but he knew his question was absurd. Wiley was unresponsive and appeared dead; still Corporal Thunder quickly prayed he was alive and only in shock or resting. Carefully sitting beside Wiley, he checked his vitals and prayed, again, for a pulse—for any sign of life.

"Jesus, Wiley's shot all to hell and bleeding everywhere," Hawkins exclaimed, slamming into the crater as the next to arrive. Noting the severity of Wiley's multiple wounds, he asked Corporal Thunder anxiously, "He gonna be okay?" He, too, realized it was a preposterous question considering Wiley's status, but he was hopeful. All too often, all they had was hope. Kneeling, he held Wiley's huge hand. *Combat and killin' and death make me feel small, but my two small hands don't begin to cover Wiley's enormous fist. Talk about feeling small,* Hawkins thought.

Wiley's eyes slowly opened, but he was temporarily confused and unable to speak coherently. "Yep, I knowed it," Hawkins teased. "Wiley's playing opossum. He's catching a few winks while we're out busting our asses. Okay, sleeps time is over, Wiley. We got work to do."

"Hawkins, is that you?" Wiley sighed as he began to recover and regain his senses. "Can't a guy take a nap in peace? You know I like my sleeps." Corporal Thunder and Hawkins glanced at one another relieved he was okay. Wiley always said *sleeps* instead of *sleep*.

Corporal Thunder and Hawkins purposefully talked and laughed with Wiley to help him become conscious of his location and the situation. When

Wiley seemed more lucid, they simultaneously asked, "Where's Clary?" They looked at one another and shrugged.

Sprinting into the area and executing an awkward belly flop for cover amidst a cloud of dust and hail of bullets in close pursuit of his meandering and twisting jaunt, Clary was the last to arrive. He slapped dust from his uniform and grabbed Wiley's huge shoulder and held it lightly.

"Okay, gather round. We have updates to share," Corporal Thunder smiled. "Let's be fast. Clary, you have the center. You update first." Time was of the essence and they knew it.

Clary summarized the organization of the Marines in the center as he occasionally peered over the crest of the crater's berm while reloading his magazines. "At first, we took a lot of casualties. We lost a lot of senior leaders. We were bogged down. We had no officers and no Staff NCOs. But we formed teams. Now we're back up. We're advancing to within about twenty or thirty meters of the tree line at the northern edge of 881 South." Clary hunkered lower as another barrage of rocket propelled grenades screamed overhead and continued, "We'll halt there for artillery and air strikes to prep the tree line and beyond. Then we'll continue to attack and secure the objective." He softly wiped sweat and blood from his brow while breathing hard.

"Hawkins, you have the right flank. What's your update?" Corporal Thunder inquired as they began to expand their description of the battlefield and their situation and their upcoming tasks.

"Jesus, we gotta piss pot full of NVA over there. But we're 'bout to get'em pissin' in their skivvies," Hawkins summarized. "We've stopped a few attacks to roll up our flank. We're takin' out lots of snipers. We're destroyin' bunkers one by one. We took their best shots. Now we're counterpunchin' and they ain't likin' it. They thought they had us at first, but now they ain't so sure. They're ready for the knockout, but it's one helluva fight with lots of fightin's left to do."

"Wiley, now your update," Corporal Thunder shouted as they ducked while hearing a RPG round whistle overhead. The whining sounds of the rocket propelled grenades intensified and they spoke louder and faster.

"Well, at first I wasn't doing much but getting shot up. Hell, I took an RPG, then an AK47, and then a grenade," Wiley frowned while propping himself up on his elbow and then lying back down in pain from his wounds, "but then I got going. The supporting arms are now firing okay," he summarized. "We got battalion doing 881 North and the Airborne FAC is really helping me with air and artillery on 881 South. We got the battalion's 81 mortars working the back slope of 881 South, too. The 81s are stopping any NVA reinforcements coming over from 881 North. We got a fires team together now and we're working good."

"Okay, good. Good jobs," Corporal Thunder noted above the rumbles of nearby explosions and then gave his update. "We're doing on the left flank what Hawkins' doing on the right. We took the NVA's best shot, but we've held our own and stabilized the situation. Now we have the NVA wondering. Now we have to attack and kick butt. We have to keep working together. We're fighting better now, but we have lots of hard work and hard fighting to do, too. Okay, that's my summary of where I believe we are," he grimaced as he withdrew his K-Bar to sketch the battle area in the scraggly dirt of the crater and point to specific areas while he talked and formulated their plan of action.

"First, we have lots of casualties. We have to start taking them off the battlefield and evac them so they can get good medical treatment," he admitted and turned to Wiley. "Wiley, you radio the company and ask it to organize an evacuation process. Tell the company we'll evac the casualties to the crest of the hill. Ask the company to come up and take them back down the hill. Tell them we have Marines dying and it needs to be done now."

Pausing thoughtfully, he quickly formed the rest of his plan and ordered, "Clary, after we counterattack, you help organize the corpsmen for hill evacuations. You get a team to help Cord evac the casualties to the crest here. Cord's working that now and will work with you and the corpsmen and evac team. Wiley, like I said, you then coordinate with the company evac team to move the casualties on down the hill.

"Second, we have a lot of useless M16s. We talked about how insane it was to issue new weapons in an old war. Now most of what we said could happen is really happening," he sighed as much from fatigue as from frustration with the failing M16 rifles, "but we can't do much about that now. We just have to use what we got. Maybe the AK47 is the best answer. Just kill the NVA and take their weapons. I don't know what else to do. It's a shame, but our own M16s are just jamming and quitting and dying on us. They're junk. They're our worst enemy.

"Third," he concluded looking directly into the haunting eyes of his team members who would have to search their souls for the courage it would take to do what he then ordered them to do, "we have to coordinate this final counterattack. We have to secure this objective. We have to accomplish our mission. That's why we're here. That's what we do. That's what we'll do, too. We'll accomplish the mission and secure this hill.

"I know it's bad, but it could be worse," he sighed again. "Remember when we talked after the decapitation incident about the difference between a scared or angry enemy? We got us a scared enemy right now. He's afraid. He's mostly hiding in bunkers instead of out hunting for us. He thinks he's got us and that we're done. He's not yet angry or hostile because he thinks he's going to win and live. So, he's hiding in the bunkers instead of hunting us down. He's being safe.

"But we're mad as hell. We're angry he's killed so many of us. The NVA killed Lieutenant Antoine and we got to make him pay for that. Pay for the others, too. While they're hiding, we're going hunting. We'll hunt them down and kill them, but we need to do it fast before they realize they're going down and become angry. Let's kill them while we're mad and they're just scared."

"Yeah, ain't none of 'em livin'!" Hawkins declared as he vividly recalled the brutal battlefield littered with dead and wounded Marines. "Let's hunt 'em down in their hidin' bunkers to kill 'em all. Ain't gonna be no survivors. No quarter asked; none given. They don't deserve to live after what they done to our platoon and what they're doin' shootin' our helpless wounded. They made the rules. Now we'll kill 'em with their rules."

Corporal Thunder intuitively knew that Hawkins needed no motivation to fight, but he again mentioned the scared and angry differences to illustrate the gravity of the situation to the team. Hawkins' words only reinforced it for every one of them. They were all of one accord and all nodded in agreement. Clary added, "Let's hunt 'em down. Let's show them Marines don't hide. Let 'em hide. We'll hunt." Hawkins' words reinforced their readiness to fight, Clary's words confirmed it.

With uniforms soaked in blood from wounds and sweat from exhaustion, they glanced at one another as they simultaneously grimaced in extreme pain. They were all hurting equally badly, but they understood that they had to persevere and move on. Marines were depending on them and they were depending on one another. They knew they had to take the hill now or the hill would take them. The hill was their hell and their hell was the hill. They fought their pain as tenaciously as they fought the enemy.

"Wiley, crank up the supporting arms fires," Corporal Thunder ordered as they understood and accepted that such fires would be 'danger close', but that close fires were critical because they were in such close contact with the enemy. "Target the tree line. We'll mark our front lines with purple smoke. Let'em know that. Tell them we know it's close. That's just the way it is and has to be. Tell them to take the tree line and work outboard. You observe and adjust fires for them. Just keep the fires in the trees and off the cleared or grassy part. Emphasize to them we know it's danger close. It's that way or we lose this hill—and we're not losing the hill.

"Okay, any questions? Did we forget anything? Anyone have any other thoughts?" the Corporal paused to reflect and asked. His expression was serious and determined as he stared at them individually. They stared back with an equal commitment.

Wiley, Hawkins, and Clary glanced bleary-eyed at one another. Fully focused, they said nothing. They simply nodded their heads in agreement. They were all in. Unsure if they could do more than they had been asked to do, they knew it would take all they had simply to do it.

"Okay, let's return to our positions and organize for the final attack. Be ready to attack when Wiley unleashes the artillery and air. That's the signal to advance. It's that simple. It's what we have to do," Corporal Thunder directed. "It'll then be over. It'll be over one way or the other. It'll be over and done. Then we'll see who's on the hill. It'll be either us or the NVA. Then we'll see who's still alive. We'll see who's dead, too, and it won't be us. We're surviving this hill and this hell. It's what we've been doing. We just have to keep doing it. We'll do it till it's over."

The Corporal gazed directly into their eyes again and declared, "It's now or never. Let's go do it. Let's go fight. Let's go take the hill. Let's go hunting. Let's survive. Semper Fi." No other words were spoken as the four Marines thrust their fists forward and briefly but tightly held one another's hands in a clasp of brotherhood and friendship.

Except for Wiley, who remained in his crater position, they dashed to return to their positions. Wiley immediately began coordinating the fire support. The pulsating cadence of the battle raged to increasing crescendos, but the team was oblivious to the sounds of war. They were fixated and focused on their missions. The violence and blasts and explosions were secondary to their quiet mental preparations and silent prayers for the coming attack. The hill and battlefield were absolute chaos and they sensed it would become worse before it became better. Yet, they acted calmly and courageously.

Within minutes, the final assault forces were standing by. Minutes later, the supporting arms fires engulfed the tree line. Shattering and splintering sounds rumbled over the hill. The hill shook violently from the force of the bombardments as rippling and ripping waves crossed and re-crossed and crisscrossed the war-torn plateau. It was the beginning of the end, but no one knew the ending. They knew only the beginning as Wiley prayed, *I pray we survive and we're alive to know the ending.* But surviving and living were questionable.

It seemed it was a volcano waiting to erupt. First, it belched softly and sporadically and then it erupted violently and viciously with incredibly sustained force and magnitude. Following the upheaval the Marines charged forward covered by Wiley's supporting arms fires and their fear-defying courage. The NVA either died in place or retreated. There were no NVA surrenders or prisoners. There were only dead NVA and dead, wounded, and living Marines and Navy Corpsmen. But there were more dead and wounded than unscathed living. It was fighting and killing to survive and live. There were more who died on the hill that day than lived on it. It was war and it was Vietnam in all its savagery. It was Khe Sanh.

"Okay, now we counterattack," Clary shouted to his teams above the thunderous explosions of the artillery and close air support missions Wiley was coordinating. "That's our signal. Let's move out. Let's go."

It was a virtually cloudless day, but a dense mist engulfed the hill. The smoldering grass and whiffs of smoke from splintered tree branches and shattered shrubs floated aimlessly. Burnt powder fumes from multiple weapons mixed and mingled with the stench of death. It was eerie and haunting, but the haze from countless explosions provided cover for the attacking Marines.

"Fire for effect," Wiley radioed the battalion fires team as he observed the initial artillery barrages impacting on target. "Then slowly walk them north. We got Marines advancing from the south to the north. They'll mark their front lines with purple smoke. Keep your fires north of the purple smoke." Wiley then passed similar instructions to the Forward Air Controller as the ground and aviation supporting fires began to work in unison as a team.

Marines, frustrated with heavy losses and malfunctioning weapons, gathered themselves. In the center, Clary urged, "Fire and maneuver slowly at first and then faster and faster." At first it was inches at a time. Gradually, it became a foot or two or more. Then the counterattack gained momentum and the Marines sensed the flow of the battle tilt in their favor. Clary shouted, "Let's ride this wave to victory," as he had a quick recollection of his California surfing days.

"Jesus, the artillery's close. It's just the way we like it. It's right on target, too," Hawkins yelled to his Marines on the right flank preparing to attack. "It's our signal to move out. Keep your butts down and your rifles up and firing. Let's go huntin'. It's knockdown and knockout time." Hawkins had a fleeting thought of his Boston gym and boxing days. Fighting was simply ingrained in him; a part of who he was. *Fearin' time's over. Now it's fightin' time,* he sighed.

Hawkins rallied the right flank Marines as they steadily and then more rapidly advanced. Minutes later, Hawkins hollered, "Now let's kick ass. The NVA lines are beginnin' to crumble and break. No doubt they had us at first, but now they're beginnin' to doubt. We 'bout got'em. Look who's backin' down now. Look whose lines are cracking. Look who's throwing in the towel. They're hidin' and won't come outta bunkers to fight. Make the bunkers their graves."

"There it is. There's the artillery and our signal to move out," Corporal Thunder shouted on the left flank as he heard the incoming artillery begin to impact on enemy positions. "Let's take the fight to them now. Let's move forward as fast as we can. Just fire and maneuver. Just keep doing it. The NVA's about to break. Let's break'em down good," he ordered the Marines standing by to attack as he quickly flung two grenades and fired and maneuvered forward.

Observing the battle unfold before him, the Corporal prayed silently to steel himself for the attack, *Spirit Father, we're walking into the evil and shadow of the mountain of death, but there's no time for fear now because we're Marines fighting together and for one another. We're Marines and our strength*

and comfort are in one another. Great Father, it's that simple. There's nothing else
to say or pray. There's nothing else to do. There's nothing to do now but fight. I pray
we fight true. Amen. Then he yelled a traditional Indian warpath, "Aaaaiiieee"
as he charged forward with his gleaming machete and AK47. He was back
hunting on the plains.

The NVA line started to weaken, then it cracked, and finally it broke.
Hawkins was the first to observe, "We got a crack in the line. Now, let's fill
it with Marines and roll up the flanks. We got'em runnin'. Now, let's get'em
retreatin'. Let's get'em racin' for Hanoi. Yep, the race is on!"

The final assault raged for less than an hour. Then suddenly, it was over.
Yet, for many it would never be over. While it was eerily silent, the battle
would forever rage on in the memories of the living. It was a Marine victory.
Yet, for those who perished it would always be a loss, too.

It was now late afternoon. The Marines were exhausted, but had to fight
on. Instead of fighting the enemy, the fight was now to police the battlefield,
recover the dead, and evacuate the wounded. They were gruesome tasks.
There were so many dead and wounded. There was so few living. Only a few
who survived were capable of evacuating the casualties and deceased. They
were more than the walking wounded. They were the crawling dead. It was
the most physically and psychologically fatiguing part of the day. It was war.
It was war in all its violence and brutality and ruthlessness. It was a victory,
but a costly one in human suffering and tragedy.

Corporal Thunder suddenly appeared at the evacuation site. Casualties
were cleared from the hill and taken to the trail leading back down 881
South. Evacuation teams from the company were in place to form a chain to
pass and pull the wounded and dead down the hill. It was surreal. Casualties
were placed in ponchos and drug down the steep slopes as carefully as possible. The task was completed long after nightfall, but thoughts of that night
and the day's battle would linger well into their tomorrows…they would be
with the survivors forever.

The Corporal strode silently among the corpses and wounded searching
for his Marines. The exceptionally high number of casualties was numbing
and the withdrawal from the adrenaline high of battle contributed to his
sheer exhaustion. Relief swept over him when he finally located Wiley
before he was evacuated and exclaimed, "Wiley, you did your job. You did it
well. You stepped up and you did the job of the platoon commander, too."

Corporal Thunder smiled in spite of the past hours of relentless fighting and horrific battle and exclaimed, "You once talked about leadership and jobs. You said leadership was just doing your job. You did yours and more. I'm proud of you. The NVA had us out-manned and out-gunned, but you took care of them with supporting arms fires. Your coordination of arty and air saved the day. We'd never have made it without you. God bless you, Baby Brute."

Wiley stirred and grinned remembering the sparingly used but special nickname the team had given him. He desperately wanted to briefly talk with Corporal Thunder, but multiple sudden sharp pains overpowered him and he realized it would take all the strength he could muster to simply survive. He closed his eyes in peace and powered his energy toward his survival.

"Take care, Wiley. I'll see you sometime and somewhere. Now, let's get you off this damn hill. Let's get you treated. I'm waiting here for Hawkins and Clary. I'll search for them. I'll see you later," Corporal Thunder smiled and without warning he bowed down and kissed Wiley on the forehead as a Marine and friend…*and brother*. Profoundly touched by the gesture, Wiley grinned without opening his eyes and saluted as best he could. Moving on swiftly and silently, Corporal Thunder reluctantly disappeared to perform other missions.

Wiley was eager to talk with Corporal Thunder, but simply physically unable. Plus, the Corporal had already wheeled and vanished into the night to search for Hawkins and Clary. He was recalling the Corporal's words and kind gesture, when evacuation teams grabbed his poncho and began pulling and sliding him down the hill. Thankfully, Wiley passed out from the pain and the ragged decent down the hill.

Closer to dying than living, Wiley had been in hell today. Now, he was fighting like hell to delay heaven. He was denied an opportunity to bid a true farewell to Corporal Thunder, but he hoped to see him at the bottom of the hill. He never saw him. The sighting never occurred. Wiley saw none of the team at the bottom of the hill and none of the team saw him.

Corporal Thunder then searched frantically but calmly for Hawkins and Clary. He knew the general location on Hill 881 South of each and began a systematic search of their respective areas. Hawkins was the first to be located. Drenched in blood and partially crushed inside an NVA bunker, he was as feisty as ever. Corporal Thunder, however, was taken aback by the extent of his horrible wounds, especially when Hawkins attempted to stand, staggered, and collapsed.

"Jesus, I just wanted to kill a few more NVAs and bust a few more bunkers," Hawkins confessed while smiling in pain. "I was huntin'em down. I musta got a little too far forward. Either the artillery or air blasted the bunker with me in it. I took another AK47 round in my side and another one in my ankle. Plus, I got some more shrapnel from our own fires. They hurt like hell. I can't walk. You'll have to carry me outta this shithole. Sorry."

"Yeah, well, I've been carrying you all tour," Corporal Thunder smiled jokingly. "I guess a few more meters won't hurt." Reassured by Corporal Thunder's presence, Hawkins grinned.

Corporal Thunder quickly bandaged Hawkins' new wounds. As he wrapped the two gunshot wounds, he talked to distract Hawkins from his pain, "Remember the time we talked about leadership during one of our bunker talks? You simply said a leader marches to the sounds of the guns and inspires his followers to do the same. To march to the sound of the guns—well, that's what you did all damn day long. One gun after another, you marched to the guns. You took the guns and bunkers out, too. You almost single-handedly held our right flank. I'm proud of you, but I'm pissed, too. You getting all shot up pisses me off. Be more careful next time. We need you."

"Next time my ass!" Hawkins exclaimed. "This is the last time for me. I'm outta this shithole. None too soon either. Besides, you oughta be pissed at the NVA. They the ones shot me. Here's another besides. Besides, it looks like you got shot up, too. That pisses me off."

The pain and exertion to talk were too much for Hawkins as he again collapsed into Corporal Thunder's arms. The Corporal immediately combat carried him to the evacuation site and laid him down gently and said a prayer for him. Standing over him for a few minutes, he reminisced about their talks together while remembering the wild tales and wooly times and recalling how most were tame and true compared to the often rabid and raging and real Hawkins.

As the memories warmed his heart, Corporal Thunder bent down and lightly caressed Hawkins on the forehead. He pressed his hand on Hawkins' head for an extended time. He, as well as Wiley and Clary, had become more to the Corporal than simply team members.

Hawkins' eyes fluttered open slightly in response to his leader's soft touch. Corporal Thunder whispered, "God bless you, Little Italy." Saying farewell was hard and exhausting.

Holding up two balled fists, Hawkins struck a fighter's pose as he pretended to jab and counterpunch. He smiled remembering the pride he had in the team's nickname for him. The smile and punches, however, overwhelmed him. Dropping his fists, he grimaced in pain and passed out. The Corporal inhaled with deep emotion and quickly departed to search for Clary.

Clary was the hardest and last to be located. Clary had evidently led his impromptu teams farther into the tree line than Corporal Thunder had first thought. He had penetrated deeper into the NVA lines than anyone to take the fight to the enemy. It was dark, but Corporal Thunder refused to discontinue his search. He was on a mission to locate Clary. As always, the mission was paramount.

Corporal Thunder eventually discovered Clary behind a destroyed NVA bunker. He was bathed in flowing crimson and unconscious atop a log and sandbag rampart. Initially, he thought Clary was dead until he checked his pulse. It was faint, but it was a pulse. Clary was ashen, but his ghost like coloration was splashed with blood red hues. The Corporal poured a canteen of water on Clary's face to wipe away the blood and mud and crud. He then began to treat Clary's multiple shrapnel wounds.

"Corporal Thunder, is that you?" Clary asked as he awoke briefly to a semi-conscious state.

"Ssshhh. Be quiet. You don't have to talk," the Corporal answered. "It's me and you'll be okay. Just relax. Be still. Be quiet." He recoiled at Clary's jagged shrapnel wounds while compassionately treating them and thinking, *God bless Navy Corpsmen. They have to do this all the time. Talk about a nasty duty, but talk about respecting them and that duty, too.*

"Okay, but talking helps me with the pain," Clary confessed. "The damn NVA got me with a few grenades. I saw them too late. I dove like you told us, but I was too slow. They got me."

"Yeah, well you got them, too," Corporal Thunder explained. "There's nothing but a lot of dead NVA around here. Ten at least. You got them all. Good hunting for a surfing beach boy.

"But what you really did was lead," Corporal Thunder continued, "Remember when we all gave leadership talks? You talked about organizing teams and teamwork. You talked about how sports helped you with your leadership philosophies. You talked about getting people to work together. You talked about excellence and success. Well, that's what you did today. We're all proud of you. You held the center together. You led the attack. We won, too. You're a winner."

Corporal Thunder was unsure how much Clary heard or understood because Clary lay in silence, but he smiled weakly before drifting into unconsciousness. Fear instantly gripped the Corporal. He was afraid Clary was dying or dead. He kneeled, pulled Clary up, and carefully slung him over his shoulder to combat carry Clary to the evacuation site. As with Wiley and Hawkins, he laid him down tenderly and sat with him briefly. He prayed a silent prayer before leaning over and pressing his palm to Clary's face and patting his cheek.

Corporal Thunder never knew if Clary regained consciousness, but when he whispered, "God bless you, Socrates," he swore he saw a quivering smile on Clary's drawn and beaten face. The Corporal then faded into the darkness and vanished into the night. Then he was gone. Then it truly became darker than dark…*for the NVA*.

The following morning, Company M conducted an early reveille at the southern base of 881S. The area was in shambles and littered with dead and wounded amidst the heartbreak of those still living. It was a sorrowful scene, but they set aside their sympathies for their missions. While reconstituting after the previous day's battle, the company confronted three challenges.

"We have three missions this morning," Lieutenant Abrahams announced. "First, is to medevac our dead and wounded. Second, is to locate Corporal Thunder. Third, is to prepare for our helilift back to our Payable River base camp." He surveyed the area with true sadness.

Mike Company was a shadow of what it had been 72 hours ago. "Our losses are devastating, but it's worse having a Missing In Action or MIA," Lieutenant Abrahams stressed. "We have one Marine unaccounted for. We're assembling a team to search for Corporal Thunder."

Intent on locating him, the Lieutenant had always respected Corporal Thunder. "The third platoon will depart at the earliest to search the hill. We defeated the NVA and they retreated. If there's enemy there, however, it's to abort the mission. Battalion will conduct a later operation to secure the hill with Kilo Company. It'll probably be later today or tomorrow. They'll look then. We're just too beat up now to do much more. That's why we're going back to base. We've had too many losses." He spoke cryptically to lessen the sadness of their situation.

While the company organized the dead and wounded into multiple assembly areas for evacuation, the third platoon began the exhausting ascent up Hill 881 South. Wiley, Hawkins, and Clary lay in separate locations unconscious from their wounds and loss of blood. Hawkins, however, was at times somewhat coherent. With Hawkins it was difficult for the corpsmen to ascertain his true situation because he was always gesturing wildly and rambunctious with blazing feistiness…and talking incessantly. They learned, however, Hawkins was always talking.

"Jesus, I got only one request before leavin' this shithole," Hawkins pleaded with the corpsmen. "Let me stay to the last evacuation helo. I wanna wait as long as I can. I wanna learn the news on Corporal Thunder. That's all I ask. I gotta know if he's okay."

"Okay, we'll hold you till last," Doc Lynn promised, "but then we're all going back. We'll hold you as long as we can. But then you have to go. We all have to go."

"Thanks," Hawkins sighed. Then he waited. He waited impatiently, but he waited. He talked, too, but he always talked. Talking about home and the battle and the team gave him reasons and strength to patiently persevere… *and avoid thoughts of death and dying.*

The Mike Company helo medevacs began midmorning as the mountain mist and overcast dissipated. The waiting was torture for Hawkins; it was more painful than his wounds and his wounds were excruciatingly painful. He waited restlessly and anxiously. He talked relentlessly.

Descending the mountain about noon, the third platoon leader reported to the Lieutenant, who was waiting for the word on Corporal Thunder. After talking briefly with the search team commander, he then strolled solemnly and slowly to Hawkins. Sad news was never easy.

"Hawkins, sorry. The platoon scoured the hill looking everywhere for Corporal Thunder. They couldn't find him. He's not there," Lieutenant Abrahams despondently reported to Hawkins. "He's dead or blown up or the NVA captured him. He's gone. He's just not there."

Hawkins was in dire physical pain, but his true pain was the emotional and tragic news about Corporal Thunder. "Jesus, I can't leave here without him. He's gotta be there. He's gotta be somewhere," Hawkins exclaimed as tears welled in his eyes. "The NVA're good, but they ain't that good. They ain't got my Corporal." Hawkins' shoulders trembled and he began to cry. Mafia tough and street hard Hawkins had never once cried in Vietnam, but now he cried.

Hawkins paused for a moment and asked, "Sir, they looked everywhere? They couldn't find him? They're sure he ain't there?" as the tears flowed freely before they were suddenly reined in.

"Yes, the platoon did a detailed search," Lieutenant Abrahams answered, "they just found hundreds of dead NVA. They even found about eleven with their heads cut off." Aware of the strong bond of friendship that distinguished the team, Hawkins' tears were no surprise to the Lieutenant. He understood that in war, mounting deaths eventually overwhelm combatants and emotions have to be released, must be released, either voluntarily or involuntarily.

"Sir! Wait! What? Their heads cut off?" Hawkins quickly beamed and asked. Now jubilant his tears of sadness became tears of joy and he knew with certainty his Corporal was once again on the warpath.

"Yeah, there were just eleven headless corpses with heads lying next to them. That's hard to understand," the Lieutenant replied with a puzzled look on his face.

"Sir, with all due respect, that ain't hard to understand," Hawkins smiled. "That's Corporal Thunder. He's alive. He's out there somewhere. He's still fightin'. He'll just Indian the hell outta those NVA. They're in for it now. They got him on the warpath. They got an Indian in their tepee. Damn, I should be fightin' with him. Instead, I'm laying here all shot up. Ain't I the shits? Ain't I just the livin' shits, but I ain't dyin'. Not here. Not now. I got reasons for livin' now."

"Hawkins, you're delirious," Lieutenant Abrahams whispered in stunned disbelief.

"Sir, I ain't delirious. I'm just delighted as hell," Hawkins replied. "Corporal Thunder's out there somewhere. He just don't wanna be found. Not yet anyways. Not till he finds what he wants to find. Not until he finds what has to be found. Not until he does what he has to do.

"Sir, with your permission, I'll talk with you about it later," Hawkins added with a sense of rejuvenation and respect. "Now, let's just get the hell outta this shithole. I can go now. I'm ready as hell. Let's go. I ain't got no more reason to stay now." The Lieutenant nodded and turned shaking his head with curiosity as he coordinated the company's actions for the day.

Actually, Hawkins was delirious—delirious with the good news about Corporal Thunder. He could hardly wait to pass the news to Wiley and Clary. Unfortunately, their respective medevac pipelines proceeded in entirely different directions. They were medevaced from the hill without seeing one another. They never knew the fate of one another. They never knew who lived and who died. They simply moved on. The war moved on, too, but it moved on without them.

Neither Wiley nor Clary nor Hawkins ever saw or talked with Corporal Thunder or one another in the medevac area at the bottom of the hill. None were ever able to express the thanks and farewells they believed the others so richly deserved. Some alleged Corporal Thunder later died on 881 South, but those who lived refused to believe his death. Corporal Thunder's team had its reasons for believing he lived. They could never—would never—accept that the NVA had killed him. They knew Corporal Thunder too well.

Mike Company and its Marines and Navy Corpsmen, with Corporal Thunder and his team, accomplished their mission. They attacked, seized, and secured 881 South. Corporal Thunder was confident they would succeed, but as he had expressed to them before the fight, "At what cost?" Corporal Thunder recognized that success always had a cost. Khe Sanh was no exception. It was costly.

On that fateful day, 30 April 1967, about 120 Marines and Corpsmen launched an early morning attack on 881 South. By late afternoon, 44 had been killed and 46 wounded. The vast majority of the wounded were critically wounded and far too many later died. It was an extraordinarily high casualty rate of about 85-plus percent. At that point in the war, the First Battle of Khe Sanh was the bloodiest and deadliest battle of the Vietnam War.

While Khe Sanh was no Iwo Jima or Normandy or Battle of the Bulge, for those who fought for the hill, Khe Sanh was all of these and more. It was their World War III. It was their opportunity to fight for their Corps. Yet, they fought mostly for their fellow Marines. They fought for one another. It was what Marines do and have always done.

Corporal Thunder and the Marines defied numerically superior NVA forces and substantial accompanying fire power. The battle, however, was eventually and decisively won with quality instead of quantity. The Marines staunchly fought to overcome an NVA ambush and to later launch a counterattack. They fought hard, but they protected and cared for one another harder.

Ensuring Wiley, Hawkins, and Clary were safely evacuated, Corporal Thunder then pursued his subsequent mission. It was his personally assigned mission. It was what he believed he had to do. Then he simply did it. Without orders and with no requests for permission on his part, he simply acted. Once again, he took the initiative and acted boldly and decisively.

Corporal Thunder observed the last member of his team's evacuation from the war ravaged battlefield before disappearing into the darkness. It was darker than dark, but about to become darker for the enemy. The hill was now silent, but Corporal Thunder was the epitome of silence.

Corporal Thunder believed and thought *881 South is only one part of the Khe Sanh battle. There's more that needs to be done. Maybe I can do it*, as he blinked his eyes once, then twice, for night vision and perked his ears to listen for enemy sounds. But now, in the dark silent night, there was no fear...*None. Zero. Zilch.* He had exhausted his quota of fear throughout the day. Tonight atop 881 South, amidst the charred and churned battlefield, there was only his stoic Indian resolve. *Now, I'm done with fear. After today, there's nothing left to fear*, he thought.

It was that straightforward and that simple to Corporal Thunder. He was motivated by mission. Throughout the devastating deaths and casualties of the day, however, he became motivated by more than mission. He became motivated by the possibility of contributing to the prevention of future such losses. The cost for the hill and success had been high. It was too high. Corporal Thunder now fought to reduce future costs.

~

CHAPTER 23

Khe Sanh's Triumphant Ending

You're a little unorthodox. Maybe a bit of a maverick, too.
Maybe a whole lot of a damned fool. But damned if you don't
get the job done. Damned if you don't do missions and more.

—Marine Lieutenant Colonel John David

Corporal Thunder was now alone atop Hill 881 South. It was dark and it was silent. The horrific sounds of war and the palpable fear that resounded and ricocheted throughout the battlefield during the day were now suppressed into quiet solitude. The gentle night breeze was in stark contrast to the ferocious storms of war hours earlier. Smoldering smoke from explosions and crackling brush swirled aimlessly as ghostly waifs floating and flittering into the night. The dry earth was awash in blood. Bloody swaths from splintered bones and shattered bodies and youthful innocence were scattered in the desolate dark and silent raped and ravaged landscape. Nature would heal the land in time, but the human death was for all time and forever.

Silently, Corporal Thunder softly followed the trace of the perimeter tree line to the northern edge of 881 South. Once satisfied all the Marine and corpsmen dead and wounded had been evacuated from the war torn area, he sighed. The day's battlefield, however, was still littered with NVA dead. Concluding the enemy would come to account for their dead, Corporal Thunder thought, *They might recover and evacuate any wounded, but there's too many dead to evacuate. They might just take their IDs or dog tags. But they'll come. It's what soldiers do. They'll come.*

Hill 881 North was thousands of meters to the north. Corporal Thunder believed a NVA team from 881 North was already en route south to account for their dead. The northern hill most likely remained occupied by the NVA; however, he suspected they would be retreating from 881

North after today's defeat on 881 South. He was now committed to hastening the retreat.

Corporal Thunder selected a concealed and camouflaged position near a trail intersection. Dragging two dead NVA soldiers to an area easily seen despite the darkness, he selected adjacent hide sites. Selecting multiple concealed positions, he repeatedly placed dead NVA close by trails. After separating them far from one another in isolated and unrelated areas, he paused to sharpen his machete and waited stealthily. Quiet sounds from the blade and whetstone soothed him.

In the darkness, Corporal Thunder recalled Oklahoma talks and lessons from his dad, "Son, you have to understand, we Indians had our own fighting styles and tactics. We rarely fought as nations or armies. We fought as tribes and individuals. First, we fought with bow and arrow and spears. Later, rifles became part of our arsenal, but we always had other preferred weapons such as tomahawks or knives." He recalled they always talked of fighting when his mom was absent.

Corporal Thunder vividly remembered his talks and the Indian history his dad proudly taught him. On another occasion his dad explained, "Son, Indian tactics are warrior based. We seldom formed battle lines. We fought more as individuals, but we worked together. We used the land and trees to ambush and confuse our enemies. We worked to surprise our enemies with stealth and force. We preferred quick fights and quick withdrawals. Back then we were called savages. Today, we'd probably be called guerrillas."

The one talk Corporal Thunder remembered most was his dad declaring, "Son, we Indians respected individual Indian acts of bravery more than tribe or team ones. One term we had was called 'Count Coup.' It was one Indian charging into a group of many enemy and simply touching the enemy. He didn't have to kill the enemy. He just had to touch him. Then he had to return to the tribe. It was considered as honorable, maybe more, and courageous to 'Count Coup' as to kill an enemy. It was probably humiliating and embarrassing for the enemy, too."

Alone and quiet, he sat and reflected on his dad, his Indian heritage, and his home in Oklahoma. He was at peace with himself, but he was preparing for war. Embracing warrior warfare, he tested the machete's sharpness and waited. Running his palm along the razor sharp blade, he meditated with the Great Spirit. He prayed for Wiley, Hawkins, and Clary.

While he was surrounded by death, he was more alive than he had been any time throughout the day. Alone and unafraid, he thought of the team. He was a Marine, but tonight he was an Indian warrior, too. He waited alone in silence. His Indian heritage and the Great Spirit comforted him.

After midnight, Corporal Thunder heard careful footsteps. He crouched and watched and waited. Counting a team of twelve NVA, he prepared for battle. They were quiet and cautious at first. They were the recovery team for the dead and any wounded, but there were no wounded. Corporal Thunder had made sure of that. The Corporal observed patiently. The NVA searched passively. Then the NVA divided into two-man teams and started collecting dog tags.

As they searched the area and began their grisly duty, the NVA became less cautious. They relaxed believing they were then alone. In time, they perceived no danger. Once they became even more relaxed and careless, Corporal Thunder initiated his plan by singling out a team collecting dog tags. He waited until they were far from the others. Once they were isolated and out of sight of others, he executed his "Count Coup."

The stoic Indian in him was silently lively. The NVA were loudly lethargic. Corporal Thunder dedicated himself to his task. The NVA deplored theirs. The Indian-Marine crouched and reached out and touched an NVA in the darkness. First, he simply touched his machete to one's shoulder. The NVA would turn, but never see the machete as it flashed once and then twice in two strong and swirling motions. The silent swiftness was deadly as two decapitated skulls splattered to the earth. His machete was amazingly swift and powerful and lightning fast.

Repeating his Indian "Count Coup," six NVA recovery teams were eventually decimated by decapitations. Recording eleven headless NVA with eleven bodiless heads, Corporal Thunder neither smiled nor frowned. He was on a mission and he performed it. It was war.

The Corporal purposefully spared the life of the last enemy soldier. He spared him with a violent machete strike across his back shoulder. His own left shoulder throbbed from its wounds, but his right arm struck strongly. The AK47 he then forcefully thrust into the NVA's gut assured obedience to his gestures. The machete wounds were relatively minor and non-life threatening flesh wounds, but they would probably confirm the 881 decapitations to his NVA comrades.

Stripping the enemy of his weapon, equipment, and clothing, except for his skivvies and boots, Corporal Thunder then simply pointed north with his machete. The NVA was terrified and froze. Corporal Thunder twirled his machete menacingly. The enemy soldier backed away three or four quick steps before wheeling rapidly and sprinting toward 881 North to rejoin his unit. As the enemy ran fearfully, Corporal Thunder uttered a loud and menacing guttural Indian war chant, "EeeeeeOoooooo." The lone enemy ran faster. Corporal Thunder followed slowly. The soldier was his unsuspecting and unwitting guide to the withdrawing NVA force and camp.

Silently and strongly patrolling north, Corporal Thunder was careful to avoid the trails and conceal himself deep in the jungle foliage as his contorted face winced with agonizing pain. Throbbing with excruciating and relentless aches, his left shoulder sagged and his forearm burned from tingling nerves. Pausing to occasional rub his wounds, he accepted there was no relief from the pain. It would have been more painful for him; however, to abandon the mission he was now on. As he pursued his prey with passion, he discovered his mission was medicinal.

Missions always challenged Corporal Thunder and he was now on another mission. As he patrolled farther and farther north from Khe Sanh and his company, he remembered a briefing Lieutenant Abrahams had overheard about a month ago and had shared with the platoon. Two Marine intelligence officers at regiment were discussing Khe Sanh. They were analyzing various enemy courses of actions, but both agreed the NVA intended to defeat the Marines at Khe Sanh as they had defeated the French at Dien Bien Phu. Both had emphatically agreed, "Such an embarrassing and humiliating defeat must be avoided."

The course of action Corporal Thunder remembered most was one officer detailing to the other, "The NVA have their operating bases and sanctuaries in Laos. We know that. But I'm thinking they also have a forward operating base in Vietnam. I think it's probably up in the thick jungles and high mountains north of Khe Sanh. It's far enough away to be undetected, but close enough to quickly assemble forces for a major attack against Khe Sanh."

"I agree, but so far we haven't located it," the other officer replied according to the Lieutenant. "It's a critical intel mission. We have to locate it and locate it soon."

Corporal Thunder had filed the intel estimate in his memory. He neither thought about it again nor discussed it with anyone. After too many Marines and corpsmen from Mike Company were killed and wounded yesterday on 881 South, however, he remembered it.

The remembrance ignited the embers of a plan he slowly fanned into a flame for scorching the NVA. He was now boldly acting on that plan. Employing his Osage Indian and Marine Corps warrior skills and heritage, he was somehow and someway determined to reach out and touch the NVA. The Indian Marine Corporal had a plan for a true "Count Coup" for Khe Sanh.

Tracking the lone recovery team NVA soldier north, he was deliberate as well as determined. He was weakened by severe pain, but he was strengthened by his stoic resolve and his mission.

As sunrise approached, the Corporal heard the sounds of commotion as the NVA hastened their retreat and withdrawal from 881 North. The enemy appeared to be rapidly evacuating the hill before daylight to conceal themselves in the vast and treacherous jungles and mountains to the north as quickly as possible. Corporal Thunder had hoped for this as well as expected it.

He reasoned, *So far the plan is okay. So far the mission is on track. Now, I just have to hold on. I just have to fight this pain as hard as I'm fighting to track the enemy.*

The NVA were focused more toward the north than the south. They were focused more on their advance security than their rear security. Nonetheless, Corporal Thunder tracked the retreat with patient caution. Forcing himself to patrol slowly, he avoided the easy trails and closing to close to the enemy withdrawal because he suspected the trails would be under constant surveillance. Estimating the enemy withdrawal would be protracted because of the transport of heavy weapons and supplies, he bided his time. Believing tracking the NVA would be tiring, he conserved his energy and took his time. He constantly reminded himself to track slow and steady. Such racing and repetitive thoughts were relentless more than reckless, but he recognized they required his constant attention. His mind was more alive than his body.

Higher into the mountains and deeper into the jungles it became darker and darker. It was rugged terrain, but the best terrain in which to conceal a secret and undetected forward base. Furthermore, about twilight and well into the withdrawal, he observed from a distance that the narrow jungle trail developed into what Corporal Thunder called, "a jungle expressway."

Corporal Thunder's analysis, *It's probably a work in progress, but they're working on it hard. It's probably part of their preparation to assault Khe Sanh. Once it's finished, or close to Khe Sanh, they can drive trucks and haul artillery and supplies. They can haul it fast, too. It's not really an expressway, but compared to the single file trails in these jungles it's a highway.* Corporal Thunder smiled and noted, *It's maybe eight or ten feet or so wide. Certainly wide enough for the NVA's wooden carts. Probably for small trucks, too.*

Scribbling in his notebook, Corporal Thunder paused to record the coordinates of the road. He also noted it on his map with his grease pen. Then exhaustion overwhelmed him and he had to rest. His muscles were numb. Throbbing from his wounds persisted. His throat was parched and his stomach begged for nutrition. Then he remembered Wiley, Hawkins, and Clary as he fixated on his miseries. The thoughts of his team caused him to smile repeatedly. As his face lit up it energized him and his miseries faded ever so slightly.

Corporal Thunder then collapsed for a moment to capture a measure of modest energy. Later, in the darkness, he rose and selected a concealed and camouflaged hide site deeper into the jungle and well off the trail. He had scrounged a number of Cs from the Marine casualties on 881 South and hungrily ate a partial one. He was traveling light, but he concluded he had sufficient Cs for a few days if he conserved them and maybe ate only one per day. The Cs and water from the mountain springs were his only sustenance. In minutes he was asleep, but he slept with the knowledge that tracking the NVA would be easier tomorrow. *The jungle expressway will now guide me,* he thought.

Awakening sometime during the night from a sound sleep, Corporal Thunder listened quietly. Remaining perfectly still, he listened for several minutes hearing nothing but jungle night sounds. The natural sounds of the jungle were comforting…the same as they were on the plains. They reassured him all was well. By now he was confident in the jungle and its sounds.

Corporal Thunder also considered the NVA knew this area better than him. Night movement would be too dangerous and he knew it. He knew what he had to know for now. The enemy expressway would be waiting in the morning. Tracking the retreat was no longer the priority. The priority now was simply aligning on the road and locating the NVA forward operating base. He knew that could wait until daylight. Pulsing pain and lingering grogginess caused him to sigh. He quietly drifted back to sleep. He knew sleep was his priority. Then the priority was locating the camp. But he knew he had to rest first. His mission was on track, but it would derail if he was too exhausted and too severely wounded to continue. He slept restfully despite the multitude of thoughts racing through his mind. Tiredness overwhelmed his thoughts, but his mind was active with cryptic thoughts. He urged and willed himself to maintain control. Finally, his pain and exhaustion overpowered his mind's countless repetitive invading musings and he slept at last.

Waking before daylight, Corporal Thunder quickly cringed. The NVA expressway had disappeared. He thought maybe he had been delirious, that maybe the expressway had been a mirage. After an hour of surveillance of the area, however, the expressway reappeared. It became obvious the enemy engineer units were covering the expressway with natural camouflage and netting. He observed immediately after either extending its length or moving forces over it, the expressway disappeared under fresh cut foliage and camouflage netting. It rendered detection virtually impossible. The NVA were extra careful, but Corporal Thunder was methodical.

Remembering his dad teaching him patience and still hunting tactics in the Oklahoma fields, he smiled recalling the lessons and home. He was patient and still, often preferring "still hunting" from dugouts, blinds, or concealed positions to "tracking hunting." Let the game or enemy come to you, instead of you searching for it, his dad taught him. He remained silent and stoic.

Later, once rested, he resumed his search to locate the NVA forward operating base. He sensed he was closer and closer and advanced slower and slower. He had time. He had all day. He took all day, too. Throughout the day, he observed various enemy units veer off from the main force. He considered, *They probably have a number of smaller camps in lots of valleys and maybe one big camp. Maybe they're breaking off as decoys. They're hiding this place from any air or ground recon. Maybe they're just taking lots of precautions. They're dispersing their units. This camp must be extra special and secret to them.* His wandering and wondering thoughts helped him maintain his focus while the ramblings also helped him ignore his pain.

At dusk, Corporal Thunder sighted the main NVA base. It was larger than he expected. It was well fortified, too. It was well defended, but it was fortified stronger than it was defended. It was expertly concealed and constructed to avoid detection and withstand heavy bombing.

Corporal Thunder asked, *I wonder if it can take an Arc Light strike? I bet the B-52s can take it. I hope the B-52s get the mission, too. Another Arc Light would be good.*

The surveillance on the camp continued throughout the night and the following day. On the third night, he began his trek back toward Khe Sanh. Carefully avoiding trails, he practiced caution, but his return was as fast and safe as possible. On the slow advance north he had familiarized himself with the land. Now, however, he had reason to travel faster.

The past day Corporal Thunder had listened to the bombardments he suspected as H & I, or Harassment and Interdiction fires, surrounding 881 North. He concluded Company K and the battalion command elements were firing on 881 North to prevent the NVA from re-occupying it. So, he took a circuitous and cautious route around 881 North toward 881 South.

The Corporal approached the northern base of 881 South hours before sunrise. Ascending the mountain with care and caution, he eventually observed the outlines of the perimeter defenses of the Marines. He stripped down to mostly an AK47, his machete, and minimal clothing and equipment. While looking like anything but a Marine, especially with the AK47, he constructed a temporary hide site and disappeared into the brush and was asleep in minutes.

Fatigue, bone deep, bone marrow deep fatigue, and empty sleep again overwhelmed him, but Corporal Thunder was awake and alert before sunrise. Concluding it was safer to attempt to rejoin his battalion in daylight than at night, he waited patiently. Night watches were always more nervous and edgy than morning ones. They represented the difference in darkness and daylight.

Corporal Thunder later crawled to within shouting distance of the Marine perimeter during the pre-dawn darkness. He then waited until an hour or so after the battalion's reveille to allow the day to become somewhat routine and the night edginess to wither. As the night nervousness disappeared, he yelled loudly, "Marines, it's me. It's Corporal Thunder. It's Corporal Thunder from Mike Company."

Silence. He heard nothing, especially any weapons firing. Relieved there was no firing in his direction, he yelled the introduction again.

"Wait one," a Marine guarding the perimeter shouted back. "Wait one. We got someone coming to check you out. Wait one."

Well, at least maybe the word's been passed about me missing, he thought.

Minutes later, Corporal Thunder heard a shout, "Corporal Thunder, is that you?" It wasn't a by the book challenge and password procedure, but it worked. The battalion was obviously aware he was missing and it appeared they had his records or personal data, too.

Corporal Thunder hollered, "Yes, Sir, it's me. It's Corporal Thunder," and then he stood by.

"Advance and be recognized. Keep your hands over your head," a perimeter Marine yelled.

Corporal Thunder took the bolt from the AK47 and stuffed it in his pocket to disarm the rifle as he tossed it into the brush to avoid any suspicions or confusion. Complying with the orders from the perimeter, he tucked his machete in his backside with his belt and walked slowly toward the perimeter avoiding any sudden movements. Almost home with Marines, he inhaled deeply. His walk then slowed. As he arrived at the perimeter security gate he collapsed into the arms of one of the Marines. He was in severe pain from his wounds, loss of blood, sheer weariness, and a fever. He was physically and emotionally exhausted. He was done for now, but he had done what he believed had to be done.

Quickly whisked to the battalion field medical station, Corporal Thunder never stirred. The Senior Corpsman quickly ordered, "Okay, let's check him out. Check his vitals. Clean and dress his wounds. He needs an IV. Get him some fluids." The corpsman's response was professional.

Emergency first aid and medical evaluations were immediately administered to Corporal Thunder, but he was unaware of them. He was unconscious. He had no idea how long he was unconscious, but as he began to regain his senses he heard someone say, "He's starting to wake up. Someone notify the Battalion Commanding Officer. The CO wants to be here when he comes to. The CO wants to talk to him as soon as he's able to talk."

"Where am I?" Corporal Thunder asked confused by his surroundings. The scent of raw alcohol and raw wounds and raw fear blended together in the medical tent.

"Son, you're back with the battalion. You're on 881. We have you now," the Navy Doctor answered. "You're hurt bad, but you're okay. There's nothing to fear now. Welcome back."

Corporal Thunder slowly regained his awareness. After a few health questions the Battalion CO arrived, smiled, and asked, "Corporal Thunder, where the hell you been?"

"Sir, it's a long story," Corporal Thunder conceded.

"Okay, we have time, but let me gather my intelligence Marines here before you begin your story and debrief," the Colonel interrupted and added.

"While we're waiting do you need anything?" Lieutenant Colonel David asked.

"Sir, I'm hungry and thirsty. May I eat and talk?" Corporal Thunder answered.

"Yes, but all we have is C-Rats. What one you want?" Colonel David replied.

"Sir, I'll take a ham and lima beans," Corporal Thunder grinned, "and Bug Juice, please."

"Damn, son, you must be sick. Sick or out or your mind to ask for pork and poots," Colonel David shrugged. "You sure that's what you want? You know they're nasty as all hell."

"Sir, I hate the damn things, too, but it's what my team and me always joked about. I hate them, but they remind me of my team," Corporal Thunder admitted.

"Son, they're on the way. You want them heated or cold?" the Colonel inquired.

"Sir, cold. That's when they're the worst," the Corporal frowned as he was somewhat modestly embarrassed by the Colonel's friendliness and his tending to his needs.

"Anything else?" Colonel David queried as he stood beside the elevated litter Corporal Thunder lay on.

"Sir, only one. Can I have my machete back?" Corporal Thunder asked. "Someone took it."

The machete magically and mysteriously appeared and was immediately placed on Corporal Thunder's makeshift litter by one of the corpsmen. He patted it and said, "Thanks."

"Yeah, I remember that machete from Con Thien. I remember our talk about it, too," Colonel David recalled and winked. "I started to tell you a similar story about a Samurai sword and me on Iwo Jima, but I decided to wait. Maybe we'll talk about it later when you feel better."

"Yes, Sir, that would be great," Corporal Thunder replied, "machetes and Samurais make good stories." They both winked and smiled again.

"I remember you did a good job then, too," Lieutenant Colonel David recalled, "but you scared the hell out of us just now missing like you did."

"Yes, Sir, but I had a mission to do. I did it. Now, I'm back," he succinctly responded. "I didn't mean to scare anyone, but I had a mission to do for Lieutenant Antoine."

Corporal Thunder mentioned Lieutenant Antoine's name and it reminded him of the letter.

"Sir, I apologize, but I have another request. May I have Lieutenant Antoine's home address? I want to write a letter to his widow and baby daughter."

"Son, I'll make sure Mike Company gets that to you," Colonel David promised.

"Okay, son, my intel Marines are here now. Why don't you tell us about your mission?" Colonel David implored somewhat anxiously and excitedly. "After Con Thien and what I know about you, this will probably be interesting." The intel Marines copied notes furiously as Corporal Thunder spoke slowly.

Corporal Thunder summarized the mission and included the details he remembered and then concluded, "Sir, I overheard our battalion officers talking about how serious it was to locate the NVA forward operating base. After our battle and our losses on 881 South, I knew how critical it was, too. I thought we had a good chance to locate it. So, that's why I did what I did."

Colonel David quietly and attentively followed his every word. Focusing on his actions in particular, the Colonel nodded in approval. Corporal Thunder provided vivid descriptions, except he omitted any details of the decapitations. He reserved that for later and then only if asked. He was never asked.

"Sir, I have notes and coordinates and map markings for the NVA expressway and camp if you want them," Corporal Thunder remembered. "They're in my map case."

"Son, I would expect no less," Colonel David gleamed. "Damn straight we want them."

The Colonel glanced at his intel officer and team and asked, "Okay, have what you need?"

"Sir, the division's been searching for this camp for awhile. We have more than we need and division will be overwhelmed. This is a real coup. It's a major coup," the intel officer reported.

Corporal Thunder beamed when he heard the word "Coup," but he said nothing.

The intel officer continued, "We need to pass this intel on immediately. It's highly sensitive and classified. I recommend we courier it to division. Maybe, better yet, I recommend we meet with them to talk in more detail than a written report. They'll have questions, too."

"Okay, pass a preliminary report to regiment and division," Colonel David ordered, "but prepare a more extensive report and brief. Let them know we're available to meet at the earliest."

"Son, once again you've done one helluva job. You're a little unorthodox. Maybe a bit of a maverick, too. Maybe a whole lot of a damned fool. But damned if you don't get the job done. Damned if you don't do missions and more," Colonel David smiled and placed his hand on Corporal Thunder's shoulder. "Now finish that damn C and get some rest. We'll talk later."

Colonel David turned to return to the battalion command combat operations center and to standby by for the inevitable contacts and questions from regiment and division. His battalion had won a major victory and now had critically sensitive intelligence. The Colonel was confident regiment and division would be contacting him at the earliest. He glowed proudly in anticipation.

"Son, as I recall you're an Oklahoma Indian, aren't you?" Colonel David asked as he turned one last time to address Corporal Thunder before he departed for the command center.

"Yes, Sir, I'm an Oklahoman. I'm an Osage Indian. I'm a Marine Corporal, too," he smiled.

"You damn sure are, son," Colonel David admitted. "You damn sure are. You're all those and more. Welcome back. Welcome home."

"Corporal Thunder, we've been ordered to helo medevac you to Delta Med in Dong Ha at the earliest," the physician informed Corporal Thunder about noon. "You don't have to do anything. I just want you to know so you can get ready. We're sending a corpsman back with you."

The Intelligence Officer entered the aid station moments later and briefed Corporal Thunder. "Your info and intel on the NVA base camp is generating urgent and serious attention. Regiment intel from Cam Lo and division intel from Phu Bai will meet with us in Dong Ha. They have questions. They're working hard and fast to draft an intel estimate and recommendation. Then the operators will start planning. It's all moving fast. You up for all this?"

"Yes, Sir, I'm ready. I'll need help because I feel a little weak, but I'm ready," he nodded.

Corporal Thunder suspected, but had only a vague idea, how sensitive and critical the NVA base camp intel truly was. Once they arrived in Dong Ha later than afternoon Corporal Thunder remarked to the intel officer, "Sir, we sure started a whirlwind of activity, didn't we?"

"Corporal, you have no idea. Hell, I thought I knew, but now that it's happening I had no idea either," the officer sighed. "This is getting bigger than big. It's huge and getting monstrous."

Within an hour of Corporal Thunder's arrival at Delta Med in Dong Ha he was again debriefed. This time it was by regiment and division intelligence and operations officers. The debrief was quick with few questions as it appeared the officers had most of the information they needed. They simply wanted to confirm it. Now they needed to plan and to act on it. Time was of the essence.

Within twenty-four hours an air attack plan was completed, briefed at the highest levels and approved. Within twenty-four hours massive and repeated B-52 Arc Light strikes were launched against the NVA base camp north of Khe Sanh.

A later summary of the Arc Light mission and post-strike analysis concluded with the statement, "The Arc Light strikes against the NVA base camp north of Khe Sanh on 5 May 1967 were effective and successful. The camp was destroyed, extensive damage was inflicted on an unknown quantity of NVA ordnance and weapons systems, and an estimated one NVA infantry division, two NVA engineer battalions, and an unknown number of supply, transportation, and support troops were decimated. All aforementioned units are estimated to have been rendered incapable of conducting combat operations for approximately six to eight months minimum."

The report included significantly greater detail on the planning, execution, and success of the strikes. The true success of the strikes became known only with time. Captured documents later revealed the NVA were committed to attacking and seizing Khe Sanh in the summer of 1967. But that was before the NVA were introduced to Mike Company and 3/3 on 30 April 1967.

It required eight months for the NVA to reconstitute the forces and resources required to attempt to again capture Khe Sanh. By then, the Marines were entrenched and ready for the NVA to attack. Then, from January to July 1968, the enemy initiated their infamous Siege of Khe Sanh. The courage and will of the Marines prevailed time and time again. The NVA repeatedly failed to capture Khe Sanh. The Marines repelled countless attacks and consistently succeeded in repulsing the enemy. The North Vietnamese eventually canceled their plans and operations to capture the fire base and withdrew in humiliating defeat.

Corporal Thunder, however, never knew the true extent his and his team's actions had in contributing to the Marines' success and the NVA's failure at Khe Sanh. He lapsed into a deep coma from infections to his wounds. The wounds were untreated for an extended and critical time while he remained in the mountains and jungles and searched for the enemy base camp.

Emergency airlifted and medically evacuated prior to the Arc Light strikes, Corporal Thunder was never aware of the success of the strikes. He was aware, however, he was again fighting for his life. He was aware his machete had again been taken, too. He coaxed a corpsman into sliding it next to him. Then, he was aware, vaguely aware; he was en route and receiving urgent medical care in Hawaii.

Corporal Thunder joined Wiley, Hawkins, and Clary in their meandering casualty pipelines. The extensive medical pipelines, however, went in diverse and divergent directions. The paths of the four Marines never crossed. They were now alone. They were no longer a team. They were wounded Marines fighting for survival. Survival remained their foremost mission and challenge. It was another part of war. It was another part of Vietnam. It was always about survival.

CHAPTER 24

Lifting the Veil of Darkness

Maybe war was never what you wanted to do, but you did what you believed was right and what you had to do.

—Marine Lance Corporal Aaron Wiley's Father

Corporal Thunder's, Wiley's, Hawkins', and Clary's fight for survival required varying degrees of strength and stamina. The wounds to their bodies were numerous and serious. The wounds to their bodies were those of sadness and sorrow for one another. It was the wounds to their hearts and souls, however, that inflicted the most concern and curiosity. Wounds to their bodies would eventually mend. Wounds to their hearts and souls, however, would remain a mystery. They would remain a mystery until they learned the fate of one another. Learning their respective fates, however, proved as illusive as learning the intricate complexities of limited war.

The team dissolved. It disappeared. It was gone. At a time they needed one another the most, they were alone. The opportunity to express farewells escaped them and sudden separations were regretted. While they attempted to learn the fate of one another, their own fates became paramount to them. They had to do what they had always had to do…survive and move on.

First, they simply had to survive. They had to move on before they could go back, but eventually going back was more painful and more complicated than moving forward. The moving forward was hard, too. It was, however, easier than going back. The war was over for them. It was their past. Then their individual futures beckoned them and they were forced to move on. Nonetheless, they remained curious about the fate and future of one another.

~~~~~~

"Where am I?" Wiley groggily asked, "How long have I been here?"

"You're in Yokosuka, Japan. You've been here about four weeks," a Navy Nurse answered.

"Four weeks!" Wiley exclaimed. "I have to get out of here and get back to my team." He tempted to rise up, but traction restraints prohibited his movement.

"Well, that's unlikely. Your wounds are extensive. We've had to keep you on periodic morphine drip doses to relieve your pain," the nurse replied. "You'll probably be here at least another two to three months. Maybe longer. Then you'll probably be going back to the states."

Wiley drifted back into unconsciousness. Over three months later, he was transferred to Camp Pendleton, California. Two weeks later, he was discharged from the Marines. Two days later, he was home in Mississippi. Shuffling up the dirt road, Wiley's two sisters were the first to see him. They raced to him in tears as they yelled, "Daddy! Mommy! Aaron's home. Aaron's home."

Wiley was home with family and friends. Home and reestablishing his life were his priorities now, but his first priority was the church and piano. Wiley's first request to his family was, "Can we go to the church to see the new piano?" The piano reminded him of Hawkins and the team.

The family loaded into its old farm truck and bounced along the country road as they drove to the church. Wiley asked, "Mom, will you play the piano while my sisters sing a hymn?"

Wiley's mother played the piano as his two sisters sang a favorite hymn. He recalled Hawkins and the day of his R & R forfeiture. It was the day of his piano donation. He smiled as he remembered traveling to the rear for the check and the Army club fight.

While the Wiley family sat in the church pews, he entertained them with stories of Corporal Thunder, Clary, and Hawkins. The family laughed. The family cried. The sun was setting before they realized it, but Wiley noticed it. He would forever notice sunsets. He observed his Mom's anxiousness to cook him his favorite meal, too. Wiley's mother announced, "It's supper time."

"Before we go will you play and sing one more song?" Wiley asked as he turned the hymnal to "Fight the Good Fight." *The team always fought the good fight,* Wiley remembered smiling.

Wiley's family sensed his sentimental attachment to the hymn and team. The song was sang and played with exuberant joy and solemn sadness. Wiley's dad said a prayer thanking God for his son's return home from the war. His prayer included special thanks for Corporal Thunder, Hawkins, and Clary, too. They team was invisible, but it was there with them. It was part of them. They were family.

The Wiley family lazily motored home to supper in silence, but with loud smiles of special memories. The piano was never again played without thinking of Hawkins and the team.

~~~~~~

Corporal Thunder was vaguely aware of the tropical breeze as his thoughts wandered between awareness and oblivion. He struggled for an unknown period of time before he heard someone comment, "He appears to be coming to. He's stirring slightly. He's searching to come out of his coma. Send for the doctor."

"Son, can you hear me?" The Navy Doctor asked minutes later, "Can you hear me?"

Corporal Thunder nodded, but it took him a few minutes before he could speak, "Yes, Sir, now I can. I hear you now."

"Good. That's good. You gave us a scare. We almost lost you," the doctor answered, "but you'll be fine now. It took a while to identify the rare tropical infection. Then we had to regulate your medicine, but now you'll be good as new. It'll take another month or so, but you'll be fine."

"Good enough to get back with my team?" he inquired.

"Well, that's up to the Marines. You'll have to take prescribed meds for some time. Maybe months. Maybe years," the doctor replied. "We'll have to monitor your recovery and progress."

"Then I probably won't be going back to Vietnam, will I?" Corporal Thunder sighed.

"I'd recommend against it. You'll be too susceptible to a relapse," the doctor answered.

"Well, if I can't rejoin my team, I hope they discharge me," he mournfully mumbled

Corporal Thunder was released from Tripler Army Medical Center in Hawaii six weeks later. He was transferred to the Balbo Naval Medical Center in San Diego for temporary duty and his discharge. He was home in Oklahoma for the late summer dove hunting season and fall harvest.

The bus from Pawhuska dropped him off at the section line bus stop. He marched erect and proud up the gravel road alongside the barbed wire fence toward home. His dad was plowing in the fields and was the first to see him. Squinting in the bright sun to steady his vision his dad waved. Corporal Thunder waved back. Until he reached the fence closest to him, his dad continued plowing. Then his dad ceased plowing, climbed the fence, and walked toward his son.

Corporal Thunder's dad spoke no words. He was unable to speak. Words were choked in his heart, strangled by his tongue, and wrestled by his emotions. So, he simply smiled and hugged his son. The hugs were long and hard. Holding his son by his shoulders at arm's length he again confirmed it was his son. His strong and stoic dad then turned to wipe the sweat from his face while he concealed the tears in his eyes. The sun weathered and field hand gritty face of his dad was streaked with tears as the calloused and rough hands of his dad softly patted his son's cheeks.

The two, dad and son, then strolled with their arms over one another's shoulders toward home. They spoke no words. They both knew there would be words galore once his mom learned he was home. Words galore and more was an understatement, but the words came after endless tears of joy from a relieved and loving mom. Moms often suffer the most in war.

Corporal Thunder was home with family, but before he considered himself truly home he was compelled to describe his Marine family to his Pawhuska family. As he and his brothers and sisters and dad and mom sat on the back porch in the warm Oklahoma evening breeze, Corporal Thunder shared stories of Wiley, Hawkins, and Clary with his family. They, too, laughed and they, too, cried. It was impossible to reflect on Vietnam without remembering the team.

While reminiscing about his team, tears slowly came to his eyes. He excused himself, "Dad. Mom. I just want to take a walk on the land. I want to walk the pasture alone for a few minutes. I'll be back soon." His dad nodded in understanding. His mom clasped her hands over her heart.

Corporal Thunder strolled silently as the lyrics to the concluding stanza of the state song *Oklahoma* drifted into his memory, *We know we belong to the land and the land we belong to is grand.* Accepting he was finally and truly home, he knew he was where he belonged. He was home on the grand land of Oklahoma.

~~~~~~~~~~~~~~~~~~~~~~~~~~~~~~~~~~~~~~

Clary was initially medevaced to the hospital ship the USS Repose off the coast of South Vietnam. Later, he was airlifted to Saigon and then to Guam. In one sense, his wounds were the least life threatening of the four. In another sense, however, they were the most complicated and potentially serious ones, too.

"Son, your head wound from the rifle projectile and fragments appears to be relatively minor, but it could become serious," the Navy Doctor informed Clary. "We just need to keep you under observation for an appropriate time to conduct some rather critical tests. You should be fine, but we want to be sure."

Later, another Navy Doctor advised Clary, "You have multiple grenade fragments in your body. We've been able to extract most, but a few are extremely close to vital organs or sensitive nerves. We need time to evaluate their possible movement and to assess the risk of additional surgeries. You might have to live with some war trophies in you. That's about as simple and straightforward as I can explain it."

"Yes, Sir, I understand," Clary replied and asked, "but how long will it all take and what about my team?"

"We should know in a month or two. Just be patient and work with us. But no strenuous physical activity. Not for awhile. Not until we clear you," the doctor answered, "and, sorry, but I don't know about the team."

Clary was eventually transferred and discharged from the Marine Corps six weeks later. The Marine Detachment on Guam helped coordinate his release from active duty and his plane trip to San Diego. He walked off the plane in San Diego into the waiting arms of his mother. He hugged her tightly. She sobbed softly.

Clary later pulled a wrapped gift from his sea bag and handed it to his mother. "Mom, it's a little late, but it's my Mother's Day present for the best mother in the world."

"Son, the gift's nice, but you're coming home is the best gift ever," Clary's mom smiled.

Clary attempted to persuade her, "No, mom, you're the best gift and best mom ever."

Clary's mom protested strenuously until Clary surrendered and said, "Okay, mom, moms know best. But we'll talk about it later." Clary hugged his mom softly, but with strong emotions.

Clary's father, who was standing in the background, then walked forward and hugged his son. He had purposefully stood aside for Clary and his mom to reunite before they came together as a family. Then they were one. Clary was excited to tell them about the team. On the drive home along the California coast and beaches, Clary regaled them with stories about the team, who he described as his brothers. They were immediately accepted into his California family and the experiences they shared become frequent dinner time talks.

Clary thought, *This is a part of the new and better relationship. This is how home and family should be. It's how home and family will be from now on. It's how home and family will be forever. My Marine family is making this possible.*

~~~~~~

"You shoulda saw Corporal Thunder," Hawkins disclosed. "He machete chopped the damned NVA's head right off. Later, he did it to a whole shit pot full of enemy, too."

Hawkins was initially medevaced to Da Nang and later to the Oakland Naval Hospital in California. He lay in traction confined to his bed. His ankle and hip were in casts and he was essentially immobile, except for that part of his anatomy the matronly Navy Nurse referred to as "his tongue and lips and nonstop motor mouth."

With no apparent adverse effects to his storytelling, the nurse sighed, "Hawkins, you're entertaining this ward with stories from sunrise to sunset, from reveille to taps."

"Yes, Ma'am, but ain't they good stories?" Hawkins boasted unfazed. "They're all true, too."

"That I don't doubt," the nurse answered gleefully. "If the enemy is in half as bad a shape as you are, then they must be true. But I'm a little suspicious about that Army club brawl. Corporal Thunder, Wiley, and Clary killing thousands seems an exaggeration, too."

It was obvious by now the nurse was intimately familiar with Corporal Thunder, Wiley, and Clary. She was probably all too familiar with Hawkins, too, but as she confided to him, "Young man, you've sure livened up this ward. Your stories make it fun to come to work now. Despite all the terrible wounds everyone has, the ward is different and fun with you."

None too soon for the sanity and serenity of the ward, Hawkins was discharged from the hospital in late summer. He had endured extensive rehabilitation and was now as strong and feisty as ever. Hawkins had even trained with the local Marine boxing team as part of his rehab.

Marine Corps Barracks, Treasure Island in San Francisco coordinated his Marine discharge and return to Boston and home. The hospital was glad to bid farewell because it meant he had survived. The boxing team farewell was sad because he had become its best fighter.

Hawkins arrived at Logan International Airport in Boston to no family or fanfare. He planned to take the bus home to the North End. Then he planned to surprise his mama by simply walking into their home unannounced, but his plans were derailed.

Proudly strolling in his Marine uniform, Hawkins was accosted by gang types a few blocks from his home. He paid them no heed until one shouted, "Hey, jarhead, kill any babies today?" Hawkins smiled in devilish anticipation. The thugs missed the smile. Hawkins missed nothing.

Hawkins initially ignored the three thugs, which seemed to only embolden them. Then the thugs crossed the street to confront Hawkins. Hawkins was toting his sea bag. Once the thugs were about six feet from him he lobbed it up in their direction. It surprised them. Then all three looked up as they prepared to catch it by its two ends and center to avoid being bowled over.

The thugs glanced up and Hawkins delivered a swift powerful kick to the center one's groin. Flattening his palm, he powered the heel of his hand upward immediately below the second thug's nose. Finally, he stomped on the third thug's foot arch and the victim hopped about frantically. Hawkins delivered upper cut after upper cut and jab after jab into solar plexuses and battered and bleeding faces. As he glanced into one's face he thought, *Damn, looks like your face has been to the meat grinder* and frowned remembering Con Thien.

Stopping the fight was probably what Hawkins should have done, but he was having too much fun defending his team. He recalled he departed Boston for fighting, only to fight worse fights in Vietnam. Now he was back home in Boston and fighting again. He was defending all who fought in Vietnam, too. Hawkins had all three down and he was kicking them into total submission when the police arrived somewhat belatedly. One of Boston's finest was a former Marine and cautioned his partner to wait even longer before intervening to stop the fight.

Hawkins and the thugs were escorted to jail. The thugs were handcuffed and sat in the rear seat of the police car while Hawkins sat up front with the police officer and shared stores of Vietnam and the Corps with him. At the police station, Hawkins made his phone call. Within the hour, his priest uncle arrived accompanied by a Mafia neighborhood underboss. They were an odd couple and the station desk sergeant's undivided attention was immediately assured. The precinct captain cordially hailed them into his office, which also seemed odd to the desk sergeant. Hawkins was released. The thugs jailed. Hawkins' priest uncle and the Mafia underboss drove him to within a block of his home and urged, "You got one block until you're home. No more fights."

Strolling the final block in peace, Hawkins opened the door to his home, and shouted loudly, "Mama Mia, I'm home." You had to know Italian to understand the laughter and language from then until long past midnight. Regardless of your language, you would have known it was a special homecoming. The Italians seemed totally disinterested in Corporal Thunder's admonition to listen as well as talk. Everyone talked; no one listened. It was pure *Little Italy* night in Boston.

Within seconds, the entire neighborhood knew Hawkins was home. Minutes later, the homecoming became a neighborhood coming out party. Within an hour, Corporal Thunder, Wiley, and Clary were heroes and household names in Boston's North End. The team was absent, but it was always present in Boston. Hawkins assured it with story after story after story; accompanied by beer after beer after beer.

~~~~~~

Corporal Thunder, Wiley, Hawkins, and Clary were all safely and securely home by late fall 1967. The Vietnam War was now in their past. They were no longer a part of the war. The war, however, would forever be a part of them. They had done their part, but their part would never be done. The war helped define them and distinguish them. It helped them become who they would become, too. The war became as much a part of their future as it was their past.

Once home, the Vietnam War was inescapable for them and all who served in it. It became over-publicized and was often referred to as a media war and spectacle with the nightly news broadcasts and daily print media battling for ratings. It became a part of family dinner talks, Sunday sermons, and classroom debates. It became part of the fabric of America's idle talk and contentious opinions. It dominated virtually every aspect of American life.

~~~~~~~~~~~~~~~~~~~~~~~~~~~~~~~~~~~~~~~

Corporal Thunder confessed to his dad in their Oklahoma barn that winter, "Dad, I feel like I failed in my mission. I wanted to help the South Vietnamese remain independent and free. Worse, I feel guilty those fighting and dying now are there because I didn't do what I was supposed to do. Sometimes I feel guilty because I'm home safe and they're still there in danger."

"Son, you did what you could do. You did all you could do. You acted honorably. Maybe it was our nation that failed. Maybe it was us as a people who failed," his dad responded. "We never seemed to know the type of war we were fighting. We never seemed to come together as a nation. Our government never convinced us as a people the war was right and just for all of us. But you and those who fought, you fought well. I'm proud of you."

~~~~~~~~~~~~~~~~~~~~~~~~~~~~~~~~~~~~~~~

One day in the Mississippi fields Wiley spoke solemnly with his dad, "Papa, sometimes I feel shame because I couldn't do more for the South Vietnamese people's freedom. Other times, I feel sorrow because so many have done so much. Our people know what it's like to struggle for freedom. It's hard and we needed help to gain our freedom. I wanted to help more than I did."

"Son, the shame would have been to do nothing. You did something. You did your duty. Maybe war was never what you wanted to do, but you did what you believed was right and what you had to do," Wiley's father consoled. "You never thought of avoiding the draft or protesting. You never thought about taking the easy way out. You did the hard right. I'm blessed to have you as my son."

~~~~~~

On an early winter drive along the California coast, Clary once admitted to his dad, "Dad, sometimes I wonder if I was too idealistic about Vietnam. You were back here when the protests really began and spread. How could our nation refuse to help those who needed our help? How could they ridicule those of us who were fighting and dying? It seems we may have forgotten who we are as Americans and forgotten how we came to be us."

"Son, a sense of idealism is what created freedom and our country. The United States neither created freedom nor independence. Instead, mankind's quest for freedom and independence created America. Sometimes we forget freedom is a continual struggle. Sometimes that struggle, unfortunately, involves war. Idealism is a part of that struggle, too. Freedom is the ideal. We abandon our ideals and we abandon our freedoms. Our country needs idealists. I respect your idealism. More than that, I respect you and I'm honored you're my son."

~~~~~~

"Mama, you know me. I'm a fighter. I fight to win, but sometimes I lose. But I lose fighting hard. I never give up. I never quit. I just fight my best," Hawkins conceded at a Thanksgiving dinner table talk with his mama. "In Vietnam I fought hard, but it seemed sometimes the politicians and the generals wouldn't let us fight as hard as we could have or should have. But the worst part is our people weren't ready or willing to see the fight through. The worst part is we just threw in the towel. We just quit. Nothing's worse than quitting."

"Dominic, you know me. I know little about war, except it's often very painful. I know a lot about being a wife and a mama. I lost a husband because of a war. I almost lost my only son in a war, too," Hawkins' mama sighed. "I knew you'd never quit. So, I prayed for you and for the end of the war. It's what mamas do for sons. But I never prayed for us to quit the war. It would have been disrespectful to you and to your friends in the war. We came to America to be free. We'll do what we have to do to help America be free.

God knows I don't want to lose my son, but I don't want my son to lose his freedoms either."

~~~~~~

Corporal Thunder's, Wiley's, Hawkins', and Clary's occasional conversations with parents, relatives, and friends revealed the challenges of understanding the political and military aspects of limited war. In the remaining years of the Vietnam War they became personal witnesses to the misunderstanding and misinformation of limited war. They were home in America; however, the darkness of the war for them was as dark in America as it had been in Vietnam.

Within a year of their homecomings, Hawkins shared his thoughts with a Mafia underboss, "We just kicked the shit out of the North Vietnamese during the 1968 TET. The VC infrastructure was irreparably damaged, but instead of celebrating our battlefield success the celebrity newscasters criticized the victory. We won the battle, but we lost the public opinion war. We won on the battlefield, but lost in the media. Ain't that a helluva way to lose."

One of the most controversial issues was the 1968 M16 Congressional Report. Corporal Thunder discussed the report with his dad. "Dad, Congress reported the M16 had poor reliability and malfunction rates. It was tested and approved with one type of powder, but it switched to another cheaper powder that produced fouling and jamming. It failed to eject. Ammo magazines were made of pressed aluminum instead of durable and stronger metal. At Khe Sanh, we had all those problems with the M16. A lot of Marines died because the M16s let us down. The report was very critical and negative and true, but no one seems to care."

Hawkins read the negative report, but years later a controversial positive report disturbed him even more. The March 1970 President's Blue Ribbon Defense Report lauded the M16. In a college class Hawkins declared, "I know the M16 was a piece of horseshit. Pardon me professor, but it was. I also know a lot of Marines were killed because they had M16s. Maybe it's better now after lots of fixes, but back then it was a lousy rifle.

"I read about the Paris Peace Talks in January 1969. I was hoping for peace," Wiley admitted in another later discussion with his dad, "but the delegates fussed over the shape and size of the table and stupid issues for months. They danced their kabuki dance while America's sons died.

"We began inflicting severe losses on the NVA in early 1969. We destroyed their sanctuaries in Cambodia and Laos. Yet, that only caused the protestors to rally and to sympathize with the North Vietnamese," Corporal Thunder observed in media reports as he and his dad discussed the war. "The politicians then halted the strikes to appease the protestors, but it cost the troops on the battlefield. Imagine that! Pleasing protestors at the expense of supporting the troops."

"We thought the peace talks would end the war, but the talks seemed to make the war last longer," Clary calculated and admitted to his dad in another conversation, "The war lasted longer after the talks started than the war did before talks started. Then, for over a year, from mid-1969 to late-1970, the war raged on with Americans dying on ruthless battlefields. The talks and the protests raged on, too, but in plush hotels and resorts and police protected streets."

"We were fooled again in January 1972 when President Nixon announced another peace plan," Wiley declared to his family after a Sunday sermon, "but the plan was snubbed by Hanoi. The North launched the 1972 Easter Offensive months later and the talks collapsed. We continued to withdraw our forces, but the South eventually defeated the North's Easter Offensive without us. We had our freedoms and we quit, but they continued to fight for theirs. I'm thankful no one quit on us Blacks and helped us gain our freedoms."

"One of the damnedest things in the summer of 1972 was Jane Fonda visiting Hanoi," Hawkins smiled as he and his uncle talked after mass. "She criticized the war and America. She had her picture taken on an NVA anti-aircraft battery and sang a peace song for NVA troops. I wonder if she had a peace symbol with her. You know, the horse turd with a chicken track on it.

"But the dumbest thing was Ms. Fonda claiming the NVA manipulated her," Hawkins laughed. "Well, no shit, Ms. Fonda. What the hell did you expect? She said she was exhausted and did things she might not have otherwise done. Well, no shit, Ms. Fonda. You think the forces fighting weren't exhausted? You think they weren't tired of fighting? You think they wanted to be doing what they were doing? But they had to do it a lot longer because of you. You helped the North and it used you to prolong the war you claimed you wanted to end. Ain't you the shits?" While nodding in agreement, his priest uncle genuflected and prayed for his nephew's language.

"In November 1972 President Nixon was reelected," Wiley observed in a later news story he shared with his dad, "and he became so frustrated with the lack of progress with the Paris Peace Talks that he finally focused on forcing Hanoi to negotiate. President Nixon finally said enough is enough. Finally, we had enough limited war. Finally, the U. S. did its total war bombings."

"In December 1972 the United States' air power unleashed the most concentrated and devastating aerial bombardments of the war. The destruction to North Vietnam was prohibitive," Corporal Thunder read in press accounts he discussed with his University of Oklahoma classmates. "The peace talks reconvened on 1 January 1973 and within two weeks they concluded with peace." Unfortunately, the North Vietnamese later broke virtually every peace accord. The United States, however, never held them accountable for defying and defaulting on their broken promises and pledges.

"Jesus, what a waste," Hawkins exclaimed to his sister, Maria, at a Red Sox game later that summer. "We fight a war for over seven or eight years and never use the force we could have and should have used. People died for over eight years. Then we bomb the piss out of them for about eleven days and suddenly Hanoi wants peace. More than four years of negotiations were concluded in less than two weeks. Maybe if we'd used more force to begin with, it would have been a different war. Maybe a lot fewer people would have been killed, too. Jesus, why did we wait eight years to do what should have been done in the first year? Ain't limited war something?" By then he had had his share of limited war as well as Fenway beers.

The Vietnam War eventually concluded, but it was never forgotten. Then, almost thirty years later, an event occurred to recall the tragedies of Vietnam. In 1995, Robert McNamara published his memoir *In Retrospect*. It was his personal reflections of the Vietnam War. As the Secretary of Defense during the early years of the war he was one of the prime architects of its failed policies and strategies. In his memoir he confided the war and his strategies were, "wrong, terribly wrong."

Clary read the book and discussed it with his dad. "Dad, if one of the most brilliant minds and scholarly intellectuals of our time makes such mistakes, it illustrates the complexities and contradictions of war. Corporal

Thunder, Wiley, and Hawkins, and I had nowhere near the knowledge and experiences of our senior officers and politicians and Pentagon experts. We did, however, try to understand the war and fight it right."

"Son, there are misunderstandings in all wars. There are miscalculations that characterize all conflicts," Clary's history professor father confessed. "Let's hope from misunderstanding will come understanding. We owe that to our freedoms and to our nation."

~~~~~~

Secretary McNamara's memoirs resurrected Vietnam for Corporal Thunder, Wiley, Hawkins, and Clary. It recalled the tragedies and the triumphs of the Vietnam War for many who had served in it. It was an invitation to reflect on the good, the bad, and the ugly aspects of the war. Some memories hurt and some memories healed. The vast majority of memories were either heartfelt or hard-hearted…*maybe both.*

If Secretary McNamara's memoires were a resurrection, however, so too were they an inspiration. Corporal Thunder and his team members, somewhat individually and somewhat independently, reflected on their time together in Vietnam. The more they thought about one another, the more they thought they should come together again. It had been almost thirty years. They thought maybe it was time. They thought it was time to lift the veil of darkness.

CHAPTER 25

~

But Forever Takes Time

"Thunder, is that the machete? The real machete?"

—Marine Lance Corporal Aaron Wiley

Thunder, Wiley, Hawkins, and Clary came together in war. They became separated in peace. The war united them. Peace divided them. They became one, a team, a family, in the horrors and miseries of war. They became strangers in the goodness and comforts of peace. Geographic, cultural, and personality diversities were overcome by the exigencies of war. Without the war such differences and dissimilarities, however, surrendered to more conventional norms. Yet, there was the creation of a life-long bond that defied distance and division. Forever they would be one—*but forever takes time.*

In the aftermath of their Marine Corps discharges and return home, the team members devoted themselves to re-establishing their lives. They did so in distant locations: in Boston and San Diego as well as Oklahoma and Mississippi. They struggled again. In war, the struggle was simply to survive. At home, the struggle was to create and live meaningful lives. This became their new mission.

Initially, the team attempted to learn the fate on one another, but bureaucratic complexities and challenges frustrated and denied them. They planned on exchanging contact data, but emergency medevacs and unplanned and untimely separations precluded such exchanges. Now they had new lives to live and they began living them.

After a number of futile attempts to locate team members, Thunder expressed it best when he proclaimed to his dad, "Maybe it's easier to live with the uncertainty of their being alive than to live with the certainty of their deaths." Thunder and his dad were deer hunting during a cold rainy late fall day on the Pawhuska prairies. The wet cold always reminded him of Vietnam and the team.

Meanwhile, Hawkins similarly confided to his mama, "It's easier to think they're alive. It'd be harder to know their dead. Maybe I should let it be. Maybe I should just remember them as they were. Maybe I should just remember them in life." Hawkins and his mom were kindred spirits. His mom had lost a husband to war and now Hawkins had lost the team. They became closer than ever.

In time, however, there was one person who became committed to learning the fate of the team members. There was one person who was determined to learn more about her dad and his experiences in the Vietnam War. Her quest started as a high school history class project. It ended as a reunion of the team. A daughter's love for her dad reunited the team and it came together again.

~~~~~~

The beginning of the team's reunion began with a simple question. "Do any of you have parents or relatives who served in the Vietnam War?" the Pawhuska high school history teacher asked. "And would you be willing to ask them if they would speak to our class on their experiences in the war?"

"My dad was a Marine in Vietnam. I'll ask him," answered Kwanta Maka Thunder. "He rarely talks about it, but he'll talk if I ask him. He's my dad and he'll do anything for me."

Weeks later, in January 1997, Thunder visited Kwanta's senior history class. Later, that evening at home, Kwanta explained and asked, "Dad, thanks for talking to my class today. It's a part of your life we're never really talked about much. Our class enjoyed it, but why haven't we talked about it before?"

It was a simple question, but it opened the flood gates. Dad and daughter adjourned to the cozy family room and warm fireplace. The stories began as a torrent of entertaining narratives and emotions. In time, Wiley, Hawkins, Clary, and Swede, became part, an integral part, of Kwanta's family. Yet, an important part was missing. It was the team. The team was missing.

Thunder's talks and Kwanta's questions continued and created a base of information from which Kwanta launched her investigation and search into locating Wiley, Hawkins, and Clary. She probably could never have located them without the new technologies of the computer and Internet.

Kwanta's history teacher was recruited as a secret advisor and an accomplice as well.

"It's taken months, but I've now talked personally with all three of my dad's friends," Kwanta confided to her history teacher one day after class. "I've done it all in secret. None of them know I've contacted any of the others. Plus, I've located Sergeant Hedquist, or Swede as they call him. He was the squad leader and he lives close by in Lindsborg, Kansas. I've invited him, too. They all seem to think Swede was killed and it'll be another part of the surprise."

"What do you intend to do now or next?" the teacher asked.

"Well, I'm thinking of inviting them all to our Pawhuska home this fall for a reunion," Kwanta answered, "but I want to do it as a surprise to them and to my dad, too."

By September, the planning was complete. By October, Kwanta was ready to execute the plan. By November, it was impossible for Kwanta to contain herself. The plan was coming together. Now it was time for the team to come together. Thirty years of doubts and questions were about to be resolved. The reunion was near. Yet, it was too far away until it actually arrived.

~~~~~~

It was a late Sunday afternoon. It was 9 November 1997. Brisk late fall days on the plains were always special, but this day would become truly special. It was church in the morning, but it was work in the afternoon. The weekday fall schedule was busy and devoted to Thunder's full-time job. The weekend schedule was for the farm. It was part-time work for the land and for the livestock. It, too, was a busy schedule...more full-time than part-time. But it was what Oklahoma farmers and ranchers tended to in the fall. They worked their farms and the land.

Thunder was planting winter wheat in the newly furrowed and cultivated fields. As he turned his tractor to the west he noticed Kwanta's Jeep Cherokee driving up the dusty gravel road.

Squinting to steady his vision in the bright but fading sun from the west, he thought, *Kwanta's supposed to be at college. What's she doing home?* Thunder noticed a Dodge pickup following Kwanta and asked, *I wonder who's with Kwanta?* Dust clouds followed in trace.

Kwanta drove to a spot near the fence where her dad would end his westward trek. Emerging from the Jeep, she waved and her dad waved happily in return. It was an unexpected surprise and Kwanta's coming home from college was always a happy and joyful occasion.

Thunder braked the tractor at the fence, climbed down, and leaped up and over the fence. Hugs and greetings were shared as he asked, "Kwanta, what a surprise. Is everything okay?"

"Dad, I hope it's the best surprise ever. I'm better than okay, too," Kwanta beamed.

Thunder was so pleased to see Kwanta, he initially failed to notice others in the vehicles. Kwanta signaled and from them emerged Wiley, Hawkins, Clary, and Swede.

It was stunning disbelief at first. Then it was absolute chaos. It was joyful greetings and hardy handshakes. It was hugs and pats on the back. It was talking and yelling. It was smiles and tears, but it was mostly disbelief. It had been thirty years since they had seen one another. It took them seconds to overcome their disbeliefs. It took them the remainder of their lives, however, to comprehend what transpired that day and that weekend. The team was no longer alone.

As the sun slowly faded and with reunion greetings well-established, Kwanta ordered, "Okay, everyone gather round. Listen up. I have word to pass."

Thunder's expression was one of shock and surprise as the remainder of the team laughed. "Dad, don't look so surprised. On the drive from the Tulsa airport, Mr. Hawkins said that's how you gained the attention of the team. Well, I have word to pass. So, listen up," Kwanta urged.

"Well, hell, Kwanta, we're already gathered," Thunder replied. "We're already here. I doubt Mr. Hawkins told you that's how he always responded to my requests to gather. I hope there are a lot of things he forgot to tell you, too." Thunder playfully hugged Hawkins in jest.

"Dad, come to think of it, Mr. Hawkins said he has a lot to tell me later," Kwanta smiled, "but he said that will take time. Lots of time because there's lots to tell." Hawkins only nodded.

"Kwanta, you need to know most of it will be total bull. We could probably fertilize the whole farm with the bull he'll spread the next few days," Thunder laughed and frowned.

"Okay, dad, but this is the duty schedule for the next few days," Kwanta summarized. "Tonight's a cookout. Tomorrow's a duck hunt and evening Marine Birthday celebration. The last day's Veterans Day. We'll have a sunrise memorial service before afternoon departures."

The Marines shrugged their shoulders and nodded in silence. Wiley broke the silence with his declaration, "Well, we have us another sunset," as he glanced at the multi-colored horizon.

"Jesus, to hell with the sunset. Let's have a beer and eat," Hawkins exhorted, "but no Cs."

The Jeep Cherokee, Dodge, and tractor then drove up the gravel road toward the glistening white farm house with the wraparound porch adorned with rocking chairs and a swing. The reunion then truly began. It had been thirty years, but it seemed like yesterday they had been together. Friendships defy time. They endure time. It was now friendship time.

"Okay, the barn's your bunker during your stay. You need to take your gear and stow it in the stalls marked for you. Then square it away so you'll know where it is in the dark. There are only a few dim lights in the barn except for flashlights," Kwanta ordered as she drove to the classic weather-beaten faded red barn, "We made beds of straw with a poncho and poncho liner as your linen. There are sleeping bags if you need them. No complaints. It's warm and it's dry. It's quiet, too. No one's shooting at you either. It's better than it was in your Vietnam bunker."

"I thought I was coming to Oklahoma, but damned if I don't feel like I'm back in Vietnam," Hawkins mumbled. "I ain't complaining, but ain't this just something else?" He checked his profanity…most of it, but a little profanity was a lot of Hawkins.

"Mr. Hawkins, it's something none of you have probably ever forgotten," Kwanta smiled. "Dad's told me the stories about your bunker and talks. I wanted to make you feel at home.

"You can use the bathrooms in the house, too, for showering and whatever," Kwanta added.

"Kwanta's spoken," Thunder conceded. "Let's square away our gear. Then we'll eat."

"Dad, Aunts Moon Beam and Bright Star helped prepare the meal. We're having steaks, baked potatoes, baked beans, and salad. It's all ready except you have to charcoal the steaks," Kwanta explained. "The grill's ready and I'll bring you the steaks when you're ready for them."

After squaring away gear they assembled at the bottom of a slight slope behind the farm house. It was twilight and the sky was streaked with multiple shades of pale pinks and blues, glowing oranges and lavenders. A fire pit was glimmering with bright burning red embers and smoke drifting lazily into the dark night to mingle with a countless array of brilliant stars.

"Is this one of those Oklahoma Indian Summer evenings?" Wiley asked in awe of the prairie plains and weather.

"It is," Thunder answered proudly, "but in Pawhuska we call them Osage Summer evenings. This is Osage County. This is Osage country. Pawhuska is the Opal of the Osage."

"We have beautiful ocean sunsets in San Diego," Clary declared, "but this is spectacular."

"Grab a stump around the fire," Kwanta suggested while delivering steaks to her dad, "The beer's iced down in that old wash tub over there. Help yourself. Mr. Hawkins, we have sodas for you," she giggled. Hawkins grabbed two beers exclaiming he had best grab them before Wiley stole them all. Wiley smiled and took a soda from the tub while splashing water on Hawkins.

Kwanta then disappeared back into the farmhouse while her dad charcoaled the steaks. She listened politely from afar as the team reminisced about Vietnam and the experiences that united them as one. The Marines were happily in a world they thought they had left forever. Yet, they understood that world had never truly left them. It would remain a part of them forever.

"Dad, here's the potatoes and beans and salad. I'll put them on the picnic table for you," Kwanta remarked. "I'll be back with the plates and silverware."

"Okay, here are some old field mess metal trays," Kwanta reported as she delivered more items to the cookout. "I found them at the Army and Navy Surplus store in Tulsa. I thought they'd make the meal memorable." Thunder smiled in awe of Kwanta's planning skills.

"Yep, you're my favorite daughter," Thunder quipped. Kwanta was his *only* daughter and the *favorite* remark was a standing joke between them. She knowingly glanced back at her dad.

"Gentlemen, I'm going now," Kwanta explained. "If you need anything holler. I'll be close."

As Kwanta turned to return to the farm house the Marines stood politely. Clary then said, "Kwanta, thank you for arranging this reunion. We didn't quite know what to expect. Whatever we thought, it would never compare with the surprise you've actually given us. Thank you."

"Gentlemen, you're welcome, but the true thanks are from me to you. I know how much this means to my dad. I know it means the same to you," Kwanta replied. "I'm proud I could do it for my dad and for you. Your sharing this reunion with us is special for all of us. Thank you."

"Before you go in for the evening may I ask a question?" Wiley inquired.

"Yes, Sir," Kwanta answered. "I'll do my best to answer it."

"Your name is Kwanta Maka. What's its origin and what does it mean?" Wiley asked.

"You know my dad's part Indian, part Irish, and part Marine. But he's all dad. He's one hundred percent dad. Since mom left to follow a different path, he's been one hundred percent mom, too. My dad named me. Kwanta is Native American for 'God Is Gracious'. Maka is Indian for 'Earth'," Kwanta explained. "My first name honors Indian spirituality. My second honors the land. My dad's taught me to honor both. Dad says I'm God's grace to him and to the land."

"I've been helping run the land and farm for years, too. We've been a good team. We've been a good family of two. Now, I have a whole new family of uncles, too," Kwanta boasted and quickly changed the subject. "Breakfast will be in the morning at sunrise or whenever you're ready. Remember, you have your hunting during the day and the Marine Corps Birthday dinner in the evening. Good night, gentlemen." Kwanta then vanished silently into the dark night.

The remainder of the evening the team entertained one another with talks of college, careers, families, and interests. In time, they began to become reacquainted, but they had never truly been strangers. They had always been friends. The friendly conversations continued until almost midnight. Then a light rain began to fall as Swede asked if he could speak briefly.

"I never had the opportunity until now, but now I just want to thank you for what you did for me in Vietnam," Swede began. "When I took that AK47 to the chest I thought I was a goner. I couldn't feel much of nothing. I was kinda numb and out of it. Truthfully, I thought I was dying.

"But you guys wouldn't let me die. I had a hard time that first night. I kept drifting off," he remembered. "I sensed one of you was always there with me. I was never sure, but it seemed that way. Later, it seemed I lost it. I just went into another world. It was like I was with spirits and one was guiding me. I thought at first that I'd just passed into another place, but the spirits brought me back." Swede paused remembering the mysterious near-death feelings he had experienced.

"Then you all carried me to the medevac zone. I remember parts because you kept dropping me. I'd sometimes come to and babble, but it probably made no sense. I was just hanging on as best I could," he admitted. "Then, the next thing I remember, I was in the hospital.

"I was in a dark place and I was hearing strange words, but then I started to wake and open my eyes. Then it was light and quiet," Swede recalled. "That's when I saw the Navy chaplain priest. Then the Navy nurse came in quickly. She later told me the Chaplain was doing last rites because he thought I was dying. I guess the strange words were Latin.

"Days later, I started getting better and the doctor came in to talk to me about my recovery. He told me I probably survived because of the medical treatment and care I'd received in the field," Swede reported, "but he told me he was unable to explain one of my wounds.

"I asked, what wound?" Swede said, "and that's when the doctor took my left hand and turned it over and pointed to the cut and scar on my palm. The doctor said he couldn't explain that wound." Swede then opened his left hand to show the scar to those around the camp fire.

Without a word Thunder stretched his left arm out and opened his hand with his palm toward Swede. Thunder had an identical scar. Swede was familiar with numerous Indian customs and he instantly understood the Indian Blood Brother ritual. Standing without speaking, he lumbered to Thunder and the two shared a long and tight hug before Swede returned slowly to his stump.

"Well, I'm honored you invited me here for this reunion. I'm here because of you. I survived because of you," Swede concluded, "and I want you to know how much you mean to me and to my family. Without you there would be no me and no family. Thank you. I love you guys."

The bunker stump talks continued while the drizzle became a steady rain. "Jesus, it wouldn't be a reunion without a little monsoon action," Hawkins declared, "but at least it's quiet and peaceful."

"Well, I'm sitting right here until I'm soaked," Clary noted, "because, unlike Vietnam, tonight I can change into dry clothes and sleep in a nice warm and dry barn. It can rain from hell to breakfast for all I care. We're together and we're home. To hell with the rain."

"You can stay here all night if you want, but I'm going to the barn for my sleeps," Wiley announced. "It's late and we'll be up early for the hunt. You know me and my sleeps."

"Wiley, remember to set the night watch schedule," Thunder ordered. "We have all sorts of night critters here on the farm. Some are downright dangerous." The five aging Marines joked and laughed as they shuffled toward the barn and bed. It was a day and night they would remember forever.

Reveille came early the next morning. "We have an ambush patrol today. We're going to ambush some ducks. It's a ceasefire day and sanctuary...*except for ducks*," Thunder announced as memories of their patrols, ambushes, and ceasefires seeped into their consciousness. Memories assaulted the barriers of time and floodgates dissolved into a torrent of reflections.

The five Marines strolled to the farm house kitchen for a breakfast of eggs and bacon, grits, biscuits and gravy, and coffee and juice. Clary asked, "What, no C-Rations?"

"We're saving those for lunch," Kwanta smiled. "It wouldn't be a Vietnam reunion without Cs. But you'll have to wait."

"Damn, Kwanta, you serious? You don't miss a trick do you?" Hawkins laughed.

"Its part of the Marine Five P's my dad taught me," Kwanta answered, "You know: Prior Planning Prevents Poor Performance. Dad taught me to pay attention to the details."

After breakfast, the five Marines loaded into Thunder's pickup for the ride across the pasture to the duck blind for the hunt. They lay their gear in the bed of the truck and noticed two old and weathered wash tubs of beers and sodas. The tubs were obviously another of Kwanta's details.

Wiley noticed Thunder's rifle rack with no rifle. Instead, it had a long spear, a tomahawk, and a machete. "Thunder, is that the machete? The real machete?" Wiley incredulously asked.

"Yes, it's my only war souvenir," Thunder replied. "The corpsmen helped me get it through customs. They tagged the machete as an NVA surgical instrument. It was a joke, but it worked. It still works, too."

Hawkins took the machete from the rack and ran his finger across the blade and exclaimed, "Damn, it's as razor sharp as ever," as he sucked a thin stream of blood from his index finger.

Clary smiled with the knowledge Hawkins still had to check things out for himself and asked, "Hawkins, you didn't think he'd let it go dull did you?" Hawkins started to rebut, but had no good rebuttal to the foolish act of slicing his finger open. Instead, he licked the blood streaming from his sliced finger. He later let his hand linger in the iced tub to stop the bleeding and then withdrew two beers for what he alleged were post-breakfast "medicinal purposes."

"No, Hawkins is just going for another Purple Heart," Wiley laughed. They all laughed.

Once the Marines and truck were loaded, Kwanta appeared and explained, "Dad, I'll bring lunch out to the blind before noon. You want me to bring anything else?"

"No, we'll be fine. It's only about ten minutes away. If we need anything, I'll come back for it," Thunder answered as he completed loading the truck.

"What about hunting licenses?" Swede asked. "I hunt all over Kansas and game wardens are always poking around." Hunters always, at least usually always, respect hunting rules.

"This is Oklahoma. Today the Thunder Ranch is a Marine Corps free fire zone and Thunder Team sanctuary. We have our own rules of engagement in Pawhuska," Kwanta smiled. "It's just like the NVA sanctuaries in Vietnam. It's off limits to the game warden. Besides, an anonymous tip alerted the game warden to poachers on the other side of the county.

They'll be busy there all day. Also, we electrified the fence as a barrier." The memories flowed freely.

"You're right, Hawkins," Clary said. "Kwanta doesn't miss a trick. Don't pee on the fence."

"Dad, here's guest hunting licenses for your team," Kwanta whispered as she secretly passed an envelope to her dad, "I doubt you need them, but just in case. Uncle Blue Bull bought them. Don't tell them unless you need them. They'd probably rather think they're bending a few rules like you did a time or two in Vietnam." Thunder smiled and slipped the envelope in his truck.

Thunder whistled and two black Labrador pups came running and leaped into the bed of the truck. "What's their names?" Clary asked as he petted the frisky pups.

"Marina and Cora," Thunder replied, knowing his namesake Marine Corps pups would generate a few smiles from the team.

"Jesus, nobody misses a trick around here," Hawkins sighed. "This must be Marine Corps Base Pawhuska." The Marines roared as they drove away.

Kwanta waved goodbye as the truck pulled away and headed toward the duck blind. She grinned knowingly. Kwanta had coordinated another surprise or trick for her dad and the team. She and her two uncles, White Horse and Blue Bull, had constructed a Vietnam bunker type duck blind at the pond. She even located a tarp at the Army & Navy Surplus Store similar to the one her dad described they had in Vietnam. Kwanta imagined their surprise.

"We seem to be telling more sea stories and drinking more beers than shooting ducks," Thunder observed after a few hours in the duck blind.

"Yeah, talking we always did pretty good," Hawkins replied, "now we're making up for all those beers we missed in Vietnam, too. Besides, I ain't too much into killing anymore."

"Dad, here's a case of C-Rations," Kwanta announced as she drove up to the blind at noon.

"You gotta be kidding us. You gotta be joking," Hawkins moaned. "Jesus, these must be twenty-five or thirty years old. Since Vietnam, I ain't never been hungry enough for me to want another C-Rat. Ain't never been that hungry."

You don't really expect us to eat these, do you?" Wiley asked hopefully.

"Wiley, open them up and pass me the ham and lima beans," Hawkins ordered before Kwanta could respond, "I'll show you what we're gonna do with'em."

Wiley tossed the pork and poots to Hawkins. Hawkins tossed the can toward the pond and blasted it with his shotgun. "Damn, that's just what I always wanted to do to Cs," Hawkins confided. "Throw me another one and I'll murder it, too. They damned near killed me in Vietnam 'cause they were almost as deadly as the NVA. Now I'm killin'em."

Kwanta and the Marines laughed hysterically while Hawkins blasted the C-Rations and shouted, "Okay, anything worth killing once is worth killin' twice." He kept firing.

Kwanta then delivered them bag lunches and requested, "Dad, supper will be ready about six o'clock. The family's helping me cook it and they'll wait to say 'hi' to everyone."

"Thanks, we'll be back and washed up by then. We may be three sheets to the wind, but we'll be there by six," Thunder smiled.

The Marines were punctual and strolled into the farm house a few minutes before six o'clock. Kwanta took charge of the introductions of her Aunts Moon Beam and Bright Star and her Uncles White Horse and Blue Bull and their respective families. "Most all the surprises and tricks are thanks to my aunts and uncles. They've been a great help in planning this reunion and helping out," Kwanta acknowledged. "Dad and I are blessed by them everyday."

After introductions and social exchanges, Kwanta's uncles and aunts excused themselves and politely departed. Kwanta then suggested, "Okay, everyone take a seat in the dining room. I'll bring in supper, but remember to save room for the Marine Corps Birthday cake. I understand that's the tradition."

"Dad, you sit at the head of the table and there are place cards for our friends," Kwanta advised. "But leave the other end of the table and the full place setting open. It's for those unable to be with us tonight. It's in remembrance of those who never came home. It's for those who gave their lives for us and our freedoms." The empty place setting created an empty place in their hearts as they remembered those who gave their lives for freedom.

Kwanta then delivered the food to the table and stood to the side as her Dad asked, "Wiley, will you please offer the blessing?" They held hands remembering the long ago time they had held hands while preparing for the final counterattack at Khe Sanh. It was the last time they had been together as a team; the last time they had held one another's hands…until tonight.

"Our Father who art is heaven, we thank Thee you for the many blessing Thou has bestowed upon us. We thank Thee for the love that abounds on this farm, on these plains, on these prairies, on this proud land we know as Oklahoma and America. We thank Thee for the freedoms we have as Americans. We especially thank Thee for those who serve and sacrifice for those freedoms. We ask Thee to bless those who serve and their families, especially those who have never returned home to families. Tonight we're home with our team and our family and for that we're very grateful and thankful. We're a team again. Tonight we're finally with our special family. In the name of Jesus Christ we pray, Amen," Wiley prayed.

The Marines reminisced while Kwanta waited silently in the kitchen. Kwanta cherished the remembrances the Marines shared. She was at times laughing. At others crying. Some stories were hilarious. Others were heartbreakingly sad. All increased her love and respect for her dad, the team, and those who sacrifice and fight in war. She became acquainted with a part of her dad's life she never knew. She was proud. She was grateful.

"Let's adjourn to the fire pit out back," Thunder suggested at the meal's conclusion.

Kwanta had anticipated the suggestion. The fire pit was roaring with embers drifting lazily and erratically into the night, which were decidedly different than the precise trails of red tracers' fired from weapons into their Vietnam combat nights years ago.

"Jesus, that's just what we need. We need to kill a few more beers," Hawkins groaned. "Today we killed a helluva lot more beers than we did ducks. Yep, a helluva lot more beers than ducks. But there's more beers to kill. Pass the beers. To hell with the ammo and ducks."

Where does our nation find such men as these? Kwanta asked herself as she sat in the night shadows on the farm's back porch wooden rocking chair. *How does our nation produce such men as these?* These were her reoccurring questions as she sat silently and listened to the humble exploits of the team. It was obvious they were heroes, but the only heroes they ever considered heroes were those who never came home.

"Please remember we have a sunrise Veterans Day service in the morning," Kwanta reminded the team. "Now, please excuse me. I'm exhausted and heading to bed. Goodnight."

Goodnights were exchanged as the five Marines strolled or staggered to the barn. Once in their barn stalls they talked briefly before taps. Talking was still simply a part of the team.

Thunder spoke softly, "People are always arguing or debating whether the United States won or lost the Vietnam War. We lost a lot of good friends. I pray for them to this day. They're the ones who lost. We lost them, but I'll always believe we won because of them. I remember those we lost because we survived thanks to them." His glance and gesture upward to the Great Spirit was simple but devout and sincere.

Hawkins quickly agreed, "Yep, I'll take survivin'. War's about survivin' and we survived. Don't now much care about the winnin' and losin' part, but we sure cared about those we lost." He knelt in the stall in prayer before he nestled into the hay and settled into his sleeping bag.

"Yeah, but our surviving is part of those we lost surviving, too," Wiley declared. "Once we talked about us surviving. Remember? We agreed that as long as one of us survived we'd all survive. A part of us would always live and survive in any of us who lived. I fought and prayed like hell to survive, but if I'd died I was praying I'd become part of Hawkins. Can you imagine that?" They laughed until they cried thinking of Hawkins and Wiley as one. It was totally unimaginable, yet so believable in so many ways, too.

"Maybe more important than winning or losing is that as a nation we learned lessons from Vietnam," Clary exclaimed. "If we now better understand war, maybe what we sacrificed and endured made a difference. Maybe that's winning. Maybe that's the best win. Maybe what was done wrong then will be done right now and in the future. That would be a good legacy for us and for our nation." Clary slipped off cowboy boots he had purchased especially for his trip to the prairies. He thought of mentioning cowboys, but was too tired for a Hawkins cowboy rant.

"But despite the deaths and miseries of the war," Thunder proclaimed. "I wouldn't trade our worst day in Vietnam for the least of our freedoms. We fought for freedom and our nation. I'll never trade that. We're living free today. I'll take living free. We're Americans, we're Marines, and we're free. I'll take that as winning." The team nodded in agreement. They spoke no other words. There was nothing else to say.

Within minutes they were asleep. Five aging Marines, who had survived because of the actions and love of one another thirty years earlier, were asleep in peace. But what had truly survived were their friendships. Without having to fear for their lives as they had decades earlier, tonight they were comforted by peaceful sleeps and the knowledge they were safe. Slumbering in friendship, they slept with the remembrances of those friendships and that peace. They slept soundly and peacefully without interruptions. They were good with that.

EPILOGUE

It's like when the reporter said he wouldn't do what we Marines do for all the money in the world. We just said neither would we. We said there wasn't enough money in the world to pay us to do what we do. We just said it was our job and our mission. Then we simply said we did it for love. We did it because we love one another. It's that love I remember the most.

—Marine Lance Corporal Aaron Wiley

"Reveille. Reveille." Kwanta shouted as she banged repeatedly on the barn door. It was dark with only hints and slivers of sunrise sparkles beginning to announce daybreak and a new day. She was determined they would be at the memorial site by sunrise. They were, too.

Kwanta wore her best cowgirl boots and hat, with jeans and a soft plaid shirt, and pale blue jacket. Her silver belt buckle glistened brightly as the sun rose, but her smile shone decidedly brighter. She personified the optimism of young people committed to conquering the world.

Thunder was attired in his horsemen boots and hat, as he now affectionately referred to them in deference to Hawkins's cowboy rant of years ago. He wore a beige and tan western suede jacket, scarlet Marine Corps colored shirt with blue jeans, and matching decorative leather Indian bolo tie and belt. The chalk on his jacket was either from his Pawhuska high school math classroom or from his football head coach duties, which included chalking the field. He remained a teacher and coach at heart, but was proudly connected to the land by ranching and farming, too.

Dressed in his Sunday sermon best, Wiley's dark suit and Marine gold tie confirmed his past as a Marine and present as a part-time preacher. The black corfam shoes, however, signaled his full-time career with the Natchez Police Department as a former beat patrolman and now a lead detective. His physical presence was a natural for law enforcement, but his Boys & Girls Clubs lapel pin revealed his true passion and volunteer work with underprivileged and at-risk kids.

Swede's clothing was the most eclectic, combining contemporary and traditional as well as functional and decorative. His beige herringbone shoulder padded jacket and leather trimmed safari hat with one turned-up side revealed his passion for hunting and fishing. The blue vest with yellow suspenders in Swedish flag colors were pure Swede. It was the Lindsborg Ol Stuga Sports Bar's black and gold tie, however, that announced him as the most famous barkeep in Kansas by night and the most successful truck salesmen in the midwest by day.

Clary's cream jacket and maroon slacks, with beach print satin shirt, were California casual. The tan alligator shoes with no socks revealed his carefree but impressive persona as the CEO of a high-tech juggernaut in San Diego. The top two buttons of his shirt, stylishly unbuttoned, revealed a partially tied lily pink ascot, which he wore to harass Hawkins and quickly discarded. Hawkins thought of asking, *Clary, are you straight from GQ, Gentleman's Quarterly, or simply GQ, genuinely quirky?* But he refrained…reluctantly. They were forever friendly antagonists.

Hawkins was dressed in black. His black leather jacket, dark coal polyester turtle neck, and raven black felt fedora masked his true profession. *He looks like either a Mafia henchman or Catholic priest. He's missing only the white collar,* Clary smiled. Hawkins remained illusive and mysterious, but he was actually a bit of both. He was the director of the local parish youth center sponsored and funded largely by the Mafia. While it was part-time work, he devoted his full time to the kids. Hawkins had other part-time employment assignments, but no one knew exactly what they were and no one asked—despite more than modest suspicious curiosity.

The team was as diverse as ever with their distinct personalities and lives, but it was their common bond of friendship that still united them after three decades. Clothes or careers would never define them as much as the team itself. They remained family.

The Marines and Kwanta strolled along the path for one hundred meters to the rear of the farmhouse. The huge pond and meandering creek and tall oak trees had always been a place of solitude and fun. Thunder taught Kwanta to swim in the pond. She caught her first fish and shot her first squirrel there, too. The rope and tire swing had always been a favorite during her youth.

It was also where Kwanta suffered her first swarming wasp attacks. She was only three when stung with over twenty red and swollen whelps. Catching her breath and choking back tears Kwanta urged, "Dad, tomorrow let's kill them all."Thunder remembered Hawkins' thoughts on "no quarter given" killing. He and Kwanta ambushed and killed the wasps at sunset the next day. It was indicative of her battling competitive spirit, which distinguished her in sports and school.

Thunder called Kwanta his "Triple *S* Threat"—Swimming, Soccer, and School. She was a star athlete and honor roll student. Somewhat subconsciously, yet conscious of Clary's intellect and team nickname, he often called Kwanta *Socrates* after she received a Straight "A"report card or excellence on a test.

Thunder later added a fourth *S* for "Sleeps"because she loved her naps as much as Wiley loved his sleeps, especially on long pickup drives to swim meets or soccer games. Vietnam memories persisted and manifested themselves in the post-war lives of the team. As with Hawkins' zest for living and battling and Clary's idealistic intellect, Wiley's use of the term *sleeps,* for example, became a part of Kwanta, too. Over the years the team lived on in Kwanta.

Over the years various memories and names from Vietnam emerged from their past to become a part of their present. In the collards and grits and fried chicken south, Wiley instituted a *Little Italy* night the first Friday of every month at the Boys & Girls Clubs. With support from the Natchez Police Department and local Baptist churches the special pasta nights helped unify the youngsters, parents, and community. They were family affairs to bond families and they made families and the community stronger.

The Catholic Church and Mafia funded youth center that Hawkins directed held an annual awards ceremony for fighters and students. Championship boxers and honor roll students were presented special awards. Boxers received the *Thunder Fists* award for fighting prowess and warrior skills. Honor students received the *Socrates* award for achievements in academics and school activities. The Catholic and Mafia connection Hawkins professed years ago remained strong. The awards ceremony was special in the community and unified parents and children with special memories and an increased sense of family. In his youth, Hawkins believed one reason for living was fighting, but with age he developed an appreciation for education, too.

Clary's innovative high-tech futuristic firm was rooted in the past by a name from Vietnam, too. As a CEO and leader deeply committed to the creation of new and exciting products, he pioneered the concept of newer, smaller, more compact designs to the older, larger, ponderous technologies. They were marketed as *Baby Brutes.* They were as strong and childproof as Wiley's strength and kid-like love of life. The *Baby Brutes* revolutionized the tech industry.

These were the remembrances and connections that continued to unite the team over the years; that forever ensured they remained a part of one another despite time and distance. They smiled reflecting on the memories and names until hearing the creek's soft and steady flow.

The pond and shade were often welcome reliefs from the hot spring, summer, and fall days of plowing, planting, and harvesting. In the winter, it was sometimes frozen for ice skating or sledding on the creek's slopes. It was their oasis on the prairie. It was their Pawhuska bunker for many of Thunder and Kwanta's dad and daughter talks, too. Kwanta smiled remembering them.

This morning, however, it was a memorial site for Veterans Day. Hawkins was the first to observe the traditional boots, rifle, and helmet. Scuffed and dirty and worn, the boots were combat weathered and sat atop two sandbags. They were unpolished. Hawkins grinned slyly remembering the Army club brawl that began because of unshined boots. They all beamed.

An M14 Rifle with attached bayonet was trust into the earth and stood proud and at attention between the boots. They noted it was an M14 and not an M16. They smirked remembering the disastrous debut of the M16 Rifle at Khe Sanh.

A camouflaged helmet rested on the rifle stock. This traditional representation of fallen comrades caused sad recollections of the frequent deaths and memorial services in Vietnam.

Wiley nonchalantly glanced toward the east to witness the incredibly beautiful fall sunrise glistening across the frost covered fields. Early morning hues of pale pinks, golden yellows, and soft pastels drifted lazily across the Pawhuska sky. The frost sparkled in the sunlight as heavenly stars sprinkling across the land, as flowing plains and prairies stretching upward to the horizon to merge heaven and earth into one. Wiley said nothing, but they all thought, *It's another sunrise*. It was an irrepressible memory...*another sunrise*. It was what had helped them survive Vietnam.

Sensing the solemn mood, Thunder proposed, "Maybe it's best there are no speeches. Let's remember to ourselves what we want to remember. Let's remember both the bad and the good."

Standing straight and proud and somber as they respectfully gazed upon the boots, rifle, and helmet memorial, the Marines' facial expressions alternated between sadness and gladness as their memories of Vietnam surged and swirled in remembrances now and forever a part of them.

Doc Roman's severed legs at the Razorback river bank was probably the worst I saw, Wiley thought. *Watching him plastering mud on his bloody stumps to stop the bleeding was hard to watch, but the Doc was fighting to live and help save us while knowing he was dying.*

Jesus, the damn rockets and mortars at Con Thien and Khe Sanh were really bad, Hawkins remembered. *I hated just having to get down and get flat. I hated being unble to fight back. That and the M16 was the worst. But the true worst was thinking Corporal Thunder was dead.*

Lieutenant Antoine's death was the worst for me, Thunder recalled. *He was expecting his first baby daughter. They never saw one another. I see Kwanta everyday. I know how blessed we are to share our lives together. But they were never able to share even one day.*

The medevacs were the worst, Clary reflected. *I thought my first medevac at Con Thien was bad, but Khe Sanh was worse. We were all fighting so hard to live and to survive, but we were so close to dying and dying alone. The loneliness and not knowing about the others hurt the most.*

Thinking I was dying was the worst for me, Swede trembled. *It seemed I went to the spirit world but somehow came back. But then the priest's last rites really scared me, too. Thinking you're dying ain't a lot of fun. No fun at all.*

The Vietnam War, however, was about more than tragedies. It was also about triumphs. Its tragedies were its brutality and ruthlessness. Its triumphs were its friendships and camaraderie. The team remembered the bad as well as the good. The bad was painfully bad, but it was never so bad that it destroyed the good. Remembering the good was what helped them survive the bad.

The steeple destruction is one of the good memories, Clary reflected. *The steeple caused a lot of Marines to die or get wounded, but we ended it. It never again hurt any Marines. Never!*

Corporal Thunder and I having to see the Battalion Commander was a bad turned good, Swede smiled. *We thought we were going to have our butts kicked, but we had our backs patted. Corporal Thunder did his magic explaining our actions to Colonel David.*

Our bunker talks are what I remember as one of the best, Thunder reminisced. *We talked about home and family. We talked about tactics and leadership and calling for fires. They all helped us learn and survive, too. We became friends and family because of the talks.*

Damn, my best memory came when I felt the worst, Hawkins recalled. *I was lying there damn near dying at Khe Sanh waiting for word on Thunder. They searched the hill and couldn't find him. Then the Lieutenant just happened to mention eleven headless NVA. I knew it was Thunder. I knew he was out there alive somewhere. I knew he was on the warpath, too.*

Hawkins refusing R & R to make a donation for a piano for my dad's church really touched me, Wiley thought, *but Hawkins was always Hawkins. It's like when the reporter said he wouldn't do what we Marines do for all the money in the world. We just said neither would we. We said there wasn't enough money in the world to do what we do. We just said it was our job and our mission. Then I simply said we did it for love. It's that love I remember the most.*

They're all older now, but I can picture them then, Kwanta beamed as she glanced at the five aging Marines. *Back then they were all about the same age I am now. They were all about eighteen or nineteen years old. They were so young then, but they're the ones who have always fought for us and our freedoms. They're the best part of all of us.*

In the silence of their thoughts, Thunder whispered, "Okay. It's time to go. Let's saddle up. It's time to move on." Individually, they shared a final prayer of reverent remembrance.

Without speaking the Marines and Kwanta retraced the path to the farmhouse for an old-fashioned country breakfast. Afterwards, as they packed in the barn, they spoke thoughts they had all struggled with over the years.

"We worked hard to understand our war, but the limited war part frustrated us. The part about the use of force was really hard to understand.

How much force to use? When? How? Where? Why? They were hard issues," Clary philosophized.

"Yeah, but war is hard. Ain't nothin' easy about it. Ain't nothin' easy for any of us. Ain't no one to blame unless we're all to blame," Hawkins groaned. "Our military, our government, our people. All of us. We're all one. Can't blame anyone without blamin' everyone. But we can't just send our military to war. We gotta send our nation to war. We gotta be all in to win."

"It seems war often unites America...*initially*, but in time it seems it often divides us, too," Thunder exclaimed pensively. "When we're united as one we're at our best, but when we're divided we're less than our best. Yet, both are part of us. It's democracy. Let's hope and pray our nation and people learned good lessons from Vietnam."

"By the grace of God, we're alive and free," Wiley concluded. "God answered our prayers. Freedom's worth the fight." Wiley remained the optimist, but understood the noble cause of freedom was often costly.

They nodded in agreement, but no other words were spoken. There was nothing more to say than what they had already said. There was nothing more to do than what they had already done. They had over the years hoped and prayed for better understanding in the future. Peace was always part of their prayers, but they understood the responsibility to war, too, because war was what helped make them free. They were good with that. They were good with freedom.

"I'll drive everyone back to the Tulsa airport," Swede volunteered as they exited the barn with lighter suitcases than their combat packs in Vietnam, but with heavier hearts from the memorial service and from having to bid farewell, "so Kwanta can return to her classes at the University of Tulsa. Thunder can continue his plowing we interrupted, too."

"Okay," Kwanta smiled, "but remember, we'll do this again either next year or the following summer. Next time, however, the families are to come, too. We can do it here or in Kansas or maybe Mississippi or San Diego or Boston or wherever. But we'll do it and with families, too."

The Marines agreed and saluted smartly. Kwanta had issued them their orders. While hugging one last time, they loaded into Swede's truck and drove down the dirt drive to the gravel road. They waved dusty good-byes until they disappeared over the rolling Oklahoma hills and veered south toward Tulsa. The sun shone brightly as the prairies glowed golden beneath the radiant autumn weather. *Fall is beautiful in Oklahoma*, Kwanta thought, *but this one is special.*

Thunder and Kwanta waved back as they stood with arms locked around one another's waists. Standing silently for a long time they shielded their eyes from the radiant sun. They stood without moving long after the truck had disappeared across and into the lonesome prairie. The world was totally silent except for the soothing sounds of the Oklahoma wind drifting across the lonesome prairie and the fluttering wings of a scissor-tail flycatcher, the Oklahoma state bird.

In a barely audible tone, Thunder whispered, "Semper Fi. Semper Fi." It was probably the only Latin Kwanta knew. Thunder had taught her when she was a little girl that it translated, "Always Faithful. Always Faithful," and that it was the Marine Corps motto. She knew they were words her dad lived and lived by every day. She was confident they were words for which he would have died, too. Kwanta shuddered at the thought and pulled her dad closer.

The words epitomized her dad and the team. They were her dad. Kwanta realized the worst of Vietnam helped make her dad his best; helped make Wiley, Hawkins, Clary, and Swede their best, too. She glowed with the certainty that their love was stronger than ever. She believed darkness always surrendered to light. Suddenly, it was lighter than light. Splashes of brilliance from the light literally glowed with heartfelt emotions as the darkness faded. The light was the love the team shared. It was also the love dad and daughter shared. It was the light and love of freedom, too. Freedom and love shone brightly. They were good with the light and the love.

Thunder and Kwanta slowly spun and sashayed hand-in-hand toward the farm house. Their happiness was revealed in a few light Oklahoma line dance steps as they bounced briefly along the dusty drive before settling into a western stroll. Sounds of their boots crunching gravel and the ever-present prairie winds were soft echoes rippling across the silent plains. They spoke no words. There was nothing to say. The almost *imperceptible* tears from their gleaming eyes and smiling faces said all that needed to be said. They were home and they were free and they were family. They were good with that.

CPSIA information can be obtained at www.ICGtesting.com
Printed in the USA
LVOW07s0722230415

435641LV00003B/3/P